STAR TREK
THE RETURN

William Shatner

STAR TREK THE RETURN

with
Judith and Garfield
Reeves-Stevens

WHEELER
PUBLISHING, INC.
ROCKLAND, MA

★ AN AMERICAN COMPANY ★

Published in Large Print by arrangement with Pocket Books,
a division of Simon & Schuster in the United States and Canada.

Wheeler Large Print Book Series.

Set in 16 pt. Plantin.

Library of Congress Cataloging-in-Publication Data

Shatner, William.
    Star Trek : the return / William Shatner.
        p.   cm.—(Wheeler large print book series)
    ISBN 1-56895-359-3
    1. Kirk, James T. (Fictitious character)—Fiction. 2. Picard,
Jean-luc (Fictitious character)—Fiction. 3. Large type books.
I. Title. II. Series.
    [PS3569.H347S73 1996b]
    813'.54—dc20
                                            96-32272
                                              CIP

I have another lie having nothing to do with acting, directing or writing. It involves my universe of horses, those beauteous creatures whose form and function fill me with delight.

So to that world of horses, to the people who train and care for my four-footed friends, to the driven, excuse the pun, fellow competitors who try to take the blue ribbon away from me, but most especially to my pals, the horses, I dedicate this book.

ACKNOWLEDGMENTS

My thanks to . . .

Gar and Judy Reeves-Stevens, whose creative skills made the book possible.

Kevin Ryan, who as they say in the biz, "put the package together."

Carmen LaVia, who did his thing.

PROLOGUE

He fell. . . .

Alone.

Twisting through the air of Veridian III. The shriek of the metal bridge echoing in his ears. Spinning. The sun flashing into his eyes. The shadows engulfing him. One following the other, over and over as he fell. Light. Shadow. Light. Shadow. Like the beating of wings. Like all the days of his life. Intersecting . . .

In an Iowa cornfield—he sees the stars. A boy of five in his father's arms. I have to go there, he says. And you will, Jimmy, his father answers. You will . . .

In Carol's arms, in their bed—even as he knows he must leave her, the son they had created quickening within her . . .

In Starfleet headquarters—Admiral Nogura reaching out to shake his hand: Congratulations, Captain, the Enterprise is yours. . . .

In Spacedock—Captain Pike beginning the introduction: Your science officer, Lieutenant-Commander Spock . . .

On the streets of old Earth—squealing brakes, Edith, haloed in the headlights of her death . . .

Through all these days and more, alone he fell, hearing the whispers of the past. . . .

I am, and always will be, your friend. . . . Dammit it, Jim- I'm a doctor not a bricklayer. . . . Let me help. . . .

I've always known I'll die alone. . . .

Then one shadow blocked the light. Broke his fall. Ended the kaleidoscope of days. He turned his head, looked up, saw a face he recognized, not from the past, not from the present.

From the future.

"Did we do it?" the falling man asked. "Did we make a difference?"

The other, in his odd uniform, but with the familiar touchstone of Starfleet on his chest, knelt by his side.

"Oh, yes. We made a difference. Thank you."

Somewhere within him, the falling man was aware of pain, deep and incurable. Somewhere within him, he became aware he couldn't feel his legs, his arms, as if he and all existence were evaporating together.

The edges of his vision blurred, darkened, joined one final shadow deep enough to swallow whatever else remained.

But the other, this stranger, this . . . Picard, had offered his friendship. In another lifetime, perhaps it might have been so. So much might have been. So many possibilities.

"Least I could do," the falling man said, ignoring the final shadow for the sake of his friend, "for the captain of the Enterprise."

Voices called to him from the darkness then, their summons more than whispers.

Through the latticework of the twisted metal above him, he glimpsed the edge of something moving, coming closer.

He closed his eyes.

What was it he had said to Picard when they had met? When Picard had challenged him to return for one last mission?

He remembered. His eyes opened.

"It was . . . fun," he told Picard. He tried to smile. To spare this friend.

What lay beyond the bridge swept closer, chasing him as it had always chased him.

Through the mangled steel the shape was clearer now. Closer. Known.

He gazed up at it, amazed Picard did not see, did not know.

He tried to warn Picard. To help him escape what he no longer could.

But the momentum of his days had crested. The dark well of his vision swirled inward. Too quickly. And the face of that which chased him, caught him, claimed him.

The final wisps of existence lifted from him in a feathered haze of light, revealing all that lay beyond, still to come.

"Oh my," he whispered.

As he saw.

As he knew.

And then he fell again.

Alone . . .

ONE

James T. Kirk was dead. . . .

As Commander William Riker resolved from the transporter beam beside the grave of that Starfleet legend, he was surprised by the sudden thought that had come to him. Of all that had happened on this desolate world of Veridian III only a month ago, inexplicably, the fate of James T. Kirk weighed most heavily on his mind.

Half a planet away, the shattered hulk of the *U.S.S. Enterprise* lay in ruins, slowly being carved into transporter loads of recyclable scrap by a team of Starfleet engineers. Though the ship was beyond salvage, in accordance with the Prime Directive no trace of it could remain on this world. A primitive civilization existed on Veridian IV, the next planet out from the Veridian sun. If someday voyagers from that world landed here, they must find no trace of advanced technology which might affect the natural development of their science.

Riker had expected that the full emotional consequence of the great ship's loss would have consumed him by now. She had gone before her time, and in his dreams he had always hoped to one day sit in her captain's chair.

But in the days that had passed since the *Enterprise* had blazed through the atmosphere of this world to her first and final landing, Riker's thoughts still kept turning to the fate of the captain of an earlier *Enterprise*. The first *Enterprise* . . .

"Sir, is that . . . *him?*"

Riker turned to Lieutenant Baru. The seam ridge that bisected the young Bolian officer's deep blue face pulled taut as her eye ridges widened. She looked into the distance, past the grave.

Riker nodded, smiling inwardly at her reaction, recognizing the earnestness of youth. The *Farragut*'s chief of security had personally recommended Baru, and the three other officers accompanying Riker, to be part of the honor guard to escort Kirk's remains to Earth. Riker knew what she saw. What they all saw now.

A lone sentinel on a distant outcropping. The dry desert wind shifting the elegant black robes he wore. The reddening sun reflected from the silver script embroidered in their folds.

He had come.

From Romulus.

Against all logic.

"Spock," Baru said. With awe.

Riker understood.

He knew the Vulcan ambassador—had worked with him—as a living, breathing individual. Yet Spock was as much a legend as Kirk.

As much a legend as the friendship that had bound those two on the first *Starship Enterprise*.

The officers of the honor guard stood at ease, respectfully refraining from staring at the distinguished visitor. Instead, they faced the simple cairn of rocks Jean-Luc Picard had built for Kirk's remains. The setting sun drew long shadows from it and caught an old-fashioned Starfleet insignia pin with a gleam of dying light.

Riker breathed the still, dry air of the Veridian desert. He glanced upward to the darkening sky, as if he might see the *Farragut* sliding into orbit far overhead, come to claim Starfleet's honored dead, to bear Kirk home.

From his sentinel's position, Spock remained as motionless as the time-smoothed stones of this place.

What could it be like, Riker wondered, *to lose your closest friend, then seventy-eight years later, to lose him again?*

A hint of the power of that answer existed in the extraordinary circumstances that had brought Spock here. In fewer than four days after the crew of Riker's *Enterprise* had been rescued, Starfleet Intelligence had mounted an emergency extraction mission to bring Spock from the homeworld of the Romulan Star Empire to Veridian III, so he might accompany his friend on his final voyage.

The extraction was not an operation to be undertaken lightly. Relations between the Romulans and the Federation had been strained for centuries. Spock had become instrumental in the efforts to reduce those tensions by decades of secret negotiations intended to reconcile the Romulans with the Vulcans and, hence, the Federation.

Though the Romulans were an offshoot of the Vulcan race, they had rejected the logic which had saved their Vulcan ancestors from succumbing to their primitive, passionate, blood-drenched beginnings. So who better than

7

Spock—a child of emotional humans and logical Vulcans—to understand both sides and work for unification?

Riker had spent many long evenings discussing Spock with Captain Picard. Both understood that the process Spock was involved with was simply the playing out on a larger scale of the struggle he had faced in his own divided heart.

But whatever extraordinary actions Starfleet had taken to bring the ambassador to this world at this time, Riker knew that none of them would have been questioned, even given the Federation's need to officially remain ignorant of Spock's activities.

Starfleet, the Federation, the galaxy itself, owed Spock too much to deny him anything.

Just as they owed too much to Kirk.

On the horizon, the last radiant spike of the dying sun flared, then vanished behind a distant peak.

Overhead, stars emerged from the deepening twilight.

Far away, Riker saw Spock bow his head, as if lost in memory.

What would it be like? Riker wondered.

A warm breeze stirred the small branches and dried leaves of the lone bush that shared the outcropping.

Lieutenant Baru caught Riker's eye.

"Yes, Lieutenant?" Riker realized he had whispered his inquiry. In the fading of the day, this forsaken plot of alien rock had become a solemn place.

"Sir, shouldn't we have heard from the *Farragut* by now?"

Riker tapped his communicator badge. "Riker to *Farragut*. The honor guard is in position."

No response.

"We arrived ahead of schedule," Riker told the lieutenant. The *Farragut* had been the workhorse of the rescue and recovery mission on Veridian III. Riker was not surprised the overburdened starship might be running late. "We'll give Captain Wells a few more minutes before we sound general alarm." He smiled at her.

Lieutenant Baru was too new to her rank to return the smile. She nodded once in silent acknowledgment, then returned her gaze to the cairn.

Silent minutes passed.

The night grew darker.

His communicator chirped.

Riker smiled again at Baru as he tapped it. She was too tense. He'd have to talk to her about that. Not every day in Starfleet brought life-or-death decisions.

"Riker. Go ahead."

But his smile faded as he realized the garbled, static-filled call did not come from the *Farragut*.

"Commander Riker! This is Kilbourne! We're—" An explosion of static washed out the rest of the transmission.

Riker held his fingers against his communicator, forcing an override. Kilbourne was the chief engineer at the salvage site. The honor guard stepped closer, on alert.

"Kilbourne, this is Riker. Say again."

9

Static whistled. Riker didn't understand the cause of it. There was nothing in this planetary system that could cause subspace interference.

Then, for a heartbeat, the static cleared and Kilbourne's distraught voice cut through the Veridian night.

"—can't tell where they're coming from! Two shuttles gone! We need—"

Then nothing.

Not even static.

Riker's communicator chirped uselessly as he tried to reestablish a link.

Riker looked at the four officers gathered around him. Their Starfleet training came to the fore. There was nothing youthful about the intent expressions they wore.

"This will have to wait," Riker said. He tapped his badge again. "Riker to Ambassador Spock."

A moment passed. Then the deep, familiar voice answered.

"Spock here."

"Ambassador, there appears to be some trouble at the salvage site. I'm going to have to ask you to remain here while we beam back to check the situation."

"Of course, Commander," Spock agreed calmly. "What is the nature of the trouble?"

"I'm not sure," Riker replied. He looked through the darkness that now blanketed Kirk's burial mound to where he knew Spock waited. But in his black robes, the ambassador was invisible. "It almost sounds as if they're . . . under attack."

Spock did not respond. Logically, Riker knew, he required no response.

"Riker to transporter control—five to beam to salvage site."

With Kirk's honor guard beside him, Riker tensed with anticipation as the computer-controlled satellite transport system reacted at once. "Energizing. . . ."

In the cool tingle of the transporter effect, the gravesite shimmered. There was an unsettling moment of quantum transition. . . .

And then Will Riker beamed into Hell.

TWO

Driving rain sprayed through the ragged hole in the canopy of the portable transporter platform, drenching Riker the instant the transporter's exclusion field shut down.

The platform shuddered in the concussion of a nearby flash and bone-jarring thud.

There had been thunderstorms at the salvage site for days now.

But the flash hadn't been lightning.

The concussion hadn't been thunder.

"Move! Move! Move!" Riker shouted over the storm and the nonstop roar of explosions. The platform shuddered again. Sparks flew from one of the pads. Riker shoved the honor guard ahead of him, toward the steps that led to the duraplast

11

walkways linking the buildings of the salvage camp spread out before him.

When the guards were clear, he charged after them into the storm.

It was night in this region of Veridian III, and Riker had been prepared for partial darkness. But the emergency lights weren't operating, and the bombarded camp had become a collection of looming shadows, black against black, hidden by night and rain.

Except when the sky blazed with alien fire.

Riker caught up with Baru. She leaned over the walkway railing, staring to the east where a sputtering ball of plasma flared against the duranium skin of the *Enterprise's* lifeless saucer. The starship's primary hull rose from the raw mud like a cliff of glacial ice, two hundred meters distant. All around the ship, energy beams and the flash of chemical explosions played like crazed lightning over the towering cranes, personnel barracks, and hastily constructed shuttle landing pads to the west of her.

"What's happening, sir?" Baru shouted, her voice almost lost in the deafening barrage.

Riker angrily pushed his rain-flattened hair from his eyes. "We're under attack!" he yelled back. A sudden wind caught him and spun him off balance—the wake of a low-flying craft, he knew. Released from its grip, he grasped the railing to steady himself, then looked up. But he saw nothing except low storm clouds, flickering with their own lightning and the explosions that bloomed beneath them in the camp. Baru still clung to the handrail, mesmerized by the infernal spectacle before them.

A wave of heat blasted him from the side as a barracks building detonated in a rocketing fountain of blinding plasma fire. Flaming debris arced downward, its flame untouched by the rain. Riker rapidly calculated that they were within range of the downfall. He grabbed Baru's arm, yanking her off the walkway, into the mud. "Let's go!"

Riker jabbed at his communicator as they ran, their boots caking with thick mud each labored step. *"Riker to Kilbourne!"*

An enormous thunderclap reached out and scooped them up from behind, tossing them into the rain. Baru's arm flew away from his grasp.

Riker twisted as he fell through the hiss of crisscrossing shrapnel, in time to see the transporter platform engulfed by plasma. As he struck ground, columns of steam shot up all around him where molten metal hit cold mud.

Riker lay face-down in the mud, lungs aching with the need to breathe. His ears rang with the thunder of whatever had hit the transporter platform.

A double pulse of wind shocked him into action. As he fought to lift his arms from the mud, he heard the sound of air being sliced by fast-moving vehicles.

He wrenched his back as he rolled free and struggled to his feet. His uniform clung to him, with ten extra kilos of thick clay that not even the stinging rain could dislodge.

Riker brushed his hair again without thinking. Mud stuck to his forehead.

"Lieutenant Baru!" he called.

A thick shaft of green energy stabbed through the night and the storm, piercing the *Enterprise's* hull. The impact point was close to a wedge already removed by the engineers. Riker saw the inner decks lit up with the discharge of whatever type of weapon was being used. He saw no trace of Baru or the other members of the honor guard.

The beam sliced through the *Enterprise,* pivoting from its origin point, fired by a flying craft.

A chain reaction of explosions started deep within the hull of the *Enterprise.* Instinctively, Riker knew that some of the ship's self-destruct charges must have been triggered. They had been deactivated by the engineers, but not all of them had been removed.

"Commander!"

Riker wheeled to see Baru struggling toward him. She was layered in mud, its dark wetness shimmering fitfully in the strobing flares of the attack. She limped, one hand wrapped tightly over her shoulder. Her other arm hung uselessly.

An enormous gout of flame flared from the *Enterprise's* hull. A second later, another gout blasted out through the saucer's side. Even through the wind and the rain, Riker could feel the heat.

"Who's doing this?" Baru cried as she reached his side.

Riker shrugged. He had no idea, nor even suspicions.

"We have to get to a shuttle," he said.

There was nothing they could do down here.

But some of the engineering shuttles were armed. He had to go up. To fight back.

Baru's gaze swept the camp. The mud around them glistened in firelight, lightning, and plasma bursts, as if they stood in a sea of flames. "There won't be any shuttles!" she said.

Riker took hold of her good arm. "We won't know till we look. This way."

Bodies lay scattered around the debris of the burning communications center. More explosions shook the saucer hull. Riker's jaw tightened as he heard screams blend with the roar of the unseen craft, the hum of their weapons, the roar of the flames.

But there was no way to know from where the screams came. No time to search for whoever made them.

Never enough time . . .

They skirted the burning mound of wreckage that had been a storage warehouse. Beyond it, Riker could see the smoking pits that were all that remained of the shuttle pads.

Two *Tesla*-class shuttles lay in pieces nearby, split open like used packing crates. A third shuttle was intact, though its frame was out of alignment where it angled into the mud, hurled there by an explosion not quite near enough to destroy it. Ragged figures milled about it. Riker and Baru fought the mud as they staggered closer.

Kilbourne was there. Four engineers worked with him. Two still in their sleeping robes. The attack had been that sudden.

"Who are they?" Riker asked as he leaned gratefully against the shuttle's hull, leaving a muddy handprint to be washed away by the pounding rain.

Hunched over his tricorder, Kilbourne looked up at him with shadowed eyes. "I don't know. They . . . they took out the *Farragut.*"

Riker felt acid course through his stomach. The only other Starfleet vessels in the Veridian system were a handful of transport freighters and engineering support cruisers. Without the *Farragut,* the survivors of the salvage camp—and Deanna Troi—were at the mercy of its attackers.

Kilbourne returned his attention to the small screen of his tricorder. Riker touched Kilbourne's shoulder. "Then what are they after?" Both of them glanced over at the looming mass of the *Enterprise's* saucer. The open ground between it and the camp was a nightmarish field of destruction. The saucer itself still crackled with energy discharges, long bolts of plasma sparking out as if in combat with the lightning.

"I don't know," Kilbourne repeated wildly. "There's nothing important left in her. All the tactical computer cores were pulled on the first day. Phasers . . . shields . . . everything classified has already been taken out."

The ground shook as a blinding flash of light exploded from the saucer's interior with a booming echo.

Kilbourne held out his tricorder. Riker recognized the traces on its display.

"Whoever they are—they're flooding us with sensor scans. They know where each one of us is." Kilbourne stared up at Riker. His haggard face was streaked by blood and rain and mud.

16

"We've got to retreat, Commander. Into the forest."

Baru stiffened at Riker's side. Riker looked at the engineering shuttle. It couldn't fly. But that wasn't all it was good for.

"Does this shuttle still have demolition charges?" Riker demanded. They were low-yield photon torpedoes designed for clearing orbital wreckage. The shuttle would normally carry four and be capable of firing two at a time.

But Kilbourne looked at him as if Riker were mad.

"You can't be serious."

Riker grabbed the chief engineer by his shirt-front, twisting the sodden fabric in his fist. He ignored the startled protests of Kilbourne's staff as they gathered around him. "Starfleet doesn't run," Riker spat at him.

He grabbed Kilbourne's tricorder and thrust it at Baru. "I want both torpedoes prepped for atmospheric detonation. Do it manually so they don't show up on the enemy's sensors."

Kilbourne's agitated voice shook. "The second you turn on the shuttle's targeting system, whatever's attacking is going to incinerate us!"

Riker smiled grimly. "Probably." Then he turned his back on Kilbourne and told Baru how to use the tricorder to open the shuttle's torpedo bays.

It took less than two minutes to prepare the torpedoes for simultaneous activation, target lock, and launch. Throughout that time, the unknown assailants' attack never lessened. The

Enterprise's saucer crumpled in on itself in three sectors. Fires blazed inside every open level.

One of Kilbourne's junior staff huddled against the side of the shuttle, hands pressed tight to his ears, eyes clenched shut, rocking, trying to shut out the assault on his senses.

Baru handed the tricorder back to Riker. Her expression was unflinching. "That's all we can do with the tricorder, sir. If you want to launch those things, we're going to have to do it from inside."

Riker met her gaze. He nodded his understanding.

The torpedoes could be launched only by the controls on the shuttle's flight deck. But the instant they were brought online, the enemy's sensors would detect them, target them, and direct fire at them.

And at whoever was on the flight deck.

"Get your people out of here," Riker ordered Kilbourne.

Riker felt Baru's hand on his arm.

"Sir . . . you can't do this alone."

Riker watched as Kilbourne and his engineers fled into the rain. The ground shuddered in a series of explosions. Riker wondered what was left to explode in the camp.

"Don't worry," Riker said. "I plan to live forever."

He punched a command sequence into the tricorder. Then he hefted the tricorder in his hand, paused for a moment, and threw it into the storm. It landed fifty meters away, disappearing into the mud.

Riker answered Baru's unspoken question. "In thirty seconds, that tricorder's going to put out a signal that makes it look like a phaser bank coming online."

"A distraction," Baru said. She smiled. Riker had no time to smile back.

He jerked his head to the side. "Follow Kilbourne. Take cover in the forest." Then Riker pulled himself through the off-angle door of the shuttle, out of the rain.

Inside the shuttle, the flight deck was at a twenty-degree slope. Riker braced himself on the copilot's chair as his mud-coated boots slipped on the traction carpet. He forced himself to finish counting out the thirty seconds in his head. He counted out an additional five to give the enemy time to react. Then he activated the shuttle's torpedo substation.

Swiftly, he set the torpedoes to target any moving object one hundred meters in altitude or above. As soon as the panel confirmed his input, he hurried back through the shuttle's cargo hold to the airlock door.

The instant he appeared in the doorway, a green bolt of energy hit the mud fifty meters in front of him, vaporizing the tricorder in a spray of steam. Riker felt the rush of relief. The distraction had worked.

But the beam did not shut off. It pushed on through the mud, rending it like water before the prow of a ship, closing on the second weapons signal—the shuttle.

Riker gripped the sides of the door and pushed to leap free.

His boots slipped.

He fell, chest slamming into the raised ridge of the airlock seal.

He felt a rib crack, lost his breath, looked up to see the inexorable green bolt crackling toward him, ten meters away, wreathed in steam.

He pulled himself up even as he knew he wouldn't make it.

Never enough time . . .

"Deanna," he gasped, willing his final word to her, his final emotion. *Imzadi . . .*

He thought of Kirk.

Falling . . .

The beam reached out for him.

A hand grabbed his wrist.

"Commander!"

She hadn't left him.

Riker's eyes met Baru's as she hauled him out of the shuttle with desperate strength.

He saw what she saw. Knew what she knew. All in that one terrible moment as he was hurled away from her to safety.

And heard her cry . . .

Heard the hiss of vaporized flesh . . .

Heard the hum of torpedoes launching . . .

The shuttle sliced in two . . .

The taste of Veridian mud for a second time as the shuttle erupted.

Too late for Baru.

But not too late for the torpedoes.

Riker rolled onto his back in time to see two ionized streaks of plasma exhaust bank into the storm clouds as the torpedoes sought their targets.

The clouds lit up like dawn.

A heartbeat later, the concussion of the torpedo detonations shook Riker deeper into the mud.

For a silent moment after, even the rain stopped.

When it began again, it felt gentle. Warm. Slow as tears.

Riker carefully, painfully, drew himself up into a sitting position. He strained to breathe. He choked on mud.

He saw Baru's hand, reaching for him, out of the mud. In relief, he gripped it. Pulled.

And the hand and forearm and nothing else of the young Bolian slipped from the mud.

Riker dropped the hand in horror.

In the awful silence, he heard it hit the mud.

He sat alone in the night. Hellish fires from the camp and the saucer still lit the low roiling clouds. But there were no more explosions. No more screams of low-flying craft. The warm rain bathed his eyes.

The attack was over.

Then Kilbourne was beside him. One of his engineers, still in a sleep robe, held a medikit. They helped Riker to his feet.

"Why?" Riker asked. Though he expected no answer. Certainly not from Kilbourne.

"I . . . don't . . . know," Kilbourne said grimly as he broke open a hypospray. "There was nothing here to steal. No secrets left. No . . . nothing. If you hadn't launched those torpedoes. . . ."

But Riker knew that part wasn't true. "They didn't stop the attack because of two demolition torpedoes."

"Why else would they?" Kilbourne jammed the hypo against Riker's neck. Its cool tip hissed as it delivered its healing agents.

"For the same reason all successful attacks end," Riker said, rocking as the painkillers flooded his body, as he finally surrendered to the overwhelming exhaustion he had held at bay. "They accomplished their objective."

"What objective?" Kilbourne raged. "Name one thing on this stinking planet worth dying for!"

For that question, Riker had no answer.

But somewhere, someone did.

And Riker knew he couldn't rest until he had found those responsible, and answered that question for himself.

THREE

Alone in the darkness by the gravesite, Spock had found a rock to sit on, the better to preserve his strength. Once settled, he had rearranged his robes, the better to conserve his body heat.

He was 143 standard years old. Advanced middle age for a Vulcan in good health. But whatever encounter Riker and his officers had beamed into, those days of action were behind him.

Quite illogically, he found he missed them.

For almost half an hour, he maintained his position, observing moving points of light against

22

the stars, and the streaks of multicolored light that were exchanged between them.

Starships in orbital battle.

"Fascinating," Spock murmured.

As his eyes adapted to the distant discharges, he recognized the distinctive blue signature of Starfleet phasers.

But the return fire was unidentifiable. He had never seen its like before.

The situation presented an interesting set of problems. In his mind, Spock began to analyze them as a series of logical arguments, attempting to identify likely attackers, their motives, tactics, and probable odds of success.

But he was interrupted in his calculations.

The night air thrummed. Something large was approaching through the sky.

Spock rose slowly to his feet. He scanned the dark horizon, searching for any occultation of stars that would indicate the presence of a flying craft operating without running lights.

The thrumming increased.

He could see nothing, but his robes began to swirl around him, blown about by some kind of backwash.

Spock raised his hand to shield his eyes from a rising whirlwind of dust.

Directly above him, the stars wavered and then disappeared, blacked out by a silhouette of something he couldn't identify. A sudden light danced at the edge of his vision.

Spock looked down the slope toward Kirk's grave.

Amber rays spiked out from between the rocks of the simple cairn.

Above the thrumming and the wind, Spock heard an oddly musical chime.

The light emanating from Kirk's grave brightened, then began to fade. Spock clearly heard the sounds of rocks falling against themselves.

The logic of this situation was inescapable, yet made no sense.

Among the stars, the signs of a space battle ended. Above Spock, the watching stars returned and the thrumming backwash ceased as suddenly as if a ship had gone to warp.

Spock drew an emergency light from his belt. He began to descend the slope to Kirk's grave.

He played the light against the cairn.

The rocks *had* fallen in.

The grave was empty.

Spock looked to the stars.

It was not at all logical, but for a moment, a most improbable thought came to him—

Perhaps some journeys were never meant to end.

"Jim . . . ?" he said.

There were *always* possibilities. . . .

FOUR

High above Veridian III, flashing in sunlight, a thirty-meter-wide slab of curved duranium hull metal slowly spun in the silence of space. The black letters etched into its surface read *U.S.S. Faragut* NCC-60597.

It was the largest piece of debris that remained of the starship. The rest was a cloud of dazzling shards, slowly dispersing.

Aboard the *Avatar of Tomed,* the Romulan commander, Salatrel, watched the hull metal impassively on the main viewscreen of her bridge. Beside her, she could sense her subcommander's elation.

"A great victory, Commander," Tran said.

Salatrel turned in her command chair. One upswept eyebrow arched, disappearing beneath the dark bangs that framed her aristocratic features, pointed ears, and full lips.

"This was no victory," she said. "They had no reason to expect us. They had no warning. It was an operational procedure. Nothing more."

But the young Romulan officer held her eye in a way he would not dare if this ship had still been a part of the Empire's fleet. With an insincere inflection of servility, he said, "They were expecting *something,* Commander. We lost two attack craft to torpedoes at the secondary target site. We are at war."

"I have not yet given that command," Salatrel replied sharply. "Don't make me remind you again."

An instant too slowly, Subcommander Tran dropped his gaze in response to the icy threat in his superior's tone. The most common language of the Romulan homeworld conveyed precise meaning by word and by inflection, and the weapons officer knew how close he had come to insubordination.

The communications officer's voice rang out, across the expansive bridge. "Commander, the second wing has confirmed transport at the primary target site."

Salatrel rose from her command chair. How long had she waited for this moment?

"Kirk?" she asked. The harsh and hated human name felt odd in her throat. Alien.

Her science officer answered from the engineering console where transporter displays flashed. "DNA analysis confirms identity of the remains, Commander. When the attack craft dock, the remains will be beamed directly into the stasis unit."

For the first time since this mission had begun, Salatrel permitted herself a small smile. She sat back in triumph.

"Decloak," she commanded her crew, "and prepare to receive incoming craft."

She glanced up at Tran, who remained standing beside her.

"You'll have your war soon enough, Subcommander."

Tran's eyes narrowed with predatory anticipation. "War, and victory," he said.

On the viewscreen, the frozen cloud that was the *Farragut* sparkled in its death throes.

Closer in, amongst the spinning, twisting wreckage of the *Farragut,* a handful of shapes moved of their own accord.

Some of the starship's crew had managed to

26

don environmental suits as their ship was torn apart around them in the unexpected attack.

Now they moved toward each other in the maelstrom of debris, homing in on each other's rescue beacons. Circuit panels, bulkhead sections, chairs, blankets, and frozen bodies sailed lazily past them, glittering with ice crystals.

Some larger pieces, intact equipment operating on self-contained power sources, still sparked.

The survivors avoided them. Using their maneuvering thrusters, they each eased out from the slowly tumbling ruins until they could see Veridian unobstructed.

From the voices on the emergency channels, six had survived. From a crew of six hundred forty.

Gradually, they floated free and toward each other, linking hands, exchanging information, until they formed a single six-spoked star.

But as they linked their communicators and broadcast their position to whatever fleet vessels had survived the attack, their view of Veridian III once again became obstructed.

By a wavering green mass that shimmered like a mirage, until it solidified into the double-hulled, raptor-prowed form of a *D'deridex*-class Romulan Warbird.

The *Avatar of Tomed*.

The veterans among the survivors knew they only had seconds remaining to them.

The Romulans were not known for taking prisoners.

As the monstrous starship—almost twice the length of Starfleet's *Galaxy*-class vessels—

smoothly changed its orientation, the twin hangar bay doors in its lower hull slid open.

Like flashes of verdant light, seven sleek attack craft, no larger than transport shuttles, returned, slipping easily through the forcescreens that held the Warbird's internal atmosphere.

The hangar doors slid shut again.

For a long heartbeat, the first visual discontinuities of the Romulan cloaking field began to warp the edges of the Warbird's silhouette.

And then, almost as an afterthought, a particle beam spun out through space and vaporized the six survivors.

By the time their incandescent atoms had dispersed in the vacuum to join the remains of their crew and their ship, the *Avatar of Tomed* had vanished as simply and as swiftly as it had appeared.

The hull metal fragment spun slowly in the silence of space.

The name of the *Farragut* faded into darkness.

Phase One was complete.

FIVE

Most Starfleet vessels were duranium white, proudly bearing the Federation's colors, boldly lit by running lights and identification beacons so all would recognize them on their missions of exploration.

But not all Starfleet missions involved exploration.

And some Starfleet vessels were as dark as the void between the stars, intentionally coated in microdiffracted carbon to absorb all visible radiation that fell upon them.

The *U.S.S. Monitor* was one such vessel, the latest in the *Defiant*-class, space black, on silent running, closing in on a dying, ancient world deep in the Core Frontier. Its destination: New Titan.

The ship was little more than an armored command saucer with integral warp nacelles. Over-powered, densely shielded, excessively armed, carrying more weaponry than three *Galaxy*-class starships. She was the result of Starfleet's fevered preparations to fight a war against the Borg. A war that had yet to come to pass.

But there were always possibilities. . . .

The *Monitor* eased into a nonstandard polar orbit over New Titan. The only sign of its presence was the winking out, then reappearance, of the stars it passed.

Its double-sealed hangar door opened.

A small personnel shuttle emerged, propelled by low-gain tractor beams, undetectable past ten kilometers.

The shuttle was aerodynamic, designed for unpowered atmospheric gliding. Like its base ship, it carried no markings, no operational running lights.

Its mission was not exploration, either.

The shuttle swiftly twisted through three axes at once, setting its course. Its impulse engines glowed faintly, tuned to emit in the almost invisible ultraviolet instead of the visible blue spectrum. Much less efficient, but far less noticeable.

It moved away from the *Monitor,* dropping for New Titan like a falling lance. In less than three minutes, hidden within the coruscating aurora of the planet's north pole, the shuttle met atmosphere and began to leave its blazing trail.

Inside, the craft shuddered heavily. Artificial gravity and inertial dampening had been turned off to reduce the risk of stray radiation being detected on the planet's surface.

The pilot, tightly strapped into her seat, maintained her calm expression and kept her hands steady on the controls. Behind her, her five passengers hung tight to the bench seats running along both sides of the shuttle's hold.

Their expressions were unknown, for each wore a carbon-black combat helmet with an opaque blast shield in place, capable of deflecting a full force beam from a type-3 phaser. The rest of their black uniforms were as heavily armored.

Their seat webs creaked as the shuttle slowed, increasingly buffeted by the thickening density of the air. Equipment swung from straps, metal clips creaking.

Three of the passengers braced themselves with phaser rifles, wedging the stocks against the shuttle's deck. The only identifying insignia they wore was the Starfleet delta slashed by a bolt of red lightning—the unit crest of Starfleet's newest intelligence division. That, and their nametags: WEINLEIN, BEYER, KRUL.

The other two passengers also wore carbon-black commando armor, though not the lightning-bolt insignia. Instead of weapons, their equipment harnesses carried sealed carryall pods.

But they also wore nametags: CRUSHER, PICARD.

Jean-Luc Picard felt himself shift as the shuttle slowly banked. The hum of its engines shut off, making the hold eerily free of sound. Picard knew that he and his team were in glide mode now, covertly traveling where a transporter beam couldn't be risked.

Through the heavily filtered blast shield he wore, he saw the subdued overhead lighting switch from full-spectrum to red.

It was almost time.

He opened his helmet.

Across from him, Weinlein lifted her own blast shield, and yanked open her helmet's visor. She was mostly human, though there was a hint of alien heritage in the assured gaze of her dark eyes. Picard regretted there had been no time to train with her directly. But then, events had moved too quickly for even Starfleet to be completely prepared.

With a black-gloved fist, Weinlein tapped the helmet of Beyer beside her. He opened his helmet as well. Fully human. And surprisingly young to wear the intelligence section's delta, Picard thought. Though the very idea of Starfleet forming a unit of this nature had been an even greater surprise.

But he knew it shouldn't be. Starfleet had given Commander Elizabeth Shelby a free hand to develop whatever systems and technologies she felt were necessary to fight the Borg. Both the *Defiant* class of starship and this unit were the results of that mandate.

Beyer tapped the helmet of the third commando.

Krul lifted his shield, opened his visor, and grunted, sweat gleaming from the ridges of his crested forehead.

Years of working with Worf on the *Enterprise* were responsible, Picard knew, for the sense of confidence he felt now in the presence of a Klingon on a mission such as this.

Weinlein looked past Beyer at Krul, responding to his growls with a grin. "Are you still complaining?"

Krul bared his teeth at her. Unlike Worf, he wasn't Starfleet. He was an exchange officer from the Klingon Defense Force, just as Shelby had drawn the other members of the unit from independent planetary defense forces throughout the Federation. "Human battle gear," Krul snarled. "Too much protection. Not enough weaponry."

Picard hid a smile as Weinlein and Beyer exchanged a puzzled look. Each commando carried the equivalent of two kilotons of explosive force. In addition, Krul carried extra Klingon munitions. Just in case, he had said.

Weinlein unfastened her seat web, stood up, holding one hand against the shuttle's low ceiling as she leaned over to tap Beverly's helmet.

The doctor fumbled with her shield and visor, and looked up at Weinlein grimly. Mutely.

Picard could see the unasked question in

Beverly's eyes. "How much longer?" he asked for her.

"You in a hurry?" Beyer asked.

"Stow it, Jerry," Weinlein ordered. She checked the read-out on her wrist-mounted tricorder. Picard recognized it as a heavy-duty model, specially hardened for use in non-Class-M environments. "We'll be over the drop zone in three hundred seconds." She strapped herself back in her seat web.

Beyer held up his fist. Beside him, Krul reached up to meet it with his own. The salute of warriors ready to face death.

Picard and Beverly looked at each other past the confines of their battle helmets, uncertain of how to respond to the bravado of their support team. "This isn't a side of Starfleet we see very often," Beverly whispered.

Picard caught sight of the equipment pod strapped to her waist, marked with the Starfleet caduceus. It was the interface, he knew. He had thought of little else since Shelby had first proposed this mission to him. . . . .He forced himself to smile. "It's a big galaxy, doctor."

But Beverly frowned as she followed his gaze to see what he looked at.

Awkward in her battle armor, she reached out to put her hand on his. "It will be all right, Jean-Luc. We won't have to use it."

It was Picard's turn to recognize the lie in Beverly's smile.

Their team leader unfastened her seat web again. "Thirty seconds," Weinlein announced. She stood up, then moved to the rear of the shuttle and pulled down three times on a side-mounted, manual release lever.

With a sudden roar of wind, the rear decking of the cargo hold dropped open onto darkness.

Exactly as they had trained, Picard and Beverly sealed their helmets and got to their feet.

Weinlein watched the readout on her tricorder. She raised a finger, paused, brought it down, pointing to Krul.

Without hesitation, the Klingon stepped over the open deck and dropped through it.

Weinlein was already pointing at Beyer. The human followed Krul two seconds later.

Picard approvingly noted the precision of Weinlein's command of her troops. Perhaps her combative approach was necessary, given the nature of the personnel she led. He would remember that when they reached their objective and command authority switched to him.

Then Weinlein pointed at Picard, and as he had done a dozen times in the *Monitor's* holosuite, he stepped out into nothingness. Trying not to dwell on the fact that he had never done this before, in realtime.

For the first few seconds, Picard had no sense of movement or direction until he felt the abrupt tug of the antigravs pulling on his equipment harness.

He flipped over, dangling feet first, with still no sensation of falling, though he knew from the training simulations that the surface of New Titan was rushing up at him at ninety kilometers per hour.

He looked up and saw the densely packed stars

34

of the galactic core, blazing in the cloudless night sky, brighter than the Earth's full moon. A dark object moved against them, then slowed, becoming the silhouette of Beverly, he decided. Or Weinlein.

He felt a gentle tugging to one side and wheeled slowly as he descended. Weinlein had told them she'd be using discontinuous sensor sweeps to monitor their position and rate of fall. The antigravs would step up their displacement effect fifteen meters off the ground, so that the actual landing would be no more jarring than stepping off a curb.

At least, that's what the holosuite technician had told Picard during the simulations.

He recalled the technician's grin as he had said it.

Picard rocked in his harness as the antigravs on his back began to work harder, changing his angle of fall and rate of descent. He tried not to speculate if it had felt like this on the *Enterprise,* as she had fallen through the atmosphere of Veridian III.

Tradition held that the captain must go down with his ship.

But Picard had been on the surface with Kirk.

He still awoke at night, these past weeks, anguished, sweating, wondering if he might have made a difference had he stayed aboard, in command, as every regulation in Starfleet had stated he should.

But then, he and Kirk would not have had their chance to make a difference on the planet's surface, as they indeed had done.

So many possibilities, Picard thought. And never enough time to explore them all.

The harness dug into Picard with a sudden, sharp snap. His simulated training paid off as he reflexively swung his legs together and bent his knees.

Then he slammed into dirt as if he had stepped off a three-meter wall, not a curb.

But he rolled as he had been trained, absorbing the impact along the side of his body.

A moment later, Beverly hit and rolled an arm's length away. He was about to reach out to her when Weinlein landed between them, coming to rest on her feet with no sign she had done anything more than step forward.

Before Picard could speak, he felt Krul and Beyer behind him, soundlessly detaching his anti-grav units from the back of his harness. Weinlein unhooked Beverly before reaching around to deftly disconnect her own antigravs.

Picard watched, silent. This was a part of the mission the commandos controlled. And they did their jobs well.

Krul and Beyer piled the antigravs together, preparing them for phaser immolation. Picard used the moment to pull down his visor and touch a forearm control on his armor.

Instantly, small projectors on the inside of his helmet cast a green-tinged, three-dimensional image of the people and terrain around him, created by low-level, discontinuous sensor scans. Because of the sensor emanations it produced, night-vision gear had not been safe to operate in the air. But close to the ground, there was less chance of signal scatter.

Above all else, Picard knew, they must remain undetected.

A phaser hummed. The antigravs expanded in a cocoon of light, then faded into nothingness.

Beyer was the first to break the silence. "They tracked us . . ." he hissed, pointing ahead where a Starfleet-blue phaser beam cut through the night from the horizon and found an unseen target that flared in a silent explosion.

Picard recognized the glimmer of an antimatter reaction.

"Was that our shuttle?" Beverly asked.

Weinlein nodded. "She had to activate the engines to climb out of the atmosphere. Which means the sensor fields they're using are more sensitive than we thought." She looked at Krul as the Klingon held out a small Klingon tricorder. "Give me a reading, Krul. Starfleet phaser cannon?"

Krul growled in acknowledgment.

Weinlein glanced at Picard. "That's a good sign. It means whoever's there is making do with the equipment at hand. They haven't brought in anything new."

Picard was struck by Weinlein's apparent complacency. Had she simply dismissed what had just happened so easily? "Our pilot just died. How can that be a good sign?"

"We all knew the risks," Weinlein said briskly. She pointed ahead. "Two kilometers, double time. Krul on point."

The Klingon jogged off into the darkness,

distinguishable only by the green trace he left on Picard's visor.

Weinlein turned to Picard. Her features were ghostly in the soft glow of the galactic core, overlaid by her night-vision silhouette. "Not to put too fine a point on it, Captain Picard, but move it."

Startled again by her directness, Picard started after Krul, keeping the Klingon's sensor shadow centered in his visor. He could hear Beverly just behind him. Weinlein and Beyer ran behind Beverly.

The terrain of this region of New Titan was rough, strewn with boulders. It reminded Picard of the nature preserves on Mars. But the air was different here. The terraformed craters of Mars were sharp with the tang of oxide-rich soil and lush vegetation. New Titan smelled acrid and lifeless. Whatever ecosystem had spawned the oxygen in this world's atmosphere had long since fallen into extinction.

Extinction.

As they ran, Picard's attention kept flicking ahead to their destination, to what Starfleet Intelligence projected they might find there. And how, of all the possibilities they faced, extinction was, he feared, one of the most likely.

Fifteen minutes and two kilometers later, Krul waved them to a stop at the base of a low hill. Thankful for the respite, Picard bent over, hands on his knees, gasping for breath. This short run was nothing compared to the marathons he competed in on the holodeck. But to run across broken terrain at night, carrying thirty kilos of equipment, armor, and supplies—that wasn't part of his job description.

Beside him, Beverly breathed deeply but evenly, as if she were used to this kind of exertion. Picard wondered if he should take up dancing.

Their team leader stood before them, commanding their attention. "This is it. All systems power down. Stay low."

Her hands hit the controls on her forearm padd. The green glow of her night-vision display faded from her helmet. Picard did the same and blinked as his eyes adjusted to the starglow.

He followed Weinlein up the hill, dropping to his belly a few meters from the top as she did.

Then they looked over the rise, and Picard's throat suddenly felt as dry as the rocks he lay across. In a barren arroyo, where half a kilometer away a plasteel perimeter barrier glowed in the glare of fusion-powered spotlights, lay their first objective—Starbase 804.

To the side Picard saw an equally brightly lit landing pad, safely away from the low buildings within the perimeter. There were no shuttles on it.

Studying the base, Picard could identify all the familiar structures without having to read their markings—subspace relay, clinic, recycling processor.

By the manuals, what lay before them was a type-seven, forward reconnaissance starbase, standard issue on Class-M planets when atmospheric domes were not required.

But this starbase was no longer standard issue.

Weinlein pointed straight ahead. "Captain, do you confirm what I see?"

Picard swallowed hard. The reports from Starfleet Intelligence were correct. How could he not confirm it when the jarring truth rose before him from the very center of Starbase 804?

Floodlights sprayed up its sides, bringing every centimeter of chaotic detail into hideous relief—pipes and conduits, duranium sheets, prefab housing sections, even parts of the shuttles that should be on the pad. There were traces of everything used in the construction of a starbase, now taken apart and reassembled into one of the most basic shapes of technology.

A cube.

"I . . . confirm. . . ." Picard said. His gut, his chest, his body felt packed in ice.

Weinlein brought her forearm up to her helmet and tapped a single control. Picard knew her words would be recorded, compressed, then transmitted in a theoretically undetectable microburst to the *Monitor,* far above them in polar orbit.

But her words would also be forever burned into his mind.

"Archangel, this is red leader. We have positive confirmation. Repeat, positive confirmation."

Picard kept his attention riveted on the cube in the center of the starbase. He thought of the equipment Beverly carried. Of her assurance that it would not have to be used.

But all that had changed.

Beside him, Weinlein completed her report.

40

"Starbase 804 has been assimilated by the Borg."

Within their armored gloves, Picard squeezed his hands into fists.

He was running out of possibilities.

SIX

Over the centuries, the Dante Field had been mapped, explored, and abandoned by every spacegoing culture in the sector. Drifting in inter-stellar space, dozens of light-years from the nearest star, it was simply a collection of aster-oidal debris, the castoffs of some unknown system's Kuiper Belt, perhaps even the remnants of a solar system which had never formed.

Whatever its origin, each of the thousands of asteroids in the field was worthless and without interest. Devoid of minerals, too far from the trade routes to even qualify as a hazard to naviga-tion.

But being worthless had become, to some, its greatest value.

The *Avatar of Tomed* decloaked as she dropped from warp on the outskirts of the Field.

Moving with deceptive grace, the giant Warbird effortlessly banked through the cloud of frozen rocks, avoiding the larger bodies, scat-tering the smaller ones with her shields and tractor beams.

But her course was not intended to avoid *all* the asteroids.

Near the field's center, one asteroid remained in the *Tomed*'s heading. It was more than three kilometers long, a slowly spinning shard of rock, scarred by millennia of impact crates.

The Warbird closed on it, without slowing, until a new impact was inevitable.

But then one small part of the asteroid's surface rippled with holographical distortion as the Warbird made contact and—

—passed safely through.

Inside the hollow body, beyond the holographic camouflage, the rough interior was studded with directional grids of docking lights.

Eight other Warbirds were docked within the main cavern, with twenty-seven Romulan Birds-of-Prey, more than a hundred scoutships, and uncounted other, smaller vessels.

The *Tomed* followed the line of pulsing lights that guided it to its bay. It expertly slipped between two other Warbirds and made precise contact with the docking conduits that would hold it in place.

On the *Tomed*'s hangar deck, Commander Salatrel stood with her senior officers as the artificial gravity fields of her ship and the asteroid base were brought into phase. Then, with a rumbling hiss of air, the hangar doors opened into the main conduit leading to the station corridors. A sudden wind rushed past her as the atmospheric pressure of the *Tomed* equalized by expanding into the endless tunnels of the base. The folds of her uniform were disturbed, and her dark hair fluttered for just that instant of equilibrium being sought.

Before the sudden wind had died, service technicians on wheeled cargo haulers rumbled in, bringing new armaments and supplies for the smaller craft parked on the *Tomed*'s deck. Shouted commands echoed back and forth. Mechanics' tools whined. Induction motors roared. Metal clanked against metal as the hangar filled with the smells of ozone, lubrication sprays, and carbon.

Salatrel took a moment to contemplate the sudden onslaught of activity, then walked through the maelstrom, an eye of calm.

She had not yet given the order, but there was no mistaking the swell of anticipation and excitement that flooded the station in her wake.

Without doubt, Dante Base was now on a war footing.

Deep within the hollowed-out asteroid now designated Dante Base, Salatrel ignored the tunnels that led to her private quarters. There would be time enough for rest when the mission was under way. Or when she was dead.

Instead, she headed through two sets of blast doors to arrive at the ultrasecure secondary docking cavern.

Where the other ship waited.

What the other ship's ultimate configuration had been, Salatrel could not be certain, for its forward hull covered the observation ports beside the main airlock portals, obscuring everything beyond.

Even its method of docking had been unorthodox. Instead of the clean seal between adaptable docking rings, the other ship appeared to have grown into the metal and rock of Dante. Tendrils of cable and connecting conduits spread out of the portal like connective tissue, anchoring the ship to the asteroid not in one place, but in hundreds.

Salatrel walked from the corridors of the asteroid to those of the ship without ever seeing a clear line of demarcation between one and the other.

But once she was without doubt within the ship, Salatrel followed the Romulan markings that had been affixed to the bulkheads, to lead her to the security doors protecting the cavern's central chamber.

As the doors unfolded, grinding on their metal hinges, Salatrel stood for a moment in the entrance, scenting the slightly fetid liquid that pulsed through the twisted pipes lining the chamber. Overhead, where the arching dome of the chamber's ceiling swept into shadow, there was nothing to see. But ahead and to the sides, an overlay of technology, both alien and Romulan, defined the chamber's circumference and its roughly textured walls.

Directly ahead, sunken into a central, circular deck, was the control pit, where Romulan computers had been installed. The shafts of light from their screens and operational surfaces spiked up through the haze that filled the chamber, mercifully hiding those who worked among them.

Her eyes traced the myriad light channels that snaked along the curved walls, angling in through the empty air to converge like a web on the immense machine at the heart of the chamber. Here and there along the machine's alien outline, she could see, Romulan devices had been attached to its ancient golden metal. The haphazard patches were based on incomplete knowledge, she was certain. Still less than a quarter of the machine's inner workings were understood to any degree.

But those were merely details.

Her scientists had assured her that as far as results were concerned, the restored machine would perform as promised.

"Commander Salatrel?"

Salatrel turned to acknowledge Tracius, her centurion. She accepted his salute with sincere warmth.

The elder Romulan was taken aback, as always, by Salatrel's familiarity. His family and hers were joined by centuries of common purpose, but he was old fashioned enough to still believe that their familial association and affection should not be part of their professional relationship.

"I understand you have had great success," Tracius said stiffly.

Salatrel smiled at his predictability. "That remains to be seen." Then she noted the diplomatic padd he carried—a small computer device programmed with the stolen codes of the Star Empire's diplomatic corps. "You have news?" she asked.

Tracius held up the padd. Its compact screen

glowed with Romulan script. "Spock is no longer on Romulus."

Salatrel stared at the padd, intrigued. "Dead?" Though she knew that was too much to hope for.

"Extracted. Starfleet Intelligence mounted a most extraordinary operation. Beamed him out of the capital."

Now Salatrel was more than intrigued. "How is that possible?" The government maintained strict control over all transporter activity in Dartha.

"Apparently, Starfleet has developed methods of circumventing our security precautions."

"And they risked exposing those methods to recover one aging ambassador who does not even have official status?"

Tracius offered Salatrel the padd. "Spock is gone. More than that is supposition, my commander." His bearing was rigid with disapproval. As if she were still a child and he still her tutor.

Salatrel graciously declined Tracius's unspoken offer to check his conclusions.

"Perhaps I should have asked: What is your interpretation?"

The centurion paused—a delaying tactic, Salatrel knew, which allowed him to gather his thoughts. In that moment, she studied Tracius pityingly. His white hair, cut short in the old style, looked dingy and limp in the dull amber light of the chamber. He deserved better than this. At his age, he should be writing his memoirs in a country estate, revered at court for his hand in guiding the history of his people.

But history had not unfolded as it should.

Because of one man.

One human.

"I believe it is connected to Kirk," Tracius said.

Salatrel waited for more.

"They were friends."

"A long time ago, Tracius."

Tracius's eyes didn't waver from her own. It was not a challenge of insubordination, as Subcommander Tran had proferred so daringly. It was a reminder of an unpleasant lesson taught long ago.

"What is time between friends, Commander? Is that not why we are here today? Because of the past?"

Salatrel drew herself up and smoothed the silver mesh of her command tunic. The lesson this time would be for Tracius to learn. And he would learn it from her. "We are here only for the future."

She turned from him, then, and was surprised to feel his hand on her arm.

It was not proper behavior for a centurion. But it was for a friend.

"Spock, with his insane dream of unification, is more dangerous than you know. And what you're planning can only serve to involve him in our plans. And for what?" He waved his hand to the murky outlines of the waiting machine. "This . . . abomination? It is without honor, Commander. This *new* plan of yours—so hastily conceived of—once put in motion, can end in only one of two ways."

47

"No," Salatrel said. "It shall end in only one way." She lifted Tracius's hand from her arm. Defeat was not an option.

Only victory.

This time when she turned, Tracius did not stop her.

Unaccompanied, Salatrel approached the ark. That was the name her scientists had given to the alien machine's central component—an elongated container, three meters along its widest axis, made from bulging, asymmetrical panels of a transparent mineral, bound by gilded struts of tarnished metal, like some grotesque inner organ trussed in gold wire.

Salatrel studied the curves and swellings of the machine that cradled the ark—the forms of flesh and technology combined as one. It was no wonder her scientists could not fully comprehend its workings. Even those who had supplied it said it was tens of thousands of years old, removed from the ruins of a race so obscure they had no name, as if fate had wiped them from the memory of the universe.

She glanced into the shadows of the control pit facing the ark. The Technicians worked among their Romulan computers there in the dark center of the chamber, precisely moving silhouettes, pinpointed by red dots of coherent light shining from their various arrays.

A scientist's voice echoed from hidden speakers. "Transporter systems are online."

Another replied, "Locking on to stasis unit. Commander, it is time for Phase Two."

Without knowing it before, Salatrel now realized she had waited all her adult life for this moment, never expecting it would be so perfect, so personal. Yet it had come and gone in less than a heartbeat. "Proceed," she said. As simply as that, the shape of the galaxy would now change.

Responding instantly, the alien machine began to vibrate. Thick conduits, formed of fleshlike plastics, not metal, swelled as their internal pressure increased. A rhythmic thudding began to shake the scarred metal deck.

"Backup buffer initialized," an unseen scientist announced.

The deeper, duller voice of a technician intoned, "Phase transition coils are online. Temporal translator is phase matched."

An electrical hum spread thrillingly through the moist air of the chamber. Mist spilled out of the control pit where the Romulan computer consoles had been installed to operate the device, bypassing the original alien controls that appeared to require direct implantation into a living nervous system.

Salatrel's chest tightened. Despite her bravado before Tracius and the station crew, she knew she had gone into battle feeling less tense than she felt now. She had led a mutiny against her own admiral and hijacked her warbird with less fear and less doubt than she felt now.

Ever faster, the broadcast voices of the scientists and the technicians rattled through the rest of the systems check until the phase transition coils were synchronized with the pattern buffer and the temporal isolation conduits.

Salatrel fought to compose herself by picturing the subspace pathways now linking her warbird with this device, and the unimaginable pathways through sidestepped spacetime that reached back into the past. She forced herself to focus on the one final command that remained to be given.

The deadened voice of Vox, the warrior who once had been her lover, reached out to her through the sounds of machinery and power, gushing liquid and hissing steam. "Commander . . . ?"

Salatrel stared fixedly at the ark, now suffused with a blue-white glow.

"Energize," she ordered.

It all happened at once.

A soaring exhalation filled the chamber, disconcertingly like the cry of a living thing. It came from the machine.

The slow wave of light within the liquid-filled ark quickened rhythmically with an orange gleam that fractured into stabbing golden flickers.

The conduits labored, pulsing erratically.

A harsh, warning alarm sounded sharply on a Romulan console.

"Primary matter stream confirmed."

"We have initiated temporal lock."

A second warning alarm sounded.

"Switching to backup emitter."

"Secondary matter stream confirmed."

An energy discharge crackled off a resonating coil a hundred meters away, lighting the vast chamber with the uncontained fury of a storm.

"Matter streams blending. Temporal consolidation is confirmed."

Salatrel realized she was digging her thumbnail into her palm.

Retrieval had been the easy part.

The light in the ark began to fade. A shadowy mass now became visible in the dense, murky liquid.

Desiccated, corrupted, monstrous remnants of the hated past, floating before her.

Awaiting invasion.

"Now confirming nanite transmission," a Technician stated.

Salatrel glanced up. Above two of the consoles in the control pit, holographic images of DNA helices spun through the air faster than she could read their base pairs.

Three alarms shrieked at once. A siren warbled, filling the chamber with its desperate song.

The projected DNA models lost focus and cohesion.

"Vox?" Salatrel called out to the darkness.

A sudden flash and explosion from the machine's flank sent sparks cascading through the chamber. The machine had rejected one of its Romulan devices.

"*Vox!*" Salatrel shouted, poised to run to the control pit where the silhouettes of the Technicians still moved at the same plodding, deliberate pace.

"Medical team to the ark," Vox calmly announced.

Three Romulan scientists charged out of the darkness toward the small scaffold platform built around the transparent container. Salatrel ran to get there first.

She ducked as a nearby conduit burst, spewing thick green liquid through the air that splashed noisily on the rocky floor. The Second Complex now reeked with the unlikely stench of chlorophyll.

Salatrel reached the scaffold first. The ark was two meters above her. She stared up into its darkened heart, saw the shape within.

Saw that shape *move*.

She leapt for the ladder, two of her scientists close behind her.

"Open it!" she commanded as they reached the top of the ark.

The two scientists attached a polyphasic grappler to unlatch the metal clamp holding the topmost panel in position.

The shape within the ark struggled, arms flailing.

"No!" Salatrel shouted. She grabbed the tool from the startled scientists' hands, spun it around and smashed it handle first on the transparent panel.

The panel cracked.

She swung again.

A gout of liquid sprayed into her face. She lost the grappler in the depths of ark.

She clawed at the edges of the shattered panel with her hands.

The shards of it slashed her palms. The dark liquid streaked with the green of her blood. But the pain could not stop her.

Salatrel tugged at the metal band between the

broken panel and the next. Her scientists saw what she was doing and pulled on the opposite side.

The few remaining Romulan controls and devices exploded spectacularly in the pit and on the machine. Salatrel and her scientists held fast to the scaffolding.

Salatrel's face was smeared with the ark's nutrient fluid. Rivulets ran into her mouth. It tasted bitter, salty, like an ocean choked with life.

"Get him out! Get him—"

She gasped as a hand shot up from the ark, grabbed her arm.

She felt something sharp slice along her arm, into her shoulder, as the unexpected power of that hand drew her against the ragged edges of the panels, toward the suffocating depths of the ark.

But to die now, here, with him, was not why she had risked her life, her name, her world.

With the strength of primal rage, Salatrel pulled back, bracing herself against the ark itself, feeling it bend and buckle until the terrible hand slipped off her arm and she stumbled back, free. Except . . .

The hand was gone, swallowed again.

The dark shape settled in the fluid, no longer moving.

The scaffolding gave way in one corner, sending the two scientists tumbling to the deck below. But Salatrel did not fall.

"No," Salatrel choked.

Flashing lights and sirens blended with the

spraying mist of chaos and the roaring liquid from the dying ark.

"No," Salatrel shouted.

Dark liquid erupted from the ark.

"*Live!*" Salatrel screamed, daring to command even him.

Then above it all rose the soul-shattering wail of pain, of confusion, of . . .

. . . *life*.

For a moment, Salatrel stopped breathing.

And then she felt the hand return.

This time grabbing her neck.

Pressing, squeezing, crushing.

Salatrel gripped the muscled forearm with her own torn hands. And saw—

Kirk.

Eyes alive with a madness she could not comprehend.

The flesh of his shoulders and neck twisted and shimmered as its contours changed, reformed and realigned by the microscopic nanite devices that still worked within him, restoring him, rebuilding him.

His mouth gaped open as he heaved with deep, desperate gasps for air.

But Salatrel could hear only the pounding of her own blood, thundering in her ears as her creation increased the pressure.

His mad eyes bore into her. His mouth moved, awkwardly, trying to form a word.

. . . *why* . . .

Salatrel's vision flared with searing silver dots. She felt herself spinning into darkness, saw the shadowy shape of her grandfather reaching out to welcome her as this monster's next victim, as—

A different hand joined hers in the struggle.

She saw that hand squeeze and twist on the iron-muscled forearm that held her, and suddenly the pressure was gone.

Salatrel pawed at her neck, felt the acid pain of air rushing into her ravaged throat.

Vox had saved her.

He stood before her, in profile, his noble Romulan brow high and defiant, his ear fiercely pointed, his eye dark and piercing. He held Kirk in place without effort.

Salatrel shook her head as her vision cleared.

For a moment, she was confused. Her beloved was before her, standing in profile.

She touched his shoulder, about to say his name.

His real name.

And then he turned to her and the nightmare returned.

Half his face was gone.

Obscenely replaced by black circuitry patches, laser sights, tubes and coils of bioneuronic implants—the inescapable hallmarks of assimilation.

His old name was no longer a part of him, along with everything else he had been.

He was Vox, now.

Romulan speaker for the Borg collective.

The alien machine stirred, rumbling ominously.

"We must leave the chamber," Vox said impassively.

Salatrel nodded, unable to speak.

Kirk's body was frozen in a contorted posture, his strength no match for the implanted manipulator that had replaced Vox's right arm.

The other technicians came then. Their proud Romulan features also torn apart by the machinery that had claimed them.

The technicians were Romulan no longer.

They, too, were Borg.

Like Vox.

But for now, they served Salatrel.

"We will take him to the medical facilities in Dante Base," Vox said.

Manipulator arms swung up. Drill bits and cutting blades spun. What remained of the ark was disassembled in seconds.

"We should save these components," Salatrel said distractedly. The ark's transparent mineral still hadn't been identified by her scientists or the Borg technicians. It seemed to have a dilithium-like fourth-dimensional molecular branch. Her scientists had told her it helped the reanimation machine focus the necessary temporal transference. Without the temporal capture of Kirk's final pattern of brainwaves from the moment of his death, this machine would have produced nothing more than a mindless, biological reproduction of the original.

But Vox stared blankly at Salatrel, not answering.

"So we can use it again," she explained.

"This device cannot be used again," Vox said. "It will be assimilated."

Salatrel sighed, but she knew resistance was futile.

With Vox beside her, she watched as her attacker, her monster, her creation was taken away, staggering, unable to speak. Kirk's ancient uniform hung in tatters, destroyed by the energies that had coursed through him once his body had been transported into the ark. He walked stiffly, like an *auroto*—the living dead of Romulan myth. Salatrel found that fitting.

"Amazing," Salatrel whispered. She felt herself begin to tremble as the enormity of what she had done began to filter into her consciousness. "In ten days, that creature will cause the Federation itself to fall before me."

"You are wrong," Vox said.

Startled, Salatrel forced herself to look into her former lover's left eye, trying to ignore the hideous visual sensor that had replaced his right one.

"We have made an agreement," Vox said. "The Federation will fall before *us*."

Salatrel nodded, relieved that Vox had meant nothing more than what she had already accepted.

Romulans and Borg working together.

It was the price she had paid to restore the hated James T. Kirk to life.

In ten days, she would know if it had been worth the bargain.

SEVEN

Come back, Jean-Luc. . . .

Picard ignored the distant whisper deep within his mind and walked among the Borg alone.

His heart raced. He felt sweat trickle beneath the combat armor he wore. His hesitant breaths thundered in his helmet behind his closed visor.

But the Borg ignored him.

All around Picard, they went about their task of assimilating Starbase 804. Teams of them worked as little more than ants or termites, using their biomechanical implants and augmentations to carve up the prefab buildings, remove the Starfleet equipment, and process everything for the greater good of the collective.

Picard tried his best to ignore them in return.

To his left, where the infirmary had been, a heavy construction Borg—a configuration Picard had never seen before, with four arms and thick, double-kneed legs—fired microbursts from an implanted energy weapon into a diagnostic bed that was balanced precariously on a pile of rubble.

To his right, a severed human leg was draped across half of a transport cart.

Two dogs—sleek Dobermans, pets of the personnel who had been assigned here, no doubt—trotted past. But they did not stop to investigate. Bioneuronic implants studded their skulls. Biomechanical tubes were grafted to their chests.

One dog turned to look at Picard as it passed. One eye clear though expressionless, so unlike the breed. The other eye had been replaced by a laser sensor.

But Picard was alone, and the Borg were not concerned with individuals. The dogs trotted on, into the smoke that still clung to the ruins of the starbase, echoing with the sounds of machinery.

With the same icy control which had let him face the unknown for decades on the bridge of a starship, Picard grimly kept one foot moving after the other, as if he were no more than a machine himself.

It was his greatest fear. But one he would have to face—if not for his own sake, then for that of Starfleet. Or even the Federation.

After Veridian III and his encounter with the Nexus, by the time he had been evacuated to a Starfleet facility with his crew, Picard had been sure he would draw at least a year behind a desk.

A *Galaxy*-class starship had been lost on his watch. The flagship of the Fleet. The boards of inquiry alone would take months.

But Starfleet was nothing if not responsive, and realistic. True, the *Enterprise* had been lost, but three other of her sister ships had also experienced catastrophic failure in less than a decade since the *Galaxy* class had first flown. Clearly, there were matters of design and technology implementation to be addressed by Starfleet's Engineering sections.

Picard felt fortunate that the *Enterprise's* flight

recorders had been recovered intact. His bridge crew had given their reports to investigation teams staffed with Betazoids, to whom no lie could be told. And acting on depositions given by Guinan, other El-Aurian survivors of the *Lakul* disaster had been located and interviewed. Thus the power and the nature of the Nexus had been confirmed by the El-Aurians, if not fully comprehended by Starfleet.

And neither Starfleet nor the Federation Council could forget the millions of innocent lives which had been spared on Veridian IV by the actions of Picard, his crew, and, most notably, James T. Kirk, in keeping with the highest and most noble ideals upon which the Federation had been founded.

By the time Picard was asked to testify before the formal hearing on Starbase 324, Starfleet already had all the information it needed to begin an overhaul of starship defensive-shield systems. Antique scows like an almost century-old Klingon Bird-of-Prey would no longer threaten the Fleet's most advanced, state-of-the-art vessels.

Given all the ground that had been covered behind the scenes, Picard's testimony had taken less than half a day.

He was still reeling from the speed of the inquiry and its conclusion as he and Will Riker had left the hearing room.

And only when Picard saw Commander Elizabeth Shelby waiting for him did he understand that Starfleet had its own reasons for dealing with the *Enterprise* hearings so quickly.

The young commander had been as brusque and efficient in that hallway as when she had been temporarily assigned to Picard's *Enterprise* after the destruction of the colony at Jouret IV. She waved Picard into an empty office and bluntly stated the facts.

Starfleet Intelligence had reason to believe that a series of distant outposts on the Core Frontier was being raided by the Borg.

"But the Borg are defeated," Picard had protested. He had seen it himself. Hundreds of the once-mindless creatures had been awakened to their own individuality. The threat of the collective had been removed.

But Shelby had looked on Picard with an expression almost of pity. For a moment, Picard had felt as if he were withering into doddering antiquity, faced with the clear-eyed judgement of youth.

"Captain, it is Starfleet's belief that what you contacted, what you and your crew defeated, was only *one* branch of the collective. A single tentacle, if you will, of a monster that's spreading through the galaxy." She had clasped her hands together and leaned closer over the office's bare conference table. "Think of what you've seen of the Borg's activities, Captain. Starting eight years ago with the missing outposts on the Neutral Zone. Go back eighty years to the El-Aurian dispersion. Truly contemplate the unstoppable power and technology of the Borg, and their mission to destroy life."

Picard had felt the sweat break out on his forehead.

"Do you honestly think you have *changed* that by changing just the handful of Borg with which you've had . . . personal contact?"

Picard had found it hard to breathe in the cramped office. Elizabeth Shelby had taken his lack of response as an invitation to continue.

"We're not saying we believe that facing the Borg is a hopeless proposition. You *were* able to neutralize one branch. To us, that clearly implies the other, yet-to-be engaged branches can also be defeated."

At that Picard had disagreed, vehemently. "But whatever strategy we use one branch, the next branch instantly knows what to defend itself from."

Shelby had only smiled at his passion. Picard still remembered that smile. Predatory, focused, and intense. How had one so young become so cold? Almost as if there were something of the Borg in her as well.

"We're not just going after the branches, Captain," she had said, making a fist for emphasis. "We're going after the head."

Picard's lack of comprehension had been obvious.

"The source," Shelby had explained. "Somewhere out there is the central point from which all the branches emanate. We shall find that source, and we shall destroy it. And when we do, each branch of the Borg will wither and die without any further action from us. Or any other civilization unlucky enough to encounter them."

The young commander's argument had been

persuasive, Picard allowed. There was even a kind of logic to what she had told him.

But then she had given him his new orders, direct from Admiral Stewart, Hanson's replacement at Starbase 324.

Picard was to join the tactical team to be based at Starbase 804, the closest fleet facility to the threatened region on the Core Frontier. Once there, when suspected Borg activity was detected, Picard was to be deployed with Starfleet's new, anti-Borg intelligence unit, to investigate and, if necessary, infiltrate the area of enemy action. His task would then become to carry out the mission objective—the capture and return of a Borg vessel. Shelby gave him to understand that even if the *Enterprise* had still been intact, he would have been temporarily reassigned for this mission.

Picard had known the reason why as well as Shelby did.

Four years ago, Jean-Luc Picard himself had been assimilated—made part of the Borg collective and its irresistible groupmind.

As Locutus of Borg, he had actually led the collective against Starfleet in the devastating Battle of Wolf 359, giving the Borg full access to every Starfleet secret locked in his mind.

And though every trace of Borg technology had been surgically removed from his body . . .

. . . in his mind, the tendrils of the collective remained. And Starfleet knew that, too.

Shelby had put the pieces of the interface on the table then.

The latest from Starfleet R & D—special branch. The branch Shelby headed at Starbase

324 in preparing the Federation for all-out war with the Borg. The ungainly, overpowered *Defiant*-class starships had come from that effort.

Along with the innocuous-looking pieces of microcircuitry and inert silicon that lay on the table before Picard.

Pieces which he recognized.

And which filled him with dread.

One part was simply an insulated cable, containing a microprocessor on one input jack and a slender transformer on the other.

The other was a sleek power cell, coupled with a short-range subspace transmitter, small enough to be carried unseen in a hand.

But the third piece was an asymmetrical plate of silicon, curved to fit the contours of the human face and skull.

In this case, Picard's face and skull.

Together they formed a Borg-derived neural interface. Just like the one that had been implanted in Picard's flesh, and into his mind.

"You will be accompanied by Dr. Beverly Crusher," Commander Shelby told him. "She's already been briefed."

"What about Will?" Picard had asked. For what Starfleet was asking of him, he wanted to be fully prepared—to go into action with his own command crew, the best crew in the Fleet.

But the commander had only replied, "Riker has other duties." Picard had had no trouble hearing the dismissal in her young voice as she said his name. That, too, was left over from the events of four years ago. Will Riker's refusal of a captaincy in order to remain Picard's first officer on the *Enterprise* had prevented the ambitious Elizabeth Shelby from taking his place.

At the end of their meeting, Shelby had ushered Picard out a back door, where two security officers had met him and taken him under armed guard to the private quarters that had been put aside for his use.

The guards, Shelby had assured him without irony, were not because he was a prisoner. But because he had become an invaluable resource.

After all, if the Borg were indeed massing on the Federation's frontier, and if, as had been long suspected, all-out war with the Borg was inevitable, then Jean-Luc Picard had become the most important living being in the Federation. And Shelby would see to it that he would be treated as such.

Except for Beverly, Picard had had no contact with his crew since that day.

"We require your power pack."

The flat, emotionless voice startled Picard from his reverie into the past.

A Borg barred his path.

Once it had been human, female. Starfleet.

Beneath the cybernetic augmentations fused to its chest and rib cage, he could see the remnants of a Starfleet duty uniform. The fabric had been cut away over its left shoulder, heartlessly exposing a ravaged section of blue-white flesh. But its communicator was still in position. Borg wires extended from it and entered that abused skin in a seemingly random series of small puckers. A thicker red cable ran up from the communicator and into its temple.

Whatever it had been, it was a Borg now, manipulator arm extended, a cutting blade whirring.

"Are you defective?" the Borg asked.

If Picard didn't answer, he knew his remaining life span could be measured in seconds.

"I will give you my power pack," he said.

Everyone on the team had been ordered not to argue with any Borg they might contact unless hostilities had begun. Picard didn't need to be ordered. He still remembered the parameters by which individual Borg operated: Achieve the collective's goals through the expenditure of the least amount of energy and resources.

It was the same natural law which had arisen from the principles of self-organization to govern everything in the universe, from simple chemical reactions to the evolution of reproductive strategies among living creatures.

Thus, Borg were likely to first *ask* their victims to cooperate before exerting any physical effort in assimilating them. Each major Borg offensive invariably began with the selection and assimilation of a leading individual from the target population who could function as Speaker—bridging the gap between the collective and its new component.

So far, that cautious, though logical, husbanding of resources was the only quirk of Borg behavior that gave Starfleet any hope of victory.

But even as Picard hurriedly slipped his suit's power generator and battery coils from his back, he knew that, eventually, one of the many branches of the Borg collective that Starfleet suspected had spread throughout the galaxy would, sheerly by chance, discover the survival advantage of overwhelming its technologically advanced victims *without* negotiation. When that happened, when the Borg ceased being socialized ants and became blindly guided sharks, intelligent biological life was doomed.

Picard handed his power pack to the Borg.

The Borg did not take its eye or its sensor off Picard.

"We require the protective device encasing your sensory stump."

Picard blinked, taking precious seconds to realize the Borg meant his helmet.

The Borg responded by going back into its secondary programming loop.

"Are you defective?"

"I will give you my protective device," Picard said quickly, steeling himself for the result.

The mission to Starbase 804 was dependent on Picard removing his helmet and revealing himself to the Borg only at a key point in the operation. But that point hadn't been reached. Picard knew that Weinlein and her commandos had not yet determined an access path into the Borg vessel at the center of the starbase. But he also knew that if he did not remove his helmet now, the mission would be over before it had begun.

The Borg held out its living hand.

Picard surrendered his helmet, keeping his head downcast, eyes averted. He became strongly aware of the oily smoke of burning flesh, mingled with the acrid fumes of scorched plastic and synthetics from the devastated starbase.

The Borg did not step away.

"You will direct your visual sensors upward," the Borg said.

Picard took a deep breath.

What if he met the Borg's gaze?

What if he stared into that eye and . . .

"Locutus?"

The name carried such weight and importance within the collective that recognition of Picard's face had somehow triggered a deeply buried emotional response of surprise—a relic of the biological being this Borg had once been.

Picard himself was not surprised.

Starfleet had counted on him being recognized in just this way, exactly as he had been recognized by the Borg known as Hugh, years ago.

Hugh had been a young Borg, lost to the collective when his scoutship had crashed in the Argolis Sector. Picard's *Enterprise* had rescued him. Picard's crew had nurtured the nascent individuality in Hugh, and those newly formed threads of lone personality had eventually led to the total subversion of one of the Borg collective's many branches.

But the Borg who stood before Picard now was not from Hugh's branch. It looked troubled.

Picard understood the programming conflict it must be going through.

Hugh had been cut off from the collective. Because of that loss of communication, when he had first met Picard aboard the *Enterprise,* he had not been troubled by his inability to detect

68

Locutus within the groupmind. But this human Borg was still a functioning unit of whatever branch of the collective was assimilating Starbase 804. And clearly, from its confusion, the collective was troubled because Locutus was physically here, yet not present among their joint thoughts.

The Borg trained its manipulator arm on Picard. The whirring blade stopped and folded into an inner compartment, even as Picard heard the click of another compartment opening.

The thin blue rod of an X-ray welding unit glowed along the mechanical arm. Picard knew the welder could torch through duranium as easily as through human flesh.

The collective had long ago evolved the response of treating anomalous phenomena as threatening, and therefore subject to immediate destruction.

At this moment, Picard was obviously a threat.

But he also knew how the Borg functioned.

"Are you defective?" he asked.

Whatever the Borg had been about to do, its primary behavior was now circumvented by a diagnostic subroutine. A verbal order from Locutus had been enough to trigger it.

Picard looked around quickly. A work crew of augmented Borg carried pieces of a shuttle in a single file, like cutter ants carrying carved sections of leaves. Why the Borg had not simply scooped this base up with one of their tractor beams, Picard didn't know. The Borg ship that had landed in the base's center was smaller than most of the cubeships Starfleet had catalogued. Perhaps it was not powerful enough to assimilate whole installations at once, as the colony on Jouret IV had been assimilated. There the Borg ship and crew had left only a smooth-sided crater behind.

Picard could see no sign of the rest of Weinlein's commando team. Each had planned to enter the base separately, to avoid attracting the collective's attention. They were to rendezvous by the ruins of the communications building in two more hours to brief each other on what they had seen. But until then, they were to remain alone.

"No defects detected," the Borg announced. It raised its manipulator arm again.

"You will continue your work with the power packs," Picard ordered. It was a shock to discover how easily the harsh tone of Locutus returned to him.

The Borg angled its head. Communing, Picard knew. He remembered the feeling well. The sense of support. The release of abandoning power to—

"Locutus is missing," the Borg stated. "You are defective." It stepped toward Picard. Its manipulator arm rose with the hum of its internal actuators. The X-ray welder began to glow, began to whine as its quantum capacitor built its charge.

"No," Picard said, thinking fast. "You—"

Picard stumbled back as the female Borg suddenly shimmered in a blaze of phased energy, then vanished. He looked around. Saw Sue Weinlein three meters away. The stock of her phaser rifle was braced on her hip as she scanned the immediate area, paying careful attention to the long line of workers carrying the shuttle parts.

"Don't look at me," Weinlein said. Even as a group of only two, they couldn't appear to be interacting, otherwise they might become a target for assimilation.

"Have you been following me?" Picard asked. The afterimage of the phaser burst still floated across his vision.

"My job's to get you to that cubeship," Weinlein said. "Keep walking."

Picard marched forward.

"Picard!"

He turned.

Weinlein tossed him his helmet. "Save it for showtime."

Picard pulled the helmet on, closed the visor.

He wished he were somehow locking Locutus back into his deep and hidden cell, somewhere in his core.

But he knew it was too late.

All around him, he heard the whisper of the collective. Though whether it sprang from the Borg or his own subconscious, he could not be certain.

Come back, Jean-Luc. . . .

Picard marched deeper into the starbase.

Deeper into enemy territory.

And for the first time, despair took hold of his soul.

Because he knew he would no longer be alone.

Come back. . . .

EIGHT

The hull of the *Starship Enterprise* had been built to withstand asteroidal impact, Iopene antimatter streams, and the distortional stresses of warp speed.

But here, on Veridian III, echoing with the soft drumbeat of a summer rainstorm, the once-mighty ship leaked like a molecular sieve.

Riker moved carefully through the tilted corridor on deck eight. He had learned his lesson and wore engineer's grip boots, to keep from slipping on the waterlogged carpet. Beside him, Deanna Troi moved just as carefully.

The saucer creaked.

Riker's hand found Deanna's, and for a timeless moment, they held their breaths.

Then they looked at each other in the soft light of Riker's handheld torch and laughed.

"That sounded just like an atmospheric containment breach," Deanna said.

Riker nodded. "I know."

But planetbound, sliced to pieces, and half-disassembled, the *Enterprise* no longer had to be atmospherically sealed. Their sudden apprehension had been the result of training, not fact.

"Settling?" Deanna asked.

Riker nodded again. The settling of a body decaying in death.

A third of the saucer had already been removed

before last night's attack on the salvage camp. With so many support beams missing, and with no structural integrity force field to keep the immense structure in alignment, the saucer was in no shape to even support its own mass. And no additional salvage operation would begin until a Starfleet support team answered the distress calls Riker had put out after the attack.

"We'd better hurry," Riker said. He had survived the crash of this grand ship. He had no desire to die in her collapse, weeks later.

Deanna held her tricorder ahead of them. She had been trapped in her barracks during the attack, spared the onslaught of energy weapons by a well-placed locker which had struck her from behind. The locker threw her forward between two bunks, where she had been sheltered by their mattresses.

The rescue crews had found her unhurt an hour after the last explosion had rocked the camp. Riker had sat by her side until she had awakened with the dawn.

He remembered the look that had appeared on her face as she sensed his emotions at seeing her safe. She hadn't been prepared for the intensity of them.

Neither had Riker.

Wisely, at least for now, both had tacitly agreed not to mention it. The events of the past few weeks had been confusing enough without adding the extra complication of a return to the emotions of years gone by.

Riker read Deanna's tricorder's display, then looked along the corridor, past a shifting curtain of water that trickled down from the outside rain-storm, into impenetrable darkness. The emergency lighting circuits had long since expended their power. The once-familiar ship might as well have been an ancient network of tunnels and caves.

"That way," Deanna said. "One of the class-rooms."

They moved carefully down the corridor, following Riker's torchlight, sliding their feet so as not to lose their footing.

Deanna paused at an intersection, squeezed Riker's hand tightly. "I know," she said. "I feel it, too."

Sadness, Riker thought. For all the ship had been through, to end like this, in a meaningless crash that had accomplished nothing.

He thought of the other *Enterprises* which had been lost in service to Starfleet. Kirk's original, whose sacrifice had bought an unexpected victory over the Klingons at the Genesis Planet. Rachel Garrett's *Enterprise-C,* whose valiantly hopeless efforts at Narendra III had cemented the peace between the Federation and the Klingon Empire. And joining them now, the *Enterprise-D,* a random victim of a lucky shot.

Riker felt Deanna's eyes on him. "Don't start," she said. "Sometimes, things happen for no reason at all. This was one of them. Accept it, and move on."

At the end of the next corridor, near an inoperative turbolift station, Riker and Deanna found the door to classroom twelve jammed open with a fire-blackened chair. A light shone over the chair from the classroom.

"In there," Deanna said.

The corridor floor shifted suddenly. Riker almost lost his footing again. "If anyone would know better than to be in this death trap . . ." he muttered.

Then Riker and Deanna stepped over the chair and into the classroom.

"Commander Riker, Counsellor Troi. I shall be able to converse with you in a moment."

Spock was lit by the glow shining up at him from the computer display inset on the small desk top at which he sat. A handheld torch rested on the edge of the study corral.

"I'm surprised you could find a terminal in working condition, Ambassador," Riker said. Riker had no idea from where Spock had been able to draw power. But the ambassador's prowess with starship systems was legendary.

"It was not working when I found it," Spock acknowledged.

Riker and Deanna glanced at each other, not quite certain how to proceed. It was not as if either felt they could order the ambassador to do anything. But they certainly could not allow him to remain here. Whole decks had given way in the saucer. This section of Deck 8 was already unsupported at too many critical points.

Riker watched the ambassador change the configuration of his input panel from the simple controls of a child's educational datapal to that of a full-functional library retrieval terminal. He wanted to know what Spock was doing, what had compelled him to risk entering the ship, but couldn't bring himself to ask. He felt he had no right. It was the legacy of living in a chain of command.

"The children's educational computers were not tied in to the tactical cores which Starfleet engineers have already removed," Spock said. "It was a simple matter to use this terminal to access the noncritical memory cores still remaining in the ship's main system."

"We have computers in the salvage camp," Deanna said. "Whatever work you need to do can be done there. In safer surroundings."

Spock did not bother to look up. "Thank you, Counsellor, but I find I am in need of Starfleet personnel records extending back quite some time. They would not be part of the salvage system."

"Personnel records?" Riker asked. "Anyone in particular?"

Spock hesitated. But he kept his attention focused on the screen. "James T. Kirk . . . I never really accepted the fact . . . never really *believed* . . . that he was dead."

Riker saw how stiffly, almost formally, the ambassador sat in the child-sized chair. It had been a difficult admission for him to make.

"You were not the only one," Deanna Troi said softly.

Spock turned to regard the counsellor with an upraised eyebrow. "Indeed."

Deanna smiled. Riker felt bathed in her warmth, though it was directed at Spock and not him. "Montgomery Scott said the same thing," she told the ambassador. "Believed as you believed."

Riker remembered his conversations with the feisty old Scotsman. Scott had been the chief engineer on the original *Enterprise,* where Kirk and Spock had first served together. After Kirk's first recorded death, on the maiden flight of the *Enterprise-B,* Scott had led an intensive search of the sector in which that ship had been damaged by the mysterious energy ribbon known as the Nexus.

Decades later, when the chief engineer had been rescued from transporter storage and had come aboard the *Enterprise-D,* he had explained the details of his search, how he had used experimental sensors sensitive enough to detect individual molecules, let alone the body of his captain.

In his personal quest, Scott had found the remains of other victims of the force of the Nexus—shattered bodies blown clear of the ruptured El-Aurian ships. But he had not found *all* of the recorded El-Aurian dead. And, more importantly to him, he had been unable to find any trace whatsoever of a human body.

"In fact, the first thing Mr. Scott said when he was recovered from transporter storage," Deanna explained to Spock, "was that he half expected to hear that it was Kirk who had rescued him, taking the first *Enterprise* out of mothballs just to come after his old friend."

"Hardly logical," Spock replied. "The *Enterprise-A* was destroyed at Chal, long before Mr. Scott's unfortunate crash."

Deanna wasn't willing to let the conversation go. "It was what he *hoped*, Ambassador. Not what he knew."

Riker sat back against another small desktop. It had been decorated with crude, cut out crayon drawings of some unfortunate adult with a Starfleet uniform and no hair. Riker decided Picard would not be amused. "What about your inability to accept Kirk's death, Ambassador? Is that logical?"

Spock's expression was unreadable. "Yes," he said. "I have mind-melded with the captain. That process typically creates a trace impression in the minds of the participants—a fleeting sense that they still remain in contact with one another, even after the meld has dissolved, as long as both remain alive."

Deanna glanced at Riker. Her expression he could read. Spock was not being forthcoming, and she knew it. Vulcans controlled their emotions, but they still had them. And Deanna's Betazoid heritage allowed her to detect each repressed nuance.

"In all the years that have elapsed since his disappearance, I have never felt him die," Spock said. The Vulcan ambassador spoke as if to himself, as if Riker and Deanna weren't present.

Deanna leaned forward, fascinated. "Is his death something you would expect to feel?"

Vulcan and Betazoid, Riker thought, looking at the two of them. Thought without emotion, and the sensing of emotion without thought. He remembered the underpinnings of the Vulcan philosophy of IDIC—infinite diversity in infinite combination. He was looking at a strong example of it now. By such was the Federation made strong.

The computer terminal chimed. Spock turned to it without answering Deanna's question.

At least, Riker concluded, he had not answered it in words.

A multicolored image of a tropical fish darted across the display screen. Riker recognized it as something for the children.

"Program completed," the computer announced.

Riker stepped forward to look over Spock's shoulder. On the display, he saw a picture of Kirk he recognized from history tapes. In it, Kirk was a young man, wearing a century-old Starfleet uniform. It felt odd to see the same delta insignia on Kirk's chest that Riker wore as a communicator. Most images of Starfleet personnel from that era showed them with a variety of different symbols on their uniforms. At the time, each ship and starbase had had its own distinctive symbol—a historical echo from the first, primitive days of space exploration when each separate flight had been awarded its own unique mission crest.

But over time, for all it had come to mean to the Federation, the *Enterprise* delta had been adopted by all of Starfleet, so today it could be seen throughout the known galaxy. But to see it on the uniform of someone from another century reinforced in Riker the sense that when he looked at images of the original *Enterprise*'s crew, he was looking at how it had all begun.

Text flowed up the screen beside Kirk's image. Riker swiftly scanned it and recognized it. It was Kirk's service record. The key events were required reading in the academy, and Riker was once again reminded just how much of the man's career had been key events.

"Even given what you feel, is there a reason you've called up Kirk's personnel file?" Deanna asked.

Spock kept his eyes locked on the screen. He adjusted a control so the scroll rate of the text increased. Riker was impressed by how quickly the ambassador was assimilating the information. Even for a Vulcan.

"The captain was not known to exist in our present era," Spock said, still reading. "Yet, within two weeks of his unanticipated return to . . . life, a well-planned and -equipped military operation was carried out to retrieve his remains from Veridian III."

Deanna folded her arms in thought.

"Are you suggesting that someone *expected* Kirk to appear in this time period?" she asked.

Riker could see that Spock was flagging certain entries in Kirk's record, as if marking them for further consideration. But consideration for what?

"That would not be logical," Spock answered. The sound of dripping intensified in the hallway. Riker could hear water beginning to flow like a stream. But there was no sense of distraction in Spock's voice as he continued to scan the rapidly moving text. "It would imply a cross-temporal knowledge of events. If someone from the future, having learned of the captain's return on this planet, decided to travel into the past to retrieve him, then why would that observer not return to the moment *before* his death, instead of so many days after it?"

The text on the display froze in place for an instant. Spock glanced up at Deanna who now stood beside him. "Therefore, the answer to the mystery with which we are faced will not be found in the present or the future, but in the past. Specifically, Captain Kirk's past." He turned back to the screen.

The deck shifted suddenly. Riker grabbed the corral wall, without comment, trusting to the legendary Vulcan's assessment of the odds.

"But how could anyone from the past know Kirk would end up on Veridian III?" Riker asked. "I don't understand . . . the logic of it."

"Perhaps because there is no logic to what has happened," Spock said. "What this salvage camp has been subjected to was an act of unrestrained emotion. A deeply felt, indeed, uncontrollable need to wreak some sort of vengeance on the captain."

Riker was surprised by the emotion he heard in Spock's voice. "Forgive me, Ambassador, but now it sounds as if you're applying logic to emotion."

Spock lowered his head for a moment. "Believe me, Commander Riker, at the most fundamental level, they are one and the same." The ambassador imperceptibly sighed then, and Riker was reminded he was speaking with a being who had lived for almost a century and half.

"So you came here to look for the captain's enemies?" Deanna asked.

"That is correct," Spock said.

"But how many of them are likely to have survived into this time?" Riker asked.

"All it takes is one," Spock replied.

Riker watched as Spock swiftly sorted the flagged entries on the display screen. He saw an image of a human wearing what seemed to be formal wear from Earth's seventeenth century, complete with ruffled shirt front and collar. Beside him, an image formed of the twentieth-century madman, Khan Noonien Singh. Then a large humanoid with a silvery robe. And then the infamous Tholian Grand Admiral Loskene— Riker was startled that Kirk might have had dealings with that brilliant Tholian leader, who still vexed the Federation today.

After a few more unrecognizable aliens joined the collection, another human in a extravagant outfit appeared—this one a man with a large moustache and a plumed hat. Then Riker saw a Klingon commander in a uniform as old as the one on Kirk.

"Your friend seems to have made more than his share of enemies," Riker noted.

"His was a forceful and direct personality," Spock said. "Such people are loved, or they are hated. By their natures, they allow no middle ground."

"Are all these beings alive today?" Deanna asked.

More images sorted themselves on the screen. A female Romulan commander appeared in an equally antique costume. Riker remembered her face but not her name from his academy studies. She had been involved in Starfleet's first retrieval of a Romulan cloaking device. The details of that operation were still classified, but Riker decided it would make sense that Kirk had been involved. Was there nothing the man hadn't done in his lifetime?

"I do not know how many of them survive," Spock said. "These are merely the ones with the motive to hate the captain beyond ordinary reason, and the native ability or technological opportunity to have cheated the years between their time and this."

Another Klingon appeared. And another. Klingons had clearly had no love for Kirk, nor he for them.

Spock entered more commands on the control panel. Several of the images vanished from the screen as the computer apparently cross-referenced other sources and discovered who was dead.

In the end, Spock was left with four possibilities. As the program came to an end, Riker pointed at the screen, trying to be helpful.

"Khan Noonien Singh is dead," he said.

Spock turned to look at Riker. Riker could almost swear he saw the flicker of a smile form on the ambassador's lips. "I know."

The dark classroom creaked as if it were on a seagoing vessel, moored in rough waters.

Riker glanced at Deanna. Time was rapidly running out for this shell of a starship.

Spock stared at the four faces on the display

screen. Four ghosts from the past: Khan, the humanoid in seventeenth-century clothing, the human with the plumed hat, and an insectoid creature whom Riker thought resembled one of the Kraal, long since vanished from Federation space.

Deanna broke the silence.

"Ambassador, please excuse my directness. But do you honestly believe that one of those four beings is responsible for attacking this base and stealing Kirk's remains?"

Spock put a hand on the screen, as if trying to blank out his past.

"They were not his remains," he said softly.

"I beg your pardon?" Riker said.

Spock rose from his chair and tugged on his cloak to straighten its folds. The formal aspect which Riker had first noticed had returned to the venerable Vulcan.

Spock looked Riker in the eye, hiding nothing.

"I remind you that I still have not felt James Kirk die," he said.

Before Riker could respond, Spock held up a hand to silence him. "As illogical as it sounds, Commander, I still *feel* his presence. As the counsellor can confirm."

Deanna nodded at Riker. She sensed he was telling the truth.

"A mind-meld echo?" Riker asked.

But Spock slowly shook his head, almost with an expression of sorrow.

"He is out there, Commander. In some way I cannot yet fathom, James Kirk still survives."

Spock held his hand to his temple, terribly fatigued. "And he is calling to me. . . ."

NINE

Spock!

Kirk ran, calling for help, something chasing him.

His movements were slowed by liquid. Something thick.

The deck below him seemed to shift with the characteristic lag of artificial gravity. Voices called out to him.

This is the El-Aurian transport ship Lakul . . . *we're caught in some . . . energy distortion. . . .*

Someone was in trouble. Kirk had to run faster. Always had to run faster.

Their hulls are starting to buckle under the stress. . . .

Faster. Never enough time.

The young captain looked at him.

You have the bridge. . . .

Kirk took the chair. The center chair. When had he wanted anything else? Anything more?

But this time, it wasn't right.

He turned his back. Left the bridge.

Keep things together until I get back. . . .

I always do. . . .

Into the bowels of the ship.

Running. Always running.

Reconnecting the circuits. Making the

deflector arrays do what they were never supposed to do.

Changing the rules.

The way he always had.

That's it! Let's go!

The command from the bridge, the young captain: *Activate main deflector. . . .*

And then . . .

And then . . .

And then what?

Nothing made sense.

Horses. Antonia. The stars in space. Making the jump. Burning the eggs in the kitchen. The man in the strange uniform. Starfleet uniform.

Make a difference. . . .

The man from the future.

Picard?

Jumping through space. Through time.

You don't appreciate the gravity of your situation, Captain. . . .

Falling.

Yosemite.

The ground swirling up and the sudden pressure on his ankle as . . .

Spock!

He hadn't been alone at Yosemite, climbing the mountain.

But this time, he was.

Until he felt the pressure of a cold cloth on his forehead.

Kirk's eyes flew open as the shifting gravity stopped its wild movement.

The only darkness he saw was caused by the cloth.

He reached for it. Needed to take it away. To get away. Something was gaining. He had to keep running.

"Shhh."

He moved the cloth and saw . . .

He didn't know her.

"Do you know where you are?" the woman asked.

At some level, he understood she was beautiful. Dark hair. Haunting eyes. Sensuous, upswept, pointed ears. The word "Romulan" came to him, though he didn't know what it meant.

"My ship?" he asked. Somehow, he was always onboard his ship.

Wherever that was.

But the woman shook her head. So serious.

He felt she needed help. He wanted to help her. It was one way to stop running.

"Do you know who you are?" she asked.

Of course he did. He smiled. Opened his mouth.

Nothing came out.

Panic.

"It's all right," the woman said.

She soothed his forehead, his temples, with the cool cloth.

"I know who did this to you."

"Did this?" Kirk said.

"You were very brave."

Kirk felt relief. People counted on him. All four hundred thirty aboard the . . . the *Enterprise.*

He frowned.

"The *Enterprise* . . . what is it?"

"Can you sit up?" the woman asked.

Kirk did. His head swam but he hid his symptoms. It wasn't right to show weakness. Not when so many needed him. Looked to him for strength, for guidance.

He looked around.

He was on a bed. A medical gurney, he knew.

But the room he was in wasn't familiar. A black cube of a room, marked with yellow grid lines.

"Where am I?" he asked. He felt he had nothing to hide from this woman.

"You were injured," she said. "In battle."

Battle. His next question was reflexive. "The ship?"

"*Your* ship . . . it's out of danger."

Kirk sighed. Nothing else mattered.

"For now," the woman concluded.

"I have to get back to the bridge," Kirk said. He wasn't clear as to what the bridge was, or what he needed to do there. But if he could set foot on it. Sit in that center chair one more time. He knew everything would be fine.

"In time," the woman said.

She shifted her position where she sat on the edge of the gurney. Kirk was aware of a cool breeze across his chest. He looked down, expecting to see a uniform of some sort. But what kind of uniform? He saw nothing.

Nothing . . .

He gasped.

Who was he?

The woman looked at him in concern. "Are you all right?"

Again, Kirk refused to admit weakness. "You said I was injured. In battle?"

"Against the enemy."

Kirk was at a loss. "Who is the enemy?"

The woman picked up a small padd, pressed a control. A far corner of the stark room faded away, opening up into the immensity of space. Kirk braced himself for the wail of the loss-of-pressure alarms. But the air remained still.

"This is the enemy," the woman said.

The viewpoint in space shifted. A vessel came into view. Kirk felt a tugging in his heart. The vessel was magnificent.

Her forward saucer was connected by a short neck to a small, tapered engineering hull. From both sides of that lower hull, bold pylons thrust out on dynamic angles, ending in flattened warp-propulsion nacelles.

Kirk gazed at the ship, knowing every centimeter of her but not certain if he had ever seen her before.

"The *Enterprise*," the woman said, spitting out the name. "The enemy."

Kirk was surprised. This ship didn't *feel* like the enemy. He was missing something.

The woman looked at him. "Say it. The *Enterprise*. The enemy."

The woman adjusted another control on her padd.

Kirk gasped with sudden pain.

"Say it," she said.

"The *Enterprise*," Kirk gasped. "The enemy."

The woman smiled her approval. Instantly Kirk felt the pain end, a wave of pleasure sweeping through him.

"Who are you?" he asked.

89

She caressed his face. "The monsters who did this to you will not survive," she said.

Kirk took her hand, the question still in his eyes.

"Salatrel," she said.

Then she leaned forward and kissed him.

Kirk responded, surprised by the sudden explosion of emotion he felt. He heard her fingers on the padd. More waves of pleasure pulsed through him.

He looked into her dark eyes. "Are we . . . ?"

"Yes," she whispered.

She held him close. "I thought I had lost you," she said.

The thought of losing her was unbearable to Kirk. He crushed her to his chest, determined never to let her go.

He made his confession.

"I . . . I don't know who I am. . . ."

Her eyes blazed into his. Twin novae.

"They will not go unpunished."

"Who?"

"The enemy."

Kirk looked past her at the *Enterprise*. It was a holographic model, he finally realized. A wave of fear swept through him as he gazed upon it. Revulsion.

"The Federation," he said as the word floated to his consciousness.

"Starfleet," the woman said.

Instantly, Kirk felt a stab of incredible pain slice through his bowels.

"Starfleet," he gasped. The word was foul. Loathsome.

"Look what they did," the woman said, her hand busy on the padd she carried. Kirk's heart began to race with apprehension.

The image of the hated ship faded away, replaced by another—dynamic, birdlike, with a double hull and raptorprowed bridge.

The *Enterprise* streaked at it, weapons blazing.

The raptor ship erupted in plasma, in death.

"A colony vessel," Salatrel said. "Women and children. Farming supplies."

Kirk's breath quickened. Sweat beaded on his forehead.

Another image rippled into view. A fleet of raptor-prowed ships.

"A mercy mission," Salatrel said. "Defenseless."

The fleet was consumed by the fire of the *Enterprise,* one ship after another.

"And this," she said.

A planet spun through space. The holographic viewpoint spiraled in like a reentering spacecraft. Below Kirk stretched farming fields in checkerboard perfection, rolling with the gentle curves of the world. Until over a rise, a city appeared. Fresh, bold, new. A colonial capital.

Then the tractor beam struck. Scooping up the city like a handful of dirt. Within the immense tractor beam, the delicate spires of the city's temples crumbled. Kirk could hear the distant cries of hundreds, thousands.

The city ascended into the clouds, dropping huge clumps of soil. Only a gaping, scooped-out crater remained.

"Why?" Kirk asked.

"Butchers," Salatrel answered. "Remember," she said.

Another ship appeared. Kirk recognized it. Knew it was old. A foreshortened saucer with small nacelles close to its body. Its underside painted with a bird of prey.

And inside, the bridge.

"I've seen this before," he told Salatrel.

His stomach tightened. He knew how this ended.

"Was I there?" he asked.

"Yes," she said.

Kirk saw the bridge of the vessel. Other Romulans. The commander in his silver mesh and cloak of command came forward. Green blood ran from his mouth. Kirk stared at the image intently. He *had* been there. He had witnessed this himself.

The commander spoke. "I regret that we meet in this way," he said. "You and I are of a kind. In a different reality, I could have called you friend."

"Yes," Kirk said. He remembered the words. Understood the kinship he had shared with this commander. They had been the same. Yet now, the commander was dead and Kirk lived. Why?

The bridge collapsed, blew apart. The transmission ended.

"He didn't have to die," Kirk said.

Regret overwhelmed him. A regret he had harbored for years.

"A noble house fell with him," Salatrel said bitterly. "Chironsala. One of the oldest on Romulus. And all the generations that followed were cursed."

Kirk turned to Salatrel. He reached out to her face, to her ears, traced their tips.

Then touched his own.

"Am I . . . ?" he began to ask.

"No," she said. "Human. A patriot. Dedicated to peace. To noninterference."

"Noninterference," Kirk repeated. Of course. It was as if the words were engraved on his mind.

"Dedicated to the destruction of the enemy," Salatrel added.

"The *Enterprise*," Kirk said. "The Federation. Starfleet."

In the wave of hate he experienced with each word, the regret and the pain retreated from his body. Warmth returned. Understanding.

"What do you want to do?" Salatrel prompted.

"Help," Kirk said. "Let me help." The words felt perfect. As if he had always longed to say them.

Salatrel smiled. She touched the padd she held at her side.

Her smile was like the sun of a summer day in Iowa. Kirk wanted to fall into it. Find his answers there.

"How?" she asked.

Kirk thought a moment. He replayed the sickening scenes she had shared with him. The senseless brutality. The pain he felt as he recalled them was physical, as if his nerve ends were actually being fired.

"Stop them," he said. The pain lessened. Momentarily.

"Destroy them?" Salatrel asked. The pain increased.

"Destroy them," Kirk said. This time, the pain did not just fade. Pleasure took its place.

"Kill them," he sighed. Nothing sounded better. Felt better.

Salatrel moved her hand across his chest. He drew a deep breath. Every sensation felt new.

"They almost killed me, didn't they?" Kirk asked.

Salatrel studied him. "Almost," she agreed. Slowly, she drew away the thin sheet that covered him. "But I wouldn't let them take you away from me."

The coolness of the air was like water washing over Kirk. He dimly understood that his mind was full of questions. How had he been hurt? How long had he been in this place? How long had he known this exquisite woman? The very thought of her filled him with longing and antici- pation.

But he was unable to focus on any of those questions. He could only respond to the here and the now.

The pressure of her nails across her shoulders. The cinnamon scent of her dark hair as it brushed his face.

"Are you glad you're back?" Salatrel whispered in his ear. The heat of her breath pulsed into him, making his lungs falter, forcing him to inhale through his mouth.

"Yes," Kirk said. He nuzzled his face against her neck. Hungrily kissed the fine hairs that covered her nape.

"Are you ready to help again?" she asked. Her hands moved over his shoulders, squeezing the muscles there, digging in, releasing, making a promise.

"Anything," Kirk said.

"The enemy?"

"Destroy him. Kill him."

Her lips moved over his, the tip of her tongue electric against him.

"Who is the enemy?" she asked.

Kirk struggled to concentrate. He needed Salatrel. He had to feel her in his arms. It was almost as if he had never held anyone ever before. But he didn't have the answer she wanted. It was one of those elusive questions floating in the shadows. The questions he couldn't answer. Couldn't yet focus on.

"Show me?" he asked.

"Is that what you want?"

"Show me," he pleaded.

Anything to answer the question. To give her the answer. To quell the pain that rose within him again.

"Watch," Salatrel said.

She aimed her padd at the holographically blurred corner, pressed a control.

An image appeared there. Life size. A humanoid.

Kirk gasped as the figure resolved.

Kirk recognized him.

"The enemy," Salatrel hissed. "He must be destroyed. He must be killed."

"Killed," Kirk agreed. It was the only way. The only way to find peace. The only way to find himself.

The figure reached for him from the holo-

95

graphic haze, gloating, fueled by the thousand atrocities committed by the Federation and Starfleet against the Romulan race.

"Kill," Salatrel urged.

Kirk nodded. He spoke the name of the enemy. "Jean-Luc Picard."

His body arched. There could be no escape from the agony.

Until Salatrel came to him and held him, and the agony became ecstasy so incredible that nothing else mattered.

Except the single thought . . . his single purpose . . .

Jean-Luc Picard must die.

TEN

Worf, son of Mogh, groaned with pleasure as the fangs of the *krencha* lanced into his shoulder.

The Klingon shifted his mass to the side, going with the impact of the ravenous beast instead of fighting it. He slammed into the hard solid dirt of the forest path, felt the rough bite of the ragged stones pierce his flesh, even as the *krencha*, taken by surprise, flipped forward, losing the purchase its fangs had given it.

Worf continued his sideways roll, kicking his legs into the air to build momentum, then pushed with one arm to leap onto his feet.

The *krencha* was already waiting for him. Its four running legs scuffed the soft soil of the ground off the path. Its two killing legs thrust forward. Its tongue slithered out from its reptilian lips, scenting the air, to detect its prey's fear.

But there was no fear in Worf.

He reveled in his long-delayed vacation to the Almron Preserve—the boundless tract of pristine nature encircling the First City of the Klingon Homeworld, Qo'noS.

Slowly, he bared his fangs at the three-meter-long creature before him, drawing his lips back in a fierce grimace of victory as he shook his head from side to side. His tightly bound warrior's queue of hair thrashed his shoulders and spattered the blood that flowed from his wounds. The blood dripped down his bare chest to the simple belt and loincloth he wore.

In the face of death, Worf was aware of each subtle movement of life all around him—here the errant stirring of a breeze among the leaves, there the passage of an insect. He heard each crack of a twig. Each creak of a branch. And every silver-purple leaf was distinct in his peripheral vision. Even the stench of the predator before him cut into his nostrils like the exhilarating bouquet of that nectar of the gods—prune juice.

Worf was *alive.*

As he had not been since the saucer of the *Enterprise* began its long fall, since life and death were separated only by the space between two heartbeats.

Here, in Almron, Klingons could live as Klingons had always been meant to live—always in that space between heartbeats, between death and life, defeat and victory.

The *krencha* sprang.

Worf ducked forward, presenting his uninjured shoulder, again to absorb the energy of the attack and turn it back against the beast.

But the creature was not fooled a second time. Its thick, stubby tail lashed out to the right, altering its trajectory so that Worf came in too low.

As Worf stumbled, the *krencha* slashed downward with its killing legs. Its razor-sharp claws slashed at Worf's unprotected back.

The sudden shock of pain stopped him from slapping his arms to the ground to break his fall. He was out of control. Sent sprawling. Tasting dirt as the rich soil of Qo'noS filled his open, gasping mouth.

Behind him, the *krencha* shrieked in anticipation.

The forest erupted with a cacophony of *blas rika* calls—the flying scavengers of Qo'noS. *Krencha* could be counted on not to finish their kills all at once. There would be offal remaining for the leather-winged creatures of the night.

But Worf had not lost yet.

The *krencha* bent forward so that all six legs came in contact with the forest path for greater speed.

It charged forward, shrieking, rippling toward its fallen prey.

Worf was still down. Defenseless.

And he wouldn't have it any other way.

For only in this instant, this sacred still moment from one heartbeat to the next, could he step into the perfection of *K'ajii*—the warrior's path.

Worf took that first step and time seemed to slow.

He saw the creature's square-pupiled, yellow eyes lock onto him like sensors. He saw the spittle stream from its razor fangs with each jarring thump of its forward legs.

Its dense fur rippled in the wind of its passage.

Its powerful, thick tail curved up behind it, ready to change direction in a moment.

But with the way of the *K'ajii* silent and still within him, Worf chose that moment with exquisite precision.

The curled toes of his bare foot came up under the *krencha's* primary tracheae when its fangs were only a meter from his throat.

The explosion of acrid breath from the creature enveloped Worf with the stench of rotted meat as the *krencha* sailed past him, missing its target.

Then, even before his adversary had landed, Worf spun around and leapt forward, landing on the creature's midsection before it could right itself.

Its scream made Worf's ears vibrate.

Its killing legs lashed out to embrace Worf in a deadly corkscrew hold, a last attempt to crush the life force from him.

But this was no mere fight to the death. For a Klingon, no fight ever was so meaningless.

It was a fight for honor.

For if a Klingon did not have mastery over nature, then how could he expect to protect and preserve it?

Worf risked freeing one arm from around the *krencha's* right front killing leg and slapped his

99

hand forward to grab the creature's snout. At once, it collapsed its neck, trying in turn to loosen his grip so it could snap off his offending fingers.

There was a graft and cloning first-aid station at the entrance to the nature preserve, but Worf had never had to use its services. Since he had been a teenager, at least. And he had no intention of starting again now.

Then, the *krencha* paused. It was tiring. Like most predators, it had evolved for the sudden sprint and quick attack. Prolonged battle was a waste of resources.

Worf swung his other hand up and grabbed the creature's lower jaw.

The *krencha* wailed as if it knew the battle had been lost.

It had.

Worf wrapped his legs around the creature's elongated chest, locked his heel against his instep, and began to squeeze. The creature's struggles were lessening.

Then Worf pulled the creature's jaws apart.

He shimmied along the beast, bringing his face perilously close to the gleaming fangs.

His fingers pressed into either side of the *krencha's* dark gums. The sticky saliva threatened to make him lose his grip, but the knowledge that he would also lose his fingers help him focus, maintaining *K'ajii*.

Worf's arms quivered with exhaustion as he brought the creature's head around to face him. He locked eyes with the beast. Saw its soul.

And with the last erg of strength he possessed, Worf pulled the creature's jaws apart and snapped one hand forward and one hand back, pivoting its neck to hear the telltale snap.

At once, the *krencha* went slack beneath him.

Worf trembled as he pulled open the creature's jaws and inhaled deeply of its dying breath, infusing its spirit and its strength into his own body, honoring the beast as Klingon hunters had for millennia.

Then he stood respectfully beside his fallen foe. He drew his fingers through the bite wound on his shoulder and traced the blood around the *krencha's* lips, giving his valiant opponent its final reward.

Then Worf knelt and said the words of the hunter's bargain.

If Worf had lost this battle, then he would have fed the creature. But Worf had won, so he graciously accepted the creature's matching offer to feed him.

Worf took his *d'k tahg* knife from his belt, and held it over the first of the creature's two hearts.

"*jIyajbe'*. Isn't that overkill?"

Though strained and exhausted by his battle, Worf leapt to his feet, instantly adopting the warrior's first position, *d'k tahg* held ready as its secondary blades clicked into place.

The voice had spoken in the Warrior's Tongue of Qo'noS. It had been natural, not broadcast over a communicator. But Worf had heard no one approach, no transporter harmonic. How could it be possible for someone to sneak up on him here, with all his senses so refined for the hunt? He cursed himself for his lack of preparation that had made him so vulnerable.

101

"Show yourself," Worf called out in challenge.

He whipped his head around as branches moved behind him. Too late he realized they had moved because a rock had been thrown into them. When he turned back, his visitor was facing him, showing no sign of having just moved, as if he had always been there.

Worf slowly took his measure of the being who had outmaneuvered him so easily. His first impression was that the visitor was a holy man. He wore the ceremonial robes and mask of a *k'hartagh*—one who sought peace in maintaining the balance of predator and prey. They were common enough in Klingon nature preserves. The ceremonial combat Worf had just undertaken was based in part on a belief system of endless cycles in which the hunter and the hunted traded places. The *k'hartaghan* offered themselves up to nature as prey in order to return as predators. Provided a predator could be found which could defeat them.

Though Worf carried a knife, he would not have used it against the *krencha,* as that would be a violation of the balance. But what had the *k'hartagh* meant about overkill? That was a military term, out of place in the forest.

"Who are you?" Worf demanded, keeping his confusion hidden.

The *k'hartagh* made no move. His intent was impossible to read through the silvery purple and brown camouflage robes he wore. Even his eyes were shielded from view by the carved wood slit eyeshields he wore, and the cloth mask that hung from them.

"That is not important," the *k'hartagh* said in the Warrior's Tongue. "You are Worf, son of Mogh."

Worf's eyes widened with surprise. He growled softly. His retreat to this preserve had been confidential. He had a career in Starfleet to consider. And some of the more ancient Klingon ceremonies were not ones of which Starfleet might approve.

"Do not make me repeat myself," Worf warned.

The *k'hartagh*'s hands moved behind his robes, drawing something from his back. Then in one fluid movement, sliding one foot forward while throwing his robe aside, the *k'hartagh* took a stylized pose which Worf recognized as the position of Heaven's Centered Balance, First Level. And in his hands, the *k'hartagh* held a gleaming *bat'telh*.

Worf blinked despite himself. He slowly realized that the *k'hartagh*'s move and pose were part of the *raLk'jo bat'telh* discipline—an ancient school of martial combat that had not been practiced in the Klingon Empire for almost a century. The *k'hartagh*'s age notwithstanding, Worf did recognize that the difficult First-Level move had been perfectly executed.

Faced with such an ancient, stylized form of battle with the distinctive, crescent-shaped weapon, whose name meant "blade of honor," Worf dismissed the possibility that the *k'hartagh* intended the display as a provocative gesture. From his study of history, Worf knew that warriors of the *raLk'jo* discipline viewed the *bat'telh* largely as a ceremonial weapon.

Worf lowered his knife and assumed a nonconfrontational stance. "I have never met a master of the *raLk'jo* discipline," he said respectfully.

"Is that why you face me with a coward's posture?" the *k'hartagh* said with an inflection of disdain.

Worf felt his grip tighten on his knife. "Do you wield the *bat'telh* in other than a ceremonial demonstration of your discipline?" Worf asked.

"If I have to, I will kill you with it," the *k'hartagh* calmly replied.

Worf instinctively bared his teeth, appalled by the *k'hartagh's* lack of respect for an ancient school of combat.

"Control yourself," the *k'hartagh* said in response to Worf's expression. "I'm not interested in butchering you where you stand."

His arm shifted again behind his robe. Then Worf marvelled as, one-handed, he brought out a second *bat'telh,* flipped it around, and threw it to stick into the ground a meter in front of Worf.

"Does that ease the sting of my insults?" the *k'hartagh* asked.

Worf straightened and slid his *d'k tahg* back into its scabbard. The *bat'telh* was not a plaything. The *k'hartagh* was insane.

"I will not fight you," Worf said. "It is clear you do not know what you are doing."

Again, the *k'hartagh* slipped his hand inside his robe. When it withdrew, he held a disruptor. "I need answers," he said. "And how can I be sure you're telling me the truth, if I haven't beaten you in combat?"

Worf snorted at the *k'hartagh*'s audacity. Was that what this was about? He expected to *defeat* a Klingon in combat so that he would answer questions truthfully?

"Go away," Worf said. In the surrounding forest, he could hear the wingbeats of scavengers approaching. It would be dishonorable if he did not dress the *krencha* before sunset and take measures to preserve its meat. And the shadows were already lengthening.

The *k'hartagh* extended his arm, aiming the disruptor at Worf. It was a new model, Worf saw. Government-issue. He found it curious that such an advanced energy weapon was in the possession of one trained in such an old way of combat.

"Fight me," the *k'hartagh* said, "or die without honor."

"There is no honor in fighting the insane," Worf growled.

The disruptor's golden beam punched a hole in the ground five centimeters in front of Worf's feet, sending a billow of dust and smoke into the Klingon's eyes.

"There is no honor in dying without combat," the *k'hartagh* replied.

Worf's eyes narrowed. "Very well. But when I defeat you, you must answer *my* questions."

The *k'hartagh* stepped back as Worf approached the *bat'telh* imbedded in the ground. "*If* you defeat me," the *k'hartagh* said.

Worf drew the *bat'telh* and hefted it in both hands. The balance was good, though he sensed it was a mass-produced model. Something of offworld manufacture, for no Klingon would dream of owning a *bat'telh* that was not hand-crafted and thus imbued with its maker's spirit. Worf's own, which he had pulled from the ruins of the *Enterprise,* had been in his family for ten generations.

The *k'hartagh* stepped sideways, presenting his weapon in the ancient pose called the Dragon's Passage from Thought to Action, Third Level. As Worf understood the ancient discipline, it was meant to be a conservative opening, showing respect for his opponent. . . . It was not what Worf would have expected from an insane holy man.

Remembering his history tapes, Worf countered the *k'hartagh's* presentation with the Position of Unwavering Determination, Third Level. In the symbolism of this specific *bat'telh* discipline, Worf thus signified he would not give in to idle threats.

The *k'hartagh* stepped forward, now facing Worf directly, angling his *bat'telh* gracefully through the arc of the Gentle Cut, to end in the Repose of the Dragon's Teeth, First Level. Worf was again surprised.

The underlying philosophy of the *raLk'jo* discipline required that no presentation could be made unless the warrior had perfected that move in combat. If the *k'hartagh* had indeed mastered the Repose of the Dragon's Teeth, then Worf realized he was in trouble. The Dragon's Teeth was an especially savage attack, and Worf was not certain if his own defenses were adequate to deflect the attack without fatal injury to the *k'hartagh*.

Knowing he had waited a heartbeat too long, Worf countered with the point-forward pose of the Mountain's Scorn, Fourth Level. In that way, he told the *k'hartagh* he did not believe the holy man's expertise matched the boldness of his posturing. And making the presentation with his hands in the *raLk'jo's* simple, Fourth Level alignment implied that Worf believed the *k'hartagh* could be beaten at that juvenile level—a grievous insult.

But though it was impossible to read the *k'hartagh's* expression through his cloth and wooden mask, Worf did see the amused nod his opponent made. Since there was nothing amusing about the insult Worf had made, for the first time he had the sudden suspicion that the insane *k'hartagh* wasn't even Klingon.

And then the *k'hartagh* attacked.

Even as the crescent blade of the *k'hartagh's* *bat'telh* sliced through the air, Worf recognized that it was not a killing blow. Perhaps the holy man had been telling the truth when he said he merely wanted Worf to answer questions.

Rather than deflect the blow, Worf sidestepped with a modern evasive step, moving his own weapon out of the other's path, thus avoiding any chance the *k'hartagh* could turn his own movement against him.

But the *k'hartagh* had anticipated him.

His blade dipped to the side, then followed Worf in a move so swift it had begun before Worf had even made his own decision to act.

The *k'hartagh*'s *bat'telh* caught Worf's and slid along its upper length in a spray of sparks, almost succeeding in wrenching it out of Worf's startled grip when the two curved tips met and momentarily locked.

Worf reacted instinctively, pulling his weapon in close to his chest. He pivoted in place, extending the blade in midspin to bring it into slashing position, fully expecting to meet the *k'hartagh*'s blade in a defensive block.

But when Worf had spun completely around, his blade slipped through empty air. Once again the *k'hartagh* had anticipated him and had ducked, rising the instant Worf's blade had passed, swinging his own point first against Worf's arm.

Worf cried out, more in surprise than in pain as the slick blade sliced through his triceps as if his flesh offered no more resistance than a cloud.

He wrenched his *bat'telh* back into a forward defensive pose, with no attempt at fighting within the bounds of the *k'hartagh*'s discipline, expecting a savage follow-up and preparing to block.

But the *k'hartagh* had step back, breaking the rhythm of his attack. He held his *bat'telh* straight forward in the Whelpling's Lunge, Tenth Level. In the *raLk'jo*, it was one of the first poses taught to chilren. Thus, in a battle such as this, there was no deadlier insult.

"Will you yield?" the *k'hartagh* asked.

Worf bellowed a Klingon death cry and lunged forward, *bat'telh* whistling through the air.

The *k'hartagh* had not been ready for the

108

ferocity of Worf's attack. Still, he skillfully side-stepped, leaving his weapon in place to deflect Worf's blow. But Worf again did the unthinkable by releasing one hand from his weapon and striking out at the *k'hartagh*. Worf's nails raked his attacker's throat and chin, attempting to grab the ceremonial mask and rip it off.

But the *k'hartagh*'s leg came up in a completely unexpected Vulcan defensive strike, adding to Worf's momentum and making him slam into the ground.

As Worf pushed himself to his knees, he was momentarily shocked when he looked to the side and saw that the approaching *k'hartagh* wore trousers and boots beneath his robes. But then, he also carried a disruptor. Clearly, the *k'hartagh* was not what he appeared to be.

And then Worf had no more time for observations as he felt the *k'hartagh*'s *bat'telh* smash him on the back of his skull.

Worf wondered if it were just his head that fell forward as the forest floor flew up at him. No *bat'telh* master could have missed such a simple decapitation blow when his enemy's back was turned.

Worf's last thought flew to the *Enterprise* slicing through the atmosphere of Veridian III. And then, like the noble Klingon warrior he was, Worf, son of Mogh, embraced his death as *K'ajii* demanded and fell unrepentant into darkness.

ELEVEN

Thirty minutes later, Worf awoke with a hideous headache.

His arms and legs were bound by rope, tying him securely to the rough purple trunk of an *arhksamm* tree.

Worf shook his head. It was a bad idea. But the sudden increase in pain made him even more alert. And even angrier. From the lump on the back of his head he could tell he had been hit with the *flat* of his attacker's *bat'telh!* It was the ultimate act of mockery. What a teacher did when instructing a novice.

Then he smelled something burning. Wood. And . . . *krencha* meat.

Worf turned his head. The *k'hartagh* was crouched by a fire. On a purple branch, he had skewered the *krencha's* gizzard. A delicacy. Worf's mouth watered despite his outrage.

The *k'hartagh* glanced over at Worf. Saw he was awake. Got to his feet and walked over to him.

Worf glowered at him.

The *k'hartagh,* still in robes and mask, tore a strip from the gizzard and offered it to Worf. Juices flowed down from the punctured organ, dripping onto the forest floor. The scent made Worf ravenous. The cooking had restored it to

110

body temperature—it would be the same as eating right after the kill.

But Worf turned his head. "You did not kill me," he complained.

"That wasn't the point," the *k'hartagh* said. "I need you to answer my questions. Truthfully."

Worf stared back at his attacker.

His attacker waved the strip of gizzard before his face. Then he sighed. "Are you going to deny the *krencha* its reward by wasting its death? What about the hunter's bargain?"

Worf clenched his jaw. The alien *k'hartagh* was right. The flesh of the beast he had killed must be eaten, or else the death had been wasted. But the way the *k'hartagh* explained himself . . . something was wrong.

"You are not Klingon," Worf said accusingly.

"Eat," his attacker replied. He held the gizzard strip close to Worf, quickly snapping his fingers back as Worf bit into the meat.

It was delicious. Worf could feel the power of the *krencha* surge into his body. For an instant, the *arhksamm* tree to which he was tied was nothing more than a twig. The ropes that held him, mere threads.

"We can be finished in a few minutes," the *k'hartagh* said.

Worf frowned at his use of "minutes." That was an Earth term.

The *k'hartagh* studied Worf in silence for a few moments, as if giving Worf a chance to say something. When it was clear that Worf wouldn't, he began.

"Where is Jean-Luc Picard?"

111

Worf hid his surprise. He replied by asking, "Where did a human learn *bat'telh* of the *raLk'jo* discipline?"

The *k'hartagh* rocked back on his heels and held up a cautionary finger, hidden in gloves. "Know your enemy," he said.

Worf frowned. What was that supposed to mean? "Klingons and humans are not enemies."

The *k'hartagh* angled his head as if surprised. Worf didn't know what to make of it.

"Since when?" the *k'hartagh* asked.

For Worf, the interrogation was taking on a surreal aspect. He momentarily forgot his shame and discomfort. "Who are you?" he demanded.

Again, the *k'hartagh* seemed to hesitate. "Jean-Luc Picard. Where is he?"

Worf took a deep breath. "I am a Starfleet officer. I will not—"

"*What?*"

Worf blinked at the *k'hartagh*.

The *k'hartagh* held a hand to the side of his head, as if he felt the same pain there that Worf did.

"If you are in trouble," Worf said warily. "Perhaps I can help you."

But when the *k'hartagh* spoke again, his voice was harsher, withdrawn. "Where is Jean-Luc Picard?"

"Why do you want to know?" Worf asked, now genuinely puzzled by the entire situation. His thoughts of honor and death receded as he studied the stranger. His Starfleet training claimed him in their place.

The *k'hartagh's* hand shot out and grabbed Worf by the neck. "I have to kill him!"

That was all Worf had to hear.

In a sudden flush of rage—his immediate reaction to a threat against his commanding officer—Worf pushed against the ropes that bound him to the tree.

The tree trunk creaked.

The *k'hartagh's* hand tightened on Worf's throat.

Worf's blood-smeared and bared chest swelled as he drew a mighty breath to roar.

But the *k'hartagh's* hand unerringly found both sets of carotid arteries. He squeezed, blocking the flow of blood so that Worf's voice was effectively silenced.

Worf saw dark stars flicker at the edges of his vision. Knew he had only seconds of consciousness remaining. Felt his wounded arm burst through the rope and fly ahead of him to smash the *k'hartagh* across his face.

The *k'hartagh* flew backward.

Worf struggled against the remainder of his ropes. The ones tied across his chest were unbroken. He clawed at them, only then noticing he had the *k'hartagh's* ceremonial mask tangled in his fingers.

He looked across at the *k'hartagh* as he rose from the ground.

Worf felt his mouth drop open, all elements of *K'ajii* driven from his mind, so great was his shock.

He *recognized* his attacker.

Even with the bloody streaks that Worf's raking

nails had left, his face was a perfect match for that on the history tapes Worf had scanned after hearing of Picard's encounter on Veridian III, when the *Enterprise* met her death.

"What are you staring at?" his attacker snapped.

Worf couldn't think what to say.

His attacker was a dead man. A dead man twice over.

And a hero from the past. Starfleet's past.

James T. Kirk.

"Where is Picard?" Kirk demanded.

In his confusion, Worf's voice was uneven. "I . . . don't know." All he could do was stare at Kirk. At the impossibility of Kirk.

Kirk stared at the Klingon, as if searching for something in his eyes.

Then Worf began thinking like a warrior again and tugged at the ropes across his chest.

Kirk pulled out his disruptor, adjusted its setting.

But Worf refused to go quietly. He strained against his ropes. One snapped. A second. He snarled as he gathered his strength. To stand. To lunge forward and—

—the disruptor beam took the Klingon in midleap.

Kirk did not step back as the Klingon's body crumpled to the forest floor at his feet.

Despite the pain that had burned into him as he had made the decision, Kirk had set the disruptor to stun, not to disintegrate.

Kirk knelt by the motionless body. Turned the face upright to face him.

"You recognized me."

The Klingon remained silent, eyes closed, his breathing rough and erratic.

Kirk released the Klingon's massive head, letting it fall back into the dirt.

A part of him wanted to kill this alien monster. To crush the life from it. Kirk knew such an act would bring him intense pleasure.

But for a reason he could not articulate, he resisted.

Instead, he stood, reached to his belt for a communicator, flipped it.

Then stared at it as nothing happened.

He tried again to flip open its top. Then he remembered. The device wasn't meant to open. He pressed the activation control.

"Go ahead," a disembodied voice said.

"I'm finished down here."

"Did the Klingon know anything?"

"No."

"Is he dead?"

Kirk stared at the Klingon's body, lying helpless before him. He winced as he felt a sharp stab. He longed for Salatrel's caress. For her to take these troubled thoughts from his mind and make everything better.

But still he wondered why he needed to have those thoughts taken away by someone else. Shouldn't that be his responsibility? When had he relinquished it?

But the disruptor was heavy on his belt, so easy to use.

To destroy the enemy.

Starfleet.

The Federation.

Klingons were the enemy, too. He knew that without Salatrel's having to tell him.

But then, why did he find it so hard to understand why a Klingon would be part of Starfleet? If both were enemies, why did that strike him as so wrong?

He shook his head to clear it of confusion.

"Is the Klingon dead?" the voice persisted.

Kirk put his hand on his disruptor. Drew it. Set it to full disruption.

Aimed it.

It was the easy way to get rid of the confusion. The pain. Simply press the stud and it would go away, dissolving like the flesh of the Klingon at his feet.

What could be easier?

Kirk made his decision.

He pressed the stud.

The tree behind the Klingon bloomed with a wavery light, then vanished into quantum mist.

"He's dead," Kirk said.

Sharp pain still attacked him as he voiced the lie. But somehow, it hurt less than he had expected. Perhaps the pain could be controlled, at least in part, without Salatrel's touch.

And if so, what other secrets had she hidden from him? What other lies had she told?

"Stand by for beam-out," the voice said.

Kirk stared down at the Klingon lying silent at his feet.

The Klingon opened his eyes.

"Who am I?" Kirk asked.

But before the answer could reach him, the transporter beam found him and beamed him away.

TWELVE

Starbase 804 was gone.

Through the low-lying haze that blanketed the devastated site, the broken ridges of injected foundations traced out the plan of the buildings and the walkways that had once existed. Tattered clothing and fabric fluttered across the stripped ground like dying animals, snagging on snapped-off pipes and power conduits. Here and there, crumbled bricks of silicon and twisted sheets of duraplast formed random accumulations of debris. Apparently neither substance was of much use to the Borg.

Picard gazed over those ruins. Seventy-eight people had been stationed here—humans, Vulcans, a family of Klingon archaeologists, children, pets, dreams.

All gone.

Absorbed into the monstrous cube that had arisen in the center of the base, towering thirty meters above them, ominous and all-devouring. The alien graveyard of the raw materials assimilated from the starbase.

In only three days.

"This makes no sense," Beverly said. Her voice betrayed the stunning sense of loss they both felt.

She stood beside Picard in the twilight, both still in the black commando armor they had worn since their arrival. Weinlein and the rest of her team had determined that the Borg here did not view two humans together as a group worthy of assimilation, provided they kept one hundred meters distant from any other member of the team.

The long, red rays of New Titan's sun hit the starbase dedication marker lying half-buried in the ground at Picard's feet. The Starfleet delta brought back to Picard the image of the insignia on the cairn of rocks he had built for James T. Kirk.

The sun had set on a legend of Starfleet the day Picard had buried Kirk. Now he felt as if the extinction of Starbase 804 marked the end for the Federation as well. Because the Borg that had been at work here were unlike any Starfleet had faced before: Starfleet's greatest fear had become real.

There *were* indeed other branches of the Borg collective active in the galaxy. And Picard knew all too well that whatever defenses worked against one branch would not necessarily work against another.

"It *must* make sense," Picard said, though in his heart he did not feel any conviction. "They are machines. Ruled by logic. What they are doing *has* to fit their programmed purpose to survive."

He felt Beverly look at him. With the professional gaze of a physician. For three days, he and Beverly, and Weinlein's team of specialists, had had to watch as Starbase 804 melted before them. For three days, Picard had had to fight the overwhelming pull of the groupmind, never really knowing if it were truly there, or simply a manifestation of the secret doubts he harbored.

For the same three days, he had been unable to carry out his mission.

Because there was no Borg vessel here to recover.

Picard felt the vibration of the communicator in his armor. The modified versions developed for the commandos were designed to be silent in the field, and experiments on the second day had confirmed the Borg were not interested in the commandos' ground communicator signals. Weinlein, however, still used untraceable microbursts to report to the *Monitor* in polar orbit.

Picard touched the contact surface at his neck. "Picard here."

It was Weinlein. She was on the other side of the Borg structure, a kilometer away. The other two commandos were hidden somewhere else among what few ruins remained.

Weinlein began speaking rapidly, wasting neither time nor words. "Krul and Beyer have completed the scan of the cube. Absolutely no indication of a propulsion system. No field coils. No warp core. Not even any propellant."

"That proves my point. They *are* waiting to be retrieved," Picard said. That had been Krul's theory as well.

But Weinlein still didn't agree. "By what?

119

Anything that could pick up that cube by tractor or by transporter could have lifted the starbase out of here in minutes. Just like Jouret IV. Why send down an assimilation crew if they've got a vessel that could do the same work in a thousandth of the time?"

Picard frowned and glanced at Beverly. She tightened her lips in silent commiseration. They both knew Weinlein was committed to her conclusion that they had made contact with a group of Borg who had somehow been separated from whatever branch of the collective they were part of. The team leader had reasoned that however this orphan branch of Borg had come to New Titan, their actions against Starbase 804 were only their blind response to their programming. Like all Borg, they were compelled to assimilate raw material and life-forms to serve the collective. And when they had reached the limit of what the starbase had been able to offer, they had simply retreated to their cube and entered their sleep mode.

The commando leader compared the Borg to worker ants in an ant farm, who would continue to build their network of tunnels, even if they had no queen to serve. Thus, in her opinion, the primary objective of this mission could not be achieved. Without a real Borg vessel to capture, Weinlein maintained there was nothing Starfleet could learn here.

But Picard felt just the opposite. He knew, as no one else did, that if any Borg were cut off from their branch of the collective, their nature

120

absolutely dictated they make every effort to rejoin it.

The material at Starbase 804 had included two runabouts and six shuttles. But their propulsion systems hadn't been incorporated intact into the cube.

Because the cube didn't need to go anywhere.

Because something was coming to retrieve it.

"You and I have been through this before," Picard said.

"And I was willing to wait to see what the Borg would do. To give you the benefit of the doubt, Captain. But I have no more doubt. All the Borg in that cube have been in sleep mode for more than three hours. There are no further signs of construction or modification. Therefore, in accordance with our orders, we will proceed with our secondary mission."

Picard had known it would come to this. He was ready, if not enthusiastic. "Understood," he said, without further argument.

"Rendezvous in fifteen minutes, behind the barracks wall. Weinlein out."

Picard took a last look at the sun on the horizon.

Beverly tried to reassure him. "This will be easier, Jean-Luc. We won't need the interface. Only you."

But Picard didn't believe that either. "They are waiting for retrieval. And when their vessel comes and finds its assimilation crew is gone, captured by Starfleet, the result could be . . . most calamitous."

"But the *Monitor* is still here. And it was

designed to fight the Borg." For an instant, despite her words, Beverly's voice wavered.

Picard knew why. He looked into her eyes. But all he saw was the flames of war. Of destruction. "At Wolf 359, Starfleet lost thirty-nine starships. Eleven thousand beings perished. *That* is what it means to fight the Borg. Whatever Commander Shelby's intentions are—one lone starship, no matter how well designed, will not even slow them down."

Beverly met his gaze directly, but Picard could see she did not want to say what she was going to say next.

"At Wolf 359, the Borg knew each weakness in our ships and shields. They knew our tactics and our weapons' capabilities and limitations. It was as if they could read our minds."

"They could," Picard said. He would not hide from the truth, no matter how harsh. "Mine."

Beverly took hold of both of Picard's arms, to make him understand.

"You were *not* responsible, Jean-Luc! The Borg sought you out to be their Speaker. Their liaison. You couldn't resist them. No one could."

Picard felt his jaw clench. Felt emotions he had buried far too long rush up in him like magma, seeking the violence of release. "I *tried* to resist them, but . . ." Then the next words froze in his throat. Words he had never dared speak before. But words he could no longer hold back.

"What if I didn't resist them *enough?*"

Beverly's mouth curved down in confusion. "What?" She released her hold on him.

How long had he held this secret? Picard didn't

know. It had been four years since the Borg assault on Earth. But his terrible knowledge of what he believed to be his own personal failure seemed to have been with him all his life. Poisoning all his memories.

"When I was . . . taken . . ." Picard felt what was almost a wave of relief pass through him as he finally felt himself begin to say the words that might expose him for what he feared he was, what he had been. Not even his Starfleet debriefers had heard everything that had happened to him at the hands of the Borg. Counsellor Troi had known he was hiding something. Had tried to get him to talk about it over the years. But he had always resisted. Until now. When the possibility of failure rose up before him again.

And there had never been room for failure in his life. He would not allow it.

"When I was taken, the Borg . . . they put me in . . . an assimilator. A chair. A frame. Something that . . . grew from the wall of their ship. There were straps, or metal bands. Something held me there, physically.

"I fought them the whole time. I tried to get out. To get up. But they were all around me. Simply staring at me. And then . . . before . . . the process began . . . and I gave up. . . ." Picard kept his eyes fixed on the horizon, almost invisible now. "Do you understand, Beverly? Before they assimilated me, I stopped fighting."

Beverly stared at him as she struggled to comprehend what Picard was confessing.

". . . you were in their ship. We know they have drugs. Sonic and visual brainwave inducers.

123

They wouldn't *let* you fight. It was no longer your decision to make."

But Picard shook his head. "There were no drugs. No inducers. There were just Borg. Watching. Waiting. Letting me sense the . . . presence of the collective."

Picard stared into the darkness enveloping the desolate ruins before him. Like a web of shadows, spun by the monster at its center. The cube. The Borg. Enveloping everything.

"Jean-Luc, the Borg collective is a machine-based, sub-space communications system. How could you possibly sense it before they had put implants in you?"

"How does Deanna sense emotions?" he asked the darkness. "In their ship, in the face of so many of them, I knew. I felt. It—them—their overwhelming . . . presence. And I somehow watched *with* them, through them, at myself, remaining in that frame, as the machinery descended." He closed his eyes, seeing it all anew. "The blades. The needles. I felt them cut into me!" He couldn't breathe. "And I didn't *fight* them. Because . . . I *wanted* to belong. . . . I wanted so much to belong. . . ."

Picard felt Beverly's arms draw him close to her. His cheek brushed the hard surface of her armor, her soft fragrant hair. Her hand moved from his armored back to stroke his neck, the back of his head.

"It's all right," she said. "None of it was real. The Borg manipulated your mind, made you one of them, so you could do nothing *except* want to be part of the collective."

He recoiled from her support, forced his breathing to become normal, squared his shoulders, and shook his head once. "No."

Beverly's voice sharpened. "If you insist on having this argument, let me tell you that I *am* going to win it. Because you're too close to what happened to understand it." She held up her hand to stop Picard before he could protest. "But right now, we have a mission. And we will perform that mission. And we will beam back to the *Monitor* with our prisoners. And then I'm going to take you into the holosuite and . . . well, never mind what I'm going to do. But you're going to feel a great deal better."

She was so intent, so like the Beverly of old, that Picard almost smiled.

"I'm sure I will," he said. "I do already."

This time, Beverly shook her head. "You never could lie to me, Jean-Luc. But the point is, you were not responsible for your actions as Locutus. Any more than you'd be responsible if I gave you . . . ten milliliters of cordrazine."

Picard tugged on the waist of his armor in a futile attempt to straighten his cumbersome chestplate. He tried to lighten the moment. "If I have to live in this outfit much longer, I might take you up on that, Doctor."

Beverly smiled at him as if the real Jean-Luc were back. But Picard knew even her relief was a charade. The only thing that had returned was his self-control. As long as he didn't have to use the interface, surely self-control would be more than sufficient to capture ten Borg and return to the *Monitor*.

"Time to play soldier?" Beverly asked.

Picard appreciated her more in that moment than he ever had. For trying to set right what she never could.

"Thank you," he said.

Beverly regarded him seriously. "Save it for the holosuite."

Picard nodded, not even daring to think that far ahead.

Once again, it was time to engage the Borg.

THIRTEEN

Kirk held his dying wife in his arms. Over the evacuation alarms, he heard his children screaming, caught behind the sealed doors of his quarters.

"Help them," Kalinara sobbed. Half her face was ripped away by the cluster explosives that had been transported throughout the *Talon of Peace*. Her green blood smeared Kirk's hands and arms, bubbled at the corner of her torn lips. But still she thought only of the children. *Their* children.

"I can't leave you," he choked.

"For our children," Kalinara murmured, fading quickly. "For our future . . ."

He felt her grip loosen on his hand. Heard the terrible rasp of her last breath as it escaped her seared lungs.

Kirk's cry of denial overcame the sirens.

The ship shuddered all around him. The cowardly attack continued. One thousand colonists aboard Kirk's ship faced death.

"*Father!*" screamed the piteously young voice behind the door. "*He's here! He's go—*"

Kirk staggered to his feet as his child's voice stopped midword. He stumbled to the sealed door as the deck in his quarters lurched beneath his feet.

The artificial gravity generators couldn't last much longer. And after they went, the structural integrity field would fail.

He could picture his double-hulled ship collapsing in space. Its quantum core spiraling out of containment. The explosion that would result, one dying star among so many.

Everything would be lost.

But it wasn't lost yet.

Kirk joined his hands together and swung them down against on the door, trying to jar the backup battery circuit. It had to open. It *had* to release his children. There might be time to reach an escape pod. He could carry Kalinara. The medics could stabilize her. It might not be too late. It couldn't be. He wouldn't let it be.

His fists bled as he pounded on the unmoving door.

"*Lora!*" he shouted. "*Tranalak!*" Tears streamed down his face. He smelled smoke. Somewhere belowdecks he heard a rumbling explosion. The sirens wailed in unison.

His wife had just died. His children were dying. And all because of—

The door trembled beneath his blows.

He drew back. Hope soared within him. There was a chance.

But then the door ground open.

He was here.

The monster. With Kirk's children.

Five-year-old Tranalak lay sprawled at his feet, dark eyes staring up, lifeless. Eight-year-old Lora was held aloft in the his grip, her tiny feet kicking and flailing as she struggled to free herself.

The monster grinned at Kirk as his hand flew across the child's throat with a glint of Federation steel.

Then he discarded her small body, letting it fall awkwardly to the deck—

Kirk flung himself at the monster before him.

Kirk flung himself at Picard.

His hands were talons as they sought Picard's throat.

But the monster threw back his head, laughing, laughing——even as Kirk's hands grasped in vain at his fading body.Even as Kirk fell alone to the floor. No longer a deck.

The shuddering stopped.

The sirens faded.

Kirk lay gasping on the black floor, marked with its grid of yellow lines.

Alone with his hate. His rage. His pain.

"Do you remember now?" Salatrel asked.

Kirk pushed himself up, still trembling. He stared at his hands, unbloodied, unmarked.

"Your wife?" Salatrel said. "Your children?"

Kirk stood up, body aching, out of breath.

He looked past Salatrel at the entry arch behind

128

her. At the controls to the side. The closed door in the center.

"What is this place?" he gasped.

The Romulan woman frowned. She aimed a tricorder at him.

Kirk knew it was a tricorder, though it seemed too small.

"A holodeck," she said as she adjusted controls on her device. "One of the few useful contributions the Federation has made to the galaxy."

Kirk struggled to make sense of it. Some terms seemed so familiar. But the context was so wrong.

"But this is a . . . Romulan ship?" he asked.

Salatrel stepped closer. He could sense her annoyance.

"I have nothing to hide from you," she said. "You are on the *Avatar of Tomed*. It is a *D'deridex*-class starship. Just as was your own *Talon of Peace*."

"Starship . . . ?" Kirk said, grasping at the familiar word. "I had a starship, didn't I?"

Salatrel's frown eased. "You *are* remembering."

"And my wife and children?"

"Killed. Five years ago. When Picard led his cowardly attack under color of truce."

"Picard," Kirk repeated, hearing the sound of it in his own mind. He was certain he knew that name. It was from his past. But then, why didn't the context fit?

Salatrel glanced up from her tricorder. Her eyes narrowed. "Do you doubt me?" she asked.

"Why would I?" Kirk replied. "You saved my life."

Salatrel stepped closer, put a hand to his face. "Just as you saved mine," she said.

Kirk felt his heartrate slow as he gazed into Salatrel's eyes. "Will I remember that, too?"

"The doctors say you will eventually recover all your memories." Salatrel replaced her tricorder on her belt. She removed her padd. "You will be restored."

Kirk nodded. He was impatient for that to happen.

Salatrel brushed her lips against his. He felt the electricity of her contact even as he heard her fingers tap on her padd.

"Tell me about the Klingon," she said.

"Klingon bastard!" Kirk spat. "You killed my son!" He gasped and stepped back, trying to lose the distraction of Salatrel's presence. Where had that thought come from? Those words?

"No," Salatrel corrected him, sharply. "*Picard* killed your son. *And* your wife and daughter. The Klingon was his chief of security."

Kirk thought back to the forest. To the Klingon. Klingons were the enemy. At least, he thought, they had been. Once. And he *had* had a son. Who had died. Because of . . .

A wave of sudden pain and anxiety shot through him.

"The Klingon," Salatrel repeated. "Tell me."

"But I already have," Kirk said. He forced the pain from his body. He knew what battle injuries felt like. But this ache throughout his entire body was different. He didn't know where it came from.

"I need to hear it again. What did he tell you?"

The pain increased.

"Nothing," Kirk said, wincing.

Not in words, he thought.

Salatrel grabbed his chin. Forced him to look at her. "You can't hide anything from me," she said.

"Why would I?" Kirk answered. The words felt programmed into him. He said them, but he resisted them, trying to find the web that connected all the turmoil in his mind.

He knew Picard.

He knew Klingons and Romulans. Starfleet and the hated Federation.

He knew the torment of the death of his son.

But Salatrel? And holodecks? And a wife dying when a colony fleet was destroyed by the *Enterprise?*

Where were the connections?

He held Salatrel's gaze.

Where was the truth?

The only thing he was certain of was that he did not see it in Salatrel's eyes.

But he had seen it in the Klingon's.

There was a pattern here, maddeningly out of reach.

If only he could speak with . . .

An image came to him. A tall man, strong features. Pointed ears. But not a Romulan. A Vulcan. And at his side. An older man. Hands behind his back. An easy smile. A human from . . .

"What is it? Tell me," Salatrel demanded.

Kirk frowned. If he was a Romulan patriot, a human dedicated to Romulan peace, had married a Romulan woman, had two children with her, had become a hero of the revolution against the evil domination of the Federation . . .

Why did he remember a Vulcan and a human as his . . . friends?

Where was his wife in his memories? And where was Salatrel, this woman who had been his lover for the past three years, fighting at his side?

Salatrel studied the padd she held. "You must tell me what you're thinking. You know I've always been here for you."

"I know," Kirk said. And even as the words formed on his lips, he knew they were false.

But Salatrel did not seem to recognize that. As if, despite all she had said, he did have some secrets that could be hidden from her.

"Would you like to know how we met?" she asked.

Kirk nodded.

Salatrel stepped away from him, back to the arch in the wall. Kirk followed. Watched as she tapped in commands on the controls. It seemed like a simple enough system.

"Computer," she said. "Run program Salatrel four." She turned to Kirk. "We arrive at Trilex in six hours," she said. She held up her padd. "Keep trying to remember . . . me."

Kirk held out his hand to touch her but she vanished from view, even as she touched another padd control.

He heard birds singing. Felt a warm breeze. Smelled the rich growth of a forest all around him.

He turned to see an Iowa vista. Gentle hills.

Old trees towering into the summer sky, dappling the ground with the interplay of leaf shadow and sunbeams.

Kirk knew this place. It fit perfectly into the gaps, the cracks of his memories. His eyes widened at the wonder of it. The security of it.

Then he heard hoofbeats.

He wheeled, truly remembering the moment.

She rode for him, on a glorious mare, its coat gleaming in the sun and mane alive in the breeze.

He looked up at her, to see her smile. Antonia's smile as she . . .

No. Not Antonia.

Salatrel smiled back at him as she rode closer.

An automatic wave of pleasure coursed through him.

Even as he knew something was wrong.

Salatrel slipped from the horse's side, smiled at him, held out her hand.

"I'm with the peace mission," she said. "Salatrel, of Romulus."

"I don't remember this," Kirk said.

Salatrel moved into his arms, pressed herself against his body, held him tightly in the sunlight and the forest.

"It's all right," she said. "I do."

Then she kissed him.

For a moment, Kirk hesitated. Some of what he was experiencing was merely unknown. Some, he felt certain, was false. But somewhere at the core of this experience, he sensed elements of the truth.

All he had to do was sort one from the other.

But for now, the desire he felt as he held Salatrel in his arms again made rational thought almost impossible.

So he returned her kiss.

And surrendered—if not to her, then to the heat of the Iowa sunshine.

FOURTEEN

In the deepening twilight, Picard and Beverly crept across the broken ground toward the barracks wall.

The wall was a landmark in the ruined starbase, because, apart from the Borg cube a hundred meters distant, it was the largest structure remaining—a fractured plane of extruded silicon, less than two meters high at its tallest, running no more than ten meters side to side.

On the far side of the wall, closer to the cube, barracks beds and lockers were fused together, melted by whatever tool the Borg had used to extract the optical data network circuitry from the recreational computer system. The body of a young ensign in a duty uniform was half-buried in the rubble of another wall which had fallen completely.

From the pattern of damage the commando team had catalogued, Weinlein had concluded that the Borg had struck at night, spent at least four days "convincing" base personnel to willingly join the collective, and then had forcibly assimilated any who remained at large.

Picard tried not to think of what those four days had been like for the personnel of Starbase 804. He and Beverly had already been in transit, expecting to be stationed here during Starfleet's investigation of the outpost raids in this part of the frontier. What if they had arrived a week earlier? Or if the Borg had arrived a week later? It could all have been over by now, and he would have been back among—

"Get down!" Weinlein ordered.

Picard and Beverly dropped to the ground behind the wall. Weinlein, Krul, and Beyer were already crouched in position. Krul and Beyer looked as if they had just returned from Wrigley's Pleasure Planet, rested and calm. Weinlein was her usual, crisp self. Picard was irritated at his own frayed state. After three days of field rations and sleeping in armor, he felt anything but at his peak.

Weinlein jerked a finger at the tricorder mounted on her forearm. "Still no movement." She gave Picard a cold grin. "Fish in a barrel."

"You know my objections." Picard's tone matched Weinlein's own.

"Noted and logged," she confirmed. "But even if they're expecting some kind of mother ship to come for them, what are the odds that will happen in the next twenty minutes?"

"Why twenty minutes?" Picard asked. The idea of a timetable after all these days of waiting was unexpected. . . .

Weinlein pulled on her battle helmet. "Because that's how long this is going to take."

Beside her, Krul and Beyer snapped fresh power supplies into their phaser rifles.

"How many Borg are in there?" Beverly asked. As if it mattered.

"Forty-two humanoids," Weinlein said as she sealed the rim of her helmet to her armor. "Three of the multilimbed construction units. One scuttler."

"And two canines," Krul added. His smile looked almost feral.

"We only need ten of the humanoids," Weinlein went on, ignoring Krul. "Shelby's people say that's double the minimum required to maintain a groupmind when they're cut off from their branch of the collective."

"I know the theory," Picard said. He pulled his own helmet from his back harness. "But what does Shelby say the rest of the Borg will do as we . . . make off with their fellows?"

"The commander says that once they see you, they'll be trying to make contact with Locutus. That's why you'll be front and center. You'll be verbally activating all their internal diagnostic subroutines, while we collect our ten."

Picard shrugged away from Beverly's touch. Concern again flared in him that Weinlein's tactics might prove too simplistic. "You saw what happened when I attempted that with the unfortunate woman who stopped me on our first day here. I only delayed her for a few minutes at best."

Weinlein ignored his protest as she checked her tricorder. "The *Monitor* will be overhead in seven minutes, thirty seconds." She held up an emergency transporter beacon armband. "While you delay the Borg response, my people and I will slap these on our ten targets, then the *Monitor* beams us all out. The Borg will stay in stasis till we hit Starbase 324 and Commander Shelby takes them off our hands."

Picard tugged his helmet on. He looked forward to taking action at last, though he knew he also was reaching the point of invoking the authority Starfleet had given him to take control over the mission. "You obviously don't think the Borg will activate their shields."

Weinlein put her gloved hand on her visor. "Not if Locutus tells them not to." She snapped the opaque visor down and her face disappeared. Now she and Krul and Beyer were little more than machines themselves.

"We start forward in one minute," Weinlein said. This time Picard heard her on the speaker in his helmet. "Krul and Beyer go first and take up position by the main airlock. Then Picard and I sweep in."

"What about me?" Beverly asked. She tugged her own helmet into position, sealing it to her armor.

"After all four of us are inside, you take up position immediately outside the airlock. If all goes well, you just sit tight till the *Monitor* locks on."

"And if all doesn't go well?" Beverly asked.

"Whatever else happens, Picard has to come out."

Beverly snapped her own visor down.

Picard stared at the four dark apparitions

before him. One lone starship to stand up against a Borg vessel? Three commandos to go after more than forty Borg? What was Starfleet thinking? What was *Shelby* thinking?

Or was it not thought on Starfleet's part, but desperation?

Picard put his hand on his own visor. It was dark enough now that he would need night vision to make the run to the Borg cube. "Permit me one last word of caution," he said. "Once we're inside, no fast movements until we're certain the Borg have identified us as a threat."

Weinlein's helmet angled in amusement. "Captain, if we move fast enough, they won't have *time* to identify us. Fifteen seconds." She held her finger over a forearm control. "Microburst signal to the *Monitor* in three . . . two . . . one . . . mark!"

She pressed the control, sending an untraceable coded message to the starship, setting it in motion to be in position for the emergency beam-out.

"Stand by, Captain. We go in eight . . . seven . . ."

Picard began to pull down his visor.

A double flash of blue light flickered at his side.

"Resistance is futile," said the Borg.

Picard pulled Beverly away, behind him, as he turned to face the two Borg that had materialized two meters away with all the suddenness the Borg transporter was known for.

Both cybernetic creatures had arms that ended in the glowing discharge nodes of antimatter streamers. At fine focus, the devices were good

138

for careful dissection of scrap and salvage. At wide beam, they were more destructive than phasers.

The nodes swung to Krul and Beyer, whose phaser rifles were already trained on the Borg.

And even as Weinlein yelled at Picard to take off his helmet, Picard stepped forward to confront the enemy, helmet in hand. "No!" he commanded.

The Borg instantly looked at him, instantly froze.

Their red sensor lasers converged on his face. "Locutus?" one said.

Then both Borg dissolved in a slow pulse of quantum mist.

"Frequency one used," Beyer barked over the comm circuit.

"Engaging random frequency selection," Krul responded.

The individual force fields that protected combat-ready Borg constantly adapted to whatever weaponry was trained against them. No one phaser frequency could be used more than once, because the force fields around every other Borg in the collective would immediately change to repel that frequency.

Weinlein grabbed Picard's arm. "Let's move it! We need those prisoners!"

But Picard pulled back. "They know we're here."

Weinlein snapped up her visor. Picard could just make out her lean features in the soft glow of the status lights on her in-helmet display screen. "They'll be confused. We still have time!"

"No!" Picard said forcefully. This time he had to make Weinlein understand. "They've always known we were here! Think! They didn't beam to get us until we sent the micro-burst to bring the *Monitor* out of hiding."

Picard felt the adrenaline of battle sharpen, then slow his senses to a hyperacute state. The mission would succeed or fail in the next few seconds.

"You're saying this is a trap?" Weinlein asked incredulously.

"What else would it be?"

"Then where are the rest of them?" Weinlein demanded. "Why aren't they coming after us?"

Picard felt an incongruous bubble of laughter rise up in him. It was so obvious. "They don't want *us*. They don't care about *us*. They want the *Monitor*."

Weinlein stared over the wall at the dark cube towering over the devastated starbase. "But they have no weaponry installed in that thing. No propulsion systems."

"Because they're the *bait!*" Picard said. "That's all they are!" It was perfectly clear now. "That's why they didn't assimilate the base in seconds. They needed to draw out the process, to draw us in."

Weinlein muttered in an ancient Vulcan dialect. She reset controls on her forearm padd, then jabbed the communicator contact at her neck.

"Archangel! This is red leader! Override alpha alpha one alpha! You are heading into an ambush! Confirm!"

140

Picard heard all the confirmation he needed. Subspace static.

A glance at his own tricorder told him all communications channels were being jammed. The source was the cube.

Beverly looked up from her own tricorder. "We are now within a Borg force field," she announced softly. "No beam-out possible."

Weinlein looked stricken. Beside her, Krul and Beyer kept their phaser rifles in firing position, constantly scanning the immediate area.

Picard recognized the expression in Weinlein's eyes, dark and shadowed as they were.

The look of a commander who has run out of options.

In contrast, Picard felt his own control increase. "Lieutenant Weinlein, we are trapped in enemy territory, out of contact with command. As Captain, Starfleet, I am countermanding all of Commander Shelby's orders." He reached forward and pulled Weinlein's duty phaser, type-5, from her harness. "I am now in command of this mission."

In that moment, Picard saw Krul and Beyer swing their phaser rifles onto him. Beverly stepped into their line of fire, but Picard gently pushed her back.

"I'm not the enemy," Picard said. He pointed over the wall toward the cube. "That is."

Weinlein hesitated, as Picard knew she must. But in the end, she waved to her soldiers. "Stand down. The captain's in command."

The rifles lowered slowly. But they were lowered.

Picard didn't stop to acknowledge his victory. "Listen carefully. There is a working transporter in that cube, as well as a force-field generator and whatever equipment they're using to jam subspace. Our objective is to take control of all three systems."

Weinlein frowned. "If you don't want us to take prisoners, why not just blow it up?"

"Because somewhere up there is a Borg ship waiting for the *Monitor*. *That* is our target. The mission's primary objective is once again within our reach."

"But there's only one way you can take control," Weinlein said.

"I know," Picard answered, aware that somehow he had moved beyond fear, beyond anxiety. As if, somehow, this moment had always been waiting for him and he could no longer avoid its arrival.

He reached out to Beverly, handed her the phaser, and pulled the small carryall pod from her belt.

The interface.

He ran his hand around his armor's neck seal, then pulled his helmet off.

"We go back to the original plan," he said as he popped the carryall's seal.

Even in the near darkness he could see the alien, convex shape of the neuromolecular attachment plate inside.

It was cold to the touch as he pulled it out. A thick cable came out with it, designed to be plugged into the plate and the power cell already in place beneath his armor.

Momentarily, he was surprised by how little he was affected by the sight of it—its same outward size, shape, and appearance the same as the one the Borg had attached to his skull.

And then he understood why.

Above him, a starship was in danger.

Around him, Starfleet personnel looked to him for leadership.

And on the thousand worlds of the Federation, an interstellar civilization unmatched in history teetered on the brink of extinction, to be saved or destroyed by what a single individual would accomplish in the next few minutes and hours.

In the middle of action, there was no room for doubt. He could not afford it or allow it.

He was a starship captain.

It was time to make a difference.

FIFTEEN

The steady pulse of the *Tomed*'s singularity generators throbbed in the corridors of the ship. To Salatrel, the comforting sound was as much a part of her life as her own heartbeat. Even now, with her mind focused on the next stage of her plan, she was aware of the power of the ship which she commanded, and she took strength from it.

She stood in the corridor outside the Starfleet holodeck which the Borg had helpfully assimilated from one of the Starfleet vessels they had defeated since arriving in this quadrant. She had not been lying when she had told Kirk it was one of the few useful contributions the Federation had made to the galaxy—and to this mission.

Romulan holographic simulators would never have been able to re-create an Earth environment with as much convincing detail as this unit could. And judging from the way Kirk was reacting to meeting her holographic duplicate in a re-creation of his home region of Iowa, the illusion was perfect.

Salatrel watched, as emotionless as her distant Vulcan cousins, as Kirk embraced her own duplicate on the observation screen. Vox stood beside her. To her left, his cranial implants and sensor eye were what she saw. She preferred it that way. There was no chance then of confusing him with what he once was. And could never be again.

"Kirk is lying," Vox stated.

Salatrel folded her arms. "The collective's thinking is too binary. My medical scans show he is merely confused. That is to be expected at this stage of his conditioning."

"Our analysis of the regeneration device indicated that his memories should have returned intact."

On screen, Salatrel's duplicate and Kirk took a red and black patterned blanket, and some type of food container made of stiff, woven plant tendrils, from the storage units on the sides of the equinoid's rider's seat. Once again, Salatrel congratulated herself on her decision to make use of the Starfleet holodeck. No Romulan programmer could have dreamed of such an unlikely combination of artifacts and creatures. "Obviously, the regeneration device was flawed. It self-destructed before the process was completed. There is nothing sinister in that."

Vox turned to her. She glanced up at him and again suffered and banished the automatic pang of anguish. Anger was clearly, and familiarly, expressed on the half of her former lover's face that still remained Romulan.

"At your request, the collective provided the technology you required to return Kirk to functional status. He is not functional. This project should be terminated."

"You still don't understand the elegance of this," Salatrel said sharply.

"Elegance is not a useful quality. Efficiency is useful. Reduction of effort leading to increase in resources is the ideal. Life is improved when all contribute to the good of the whole."

"That is what we are doing here," Salatrel said in a more conciliatory tone. "Consider. Who is the greatest villain ever to subvert the will of the Romulan people?"

Salatrel watched as Vox's stern expression seemed to soften, as if that part of him which was still Romulan were being released from that which was Borg. "The Butcher of Icarus IV," he said by rote. "James Tiberius Kirk."

"Exactly," Salatrel said. "Just as our people were prepared to throw off the yoke of the Federation, to stand against the injustices forced upon us by the Treaty of Algeron, James Tiberius Kirk murdered the patriots who were to lead the first wave of our redemption."

145

The tragic story of the Battle of Icarus IV was known to every Romulan child: How the first cloaked Romulan vessel had set out to probe the Earth outposts belligerently arrayed at the boundaries of the Neutral Zone. And how, after her successful mission, but before her triumphant return, Kirk and his ship had defeated her commander by dishonorable tactics—feigning helplessness near the tail of the Icarus comet to lure the Romulan vessel to her destruction.

To Romulans, if Kirk had fired upon women and children who had raised their arms in surrender, it could be no greater crime.

But Borg severity had already returned to Vox. He no longer seemed touched by the story.

"James Tiberius Kirk was a soldier. He did his duty to defend his territory. We could expect no less."

"He defended a monstrous violation of our sovereignty *and* our dignity. His butchery set back our people's aspirations for generations, as the appeasers held on to power." Salatrel's voice rose in its intensity.

Vox gazed at Salatrel as if he didn't care what she said or thought. But Salatrel could read another expression on Vox's face, as well. The one that came with assimilation. It was the way the Borg had of reducing everything, and everyone, to raw material. As if they constantly calculated the return they could expect against the exertion of instantly consuming what they saw.

"These are the facts," Vox stated, and Salatrel waited for what he would say next. It was what

Vox always said when they had this argument. "Your grandfather was the commander of the first Neutral Zone penetration mission to test the Cloaking Device. James Tiberius Kirk killed your grandfather. Therefore, your involvement in this procedure is suspect."

"Kirk's name is reviled throughout the Star Empire," Salatrel retorted automatically, as she always did. "My involvement in this procedure is fortunate."

Vox brought their argument back to the present. "Where is the elegance in chance?"

Salatrel turned away as if to study the display screen, no longer trusting herself to retain self-control if she continued looking at Vox's disfigured face, with all that its ruin represented.

In the holodeck simulation, Kirk and her duplicate sat on the patterned blanket in a sheltered area beneath a tree. Despite her assurances to Vox, Salatrel frowned. It was unusual that Kirk was still involved in conversation. According to her psychographic projections, he should have initiated lovemaking by now. But an analysis of that anomaly would have to wait. She marshaled her energy to defeat Vox, if only in words.

"In regard to the assimilation of the Federation, who is the greatest threat to the will of the collective?" Salatrel asked, still watching the screen and Kirk's atypical behavior.

"Jean-Luc Picard," Vox answered.

"Once again," Salatrel said, "exactly. You sucked all the information you needed about the Federation and Starfleet from his mind when he was assimilated. And the other half of that equation is that all the information Starfleet needs to defeat you a second time is buried somewhere in Picard's mind. Can't you see the . . . logic of the situation? You and I will turn our two greatest enemies against each other. The Romulan people at last will have their revenge against Kirk, while the Borg will be able to remove the last barrier to their successful assimilation of the Federation."

"Only if Kirk accomplishes his mission in the seven days remaining to him," Vox said.

"We are working on a way to remove the nanites. He might last longer."

"No," Vox said. "The neuronic implant will kill him long before the nanites fatally reconfigure his body."

Salatrel whirled to face Vox. "*What?*"

"To construct these holographic simulations, to create a cover story he would accept and believe, we required information beyond that which was contained in available files." Vox continued as if oblivious to her stunned reaction. To understand Kirk's personality in the time we have available, it was necessary to install a neuronic interface in order to make his thoughts available to us. It was not necessary to inform you of our action."

Salatrel's body was rigid with fury and fear. What else might Vox have done without her knowledge? Her plan depended on Kirk acting as he had in the past, not slowed down by a subspace interface with a Borg hive of unimaginative drones. "You made Kirk a Borg?"

"No," Vox said. "At this stage, that would be counterproductive to the task he must perform.

He must function as a human in order to move among others of his kind. The collective is not in contact with him."

Salatrel forced herself to relax. Kirk was still hers to command. But Vox was not finished with his surprising revelations.

"Elements of his emotional makeup were downloaded for analysis." A small smile appeared on Vox's taciturn features. "He is not as easy to control as you imagine. That is why I say he is lying."

Salatrel weighed her position. As she had told her centurion, Tracius, the only possible result of her actions was victory. Any other would result in her not being alive to witness it.

And victory depended on *her* retaining control, not the Borg.

She decided to call Vox's bluff.

The collective's bluff.

"Then why don't you assimilate him? Why don't you assimilate all of us?" Her hand dramatically swept the corridor, her ship, the entire fleet of dissidents that fought at her side.

Whatever Vox thought was not apparent in his expression. "We have a treaty," he answered calmly. "The Borg and the Romulan dissidents. You assist the collective in assimilating the Federation, and we allow the Star Empire to exist unassimilated. As a . . . curiosity. Long-term study of an unassimilated culture will allow us to be more proficient in welcoming other cultures to the collective. It is an efficient use of our resources."

Salatrel searched Vox's Romulan eye for the

truth. "Do you honestly expect me to believe that?"

Vox's expression remained unchanged. "If you wish to survive, you have no choice. Resistance is futile."

Salatrel's pulse quickened at the Speaker's last statement. Her dissidents had not resisted the Borg. The Romulan Warbird crew who were assimilated at the time Vox became Speaker for the Borg retained enough of their Romulan dignity and fervor to actually suggest the treaty to the collective. And why would the Borg waste resources on the relatively small Empire when the Federation hung behind the Neutral Zone, ready for plucking?

Resistance had never been an option, or even a strategy.

So why had Vox mentioned it?

Unless it had been a signal.

From somewhere deep inside the Romulan Vox used to be.

Unsettled, Salatrel checked the display screen again. On it, Kirk gently removed her duplicate's hand from his leg. What was wrong with him? That wasn't typical of Kirk, either.

"Why is he doing that?" she asked crossly. "Resisting her seduction?"

Vox studied the screen. "He knows she is an illusion."

"Indistinguishable from reality."

"He is a man of the moment," Vox said. "Steeped in reality. He does not belong in that device, any more than he belongs in this time." Vox turned to Salatrel. For a moment, it seemed to her that his Romulan voice spoke to her. "You do not understand what you have unleashed."

For the sake of her plan, Salatrel would not, could not accept that verdict. Not from the collective. And not from Vox. Too much depended on it, and on her.

"Watch," she said to the Speaker. "I'll show you what I understand. Kirk is only a puppet to be manipulated. And I am his master."

Salatrel strode to the arched entrance to the holodeck.

"What do you intend to do?" Vox asked. Against reason, Salatrel hoped his question betrayed an interest in any answer she might make.

"Take my duplicate's place," she said. "Remove the illusion."

If she could, she would torture whatever remained of her lover in Vox.

"And I want you to observe every moment."

The Speaker looked at her blankly. But Salatrel was sure that some part of him was alive to pain. She longed for that surety.

"That is not an efficient use of my time," Vox said.

"What if Kirk and I will be plotting revenge against the collective?" Salatrel said. "If he was wired into the collective the way Picard was, then wasn't there the same sort of exchange of data? Doesn't he have the same secrets locked in his mind? Isn't he just as big a threat to you as Picard?"

"Kirk will be dead in seven days. Picard is

151

missing. Perhaps Starfleet has imprisoned him for losing his ship at Veridian."

"The Federation is not the Star Empire," Salatrel persisted. "Those cowards probably patted him on the hand and apologized for giving him a substandard vessel. He's out there, Vox. Ready to work against you. Unless Kirk stops him." She turned the knife. "And you know it. Otherwise, you never would have expended the resources you already have."

For once, Vox had no response.

Salatrel put her hand on the entrance control. "Observe carefully," she said. "We'll see if I can bring back any more memories for James Tiberius Kirk. Or for you."

Then the door slipped open with a gentle hiss of machinery, and Salatrel stepped through.

Vox watched the observation screen impassively, the holographic duplicate fading as the real Salatrel stepped up to Kirk.

Embraced by the welcoming comfort of the groupmind, Vox noted that Kirk did not react with surprise to the duplicate's disappearance. The reconstructed human was more in control than Salatrel imagined.

Vox's consciousness floated among the thousands of eyes and hands engaged in the work of the collective in this sector, sharing all that he thought and felt with so many others that a blanketing numbness was its end result. At some level, no more important than that of one small processor in a massively parallel neural network, Vox watched Kirk as Salatrel switched off the closure on her tunic, allowing it to fall from her shoulders, so she stood before Kirk, naked.

And Vox continued to watch as Kirk embraced the woman who had been his lover. But whatever discomfort the tiny spark of individual volition still left within him felt, it was insignificant compared to the bliss of the collective.

In seven days, Kirk would be dead.

Shortly after, the Federation would fall.

And then, despite their bargain, the Romulan Star Empire would also become fulfilled as it, too, received the gift of bliss.

The Borg had recently learned that lying was an excellent way to preserve resources. And this branch of the collective especially had become quite practiced at it.

Certain in his knowledge that Salatrel would join him again, Vox observed what happened on the black and red patterned blanket beneath the tree.

His sensor eye was unwavering in its concentration.

His organic eye was bathed in a distorting veil of moisture.

Emotions were futile.

The collective was all.

SIXTEEN

The Borg cube loomed in the darkness, surrounded by the glow from its blue and red

153

power conduits, illuminating the broken ground around it.

It was implacable, impenetrable.

But Picard didn't care.

He had committed himself to action without doubt.

Others depended on him.

He ran for the cube, leading his team.

In a flash of blue radiation, two Borg materialized ten meters before him, weapons already trained on him. But before they could fire, they were already shimmering in quantum disintegration.

"Random frequency selection engaged!" Beyer called out.

Beverly was at Picard's side. Beyer and Krul behind them. Weinlein covered their flank, between the team and the cube's secondary airlock.

Twenty meters from the main airlock, Picard knew the only reason the Borg hadn't already attacked was that the collective's groupmind was analyzing the loss of its first two teams of soldiers. The next response would be overwhelming, but it was still several seconds off.

Picard yanked out a handtorch from his harness and put his thumb on its activator. He didn't want to depend on the red and blue glow of the power conduits. He had to be ready.

He was ten meters from the main airlock. It was sealed, but the phaser rifles still had fourteen more frequencies to cycle through. Enough to get his team through the door.

A blinding blue flash came from the side opposite Weinlein's approach. Picard faltered, momentarily startled by what he saw. The Borg response *was* overwhelming. A configuration unlike any Borg Picard had ever encountered.

It was bipedal, but three meters tall, with piston-like legs and thick crushing disks for foot-pads, digging into the soil. Propellant gases hissed from its leg joints as it began to stalk forward. Two pairs of arms swung forward, searchingly, manipulators opening and closing with molecularly sharp carbon cutters and whirling blades. Their target: raw materials.

Phaser beams streaked past Picard and flared in a blinding halo around the Borg giant. The beams resolved into facets like a jewel carved out of energy. Disconcertingly, the sudden light revealed a small, impassive, humanoid head centered protectively in the Borg's immense shoulder plates. It was the only biological component visible. Picard saw Beverly recoil at the sight.

The phaser beams cut out. The Borg colossus advanced. Untouched.

"They've adapted to the base phaser pattern!" Beyer shouted.

"Discard phasers!" Weinlein commanded. "Krul, you're go!"

The powerful Klingon lunged past Picard.

The Borg's arms swung down on him, intent on dismembering its attacker.

But Krul fired a Klingon thrustergun first.

An antique, Picard knew, hand-tooled with intricate engravings of Kahless battling Molor. He had examined it when they had shared a meal two nights ago. It fired simple projectiles of explosive-packed metal, propelled by a centuries-old chemical-reaction technology.

The Borg's forcefield had been set for phaser harmonics.

Undetected, the metal projectile traversed the force field's perimeter and punched into the creature's implanted breastplate before the collective could reconfigure its defenses.

Sparks arced from the Borg's immense chest, along with a spray of dark liquid. One arm snapped back, flailing out of control.

Picard saw the shock on the face so cruelly embedded in the appalling construction.

Four more projectiles pockmarked the Borg's armored body. The last one caused a defensive force-field flare, but the collective had not been fast enough to save this unit.

It began to topple.

From Krul's throat rose a Klingon victory cry, as he drove his fists into the air.

Just as an antimatter stream spurted from the glowing node of one falling Borg arm.

The incandescent beam sliced neatly through Krul's legs, mid-thigh.

The Klingon fell.

Then the massive Borg construct struck the ground before him, thrown onto its back as its one good arm still sprayed a continuous stream of antiprotons so that the arc of the beam hit the side of the Borg cube.

Picard staggered back with the force of the explosion.

A particle cannon turret instantly swung out

from the cube's side and returned fire at the fallen Borg giant.

Its chest exploded and its arm fell back, useless and impotent.

Then the cannon turret swung sharply, toward Picard and his team.

Picard charged forward and threw a smart grenade, catching a glimpse of it spiraling around the cannon turret, heading for the contact point where the cannon joined the cube.

And just as he dove for cover in the dirt, he felt himself lifted up, thrown back, hitting the dirt on his back, lungs without air.

Another explosion flared above him.

His ears rang. His chest heaved.

Then Beverly was at his side, pulling on his arm.

He was aware of smoke rising from his chestplate.

He gasped, coughed. "Was I hit?" he asked. But he felt so detached, it was as if her answer were unimportant.

"Your armor was hit," Beverly said. "Good thing they went for your chest, not your head."

Picard felt stabbing pain in his lungs as he drew a breath to respond.

Beverly frowned at her medical tricorder.

Something else exploded nearby. The air was dense with sound and smoke.

"Three cracked ribs," she told him. "Here."

A hypospray tingled against his neck.

The pain melted.

Another explosion.

"Can you stand?" Beverly asked urgently.

Picard knew he had no choice. He got to his feet. His chest was numb.

"Krul?" he asked.

"His armor's life-support will cut off the bleeding and deliver stimulants," Beverly promised. "He can hold on till it's safe to get him." Then she pulled Picard's arm over her shoulder and guided him forward, into a pit carved by an earlier explosion.

Weinlein was there, setting up a photon mortar with sure, practiced movements. She glanced at him. "Are you ready?"

Picard felt around for his torch. He had dropped it. Weinlein saw what he was doing, then tossed him hers.

"Yes," he said.

"We've got one more cannon to take out, then you can get to the main airlock."

"What about you?"

Weinlein nodded into the distance.

Picard looked.

Krul scrabbled in the dirt next to the body of the Borg construct. He was roaring threats in Klingon. Battle cries. No sense of giving up.

Another explosion went off at the side of the cube. Picard heard thudding, then Beyer leapt down into the pit.

"That's the last cannon," he said roughly. "I'm going for Krul."

Picard pulled himself up and switched on his handtorch. "And I'm going for the airlock."

"Jean-Luc!" Beverly said behind him.

He glanced back for an instant. Read the worry

in her face, and the faith, and knew what she was about to say. He nodded.

"I will," he told her.

Beyer took off toward Krul. Picard sprinted for the airlock. He held the torch under his face, making his features distinct.

The cube looked badly damaged. The anti-matter stream from the giant Borg had cut a large hole through its side.

Large enough that Picard changed his strategy and ran for it instead of the airlock. It was the better entrance.

Behind him, Beyer shouted a warning.

Picard spun, then stumbled as he saw—

—the thorax of the fallen Borg construct opening like a metal flower.

Next to the construct, Krul still screamed out his challenges, unaware. Beyer struggled to wrap his arm around Krul's writhing form while he aimed a hand disruptor at the opening in the construct.

But the beam dissipated against the Borg force field. Behind it, eight gleaming metal spider legs unfurled from the thorax, as if testing the air.

Then the legs braced themselves on the fallen construct and slowly straightened to lift up the central, disk-shaped body slung between them.

A Borg scuttler had emerged.

Picard and the commandos had seen it darting through the ruined Starbase at speeds no human or Klingon could match and suspected it was a wholly mechanical device. But now that it was still, Picard could see a single organic shape resting in the center of its body—the braincasing of whatever once-living organic being had been built into the unthinkable device.

Beyer yelled at Picard to keep running as the cybernetic insect raised four of its legs, then angled down toward Beyer, metal legs flashing, as it picked up speed.

Picard groaned as Beyer dropped his disruptor and unloaded a full charge from his Vulcan pulse wand. But this branch of the collective must have faced that weapon before, and the battle was over instantly.

A green nimbus flared around the scuttler as it launched itself into the air, drew its forward legs together, and sank into Beyer like a living javelin.

Beyer flew backward, with the creature now a part of his chest.

The scuttler used its rear legs to brace itself against the fallen, limp body, then yanked its forelegs from Beyer's bloodied chest.

Picard saw Beyer's legs spasm once, then fall still.

The scuttler turned in a blur to Krul.

Krul bellowed at the creature—the machine—as it stood over him.

Picard could see the Klingon's fists strike out to pummel the scuttler's cybernetic shell. Heard the clang of armored fists on metal. The dull thud of armored fists against whatever ghastly remnant of the creature was organic.

But the scuttler was not preparing to impale Krul as it had Beyer. Two metal legs had folded up against his body and moved inside an access panel.

There was a chance for Krul.

Picard took it.

He started to run toward Krul.

"No!" Weinlein shouted. She struck him from behind, hit his legs. Dragged him down.

An instant later, the ground erupted in front of him.

Together, they rolled behind a mound of earth and silicon bricks. Beverly ran to join them.

"There's another cannon," Weinlein gasped. "The mortar can't get past the new shields they've thrown up."

Picard pushed her away. He knew the debris they hid behind wouldn't protect them for long. And Krul needed his help. He crawled to the edge of the mound to peer into the blue and red landscape.

A Klingon shriek of defiance cut the night.

Beverly moved up beside Picard. The scuttler still crouched obscenely over Krul. Two of its legs seemed to be attached to the Klingon's helmet.

"What's it doing?" Beverly asked.

Weinlein joined them, with an ancient Romulan curse. She slammed down her visor, activating her telescopic sensors. Another curse. "It's attaching an implant."

Picard froze. "They'll know our plans."

Then he grimaced as a sharp feedback whine cut through the open communicator circuit.

"Red leader one, this is Archangel—"

The *Monitor* had arrived and her more powerful equipment had managed to punch through the Borg jamming. But because her

161

commander was breaking the communications blackout, it could only mean one thing.

"—a cubeship has just dropped from transwarp. It is closing in to engage." Picard could picture Captain Lewinski of the *Monitor* secure in his command chair, ready to fulfill his duty, as well as to test the design specifications of his ship.

But Starfleet couldn't take the chance.

Picard slammed his fist against his communicator contact. "Negative, Captain. Do not engage the Borg! Repeat—do not engage the Borg! They are ready for you!"

Static and feedback whine warbled over the circuit. Borg countermeasures. Krul shrieked defiance again. And again. A particle blast hit the ground nearby, scattering some of the cover shielding Picard and his depleted team.

Lewinski's voice came back online. "Say again, Picard."

"You must withdraw, Captain! Pull back at maximum warp. Allow the cubeship time to recover their assimilation crew down here." Picard gambled that the Borg had not yet broken the constant cycling of Starfleet encryption schemes. "It will be the only chance we have to get aboard."

Picard heard the disappointment in Lewinski's voice, tempered by imperceptible relief. "Acknowledged, Captain. Godspeed."

"Aboard?" Weinlein said.

Picard turned to her. "The collective will not abandon this team. They will not abandon—" Another particle blast sprayed them with dirt and stinging silicon fragments. The sensor ghosts constantly transmitted by their armor were still confusing the Borg's scanners, but the Borg were getting closer each minute.

"They will not abandon these resources," Picard continued fiercely. "Especially if they think there are secrets to be gained from the Star-fleet computers that were here."

Weinlein lifted her visor. Her eyes bore into Picard's. "If that scuttler implants Krul, the Borg won't come near this place." She broke the seal on her helmet and tugged it off. It was the first time Picard had seen her out of her full battle gear. Her ears were pointed. Half-human, half. . . .

Weinlein reached inside her armor and pulled out a small medallion. She pressed it into Picard's hand.

It was a Vulcan IDIC. The triangle receding into the whole and expanding from it at one and the same time. Infinite diversity in infinite combinations.

"For my parents," she said. "My mother's Vulcan. They'll need to take it to Mount Selaya."

Krul's voice rose once more. This time it was weak.

Weinlein squeezed the IDIC in Picard's palm. "Live long and prosper, Captain Picard. Now get the hell into that cube!"

Then she jumped up and swung her helmet arcing into the air behind her. The instant it left her hand, she charged forward, shouting Krul's name.

Picard knew exactly what she was doing.

Exactly why she was doing it. He wanted there to be another way but there was no time. He and Beverly ran, too—straight for the Borg cube.

To one side, particle blasts chewed up the ground as the cannon closed in on Weinlein's helmet, the source of the sensor ghosts.

To the other side, Weinlein attacked the scuttler even as its legs trembled over Krul's exposed skull, as if weaving a metallic cocoon for its prey.

Picard and Beverly reached the shattered opening into the cube. There were no Borg to meet them.

"No," Beverly whispered.

Picard looked back. Saw what she saw.

The scuttler with three legs raised.

Weinlein dodged, but not quickly enough.

Picard heard her cry of protest, as powerful as Krul's defiance had been.

But as it lifted two more legs to try to impale her again, Weinlein struck it and it toppled from Krul's body, its wires still connected to the Klingon's skull.

Another particle blast lit the night. The cannon was still aimed at Weinlein's helmet.

As the rumble of the explosion died down, Picard heard the telltale whine of an overload building in a phaser prefire cell. Picard could see Weinlein. The commando leader stood tall. Her arms were not raised to deflect the scuttler's next blow.

Picard knew why. She was holding her phaser.

The scuttler brought its second pair of legs down, and this time it didn't miss.

Weinlein's legs buckled, but she did not release her grip on the phaser.

It was the only way.

"Don't look," Picard said as the overload whine reached its crescendo.

He held Beverly's face against his chest. But he watched until it was over.

White light blazed into the depths of the Borg cube stretching before them, followed by the crack of the explosion.

Picard blinked.

Only a smoking crater remained.

Weinlein and Krul were gone. The scuttler was gone. But Picard's chance to fulfill the mission still remained. Because of Weinlein's sacrifice. Beyer's and Krul's sacrifice.

"You will be assimilated."

Picard turned, ready to face the Borg standing beside him, weapon held ready.

"Resistance is futile," the Borg said.

Automatically, Picard accepted the challenge. It was his turn to act now.

"Are you defective?" Picard began. He shoved Beverly behind him.

The Borg stepped forward. "You are not qualified to assess my operational status."

Picard held the torch to his face. "Are you certain?"

"Locutus?" the Borg said.

It lowered its weapon.

"Are you defective?" Picard repeated.

The Borg's sensor eye flashed as it was compelled into a diagnostic subroutine. Picard motioned urgently to Beverly.

She approached the Borg, placed a hypospray against a small patch of exposed flesh at the base of its jaw, then pulled its cerebral cables free as it collapsed to the deck.

Beverly smiled shakily at Picard. "What do you know? It worked." She reset her hypospray, began to place it back on her harness, then thought better of it. She kept it in her hand. "What now?"

Picard looked for a way deeper into the cube. There was no way to know which—

As if a bomb concussion had moved past him, he lurched forward, slamming into a bulkhead made of mismatched pipes and metal patches.

Beverly staggered back at the same instant.

"What was that?" she asked.

All around them, the cube creaked and groaned.

Picard felt the deck angle beneath him.

He glanced back outside, past the jagged opening.

The smoking crater beside the fallen Borg construct was still there. But beyond, about fifty meters distant, there was a sharp dark line, like a horizon on an asteroid.

Picard leaned forward, looked outside the creaking cube. Beverly was beside him. Her breath drew in sharply.

The ground in a fifty-meter circle around the cube was moving skyward. In the light of the concentrated stars of the New Titan sky, Picard could see the rest of the planet's surface rush away.

They were in the grip of a Borg tractor beam.

And Picard knew it was drawing them up to the waiting cubeship, which had anticipated their every move.

"We're being retrieved," Picard said.

SEVENTEEN

The stripped-down, single-level bridge of the *Monitor* was cramped, but only because of the extra shielding that surrounded it.

Captain John Lewinski liked that about his ship. As far as her specs were concerned, she was virtually indestructible.

"Any more signals from the surface?" he asked his communications officer.

Ardev turned from his station, blue hearing stalks twisting to remain pointed at the speakers in his control console. "The Borg have completely jammed all frequencies," he whispered in his Andorian rasp.

Lewinski angled his chair toward his science officer. "Sensors?"

Science Officer T'per remained serene, as always. "The Borg are generating a sensor blanket, sir. At the time it was initiated, full life signs came from Picard, Crusher, and Weinlein. Krul's battle suit had activated emergency medical life-support routines. There were no readings from Beyer."

Lewinski chewed his lip, thinking the situation

167

through. Two casualties before the main Borg vessel had arrived. That was not a good sign.

"What is the cubeship up to, Mr. Land?"

The navigator didn't take his eyes off the main viewscreen. The *Monitor* was operating with sensors at their lowest power setting to avoid Borg detection, resulting in a low-resolution image. Though Lewinski had followed Picard's suggestion to withdraw at maximum warp, he had taken the *Monitor* behind the New Titan system's gas giant, cloaked, and returned to a geostationary orbit above whatever was left of Starbase 804.

The Borg cubeship was also holding a geostationary position, though only five hundred kilometers from the planet's surface. The power expenditure for such a maneuver must have been stupendous, though so far sensors could not pick up any sign of what kind of system the Borg were using.

"Hard to tell, Captain," Land replied. The ship's navigator had a clipped, Anglo accent. Though fully half the *Monitor's* crew was human, apart from Lewinski, Land was the only native of Earth aboard. The Federation had become that diverse. "The ship is bleeding sensor ghosts on every frequency. I am picking up strong indications of a tractor beam, though."

Lewinski glanced over at T'Per. The young Vulcan met his gaze without expression. "T'Per, which option provides the least risk? Increasing sensor gain from this position, or moving closer and maintaining low power?"

T'Per raised an eyebrow in thought. "For the least risk, we should withdraw."

Lewinski smiled at her, but drew no response. "That wasn't an option."

"Then you should have stated which option provided the lesser risk," T'Per noted, unsmiling.

Vulcans, Lewinski thought. *Couldn't live with them. Couldn't live without them.*

"The lesser risk, Mr. T'Per."

"Moving closer, but only by a factor of less than one half."

Lewinski turned his chair to face the screen. "Take us in, Mr. Land. I want to look up their tailpipe."

"Wherever that is," Land muttered. The *Monitor* surged forward at quarter impulse and was in visual contact with the Borg cubeship within seconds.

"Definitely a tractor beam," Lewinski said softly, fingering his goatee.

The increased-resolution image of the main screen showed a telltale purple beam emanating from the surface of the cubeship closest to the planet. It stretched down to the surface of New Titan.

Lewinski quickly polled his crew for power levels, sensor readings, and any indication that the Borg had sensed their cloaked presence.

But the cloaking device was working perfectly. Lewinski thought the Romulan science team at Starbase 324 would be pleased to hear that. That is, after they had gotten over their outrage that Starfleet had operated the device aboard a *Defiant*-class ship without a Romulan observer.

Land adjusted the viewscreen's image, angling it away from the Borg cubeship, toward New

Titan. There was an object at the base of the tractor beam, increasing in size as it drew nearer. "We've got a mass coming up from the surface, Captain."

"It's got to be the starbase," Lewinski said. If Picard had been right in his transmission, then they were watching the Borg retrieve the bait.

"Life signs on the tractored mass," T'Per announced. "Forty-two Borg . . . no . . . forty Borg, two assimilated animals . . . small . . ."

Lewinski scratched his fingers through his beard. "Bottom line, Mister. Any of the red team on that?"

T'Per's fingers flew skillfully over her science panel. "Medical telemetry from armor belonging to . . . Picard and . . . Crusher, sir. No injuries."

Lewinski exhaled slowly. Some of his crew joined him. . . .

If none of the red team had made it to the cubeship, the *Monitor* had orders to attack. But now, all he could do was observe.

"Intriguing," T'Per said beside him.

Before them, a half hemisphere of soil, one hundred meters across, fifty meters deep, and topped by a thirty-foot-tall Borg cube, was rising up beneath the cubeship.

Lewinski got the specs from the screen on the arm of his chair. On the screen, the tractored chunk of planet was nothing more than a dark smear against the bulk of the Borg vessel.

"Contact," Land announced when the tractored soil vanished inside the ship.

"Any idea what they're using for a power source?" Lewinski asked anyone.

"No change in energy consumption," T'Per said.

Lewinski shook his head. He was glad he wasn't attacking.

On the screen, the Borg ship began to rotate. "Keep your eye on weapons sensors," Lewinski cautioned. He leaned forward in his chair.

T'Per's voice was clear and strong. "I am definitely detecting a power surge, Captain."

"Stand by on shields, Mr. Land."

"Captain," T'Per said, "may I remind you that if we do raise our shields, the Borg will detect us."

Lewinski kept his eyes on the screen. "What if they've detected us already, and they're powering up their weapons?"

"Logically," T'Per said, "we would have been scanned."

"Those aren't logical Vulcans, Mr. T'Per. They're Borg."

T'Per's voice cooled noticeably. "There were Vulcans stationed at the starbase, Captain. Therefore, there could be some Vulcans now aboard the recovered cube, contributing their intellect, and logic, to the collective."

"I for one," Lewinski said, still keeping his concentration locked on the screen, "do not even want to contemplate what a Borg Vulcan might be like."

Land glanced over his shoulder with a grin. "There'd be a difference?"

"At ease, Mr. Land," the captain warned.

"Shields on full standby," Land confirmed.

171

On the screen, the Borg ship had rotated until it had changed its orientation to New Titan by one hundred eighty degrees.

"I'd like an explanation for what we're seeing," Lewinski said to his bridge crew.

"They're getting ready to do something, Captain," Land volunteered. "But I just don't know—what?"

On the screen, the Borg ship disappeared in a flash of light.

"Sensors!" Lewinski demanded.

"The Borg vessel generated and then entered a transwarp conduit," T'Per reported.

Lewinski sat back in his chair, amazed. "That quickly?" He hadn't even seen the multi-dimensional opening form. Only a flash of light.

"Playing it back at slow speed," Land said.

On the screen, the disappearance of the Borg cubeship played out again, this time slowed by a factor of one hundred. Sure enough, a transwarp conduit opened. The Borg ship didn't vanish; it appeared to dissolve into a spray of light, then was lost as the conduit opening collapsed around it.

In Starfleet's first encounter with Borg transwarp conduits, the crew of the *U.S.S. Enterprise* had determined that the secret to entering them had been the transmission of an encoded, high-energy tachyon pulse. However, once the *Enterprise* had used that technique several times, the conduits no longer responded to it. As if the transwarp network, like the Borg themselves, had adapted.

Lewinski rubbed his hands over his face. He

had had four hours sleep in the past three days. "Go to full power sensors and stand down from cloaked running," he said. "Lieutenant Ardev, contact Commander Shelby at Starbase 324. Tell her Picard and Crusher are aboard a Borg vessel. But that vessel is now in transwarp, and we are unable to pursue."

Land twisted around in his chair to look at his captain. "Can't we *try* to search for them, sir? We have a heading from the sensor logs."

Lewinski sighed, deeply grateful he wasn't Picard. "The way those conduits move through other-dimensional space, Mr. Land, their heading at entry wouldn't tell us anything. I'm afraid that Captain Picard and Dr. Crusher have just gone . . . where no one has gone before."

Lewinski suddenly felt the full weight of deferred exhaustion. T'Per stepped up to the side of his chair, hands behind her back.

"Then it is most unlikely they will ever be able to determine a way to return," the science officer said.

Lewinski stretched back in his chair, thinking dark thoughts of Vulcans and logic.

EIGHTEEN

"Shit," Data said. "Damn, hell, . . . *sal'tasnon!*"

La Forge sighed, and the visor of his helmet fogged up. The local temperature on Trilex was hovering around fifty Kelvin, and despite the heating elements built into his well-insulated environmental suit, he felt the chill. It didn't put him in the mood to waste time.

"Data," La Forge said, feeling the vibrations from his helmet's exterior speaker, "exactly who taught you how to curse like that?"

"Counselor Troi," Data answered. The android looked across the small excavation site from where he knelt in the ice, and smiled. Behind him in the dim red light of Trilex Prime, the eerie, corroded spires of the frozen city could be seen emerging from the ice field like fingers from a grave. "She has told me that I must feel free to express my emotions." Data's innocent grin grew larger. "Damn, damn, damn."

La Forge decided it was time for a break. The ruins of the Trilex civilization had been frozen for hundreds of thousands of years, ever since the planet's sun had gone nova. A few more minutes' delay in this library structure wouldn't make any difference. He stepped cautiously over the grid of red string that defined the excavation area to see what Data was up to. "So what's wrong this time?" he asked, though he dreaded the answer.

Data, who did not need an environmental suit to withstand the cold of the planet, wore his standard duty uniform. He brushed ice crystals from his knees as he stood up, holding out an environmentally sealed tricorder. "This *patak* piece of *flax* is no damn good," he explained.

Then he angled his head as he studied La Forge's expression inside the engineer's helmet. "In case you are not fluent in the Klingon vernacular, I was stating that this tricorder, due to bad design, was no longer functioning."

La Forge took the tricorder from Data's hand. "I get the picture, Data. But why didn't you just say that in the first place?"

Data looked confused. "I did." Then he smiled. Mercurial changes in his mood and expression were the norm these days, La Forge knew.

"Ah," Data said, "I see from where your confusion might originate. My original statement was infused with an emotional content indicating my annoyance with the tricorder's malfunction. Perhaps you have not yet become used to me as an emotional being."

La Forge took a deep breath, then flipped open the transparent covering that protected the tricorder's surface from extreme conditions. "Data, I admit, ever since you installed that emotion chip, you have . . . taken some getting used to."

"Do I disappoint you, Geordi?"

La Forge rolled his eyes. "You're my friend, Data. You can't disappoint me. But it would be nice if we could go back to having a conversation without you sounding like your mouth's a sewer."

Data looked off to the side, an indication that he was accessing his deepest databanks. He frowned, even appeared to shudder. "That is a most unpleasant image, Geordi. But I do not know what you intend by it."

La Forge scraped the tip of his gloved thumb along the inside of the tricorder's container. "Just stop cursing, Data."

"But would that not mean I was denying my emotions?" Now Data looked troubled. "Geordi, from my sessions with Counselor Troi, which I have enjoyed very much, I have learned that such a course of action could endanger my emotional health."

La Forge snapped shut the tricorder's case. He grabbed Data's hand, then slapped the tricorder into it. "You had an ice buildup inside the cover that was interfering with the control surfaces. If you had stopped cursing for a second to examine the problem, you wouldn't have had to waste our time here."

Data narrowed his eyes as he squinted at the tricorder. He pressed a few controls and smiled happily as he read the results. "Geordi, you're a *kreldanni* genius!"

"Data!"

"Geordi, do you believe I am not expressing my emotions appropriately?"

"Not all the time, Data. But . . . sometimes, yeah."

Data's mouth twisted down in a horrible grimace. "I feel so . . . so bad."

La Forge suddenly saw what was going to happen. And he didn't want to deal with it. "No, Data. Don't say that!"

"B-but I do," the android sobbed. "I've hurt your feelings."

"No, Data! No, you haven't! I feel great! I feel happy!" La Forge grabbed Data by the shoulders. "Data, whatever you do—*don't cry!*"

But he was too late.

The emotional mimetic systems designed into

Data's android body were both subtle and robust. Data was still discovering all the complex ways in which they could interact. Tears were one of their many functions.

But not at fifty degrees Kelvin.

Puffs of water vapor billowed from Data's eyes as molecular micropumps excreted saline solution through Data's tear-ducts. Unfortunately, the liquid promptly sublimated in the intensely cold and thin atmosphere of Trilex.

La Forge groaned as Data reached out blindly with his hands. Two patches of ice crystals glittered on his face, one beneath each eyebrow.

"Geordi," the android said plaintively. "I have frozen my eyelids together."

"Oh, Data," La Forge sighed. "Not *again*."

Data stumbled over to an equipment locker and sat down as if his artificial muscles had buckled. "I am such a failure," he said.

La Forge shook his head and glanced down at his in-helmet status displays. He still had oxygen for four more hours. The *Bozeman* would be back overhead in less than two. He had no excuse for not indulging his friend.

"It's okay, Data," La Forge said as he sat down beside the android. It was an awkward maneuver in his suit, but he managed to put a supportive arm around Data's shoulders.

Data slumped, going into one of his depressions. He seemed to have them at least every other day by La Forge's reckoning. The only positive thing about them was that they seldom lasted more than a few minutes. Data might have emotions now, but his internal processor's clock still ran a thousand times faster than the human brain.

"No, it is not, Geordi. We must face the facts that my emotional skills do not measure up to the rest of my abilities." Data turned his face to La Forge. His eyes were still frozen over. "I am an emotional cripple. And my eyes are still frozen over." Then he slumped forward again, and sobbed.

La Forge had had enough.

"Data, so help me, if you don't pull yourself together, I'll . . . I'll turn you off until we're back on the *Bozeman*."

Data instantly sat up again. "You would do that? Really?"

La Forge made no effort to hold back his own feelings.

"Data, I gave up my leave time to come here with you. Between us, we used up every favor anybody in Starfleet ever owed us to get passage here and permission to dig. And after all that effort, *and* sacrifice, you're costing us the chance of doing any work at all by constantly having these emotional breakdowns. If you don't stop, I'll turn you off in a Klingon minute."

Ignoring the ice crystals glittering on his face, Data took on an expression of stoic resignation. "I understand, Geordi. You hate me."

"That's it!" La Forge stood up and began reaching around for Data's hidden function switch. "You're going to take a nap."

Data was up and backing away at once. "But I am not tired."

La Forge moved slowly to avoid slipping on

the slick frozen surface of the ice. "You're an android. You never get tired. But I do!"

Data stopped trying to get away. "Geordi. Now that I have emotions, I can understand them better in others. I can *hear* the anger in your voice. It's directed at *me*."

"I *am* angry, Data. But not at you. I'm . . . angry at how . . . self-indulgent you've become. Emotions aren't helping you develop your humanity. You're so caught up in yourself, you're driving everyone else away."

Again Data's mood changed. His expression became one of delight. "In other words, I am behaving like an adolescent. Geordi, I am happy now."

La Forge sighed again. He'd pay good credits to see how Deanna Troi would handle the emotional gravity whip Data was riding. La Forge could barely keep up. But he had to try. "Why's that, Data?"

"Plotting my emotional growth against a timeline extending from the moment I installed the emotion chip, if I have now reached the adolescent stage, marked by mood swings and intense, antisocial, emotional self-involvement, then I can extrapolate that, in approximately fourteen days, I shall have reached full adult emotional maturity."

"Do me a favor?" La Forge asked.

"It shall be my pleasure," Data said grandly.

"See if you can make it through the next fourteen days without a single curse word?"

Data shrugged. "Why the hell not?"

La Forge sighed again. Heavily.

179

"I heard that," Data said.

"Well, hear this then. I'm going back to work." La Forge returned to his corner of the excavation. So far he had melted through eight squares of ice, going down a meter to the floor of the ancient structure. It was easier than the digging he had once done with Captain Picard, when the captain had eagerly tried to introduce the engineer to his hobby. At least in conducting a dig on an ice planet, there was no dirt to shovel away. A type-1 phaser on low power simply melted the years away.

"It is very nice of you to help me like this," Data said.

"I'm not being nice," La Forge said as he checked the power level on his phaser. "I'm interested in finding out what happened here, too."

He glanced up as Data aimed his own excavation phaser at his face. Ever since the emotion chip, going anywhere with Data was like being with a five-year-old. Disaster loomed at every moment.

"Tell me you're not going to do something stupid," La Forge said.

"I may be an emotional cripple, Geordi, but I have ensured the phaser is set to its lowest power level. I am not crazy."

Data fired a weak beam at his face and the clumps of ice covering his eyes vaporized. He blinked rapidly.

"So far," La Forge muttered. Then he located a new square to melt away and positioned himself over it.

As the millennia-old ice vaporized away from

the secrets it covered, Data walked over to stand close by La Forge's side.

"Be careful you do not let the beam touch the keys themselves," Data said.

La Forge kept his temper. "I know, Data." The tricorder had shown that the floor of the structure was littered with hundreds of cylindrical pieces of metal which other archaeologists had identified as data keys, designed to be placed into Trilex computer stations. Unfortunately, when Trilex Prime had gone nova, apparently without warning, all the computer systems on the planet had been wiped clean. Since the Trilex civilization had been pervasively computer-based, with artificially intelligent machines even achieving equality under the planet's laws, much of its culture had been lost beyond hope of recovery.

But the data keys had encoded information in a different way, which left them unaffected by the radiation surge of the nova. Though each held little information, Data had hoped that recovering enough of them might make it possible to place them together like a jigsaw puzzle to obtain a fuller picture of the Trilex culture.

That was important to Data, and to La Forge, because most archaeologists, including Captain Picard, had concluded that when its sun had gone nova, Trilex had been embroiled in a war between its organic inhabitants and its artificial, machine-based life-forms.

Some scholars had taken that to mean that organic life and synthetic life could never live in peace.

Since La Forge had first met Data, the android

had always had an interest in the "Trilex Question," as it was known. But upon receiving his emotion chip, it had become an obsession with him.

La Forge could understand that.

To be really human, as Data desired, meant more than just having the capacity to feel. It meant having the capacity to stare up at the stars and ask the hardest questions of them all: Who am I? What is my purpose here?

La Forge knew those questions were in Data. And if they were to have meaningful answers for him, it was important for Data to know that he was more than just a mechanical oddity built by an eccentric scientist. It was important to know that he had a place in this universe. And for him to truly know that, it was critical that whatever had happened on Trilex had had nothing to do with the impossibility of organic and synthetic life-forms coexisting.

Finding emotions had only been the first step in Data's long voyage of self-discovery. Now he had to do what every other human must—find himself, and define himself, in his own terms.

Thus La Forge had been happy to help his friend. Especially since they had been ordered to take their accumulated leave while waiting for reassignment. To a new *Enterprise,* La Forge hoped.

"I think you have almost reached them," Data said.

"I know, Data," La Forge answered, keeping his beam moving slowly over the opening he had melted in the ice, now half a meter deep. "I've done this before, remember."

"It is just that it is very important that I know if organic life and synthetic life can coexist in peace."

La Forge spoke through clenched teeth. "Not if synthetic life keeps making a pest of itself."

La Forge stopped firing the phaser. Billows of water vapor filled the area, coalescing into clouds of sparkling ice crystals.

It was almost like a slow-motion replay of the transporter effect.

He checked his tricorder to see if the data keys had been exposed. He had to scrape his helmet visor to get rid of the frost that had formed there.

"Pretty good," he said to Data. "Looks like we've got another eleven keys down there to add to the collection. Do you want to pick them out while I—"

La Forge stopped talking as he saw a sudden energy spike on his tricorder's display.

"What the hell was that?"

"Geordi, I do not believe it is fair that you require me not to curse, while you continue to do so."

"Not now, Data." La Forge changed the settings on the tricorder. "That almost looked like a beam-in nearby. But the *Bozeman* is hours away."

"Geordi—"

"Not *now*, Data. I'm trying to concentrate."

"You do not have to. It was a beam-in. Look."

La Forge slowly raised his helmet.

Data was pointing straight ahead, across the

excavation site, to where the spires of the city rose from the ice, against the dying sun of Trilex.

But for now, the ancient ruins were hidden by the swirling billows of ice crystals. Slowly settling. Not to reveal the ruins. But to reveal the shape of a stranger in an environmental suit that was not Starfleet-issue.

"Can I help you?" La Forge said.

He carefully placed his tricorder back on his belt and began to move his hand to his phaser.

Trilex was a protected historical site, administered by the Vulcan Science Academy.

If there had been any other expeditions to this world planned when Starfleet had submitted their proposal for a dig, he and Data would have been informed.

"First, move your hand away from your phaser," the stranger said.

La Forge noted that his universal translator had not switched on. The stranger spoke English.

"This is a restricted site," La Forge said.

He peered through the thinning ice cloud as the stranger stepped forward. There were two large devices clipped to his belt. One was a hand weapon. La Forge took as a good sign that it had not yet been drawn.

"I won't be here long," the stranger said. "I just want to ask a question."

"Are you an archaeologist?" Data asked.

La Forge waited for the answer. As far as he could tell, the stranger was humanoid, but his features were obscured by the reflective visor on his helmet.

"No," the stranger said. Then his hand went

for his belt. La Forge was ready to draw against him. But the stranger removed a flattened green cylinder about half a meter long, not his weapon.

"Who are you?" La Forge asked.

"I said *I* had the question," the stranger answered. Then he aimed the cylinder at La Forge and Data.

Instantly La Forge drew his phaser, reflexively resetting its power level to stun.

"Whatever that is, put it down," La Forge commanded.

But the stranger did not move the cylinder. "Where is Jean-Luc Picard?" he asked.

Of all the reasons La Forge had been prepared to hear to explain the stranger's presence, that was the least likely.

"That is a question more suited for Starfleet Command," Data volunteered. "Because of the chain of command we operate under, it is not appropriate to ask us."

The stranger's helmet angled until the visor was pointed directly at Data. "I'm surprised your ears aren't pointed," he said. Then he began to raise the cylinder.

La Forge pressed the firing stud on his phaser.

The blue beam shot out to the stranger.

Then evaporated in a blue nimbus around him.

La Forge felt his mouth open in astonishment. The stranger had a personal force field. But where was its power generator? Not even Starfleet had perfected such a device.

"Now it's my turn," the stranger said.

A puff of vapor blew out of the end of the

cylinder. La Forge shoved Data aside as he sensed more than saw a dark streak rush past him.

For a moment, nothing happened. Then La Forge glanced behind him, expecting to see the impact of whatever the stranger had shot at him.

Instead, he saw a smart projectile hovering two meters beyond.

Then it was gone and La Forge felt a giant's hand crush his chest.

He fell back into the excavation grid, tangled up in the red grid string as he tried to right himself.

But he couldn't breathe, let alone move.

Data spoke with a voice of rage. "I will not let you hurt my friend!"

"Then answer my question. Where is Jean-Luc Picard?"

Through a red haze of pain, La Forge saw Data step past him. La La Forge gasped as he felt the sudden bite of intense cold. He realized his suit must have been punctured. Though he could see only what was directly in front of his visor—nothing but the icy cliffs of ruins they worked in, looming up all around him—La Forge could still hear Data and the stranger on his helmet speaker.

"Your weapon will not work on me," Data said. "I have no need of an environmental suit. Also, my strength and reflexes are many times greater than any organic being's. You will not succeed in fighting me." It was Data's idea of a threat, La Forge supposed bleakly.

"I have no intention of fighting you," the stranger said. La Forge heard an electric crackle.

Heard Data moan.

Then saw Data fall beside him, his limbs rigid in the stance he had taken to face the stranger.

The stranger came to stand over the fallen friends. La Forge began to shiver uncontrollably as the stranger knelt beside them. He glanced down at La Forge's suit.

"I estimate you'll freeze to death in less than fifteen minutes," the stranger said.

"Th-the *Bozeman* will b-be here b-before that," La Forge bluffed.

The stranger didn't bother to reply. Instead he removed a series of cables from a pod on the side of his belt. Each ended in a universal induction sensor. "These are dataprobes," he said. "I can use them to download the contents of the robot's processors."

"H-he's an android," La Forge said.

"But if I download the contents of his processors, he will be wiped clean." The stranger gestured to include all of Trilex. "He'll be like these computers. Empty. Dead. Just like you."

La Forge saw the power overload light flashing on his in-helmet display. He didn't expect to last even fifteen minutes.

"So," the stranger continued, "tell me what I want to know, and I'll seal your suit and leave the robot—the android—intact. Your choice."

"G-go t-to Hell," La Forge said through shivering lips.

The stranger pulled his hand weapon from his belt, aimed it at La Forge.

"Didn't anyone ever tell you you shouldn't curse?" the stranger said.

Then La Forge saw a blinding blue light flash from the emitter node of the stranger's weapon.

His last thought was of all that was left when a star explodes . . .

Cold. And darkness. And death.

NINETEEN

Shit, Data thought.

Whatever the stranger had fired at him from his flattened cylindrical weapon, he felt each of his muscles and joints freeze in place. Not from the temperature of Trilex. But from an interruption in his movement subroutines.

As Data fell backward beside Geordi's prone body, he formulated a hypothesis to account for the effect the stranger's weapon had had on him. The most likely explanation was that he had been hit with a precisely focused subspace-radiation pulse. The pulse that had been created by Trilex's exploding sun had been strong enough to wipe all local computer circuitry clean of information. But the stranger's pulse had obviously been specifically modulated to interrupt only those subroutines in Data that governed physical functions.

After creating and comparing several equations which could be applied to constructing the stranger's device, Data decided it had most likely been developed as a covert device to access secured computer networks. He felt it was extremely improbable that the device had been constructed just to immobilize him. Though, he concluded, it was certainly effective in that regard.

By the time Data had hit the ice beside Geordi, his positronic brain had had enough processing time to review the contents of the last four standard years of the journal, *Subspace Multiphysics B,* and the Cochrane Institute's abstract index from 2355 to the present. As the stranger spoke to Geordi and prepared his dataprobes, Data had correlated enough information to hazard a guess as to the origin of the device.

But then Data had seen the flash of a disruptor discharge and was filled with the certain knowledge that Geordi had been killed.

For long nanoseconds, Data waited for the emotional response to that knowledge to flood through his positronic pathways.

But nothing happened.

He felt . . . empty.

He began formulating another theory to account for the lack of connection between his movement subroutines and his emotions. Could it be that true emotions were possible only when the intellect was contained within a functioning body, subjected to the stresses of daily survival? He found that a fascinating proposition. And though he did not feel sad about Geordi's death, he did regret he would not be able to discuss his new theory with his dead friend.

"What about you?" the stranger asked. The dataprobes dangled on their cables from his hand. His weapon was back on his belt.

"What about me?" Data replied. Once again he was impressed with the selectivity of the weapon. His facial muscle analogs were still able to function, permitting speech.

"Are you going to tell me where Picard is?" He held out the probes. "Or do I wipe your mind clean of everything?"

"There is no need to do that," Data said promptly. "I am in possession of no information regarding the whereabouts of Captain Picard. Furthermore, if I did, I am fully capable of erasing that information from my own datastorage so that it would be unretrievable by you."

The stranger began examining Data's head. "You won't mind if I don't take your word for it?"

"I do not mind in the sense that you mean," Data said as he heard one of his cranial access panels swing open. "Though I do regret that your nature is such that you will effectively be ending my existence for no reason."

The stranger stopped his investigation of Data's head and moved so that his visor was looking down at Data's face like a baleful cyclopean eye. "What do you know about my nature?" he asked.

Data studied his own reflection in the stranger's visor. It might be the last thing that he saw. But still, he felt nothing.

"I do not 'know' anything about your nature, as I do not know who you are. However, based on my analysis of scientific papers published over the past decade in the area of subspace multiphysics on which your weapon appears to be based, I have concluded that you are a Romulan. And I know how thorough and precise the Romulans are in their investigative work."

The stranger put his hand to his visor and pressed a control. The reflectivity faded away, leaving a clear covering in its place.

Data blinked several times to ensure his optical sensors were working properly, especially since the unfortunate freezing incident might have damaged his lenses.

"Do you still think I'm a Romulan?" the stranger asked.

"No," Data said. "But I do not believe you are who you appear to be, either."

The stranger's brow furrowed in his helmet. "And who do I appear to be?"

Data studied the stranger's pupils for the tell-tale contraction that might indicate he was lying. But there was no sign of it. Neither had the stress levels in his voice changed.

"Do you not know who you appear to be?" Data asked.

The stranger hesitated. Data could see that he seemed to be having an argument within himself. Something emotional. But Data no longer had access to his emotions. Whatever the stranger was feeling, it was a mystery to them both.

"Tell me," the stranger said.

"No," Data answered.

"Why not?"

"If I am to answer your question, you must do something for me."

The stranger tried, but could not restrain a

small smile. "I'm supposed to negotiate with a robot?"

"An android," Data corrected.

"An android. What do you want?"

"Is Geordi still alive?"

"If you mean the human beside you, no. I killed him. And I will kill you, too."

Data heard the stress levels go up. Saw the pupils dilate.

"There is a strong probability that you are lying," Data said. "I can tell from your physiological reactions."

The stranger's face clouded.

"Where is Jean-Luc Picard?"

"You are under stress," Data said calmly. "Let me help."

The stranger's eyes lost focus, as if staring kilometers away. "Let me help . . ." he whispered.

"An old starship which has been assigned to scientific support duty will be returning to this location in one hour, thirty-seven minutes," Data said helpfully. "There is a medical officer on board who could—" Data stopped talking as the stranger suddenly slammed a dataprobe lead against his open cranial circuits. "That is neither necessary nor useful," he reminded the stranger.

"I don't have time for this," the stranger said.

"Strange, you are very much like Geordi," Data observed. Then he heard a high-pitched buzzing in his auditory recognition circuits. The stranger's face and everything around him broke up into coarse pixels that swirled like a closing wormhole, collapsing into a starless void from which there could be no return.

TWENTY

Against the void, a single blazing point of blue luminescence shone forth. Hyperdimensional flares suddenly bloomed from it, their elevenfold symmetries scintillating in dynamic protest as they were forced to conform to the rigid confines of normal, four-dimensional space-time. Then the quantum-gravitational pressure between the two realities could no longer be contained and space itself was torn apart, twisting open like the mouth of a mythical sea monster.

From the center of that majestic explosion of forces which humans still could not measure, control, nor define, a single *Galaxy*-class starship flew, for all its might as fragile as a windblown seed before the awesome power of the passageway it had just traversed between the stars.

Once again, the Celestial Temple of the Prophets had allowed its mysteries to be glimpsed, and the Bajoran wormhole had been opened.

The starship, *Challenger*, banked gracefully in the solar wind, then made its way to the strange, intriguing object that glittered like a dark jewel before it.

The Cardassian mining station once called *Terek Nor*.

Now known throughout the Federation as Deep Space 9.

"And that's it?" Riker asked.

Data stepped around the frozen holographic recreations of his body, Geordi's, and the stranger's, as he joined Riker and Troi by the opening to the library structure. Except for the temperature, they were in an exact simulation of conditions on Trilex.

"Yes," Data said. "That is the extent of my memory of the incident. Obviously, the stranger connected his dataprobes at that point, canceling out my higher brain functions as he attempted to extract information from me."

Riker scratched at his beard, staring hard at the holographic stranger. "Attempted?"

"My mind was not erased as he had threatened, and my emotional routines have returned to operational status, so I must assume he was not successful in his efforts."

But Troi shook her head, unconvinced. "No, Data. Geordi's environmental suit was patched when the away team from the *Bozeman* found you. You didn't do it. Geordi couldn't do it. Therefore, the stranger must have. And since he took action to prevent Geordi from dying, it's fair to conclude that the stranger took similar action not to harm you, as well."

Spock's voice echoed around them. "A most logical evaluation, Counselor."

Troi smiled. "Thank you, Ambassador."

Riker sighed. "End program."

Data watched as the simulation of the Trilex archaeological dig faded away around him. It was remarkable how detailed the illusion had been, considering it had been created within a relatively cramped holosuite installed over the Quark's bar in DS9's Promenade, and not in a full holodeck.

Ambassador Spock stepped from the corner of the suite, hands behind his back. "However, I believe it is time we accept the facts as they have been presented and stop referring to the assailant as 'the stranger.'"

Riker regarded Spock with polite forbearance. "Ambassador, with all due respect, the assailant *cannot* be James Kirk."

Spock continued, appearing not to hear the commander. "Computer, re-create the visitor to the Trilex site."

A three-dimensional projection of the stranger appeared in the center of the room, complete with environmental suit, equipment, and helmet.

"Now access the visual records downloaded from Lieutenant-Commander Data's memory banks, and remove the visitor's helmet to show us his face."

The helmet faded out, revealing a three-dimensional image of what was, in Data's judgment at least, a striking reproduction of the stranger's face as he had directly observed it. His features were most sharply defined in the area that had been visible through the helmet's visor, then eerily melted into lower-resolution detail toward the sides, ending in a basic, polygonal wire-frame extrapolation of the back of his head.

"Computer," Spock continued, "access the personal memory archives which I uploaded to the library system from my quarters. Run from code sequence 294-07."

A holographic viewscreen formed beside the reconstruction of the visitor. On the screen, Data recognized old update footage—a recording of an actual event instead of a mere holographic simulation.

"How does it feel to be back on the *Enterprise* bridge?" a disembodied voice asked. On the screen, the subject of the question blinked in the glare of the old-fashioned spotlights that had been trained on him.

"Freeze image," Spock said.

The Vulcan ambassador walked up between the holoscreen and the reconstruction. He gestured to the screen. "This is update footage of Captain Kirk, taken hours before he . . . disappeared on the maiden flight of the *Enterprise-B*. Computer, isolate Captain Kirk's face from the update image, dimensionally enhance, and overlay onto the reconstruction."

Data observed with interest as everything on the holoscreen, except for Kirk's face, faded out. A moment later, the two-dimensional image expanded as it was enhanced to become a semi-transparent, three-dimensional portrait of the famous and infamous captain. The portrait moved past Spock and settled like a ghostly cloud over the head of the reconstructed figure of the stranger.

Then the two images merged. Detail came to the low-resolution areas at the side of the head.

Detail came to the unresolved areas at the back of the head. But in the face, nothing changed.

The images were a perfect match.

"Computer, quantify degree of fractal correlation," Spock asked.

"Ninety-nine, point nine nine nine nine—"

"That's enough," Riker interrupted. He gestured imploringly at Spock. "Mr. Ambassador, I have never denied that the assailant *looks* like James Kirk. Nor have I questioned Worf's account that the same individual is responsible for the attack on him. But . . . sir, James Kirk is dead. He gave his life to save Captain Picard, the crew of the *Enterprise,* and millions of beings on Veridian IV." Riker moved closer to the implacable Vulcan. "I'm very familiar with your . . . early exploits and adventures with your captain and your equally illustrious crew. But the fact remains, Picard buried your friend himself."

Spock's expression didn't change. "And those remains were then transported away by a group unknown."

"Remains, sir. Not a body in frozen stasis. Or transporter storage. A lifeless shell." Data saw that Riker was uncomfortable with being so blunt with the ambassador. "I'm sorry. But surely you of all people can understand that the dead cannot return to life."

Spock raised an eyebrow at Riker. "There appear to be some of my 'exploits and adventures' with which you are not familiar."

Riker looked confused. Spock did not deign to enlighten him.

Then Data heard footsteps in the corridor

outside. A moment later, everyone else turned to the door as the entrance chime sounded.

"Enter," Riker said.

The door slipped open to reveal DS9's head of medicine, Dr. Julian Bashir. Ducking and bobbing behind him, trying to peer past the slender human into the holosuite, was the eponymous Ferengi who owned the establishment, Quark.

Bashir held up a medical padd as he entered. "Mr. Ambassador, I have the results of the tests you requested. I thought you'd want to see them personally."

But Spock declined the offer. "Thank you, doctor, but I already know what the results are. I believe Commander Riker would be more interested in reviewing them."

Bashir didn't question Spock's direction. He handed the padd to Riker. "Commander."

Meanwhile, Quark was studying the reconstructed figure in the center of the holosuite.

"So what's the story on this hew-man?" he asked.

"Nothing you need to worry about," Riker said.

Quark looked around with an expression of wide-eyed interest. "I understand. Is there a reward?"

Riker didn't bother looking up as he adjusted the padd's controls. "Quark, not now."

"I just don't get it," the Ferengi complained. "Starfleet commandeers my finest holosuite—"

Troi crossed her arms. "Every OHD panel was

dirty, Quark. We had to wipe them off ourselves to get a clear simulation."

Quark looked mortally offended. "Did you bother to ask me for cleaning services? For a very small, additional fee, I could have—"

"Quiet, Quark," Riker said as he studied the padd.

The Ferengi sidled closer to Riker, peering indignantly up at him. "You'd better not be using that thing to copy my holosuite programs."

Riker looked over at Data. "Data, could you do something about him?"

Data went to Quark and put his hand on the Ferengi's shoulder. "Quark, we have paid for a full hour of use in this holosuite. That time is not yet up."

Data tried to steer the Ferengi toward the door, but Quark didn't want to go. "And that's another thing. It was Commander Riker and the Betazoid who booked the holosuite." Quark's burgundy-rimmed eyes narrowed in what even Data could see was a lascivious leer. His voice dropped to match his expression. "So I gave them the honey-moon special rate, if you know what I mean."

Data began to push the Ferengi toward the door more forcefully, gathering a fistful of Quark's lurid jacket for a better grip.

"But now," Quark went on more quickly, talking back over his shoulder as he was propelled forward, "now that I see you've turned my most sacred honeymoon program—the Mists of the Poconos—into a common orgy for four . . . for *five* of you—" Data firmly pushed Quark outside the door. The Ferengi spun around and fussily straightened his crooked lapel. "Well, I'm going to have to charge you extra!"

Data put his finger on the Cardassian door control. "If you recall, we provided our own program."

"I know," Quark muttered. "I've never seen copy protection like it."

Data pressed the control. The door began to slide shut.

"Not that I tried to copy it, you under—"

The door closed and sealed. Data was the only one in the holosuite whose ears could continue to hear what the Ferengi was saying, and he was impressed. It would add to his rapidly increasing store of curse words. When Geordi allowed him to use them again.

Data turned back to the others, just as Riker returned the medical padd to Bashir.

"I will confess," the commander said, "that some of this is beyond me."

"Well," Bashir replied, "for your purposes, the conclusions are all you need to be concerned with."

"Any your conclusions are . . . ?" Riker prompted.

"There's not *my* conclusions, Commander. DNA is DNA."

"And DNA can be cloned."

"Oh, without question. It can be cloned. It can be engineered. It can even be reproduced by transporter duplication. But each of those techniques leaves a telltale signature on the reproduced DNA helices. With cloning, even a single generation will result in measurable replicative fading. Genetic engineering shows unmistakable traces of amino acid padding at cojoined sequences. And transporter duplication always results in a slight quantum mass imbalance. A bit more tricky to detect, but the samples obtained from Worf's fingernails were large enough to yield unquestionable results."

Riker's frown deepened.

Bashir looked even more contrite.

"Commander Riker, I have cross-checked my results with the tissue profile I obtained from Starfleet Medical Archives. The person who attacked Worf on Qo'noS was, without question, James Tiberius Kirk."

TWENTY-ONE

There were long moments of silence in the holo-suite, broken only by the muted confirmation tones coming from Bashir's medical padd. Data watched as the doctor brought up a small display to show to Riker.

"It's all right here, Commander," Bashir said. "An absolute match to Kirk, James T. Born, Earth, 2233. Not a clone. Not a reconstruction. And not a transporter duplicate."

"Therefore," Spock added, "logic demands that the assailant on Trilex is also the captain." He looked at Riker, as if challenging the commander to argue with him.

Riker was up to the task. "No, Mr. Ambassador. Logic demands that Dr. Bashir made an error in his tests. Logic demands that . . . whoever stole Kirk's remains controls a cloning or replication technology unknown to Federation science. Logic demands that we exhaust every possible alternate explanation before we accept the . . . absurdity that James Kirk has come back to life and for some reason is searching for Captain Picard."

Spock remained unmoved by Riker's outburst, but said nothing, until Troi approached him, studying the holographic image of Kirk.

"Mr. Ambassador," she began, "is it possible that your logic is perhaps being influenced by . . . other considerations?"

"By my emotions, you mean?"

Troi paused, obviously hesitant to be speaking about emotions with a Vulcan.

"Do not be embarrassed, Counselor. I am aware that you have the ability to sense emotions. I have no doubt that you are sensing mine now. Which is why you have raised your concerns."

"Well, yes, sir."

Spock thought the matter over for a few moments. "I can see the irony in the situation. It does appear that because of my lifelong emotional connection to the captain, I am the only one present who can readily accept the apparently illogical premise that he is still alive."

"Then you admit it is an illogical premise?" Riker asked.

"Upon cursory examination," Spock answered. "But consider this, Commander. If some technologically advanced group did seek to create a duplicate of Captain Kirk, then why create a duplicate with no knowledge of his identity?"

"The duplication procedure was flawed," Riker suggested.

Spock gave Riker a pitying glance. "Enough is published about the captain's life to enable the most rudimentary of psychological programmers to create a convincing personality simulation. Through a combination of drugs, pain and pleasure stimuli, and exposure to holographic simulations of false memories, it is possible to make almost anyone falsely believe he is another person for a given period of time. Only the strongest personalities would be able to resist contemporary techniques."

Spock steepled his hands, as if announcing an unshakeable conclusion.

"Therefore, I submit that Captain Kirk's body has been reanimated by a technology unknown to us. I submit that what would be called, in a Vulcan, his *katra* has been retrieved by means of a temporal displacement, created by a technology unknown to us. I stand before you as a living example that the successful refusion of mind and body is possible. This much is known and must be accepted. Our only question is: Why has this been undertaken?"

Riker still wasn't convinced. "*My* question is: *Who* would undertake this . . . deception?"

Spock betrayed a slight, Vulcan hint of surprise. "Whoever they are, they are undoubtedly connected to the Romulan Star Empire."

Data was amused as Troi, Riker, and Bashir each said at the same time, "Romulans?"

Spock turned to the reproduction of Kirk as he had appeared on Trilex. "I apologize. I had thought it was obvious." He pointed to the flattened green cylinder hanging from Kirk's belt. "This is a device of Romulan design and manufacture. Developed by the intelligence service to overcome computer security systems by transmission of precisely timed micropulses of subspace radiation."

Data felt a moment of exhilaration. "Ambassador, that was exactly my conclusion."

"Indeed."

Data began talking faster. "Yes. When he used it against me, I cross-correlated ten years of scientific research papers and detected a noticeable Romulan absence in the field, implying they had made significant advances which they wished to keep secret."

"Very enterprising, Mr. Data."

Data nodded. "I cannot tell you how . . . happy this makes me feel. That my logic yielded the same conclusion as yours."

"Actually, Mr. Data, logic had little to do with my identification of the device. I have seen it before." Spock turned back to contemplate Kirk's image.

"Oh," Data said.

"On Romulus," Spock continued, almost as an after-thought, "it is a popular item in demand by illegal arms dealers. But I do commend you on your efforts."

Riker broke in testily. "So it's a Romulan

device. That still doesn't explain why the Romulans would be behind this."

"If I may," Dr. Bashir interrupted. "We are working with Romulans here at DS9. They've provided a cloaking device for the *Defiant,* and the ship has actually operated with a Romulan observer on the bridge."

Riker stared silently at the doctor.

Bashir looked confused for a few moments, then alarmed.

"Oh, yes," he added, "I suppose I should mention that what I just said is, uh, classified."

He gazed down at the yellow grid pattern on the dark floor.

"I believe that all of these events should be considered classified," Spock agreed, returning his attention to the discussion at hand.

"Classified or not," Riker said, "you still haven't explained a Romulan connection to these events."

Because his emotion chip now allowed him to see beneath the surface of most people's reactions, Data could tell Spock was untroubled by Riker's continued resistance.

"No doubt," Spock explained, "in regard to Captain Kirk's involvement, there is a personal connection linked to something in his past. As for Captain Picard's connection, I am not able to provide a hypothesis without knowing where Captain Picard is."

Data noted how quickly Riker tensed. He restrained his sudden impulse to add additional processing power to his visual and auditory senses in order to examine Riker's next words for signs of dishonesty. He had long ago decided that it was best never to do so with his friends and coworkers, unless there was a compelling reason.

"Are you now asking the same question this Kirk-clone was asking?" Riker said.

Data saw Spock tense as well, though the subtle signs of a Vulcan were far harder to discern. Some type of confrontation was building between the two, as each sought to somehow protect his own captain. But from what, Data didn't know.

"To be sure," Spock said, "this matter might be solved more quickly if all pertinent information were made available."

Riker obviously heard something in Spock's words which Data had been unable to decode.

"I'm afraid I can't tell you what you want to know, Ambassador."

"Cannot?" Spock asked. "Or will not?"

Troi stepped between them. "Gentlemen, I can sense where this is going. It might be a good time to remind ourselves that we're all on the same side."

Data saw Riker adopt the same expression he did when playing poker. "Mr. Ambassador, is it possible the people who stole Kirk's remains on Veridian III were Romulans?"

"It is likely," Spock confirmed.

"And this Kirk-clone looking for Captain Picard, he's using a Romulan weapon?"

"You are identifying the pattern I have seen," Spock agreed.

"And exactly how many years have you spent working with Romulans, sir?"

Troi looked at Riker with alarm. "Will! That is out of line."

Spock's eyes narrowed. To Data, it was a most disconcertingly human expression. "Are you suggesting that I am somehow involved in these attacks against former members of Captain Picard's crew?"

Riker smiled coldly. "You have pointed out a Romulan connection. You, yourself, are connected to the Romulans. And you *were* by Kirk's grave when the remains were stolen."

Spock drew himself up with an almost regal air. "Commander, though I am a Vulcan, it would be wrong of you to believe that what you have suggested does not cause me considerable offense."

"I'm just trying to do my job, sir. You have been out of Starfleet for many years. Perhaps you've forgotten that part of it."

Data watched Spock's fingers tightly grip the edge of his robe as he pulled it tightly closed, as if he were trying to hide his visceral response to Riker's challenge.

"Are you blind to the real pattern being developed here?" Spock asked. "Worf, Data, La Forge. You could be next, Commander."

"Is that a threat, Mr. Ambassador?"

Julian Bashir's mouth dropped open at the belligerence in Riker's tone.

Troi looked away from Riker in dismay.

Data watched with utter fascination.

Commander Riker had actually managed to enrage Ambassador Spock. Data could tell by the slight twitch at the corner of the ambassador's mouth. And Data could not help but feel that Riker had done this deliberately.

The ambassador spoke in slow and measured tones. "Vulcans never *threaten*, Commander. We only state our intentions. Good day."

Spock swept past Riker toward the door. He faltered when it did not open before him until he had pressed the control.

Then he was gone.

Troi was incensed. "I can't believe you did that, Will."

Riker looked shaken himself. "Neither can I."

"But why?" Bashir asked. He gazed at the closed door. "That man . . . he's . . . he's a legend."

Riker looked apologetically at Bashir. "I'm sorry, doctor. I'm going to have to ask you to leave. And to not talk about this with anyone. Understand?"

Bashir looked pained, as if he were given those orders every day. "I understand, Commander," he said formally. Then he left as well.

Troi folded her arms and looked at Riker. "You know, you were moving back and forth so quickly between truth and lies, I couldn't keep up."

"It was a most distressing conversation," Data added. "For all concerned."

But Riker remained silent, at a loss for words.

"You know what this is about, don't you?" Troi said.

"No," Riker answered, "I do not have the slightest idea what this is about."

Data put it together, his emotion chip at work again. "If I may be permitted an emotional insight, I believe it is apparent that you do, however, know the whereabouts of Captain Picard."

"This is not a conversation we should be having," Riker said stiffly.

Troi reached out to touch Riker's arm. "Will, *is* the captain all right? Are we in danger?"

"There are steps we can take, and will take," Riker said. "But we shouldn't discuss them here."

"You mean, where Ambassador Spock might overhear us?" Data asked.

For the first time, a smile came to Riker's face. "I mean, where Quark might hear us. If I know him, he's close to getting computer access to everything we're doing in here."

Troi gave Riker a questioning look. "Even if *you* don't know what we're doing."

But Riker did not respond to Troi's attempt at lightening the situation.

"Deanna, *I* know what I'm doing here. It's Spock's involvement I don't understand."

"Will, Kirk was his friend. They served together for decades. What we're seeing is nothing more than loyalty. The same loyalty you would show to Captain Picard in the same situation."

But Riker disagreed. "If Captain Picard has taught me anything, it's the need for teamwork. The strength of the whole crew acting together. If I were in the same situation Spock is in, you can bet I wouldn't be trying to run the investigation on my own. I'd listen to the experts at my disposal. I'd . . ." Riker shook his head, too upset to continue.

Troi remained calm. "Perhaps they did things differently back then."

"That's not my concern. Spock's involvement is. There's something . . . not right about it."

"Do you mean the Romulan connection?" Data asked.

Riker shrugged. "Spock has spent more time working for Vulcan-Romulan unification than he ever did serving with Kirk. But it's more than that." Riker looked at Troi. "The way he was acting on Veridian. Going back into the *Enterprise* to call up Kirk's service record. Always so caught up in the past."

Troi looked as if she couldn't believe the conversation were taking place. "His friend died. It's a natural time to become introspective and look to the past."

"Unfortunately, Deanna, there's nothing natural about this at all."

Not even Data's emotion chip could help him gain additional insight into whatever information Riker was refusing to share. But Data decided that under the circumstances, that was to be expected. After all, he reminded himself, as an android, he was not natural himself.

TWENTY-TWO

The *Avatar of Tomed* blazed among the stars, leaving no wake of rainbow light, nor any other sign of her passing.

She was fully cloaked.

In Federation space.

Which could be construed by some as an act of war.

Which it was.

Though declaration of that war was still five days away.

On the starboard hangar deck, Kirk circled the battered shuttle parked in the forward service bay. He ran his fingers along its duranium hull, feeling the micropits and grooves of years of interstellar erosion and outgassing.

"I don't recognize it," he said at last.

Beside him, Salatrel consulted her padd. "You shouldn't expect to. It's an old *Montreal*-class shuttle. You've never flown one."

Kirk considered the shuttle's ungainly lines. Asymmetrical landing legs balanced the craft over its single warp engine, which extended behind the flight deck and cargo cabin as if it were a last-minute addition of a handle.

"I've never flown one," Kirk agreed. "And I've never seen one." Shuttles should be blocky and solid in appearance, though he couldn't recall why he knew that.

"The controls have been altered," Salatrel said. "But you'll know how to fly it."

Kirk turned to her. The outfit he was wearing bothered him. It felt awkward. Improper. The quartermaster had explained it was a civilian outfit, popular with humans. Kirk was haunted by the feeling that he should be wearing a uniform of some kind. Salatrel, however, had been adamant that he had never worn one, because he had never been an official part of the Romulan forces. Only a volunteer, a freedom fighter against the Federation's injustices.

"So flying a shuttle is another of my forgotten skills."

Salatrel nodded.

"I seem to have quite a number of them." Kirk was still intrigued that he had been able to fight the Klingon with such confidence and skill. Where had he learned such moves? And why?

And meeting with the human and the robot— *android*, he corrected himself—on Trilex. He had felt comfortable in the environmental suit. Why? He had known how to operate the weapons Salatrel had given him, except for the subspace device he had used against the android. How?

"Are you all right?" Salatrel asked.

She looked at him, but kept glancing back at the padd she held.

"Isn't that what that thing is for?" Kirk asked in return.

Salatrel didn't answer.

"What does it do?" Kirk persisted. "Show you

my vital signs? Let you know if I'm about to remember something?"

"It *is* a medical monitor," Salatrel said.

Kirk studied her, knew she was keeping something from him.

"What's my name again?" he asked, testing her.

Salatrel held up the padd. "This tells me you already know the answer."

"Yar," Kirk said. "A fine and honorable human name." That's what Salatrel had told him.

"Yar," Salatrel repeated. As if the alien name held meaning and honor for her.

Kirk smiled, not convinced that it held meaning for him. "It's growing on me."

Salatrel checked the padd. Kirk saw she wasn't convinced either. He could understand why she might want to keep a medical monitor on him. But why did she find it necessary to use it as a lie detector?

"Perhaps we should go back to the holodeck," Salatrel said, frowning at the padd.

"No," Kirk said. He didn't need any more treatments. Salatrel kept showing him scenes from his past, trying to provoke a return of his memories. Some he had seen often enough that they were becoming familiar.

His Romulan wife, Kalinara.

His children with her, Lora and Tranalak.

The colony ship they'd been on, the *Talon of Peace*.

He was beginning to get a sense of himself in that life. Or was he?

Had he really commanded a colony ship?

Been an explorer on the deck of a starship. Lost his wife to a brutal raid? Witnessed a child—his child—butchered by a Klingon bastard who—

Kirk gasped and pressed his hand against his temple.

No, not "child"—*children*. And it hadn't been a Klingon, it had been that monster Picard who had slaughtered them.

Hadn't it?

"I will find him," he said.

Salatrel looked at him with concern, but she had already put the medical padd away.

Kirk stretched out a hand, to lightly trace the smooth skin on her neck. "Did you know my wife? Kalinara?"

"Yes."

"And would she approve?"

"Of what?"

Kirk drew her to him. Kissed her. Felt her stiffen just for an instant like an actor caught without lines, then melt against him, kissing back.

"Yes," she said against his cheek. "I think so."

Kirk released her then and stepped back. "So do I."

Salatrel's communicator chimed. Her bridge informed her they were nearing the launch area.

Kirk picked up the small civilian bag the quartermaster had packed for him and headed toward the shuttle's open hatch.

He put his hand on the frame, about to pull himself up. Then he stopped, turned back to Salatrel.

"What happens after?" he asked her.

She blinked at him, not understanding. "After what?"

"After I kill Picard."

Kirk suddenly knew that whatever she would say next would be a lie.

Salatrel smiled without any hesitation and reached up to caress his face.

"Life begins again," she said.

Kirk kept his face absolutely still, suppressing his true reaction. Another forgotten skill he vaguely remembered having been taught by . . . The name and face wouldn't come to him. "Won't the Federation want revenge? Won't someone have to come after me?"

"I'll protect you," she said. She gave his hand a squeeze of farewell.

Kirk did not question her further, letting her take his silence as acquiescence.

He entered the shuttle. He turned and held her gaze until the hatch slid shut.

Then he performed as he knew he was expected to—waiting for the *Tomed* to drop from warp. Allowing a tractor beam to position his shuttle outside her cloaking field. Remaining adrift as the *Tomed* departed without communication, undetectable by Federation sensors.

Only when Salatrel and her ship were light-years away, did Kirk permit himself to consider her final words to him.

He knew he could not have any locator beacons or micro-communicators implanted in him. The risks would be far too great that signals from any communications device could be detected.

Perhaps not on a remote planet such as Trilex. But certainly on the Klingon homeworld, and where Kirk was traveling next.

Thus he could be confident that however his thoughts affected his physical life signs, Salatrel would be unable to monitor him unless standing beside him with her medical padd.

Kirk watched the stars slowly pass the viewport of his drifting shuttle. At last reflecting on her final words.

Life begins again, she had lied.

Kirk felt certain that when he killed Picard, as he knew he must and would, his usefulness to Salatrel would end. From her actions and her tone, it was obvious she did not expect him to survive beyond the successful completion of his mission.

And how would his end come?

I'll protect you, she had lied again.

Kirk also felt certain that Salatrel saw herself as the agent of his death.

But what of now? What of his life?

His name was not Yar. Yet he had lost a wife, children . . . a child, at least, a family, absolutely.

But to what? To an enemy? To fate? Or by his own choice?

Kirk looked at his hands on the shuttle controls. They had fought a Klingon. Outdrawn a young man with a phaser. Rewired leads into a positronic brain. And he knew they could move over this shuttle's controls with equally practiced skill.

So what kind of life had he led before his

memories had been taken from him, that he could do these things?

And what kind of man had he been, that here—adrift in space, set into motion on a plan of which he had no understanding, knowing he faced impossible odds that brought death from all sides, he felt so . . .

. . . *alive.*

A time display flashed on the control surface. Kirk's right hand moved automatically to activate the shuttle's warp engine. With his left, he fired the attitude thrusters to place the small ship on its proper heading.

The action comforted him.

Perhaps he would never be able to answer all the questions that faced him in this new life.

But as long as he could still take action, he knew he could survive.

The engines came online. Kirk set his course.

For a place called Deep Space 9 and a man named Will Riker.

TWENTY-THREE

Romulus was a gray world. Ravaged by the constant tectonic stress of orbiting a double sun.

But to the first pilgrims who had landed here, refugees from the Vulcan Reformation, this bleak world had become home. And as the generations had passed, they were Vulcans no longer, but Romulans—reveling in the raw passions that had marked their ancestral race so early in its history. Using that instinctual fury to conquer this planet, instead of controlling it and themselves within the cooler paths of logic.

Spock understood what it was that had drawn those first Romulans to this world. The need to give vent to emotions too powerful to be suppressed, just as the world's fiery core released its terrifying pressures in displays of blazing, molten rock.

Sometimes Spock felt he was the only Vulcan who *could* understand the Romulan psyche. Which is why he had been trying to unify the two peoples for nearly eighty years.

But that very part of his unique nature that propelled him to such a pivotal role in galactic history was the same which now compelled him to risk all that he had worked for since he had retired from Starfleet and had last seen James Kirk.

His action was not logical.

But Spock had long ago come to terms with logic.

It was a valuable tool. Perhaps *the* most valuable tool.

But it was not the only one.

Spock had returned to Romulus because it was the human thing to do.

For his captain, for his friend, he could do no less.

"What does a Vulcan want with Romulan weapons?" Tiral asked with a sneer.

Spock glanced around the *dinglh,* a small

Romulan eating establishment with a partial view of the Firefalls of Gath Gal'thong. Most of the other customers were gathered at the small tables near the grimy windows that overlooked the continually erupting fields of fire. Spock and his guests were well isolated in a shadowed corner, free to conduct their business, bothered only by the constant tremors that rumbled deep beneath the floor.

Spock leaned forward conspiratorially and lowered his voice, forcing Tiral and her companion to listen more closely. "Technically, the micropulsers are not weapons," Spock said. "They are military devices."

Tiral snorted, letting him know she recognized an attempt to change the subject and that she had no intention of accepting it.

But Spock merely steepled his fingers and waited. In any prolonged negotiation, victory invariably came to those who could afford to act last. And he knew he had elevated patience to an art form of meditative beauty. Even for a Vulcan.

An ancient, grizzled server with a limp approached their corner with three glass tankards of *greel*. Sloppily, he thumped down a tankard before each person at the table. Their server wore a veteran's ribbon over his heart, on the far right of his chest.

Spock lifted his tankard and made a show of holding the pale yellow liquid to the light. When he replaced the tankard on the table, he took care his fingers did not smear the surface of the glass. He was determined to make this easy for everyone involved.

"I prefer water," Spock informed the old Romulan. Then he directed his gaze toward the windows and the great spouts of lava that glowed on the horizon. The server and Tiral had proven so inept at their wordless communication that Spock wanted them to be free to signal each other without fearing he could see them.

When Spock returned his attention to the table, his tankard was gone. He calculated he had three minutes, fifteen seconds before the server would be able to confirm the fingerprints and DNA residue he had left on the tankard. He had the same amount of time to present to Tiral the pertinent information she would need to devise an appropriate plan once she learned his identity.

As Spock watched, the young Romulan woman took a swift swallow from her tankard of *greel*. The yellow foam clung to the corner of her mouth, alarmingly bright against the black lipcoating she wore.

Spock enjoyed the silence and studied her calmly. In appearance, she was intriguingly unlike the others of her race he had dealt with. Except for a wild tuft of hair springing from her left temple, her scalp was shaved, the faint bristles giving the effect of a pale blue cap. In the bar's hazy green light, a metal disk gleamed silver against her right temple. The lewd pictogram on it identified it as a limbic transducer to which various devices could be attached to heighten sexual pleasure. It was a common enough device on Romulus, and on hundreds of other worlds. But for the young woman to wear it so brazenly in public signaled her desire to shock her elders.

Spock could understand that desire.

In his own way, he supposed, he had been just as rebellious as a youth. Though he doubted this child of Romulus would see the similarity between her choice of dress and his decision to enter Starfleet Academy against his father's wishes.

Tiral wiped the foam from her mouth, then wiped her hand on the *erx*-skin leggings she wore. The yellow foam was just as bright against their shiny black surface as against her lips.

Then she turned to Snell, her accomplice. He was a heavyset Romulan, at least ten years older than Tiral, in a wrinkled business suit. The stiff, upright brown collar he wore was a style that had gone out of fashion years ago, and Spock noted the almost invisible gleam of a limbic transducer beneath his black hair as well.

Even before Spock had sat down at this table, he had concluded Tiral and Snell were both transducer addicts—precisely the type of petty criminal he had sought. In any negotiation, knowing what the other side truly needed was an invaluable bargaining chip.

"So what do you think?" Tiral asked.

Snell sucked on his teeth. He rubbed his thumb and index finger together lightly, but constantly. Spock understood the significance. Snell needed to be transduced. It would be a short negotiation.

"Why?" Snell asked Spock.

With complete equanimity, Spock gave him the explanation he had chosen. "I wish to use the micropulsers to lay waste to the central hall of records, and, in the resulting social upheaval, establish myself as a dominant crime figure in the Romulan Star Empire."

Both Tiral and Snell gasped.

"You're joking," Snell sputtered.

"I am a Vulcan," Spock replied.

Tiral rubbed at her cheek, then extended her hand, moving it up and down as if trying to pull words from the air.

"Why tell us this?" she finally said.

"You asked me."

Tiral regarded Spock for a few tense moments, then leaned back in her chair, and threw an arm over its back.

Spock was pleased. Her posture told him she had accepted his story and judged him insane. She no longer saw him as a threat.

"So you want *ten* subspace micropulsers?" she said.

"To start," Spock said.

"How . . . how will you pay for them?" Snell asked.

"How do you wish to be paid? Federation credits? Starfleet requisition chits? Gold-pressed latinum? Interstellar letters of credit? Merchandise?" Spock watched the look of amazement that spread over both their faces.

He was having the required effect. To two transduction addicts such as they, a wealthy, delusional Vulcan would be a dream come true. As far as they knew, Spock was merely an aide to one of the ceremonial cultural exchange missions that periodically traveled between Romulus and Vulcan. But that would change, Spock knew. In less than ninety seconds. And then he would become even more valuable to them.

"My organization is quite well funded," Spock added needlessly.

"You know we could get a reward for turning you in to the security forces," Snell said, as if trying out the possibility of a threat.

"Undoubtedly," Spock agreed. "However, the reward would not be as great as the profit you could make by selling me the micropulsers. Additionally, the security forces would torture me to learn why I had approached you in the first place. This would place knowledge of your criminal activities in government hands. And in the event you escaped execution by Romulan security forces, my well-funded business associates would be compelled to hunt you down and kill you in a most objectionable manner as a lesson to others who might want to betray us."

"Latinum," Tiral said. She narrowed her eyes. "Five hundred bars . . . for each micropulser."

Spock pretended to think it over. It was an atrociously exorbitant price. To make his ruse look good, he would have to barter. Spock doubted that Tiral and Snell would be familiar with Vulcan customs concerning barter—all based in logic, of course.

"Thank you for your time," Spock said. He stood up from the table.

"Wait!" Tiral said. She reached out, about to touch Spock's arm.

Spock stopped her with a withering gaze.

A primary rule of interstellar etiquette was that Vulcans must never be touched without invitation. Their low-level psi powers made direct physical contact uncomfortable and unwanted. There were few races in the Federation unfamiliar with this rule. Tiral's action had been deliberate. She wished to unsettle him.

But it appeared she had judged that the threat of her touch made enough of a point. She drew her hand back, as if not wishing to cause further offense.

"That was just our opening offer. It's customary for the buyer to make a counteroffer."

Spock straightened his robe. He adopted his most logical-appearing attitude. "That is a most inefficient method of transacting business. I know how much you must pay for the stolen micro-pulsers. I know the risks you face in procuring them. I know the time it will take you to do so. Factoring in cost, risk, and time, in addition to a profit within the traditional range of illegal oper-ations on Romulus, leads me to a price, converted into latinum, of eighty-three bars per micro-pulser."

Tiral and Snell tried not to look at each other. Spock did not need to mind-meld with them to know their reaction. He had quoted a price at least twenty-five percent higher than what they would have settled for. Right now, they would be gleefully anticipating telling their friends how they had managed to outbargain a Vulcan.

But Snell couldn't let well enough alone. Even as Tiral opened her mouth to accept Spock's inflated offer, Snell raised the price.

"You've miscalculated, friend. We need

another five bars per micropulser, or there's simply no profit in it."

Tiral shifted unhappily in her seat. Spock knew she did not want to lose this incredible opportunity to her associate's greed.

Spock waited a few moments, to build their tension. "My apologies." Snell and Tiral held their breaths. "I have miscalculated. My new offer is *eighty* bars. Would you care to have me check my figures an additional time?"

Snell quickly stuck out his hand as if to shake Spock's. "Eighty bars each—sold."

His hand waited in empty space until Tiral kicked him beneath the table.

Snell clumsily changed his offer to shake hands into a gesture to sit.

Spock sat down again at the table with the two Romulans.

"I think this calls for a drink," Tiral said grandly.

"I am still waiting for my water," Spock reminded them.

Tiral waved over the server.

The server brought three more tankards of *greel* and a large access padd. Spock saw it was not the menu padd which the server had first carried, but the old veteran offered it to Tiral as if it were.

Three minutes, eight seconds, Spock thought. He had been off by seven seconds. An acceptable margin considering whose actions he had predicted.

As Tiral read the padd's display, Spock saw by her crudely controlled expression of elation that she now knew the Vulcan sitting across from her was not a second-level cultural attaché.

The server limped off.

Tiral looked up at Spock. Her grin was that of a predator.

Spock relaxed. Everything was unfolding as it should.

"So, tell us," Tiral said with a tone of condescension. "How long have you been working for the cultural exchange commission . . . Ambassador *Spock?*"

Spock made both eyebrows rise to be sure even Snell could detect his feigned reaction of surprise.

Snell's reaction was even more excessive. He spit out a mouthful of *greel* as he sputtered Spock's name.

Tiral kicked him again and slid the padd over to him.

Then she reached under her tunic and brought out a battered palm disruptor. Judging from its condition, Spock calculated the odds of it exploding rather than firing at fifty-fifty.

"What does your famed Vulcan logic tell you now, Spock? Who's going to pay the most to get you back in one piece? The Federation? Vulcan? Or our own security forces?"

"That is not a judgment I am qualified to make," Spock said. "All three entities would likely be interested in relieving you of me. However, it could be that at my age, the Federation and Vulcan would rather disavow me than risk an interplanetary incident by negotiating with Romulan street criminals. Then again, any contact you had with your own security forces could . . . put you at a disadvantage."

Spock calmly folded his hands on the table. Tiral and Snell stared at him, transfixed by their situation. It became obvious to Spock that the pair was incapable of concluding what their next step should be. It was clear to Spock he was going to have to help with his own kidnapping and ransom even more than he had anticipated.

"Speaking as an interested participant," Spock said gently, "might I suggest that the logical approach at this juncture would be to contact your superiors for further instructions."

Snell spat on the table. "We have no superiors."

Spock shifted his attention to Tiral. Evidently her transducer addiction had not yet resulted in permanent brain damage.

"From whom were you going to acquire the micropulsers?" Spock went on smoothly. No hint of tension in his voice revealed that the answer to his question was the point of this tedious exercise. Kirk had used a micropulser against Data on Trilex. If Spock could identify the source of the micropulser, he would be one step closer to whoever had retrieved Kirk's remains and had somehow brought him back from death. "Would not *they* be considered your superiors in this matter?"

Tiral kept her palm disruptor aimed at Spock as she sought reaction from Snell. "He makes sense to me."

"He's a Vulcan." Snell glared at Spock. "Why should we trust him? How do we know he's not just setting us up?" He restlessly scratched the skin at the edges of his transducer implant.

Tiral fixed her eyes on Spock's. "What about it, Vulcan? Are you setting us up?"

Inwardly, Spock sighed. "Tiral, what possible logical reason could I have to deliberately deliver myself into your hands?"

Tiral chewed the inside of her cheek. Then she shrugged and turned to Snell. "I say we pass him on to Tr'akul and let his organization handle the negotiations for turning him over to . . . whoever pays the most."

Snell stared at Spock. "Spock, how much are you worth, anyway? Factoring in risk, effort, profit . . ."

"I will endeavor to calculate a fair ransom," Spock said helpfully. He glanced over to the main entrance. Uniformed security officers were entering, most likely for a meal, though they could check identity papers at any time. "In the meantime, if you do wish to continue with this kidnapping, I suggest we leave the *dinglh* at once." He nodded at the uniformed officers.

Tiral stood and motioned to Snell to do the same. "Okay—but don't try anything. Otherwise, you're going back to Vulcan as a smudge on the floorboards."

Spock looked at Tiral's disruptor, still trained in his direction. How could these two even walk the streets?

"Please be careful with that," Spock said. "Your finger is covering the emitter node. If you fire, you will lose your hand."

Tiral moved her finger into a safe position.

Snell frowned with sudden suspicion. "If I didn't know better, I'd say you wanted us to kidnap you."

"Such a desire would be so illogical, I believe only a human could think of it."

Tiral and Snell both snickered. Romulans had no respect for humans, either.

"Humans," Snell sneered. "They're even worse than Vulcans. At least you're not one of them."

"Indeed," Spock said.

Then he suggested taking the back way out of the *dinglh* and allowed his two kidnappers to lead him to it, thinking that the sooner Romulus established ties with Vulcan, the better. If Tiral and her like were their culture's brave new generation, Spock calculated the Romulan Star Empire wouldn't last another century.

TWENTY-FOUR

After only two days, they no longer thought of themselves as stowaways, but as parasites in a living body.

Because there was no other way to think of the Borg ship.

For all the machinery it was composed of, for all the pipes and conduits, the power mesh and waveguides, there was another component buried beneath the duranium and the plasteel. . . .

Flesh.

Engineered and transfigured.

Ripped from whatever worlds and forms that had first given it life. Now woven into the mechanistic nightmare of Borg technology.

The stink of it was everywhere. Fetid fluids dripping on the metallic decks. Soft shapes glistening and pulsing at the end of darkened corridors or twisting overhead as they propelled whatever moved inside them, all to serve the collective.

Beverly Crusher had never seen a ship like it. Had never been briefed about any Borg ship like it.

But each fresh atrocity that Picard saw, each wave of revulsion that sickened his heart—each was accompanied by what he imagined was the whisper of the collective, deep in his mind, telling him that this was right, that this was good, that this was the way all should be and would be.

The ultimate union of flesh and machine.

The destiny of all forms.

To join the oneness in which all could merge.

To return to the oneness which called to them all.

Including Jean-Luc Picard.

Near the end of their first day aboard the Borg vessel, they discovered a blind corridor that Picard had concluded served no purpose. Thus, they could rest there without fear of Borg work crews disturbing them.

"Why would the Borg create something with no purpose?" Beverly had asked.

Picard didn't know. The blind corridor ran to

an exterior bulkhead. Perhaps it was some sort of airlock mechanism that would have a purpose if the ship ever docked. But for now, it was simply empty space, ignored by the collective, so it was safe. As far as that word had any meaning on a Borg vessel.

The end wall also had a viewport.

But they kept their backs to it.

Less than a minute of staring into the infinite ripples of the transwarp dimension was enough to induce nausea.

Beverly rationalized that they were looking at distortions in more than three dimensions—phenomena the human eye had not evolved to see, and thus a vista of which they could make no sense. Picard dared look into his memories of the collective, but it was clear his mind had not evolved to hold the mysteries of transwarp, either. Nothing he remembered on the subject made sense. And as he and Beverly rested, all he could think of was withdrawing. From everything.

But Beverly remained strong. For him.

Now, two days after they had come aboard, Beverly checked a readout on her wrist-mounted tricorder. They still wore their armor. The solid dark coverings helped them blend into their surroundings. At a distance, they might be Borg themselves. Picard quickly banished that image. It felt closer to the truth than he liked.

"We're coming up on seventy hours, Jean-Luc."

Picard nodded. He knew what she meant. They had already discussed it.

Given what Starfleet knew about the transwarp

231

conduits the Borg used, seventy hours of travel would take them far enough away from Federation space that they could not expect to return in their lifetimes.

Picard was ready to take over the Borg vessel. He and Starfleet felt he did have a chance at taking control by using the neural interface. But Starfleet had specifically warned him not to attempt such a takeover during transwarp travel. They had doubted if he could maintain the proper functioning of a ship that moved according to physics which the Federation's greatest minds had yet to comprehend. And a ship that dropped out of transwarp uncontrolled might find itself stretched into a single-dimensional string of degenerate matter more than a light-year long.

That type of takeover had not seemed worth the risk. Not to Starfleet. And not to Picard.

At least, not near Federation space.

But at the distance Beverly and Picard had traveled now, death was already assured. All they had to do was choose the method.

Picard held the neural interface in his hand.

Nothing more to lose.

Beverly didn't even question his decision.

Picard rose to his feet. He stood with his back to the bulkhead and the viewport as Beverly unfolded the cranial inducer from Picard's kit. It had been fabricated by Shelby's R & D team to look identical to the implant plate the Borg had given him when he had been transformed into Locutus. Shelby hoped the similarity of its appearance would aid in confusing the Borg.

But unlike the actual Borg plate, only the

center connector, just above Picard's right ear, contained working components. That was where the neural interface would be inserted, drawing power and broadcast signals from the energy cell and subspace transmitter Picard wore beneath his armor.

Picard ran his fingers along the cranial plate.

"It doesn't feel the same," he said.

"It's not supposed to," Beverly said. "The one the Borg grafted to you connected to your facial nerves, to increase the bandwidth of the signals your brain could transmit and receive." Beverly held up the slender connector of the interface. "This is designed only for limited transmission through the skin and skull. It's not even a direct connection."

That was the saving grace of the plan, Commander Shelby had explained to Picard. Over such a limited channel, he would be able to communicate directly with the Borg, but he could not be drawn fully into the collective.

At least, in theory.

Beverly plugged the power-cell end of the interface into the socket on Picard's armor. For a moment she paused, holding the other end free, still disconnected.

Picard looked at it. In the dull light of the Borg ship, it was indistinguishable from a snake, dark and glistening. He looked up and saw an organic tube pulse slowly overhead. The ultimate fate of flesh and machine. Beverly had done enough. He had to face the next step on his own.

"I'll do it," Picard said.

He took the interface from Beverly and rotated

the metal tip in his fingers, feeling for the guide slots. All he had to do was slip it into place. Then he would hear the thoughts of the collective.

And the collective would hear his.

Picard straightened his shoulders, preparing himself. This was his duty and nothing could be more important than that. There was no turning back.

He began to lift the interface to his cranial plate.

Beverly took his hand.

"Jean-Luc . . . I . . ."

Everything she had to say was already in her eyes.

"Yes," Picard said and gently took her hand from his.

Beverly looked away. He moved the connector to its socket. Beverly held her hand to her mouth. Picard wanted to reassure her again. Reached out for her. But saw she was looking at something behind him.

He turned.

And slowly lowered the interface because of what he saw.

"We're docking," Beverly whispered.

"But we're still in transwarp," Picard said.

Together, they moved to the viewport.

Their ship was moving toward what could only be a station of some sort. A Borg station.

But it was in transwarp, unmoving against the multidimensional folds that rippled behind it.

"How is that possible?" Beverly marvelled.

Picard didn't know if she referred to the impossible reality that the Borg had constructed an unmoving station in another dimension, which no stretch of Federation science had ever predicted. Or the impossible shape of the station itself.

If Picard closed his eyes, he could see an image of a central Borg cube to which six other cubes were attached, one to each face. That is the sense his brain tried to make out of what lay before them. With open eyes, if Picard concentrated on just one cube, it remained unremarkable, each surface ornate with typical Borg texture. However, he could conceive of no explanation for the source of the light that played over the station in a realm where photons could not exist because they moved too slowly.

But if Picard let his eyes drift from one cube section to another, the entire station seemed to balloon in a disorienting way that blurred his vision. Taken as a whole, each cube appeared to be connected to the next not by a single face, but by five. Yet every angle still appeared to be ninety degrees. At least, when he tried to focus on each angle.

Picard rubbed his eyes. For an instant, the cubes appeared to be hollow and he was gazing inside them. Then they rushed at him, constantly whiplashing back and forth as his senses struggled to deal with—

"It's a hypercube," Picard exclaimed, at last understanding. "A shape that can only exist in five-dimensional space-time."

"But . . . how could the Borg build such a thing?"

"More to the point, Beverly, how can they keep it at rest here?"

The writhing form of the hypercube station slowly rotated before them. The backdrop of transwarp discontinuities shifted as well, making Picard guess that it was actually their ship that moved, if indeed such relativistic concepts had any currency here.

"Jean-Luc—over there!"

Picard felt himself begin to spiral as if he were in micro-gravity. But he fought the vertigo to look where Beverly pointed.

On the outermost face of the nearest cube, the even texture of power conduits was broken by an irregular collection of shapes. By force of will alone, Picard willed his eyes to perceive the face as a solid, unmoving object, stopping its wild oscillation.

"They're ships . . ." he whispered in shock.

He identified the white saucer of a *Miranda*-class Starfleet vessel, docked in line with an old Klingon cruiser, a dozen other vessels he couldn't recognize, and off to the outer edge, where the forced illusion of stability melted into the distortions of other dimensions, ten *D'deridex*-class Romulan Warbirds.

Beverly shook her head and looked away from the viewport, bracing herself against its raised ledge. Picard did the same. He felt bile rise in his throat.

"Could this be where the Borg originate?" Beverly asked weakly.

"I . . . don't think so," Picard said. "It doesn't

seem large enough. And the Borg are three-dimensional beings like ourselves."

Picard closed his eyes to try and stop the corridor from spinning around him. Locating the Borg homeworld, the putative central node of the collective, had become Starfleet's top priority. But after years of analyzing all reports of the Borg's patterns of attack and every scavenged scrap of Borg debris, Starfleet knew only that the Borg homeworld—if there *were* a homeworld—was somewhere in the Delta Quadrant. Given current warp technology, that region of the galaxy was more than seventy years away at top speed. Completely inaccessible.

When Picard felt his equilibrium return, he opened his eyes again and risked another glance out the viewport. Their ship was closing in on that single face of the nearest cube. It appeared to bulge toward them like a huge dome, but the transformation of a two-dimensional shape into a three-dimensional shape was one with which Picard's senses could cope.

Beverly joined him again at the viewport.

"That's where we'll dock," he said.

Beverly touched the interface in his hand.

"There could be a great many Borg on that station," she told him. "We have no way of knowing how strong the influence of the collective mind might be in these conditions."

Picard understood doctor's orders when he heard them.

"Perhaps we should explore the station first," he said.

Beverly reached up and disconnected the

power-cell plug from his armor. "That would be wise."

The snap of the connector triggered a wave of relief in Picard.

Still, he took the interface from Beverly and slipped it into a storage pouch on his own armor. "But we'll keep this near." He touched the cranial plate still in position on the right side of his face and head. "And I'll keep this on."

Beverly nodded.

Together they looked out the viewport again.

They were close enough that the vista of Borg machinery looked almost normal. They were coming in near the collection of captured starships.

Picard studied the *Miranda*-class vessel. The *U.S.S. Hoagland* had been a *Miranda*-class vessel lost at the Battle of Wolf 359, with no wreckage ever found. Was it possible that the Borg had somehow assimilated it even as the battle raged, transferring it through a transwarp corridor to this improbable station?

Picard concentrated on the distant white disk, trying to pick out the vessel's name or registration. But as they drew nearer, he could see that the ship had been partially disassembled, with dark conduits and braces connecting it to the surface of the Borg cube like filaments of mold. The Klingon vessel beside it was little more than a collection of Borg pipes and panels arranged in the shape of a battle cruiser. It appeared he was looking at some type of spare-parts repository.

Their ship now travelled over the hulks, moving in toward a circular docking pad. Picard wondered how the Warbirds were faring. If he could get a sense of the state of their disassembly, he might be able to estimate how long they had been captured. He glanced off to the side, looking for the Romulan craft.

But Beverly found them first.

"Jean-Luc . . . those Warbirds. They're intact."

As their ship rotated to line up with the docking ring, Picard had a few seconds to confirm Beverly's sighting.

Ten double-hulled ships, each almost twice the length of a *Galaxy*-class vessel, were connected to the Borg station only by standard docking tunnels and mooring clamps. Each still had operational running lights. Almost all of them had the characteristic green glow between their hulls that signified their singularity drives were operational.

"They must have just been captured," Picard said as the Borg ship's rotation carried them out of sight of the Warbirds. He focused on fixing the Warbirds' location in his memory. "That means there could be thousands of Romulans held captive here."

Beverly's voice tightened. "Being assimilated."

"Not all at once," Picard said. "The process takes time. It could mean there are thousands of able-bodied Romulan prisoners here ready to fight back against the Borg."

Beverly actually laughed. For the first time in weeks. "You mean, you and I could lead a revolt, here in a Borg station?"

"I have always thought the Romulans could be a valuable resource in a galactic civilization," he said with a smile. "An alliance with the Romulans, however formed, could be a very positive development indeed."

No longer laughing, Beverly fixed Picard with a curious expression.

"You've always thought that?" she asked.

Picard nodded, not seeing her point.

"Well, let's just hope you didn't give the collective any ideas."

The Borg ship echoed with the dull clang of docking rings joining.

Picard's stomach tightened with more than vertigo.

But there was no turning back.

TWENTY-FIVE

Riker downed a shot of replicator whiskey, grimaced, then followed it with a swig of synthale.

It didn't help.

As a round of groans broke out around Quark's Dabo table, Riker turned back to Morn beside him at the bar and repeated the punch line, "Change is the ultimate solution?"

The bulky alien, with a chinless, wrinkled face that looked as if he had been partially melted, nodded. And waited. Expectantly.

Riker considered his options. He had just spent ten minutes listening to a rambling monologue which Morn had assured him was the funniest joke in the universe. But Riker didn't get it.

Option one was to tell Morn this, and possibly endure another twenty minutes of explanation. Riker chose option two.

He roared with laughter.

Morn blinked at him questioningly, but then joined in, clapping Riker jarringly on the shoulder before sliding off the barstool and wandering off to the waste-extraction facilities.

Quark stepped up behind the bar and deftly removed Riker's almost empty glasses.

"I never get tired of hearing that one," the Ferengi said.

Riker stared at Quark until the Ferengi shrugged.

"All right," Quark admitted in low tones, "I wish I could figure out some way to shut him up. He just never stops." Quark leaned closer. "Has he ever told you about his seventeen brothers?"

Riker shuddered at the thought of it. Then he noticed that Quark had set up another synthale and whiskey.

"I didn't order those," Riker said.

Quark smiled winningly with a mouthful of teeth, each tooth determined to grow in its own unique direction. "I'll put it on your tab."

"No, you won't," Riker said, returning the smile. "I don't have a tab. You're the one who owes *me*, remember?"

Quark put on a face of genuine surprise. "I thought I paid that back to you long ago."

Riker didn't say a word.

Quark couldn't handle the silence.

"You know, my brother, Rom, handles the accounts. I'll have him look into it."

"You do that," Riker said. He stood up.

"Commander—you're not going already?" Quark asked. "The night is young!" He dropped his voice again, giving Riker a lascivious wink. "And the Dabo girls are oh, so pretty."

"If you're suggesting what I think you're suggesting, I'm sure Odo's looking for a good excuse to have Commander Sisko cancel your permit." Riker returned the wink.

The Ferengi sighed. "I've missed you," he said, making sure each undertone of insincerity remained unhidden.

"I'm sure you have." Riker straightened his tunic. "Deduct the first round from what you owe me. You can upload the rest to my account with the purser on the *Challenger*."

Quark's eyes widened. "You mean the ship that just came back through the wormhole?"

Riker waited for Quark to continue.

"But you came here on the *Alex Raymond*," Quark said. His eyes narrowed again. "Is the *Challenger* your new posting?"

"What possible business is that of yours?"

Quark shrugged. "What can I say?" Quark tapped the lobe of one of his ears, each the size of a fully spread hand. "I like to keep my ears open."

Riker grinned. "Do you have a choice?"

Before Quark could reply, Riker stepped away from the bar and made his way to the Promenade entrance.

Quark had been right. The night, according to DS9's duty clock, was young, and Quark's Place was crowded. Riker counted at least twenty crew members from the *Challenger*, one of the newest *Galaxy*-class starships to be commissioned by Starfleet.

It would be a fine posting. And many of his former crewmates from the *Enterprise* would undoubtedly find their way to it. Especially after news of its recent exploits in the Gamma Quadrant began to circulate.

But Riker's stars did not follow a ship. They followed his captain. And it was for her captain's sake that he walked slowly along the Promenade, gazing in the shop windows, sampling a *jumja* stick, taking his time as he made his way to the turbolift.

A Cardassian, the only one Riker had seen aboard the station, stood outside a tailor shop, hands behind his back. He gave Riker a friendly smile. Riker nodded, but kept walking, avoiding the temptation to glance behind.

He already knew what he would see.

There had been a Bajoran monk studying the Promenade directory when Riker had entered Quark's, face shrouded by a large hood. The same monk had stepped up to study the same directory when Riker had left the bar a half hour later.

Riker didn't have to look back to know he was being followed.

The turbolift provided a swift, if rough, ride to the habitat ring. Riker stepped into the claustrophobic corridor and wondered once again what the Cardassian designers of the station had been thinking of when they had built it. With the support beams running across the floors as well as the ceilings, it was almost as if they had gone out of their way to make movement through the station difficult.

But then, the Cardassians excelled at overcoming their difficulties, so perhaps their culture encouraged erecting barriers as much as human cultures encouraged removing them. Riker looked forward to discussing that insight with Commander Sisko. Any officer who had lasted as long as Sisko had, caught in the middle of the still-simmering Bajoran-Cardassian conflict, had to understand both sides.

Riker heard the turbolift hum behind him. Another car was arriving. He hesitated at his intersection until he heard the doors just start to open, then he turned the corner and waited.

But after ten seconds, he still was unable to hear footsteps in the corridor. Had the monk missed him?

Riker decided to act as if he had forgotten something. He walked back around the corner, head down at first, heading back to the turbolift.

After a few steps, he looked up, ready to nod in acknowledgment of the monk he knew was in the corridor.

But the corridor was empty.

Riker paused. There were no other intersections between him and the turbolift.

He decided he had been mistaken. Perhaps the monk had been a monk after all. He started to turn back the way he had come.

Then DS9 exploded around him as the monk's fist hit his jaw.

Riker had no recollection of falling. All he knew was that he was lying on his back, staring up into the shadowed hood of the Bajoran holy man who had just decked him.

"What the devil do you think you're doing?" Riker demanded, giving the monk his opening.

But the monk folded his arms, making his hands disappear into his wide sleeves. He stepped back, giving Riker room to get to his feet.

Riker did, moving his jaw back and forth beneath his fingers. "Helluva right cross for a holy man," Riker said, frowning.

The monk remained still.

Riker feinted to the left.

The monk didn't move, his posture rigid as that of a statue.

Riker smiled. He enjoyed a challenge. But the effort of smiling hurt his jaw, and he frowned again.

"There are two way we can do this," Riker began.

"No," the monk said. "There is only *one.*"

The monk leapt at him, robes billowing, giving Riker no clear target beneath them.

He felt stiff fingers expertly jab in beneath his ribs, knocking the air from his lungs, even as he partially deflected the hand aimed at his throat.

Riker fell back again as the monk flipped over him.

When Riker regained his footing, their positions were reversed. Now the monk had his back to the turbolift.

Riker spun around and raced off.

This time, he could hear the clanging of the monk's boots on the metal floor of the corridor.

Riker charged past the next two intersections,

then hit the long corridor that led along one of the station's outer spokes to a docking pylon on the outer ring.

He glanced behind him.

The monk's fluttering robes made him look like an attacking sea creature—no sign of any structure beneath the dark shape pursuing him, only the embodied action of pursuit.

For an instant, Riker wondered if there such things as ghosts.

He picked up his pace.

By the time he reached the next intersection, the station's habitat sections had been left behind. Now he was in the industrial areas of the docking ring—machine shops, cargo holds, thruster control rooms.

He ran to the right, heading for one of the cargo bays assigned to Starfleet.

The monk followed in close pursuit.

Finally Riker stumbled to a stop by cargo-bay doors marked by the Starfleet delta. He bent over, hands on his knees, urgently drawing breath. He heard the monk closing in. Riker looked around, as if searching for a way out, then slapped the Cardassian wall pad and squeezed through the cargo-bay doors before they had finished opening.

Riker stepped back between two stacks of hexagonal packing modules and kept his eyes riveted on the open door.

He was relieved when the monk appeared and cast a long shadow into the bay.

Whatever the monk was, he was physical.

Though Riker once again checked his jaw, thinking that should have been proof enough.

"There's nowhere to run on this station," the monk called out. He paused as if he expected an answer.

Riker said nothing.

The advantage of this section of DS9 was that it was completely under Starfleet control. The security monitors could be turned off at their source, so that any events that transpired here would not be recorded in Odo's office or tapped into by Quark.

The monk stepped through the cargo-bay doors. The instant he was clear, they slid shut behind him.

The monk didn't even bother to examine them.

"Come out, Commander Riker."

Riker stepped into a pool of light in the clear, central section of the cargo bay.

The monk moved toward him.

"You still haven't told me what you want," Riker said.

"I think you know."

"Try me."

The monk stopped in front of Riker. "All right . . . have you ever heard of—"

The monk's hand flew out for Riker's neck.

This time Riker was ready for him.

He parried the hand, then kicked up, caught the monk in the chest, then whirled around and with his other leg threw him off balance.

The monk hit the decking on his back as Riker completed his spin. But before Riker could recover his balance, the monk kicked out, catching Riker's legs.

Riker fell to the deck.

The monk dove for him, driving his elbow into the side of Riker's head with bone-jarring impact. Gasping in pain, Riker instinctively used the monk's momentum to roll him over, flipping on top of him. The monk's legs pushed up, sending Riker rolling over his head.

When the fighters leapt to their feet, both rocked, their exertions catching up with them. Riker shook his head. Tasted blood in his mouth.

"Why don't you ask me what you came here to ask me?" Riker wheezed.

The monk's hands reached into his robes.

Riker froze. The Promenade had weapons detectors. He had counted on the monk being unarmed.

So had Riker's backup.

The cargo bay flooded with light. Riker winced.

"Do not move," Data's voice announced. "Two phasers are trained on your position."

The monk slowly straightened up. "That's a roundabout way of saying you've got me covered," he said.

Data stepped out from behind one stack of crates. To the other side of Riker, La Forge appeared. Both held phasers.

"I want to see hands," La Forge said.

Riker was startled as the monk suddenly pulled down on his robe and the fabric tore away from him.

Though Riker had been expecting what he would find since he set up this ambush, actually standing face to face with someone who looked so much like James T. Kirk was like taking a direct hit.

Again.

Picard had described to Riker his reaction to having met Kirk in the Nexus. The visceral impact of seeing someone in the flesh who up to that moment had only ever been an image on a viewscreen.

Riker knew the man before him was a fraud, a creation of an unknown science. Still, for just a moment, a sense of fleeting wonder touched him as he dared think that the person he saw, the legend he saw, might be real.

The impostor glanced at Data and La Forge, betraying no surprise at seeing either of them. Then he turned his full attention to Riker.

"You recognize me, too, don't you?" the impostor said.

Riker stared intently at the false James Kirk. "Let's just say I recognize who you're *supposed* to be."

There was a strong attitude of competence and control in the impostor's bearing, exactly what Riker would have expected from the historical Kirk. But just for a moment, something else flashed behind those eyes. An unexpressed sense of pain . . . of loss . . . Riker wished Deanna were here now. Though she would have her chance with this . . . whatever he was, soon enough.

"Tell me," the impostor said. "Who am I . . . supposed to be?"

"You really do not know?" Data asked.

The impostor turned to the android, smiling

ruefully. "Do you think I'd let myself step into this trap if I didn't have a good reason?"

Riker started. He had seen that smile before, heard that tone of voice in so many captain's log recordings that it was as if he recognized the voice of someone in his own family. It was one thing to duplicate a biological body . . . but to reproduce so exactly the tone and nature of a personality?

"What about the other question?" Riker said sharply. "What you asked La Forge, and Data, and Worf. Why do you want to find Captain Picard?"

As if a live wire had been touched to the impostor, Riker saw the false Kirk's body stiffen as a hate-filled grimace took over his face.

"Picard," the impostor spat. "He must die! *I have to kill him!*"

Then with an enraged snarl, the impostor threw himself at Riker, hands like claws, in response to some elemental fury Riker could never hope to understand.

Data's reflexes were faster than La Forge's, and it was the android's phaser that dropped the impostor.

His hands tightened reflexively on Riker's tunic, but his eyes rolled up and he began to slump, whispering one final word before Riker caught him and gently, almost respectfully, lowered him to the floor.

The three officers stood over their remarkable prisoner for a moment, one unspoken question shared among them.

Riker touched his communicator.

"Riker to Ops . . . four to beam to the infir-mary."

And even as the transporter locked onto them, the whispered word still hung in the silence.

The last word the impostor had gasped as the phaser had claimed him . . .

A word, a plea, that only James T. Kirk would use . . . Spock. ..

Riker felt a chill move through him.

And it wasn't the transporter.

TWENTY-SIX

The truck came to a stop approximately fifty-two kilometers southwest of Dartha, the capital city of Romulus. Normally, Spock would have been more precise in his estimate, but Tiral and Snell had placed a cloth bag over his head, forcing him to rely on physical sensations of speed and heading changes alone.

Fortunately, the truck was a wheeled variety, less expensive to operate than an antigrav floater in the loose shale of the southern regions around Dartha. For Tiral and Snell, the cost of energy was of utmost importance, second only to their episodes of transduction.

Spock had already endured many such episodes during his short captivity. Typically, Tiral and Snell would confine him someplace, once even in the cargo compartment of the truck, and then retire to a location where his acute ears couldn't avoid relaying every detail of their addiction.

He concluded his kidnappers were energetic, if not overly imaginative. The seven-year cycle of *Pon farr* gave Vulcan's greatest minds ample opportunity to anticipate and then experience their pleasures, and the detailed records of that anticipation and experience were still banned on more than half the worlds of the Federation. No doubt when full relations were established between Vulcan and Romulus, entire Vulcan libraries would become available throughout the Star Empire, and Spock anticipated the shock waves that would result when Romulans experienced the exquisite discoveries of suppression and discipline.

But for the last hour, Tiral and Snell had remained silent and celibate, directing the truck on a circuitous route which Spock guessed was intended to avoid security checkpoints as well as to confuse him.

At least they had been successful in their first intent.

Spock braced himself against the door of the passenger cabin as the truck swerved to a stop. They had driven off the main transport route fifteen minutes earlier, and the thunder of rocks and gravel against the underside of the vehicle had been continuous since then.

Spock felt the door beside him swing up on its hydraulic hinges. He tensed, waiting for Snell's hand to grab his arm and drag him from the truck's cabin. But instead he scented Tiral's perfume. She, at least, was cultured enough to continue to avoid touching him.

Spock had felt a sense of missed potential as he had contemplated Tiral during his captivity. However she had come to this life of petty criminal pursuits, he knew she had not been born to it. What tragedies there had been in her past he did not know. Given the hardening her present life promoted, it was quite likely he never would.

"Ambassador," Tiral said formally, "if you would step out please."

Spock swung his legs around and made certain his feet had solid purchase before he attempted to stand. His hands were tied behind his back. The shale made finding one's balance a precarious proposition.

He felt his head brush Tiral's hand as he stood. She was protecting him from hitting his head on the overhead door.

"How old are you?" Spock asked.

"Step away from the door," Tiral said.

Spock tested the ground ahead with his boot, found a secure footing, and stepped forward. He could smell the night air through the cloth over his face. There was a tang of sulfur to it. A water reclamation plant must be nearby. A billion years of almost constant volcanic eruptions had made fresh water on Romulus rarer than dilithium.

"Have you ever considered leaving your . . . line of work?" Spock asked.

He sensed a change in Tiral's movements that indicated he had caught her attention. And even her gruff tone of bravado could not hide the bitterness that underlay her words. "Who'd have me, Ambassador?"

"There are those on Romulus who study Vulcan history. They require secrecy and stealth in their pursuits, and it could be you would have skills to offer them." But then, before Tiral could even begin to reply to him, Spock relaxed his muscles and began to fall forward.

By the time it made contact with the back of his knees, Spock was already twisting to more efficiently absorb the impact of his fall.

"What did you do that for?" Tiral shouted at Snell.

"The last thing I need is you turning into a Vulcan on me!"

Spock heard more scrabbling against the rock, a grunt of surprise and exertion from Tiral, the sound of a body falling.

Then the sharp slap of flesh on flesh. A shrill cry. A guttural torrent of Romulan epithets.

And then . . . something else. Far off. Coming closer.

Spock felt Snell's hands grab his arms roughly as he was pulled to his feet. Spock slipped, almost fell again, caught himself.

He felt his head forced back by pressure on the bag over his face.

"Careful," Tiral said faintly. Her voice was thick with liquid. Blood, Spock knew. Snell's blows had hurt her.

"Why?" Snell challenged.

"Cause he's not worth anything to us dead!"

Snell's hand struck the side of Spock's head. Next, Spock felt the cloth slide up and off his face.

It was night, but he blinked under an onslaught of sudden light, so bright his inner eyelid slid shut to ward off blindness.

The air trembled around him. A craft was approaching. Blazing its way with powerful searchlights which spread across the bleak land-scape, as if looking for any others who might be hidden nearby.

Spock stared upward, eyes slits as the beam played across him.

He saw it pick out Tiral and Snell. In the harsh blue cast of it, the green blood on Tiral's face was dark, almost black.

A wind picked up. Small stinging bits of stone danced through the night, stirred up by the craft's backwash.

It was some kind of civilian runabout, Spock noted, aerodynamically sleek for atmospheric travel, large enough for four or five passengers. But even his heightened eyesight could not pene-trate the glare of its searchlights to identify the actual model.

It set down twenty meters away. The shale crunched beneath it. Its pilot kept its engine operating on standby. Then the access hatch opened and a set of steps folded down.

Spock's hair streamed in the wind. Tiral and Snell stood to either side, equally mesmerized by the searchlight beam that targeted them.

The shadows of the three people from the craft rippled in that light as they approached, as dark as wraiths, as ill-defined as smoke.

But Spock did not need to see the features of those who approached to know that one was

Tr'akul, one of the most notorious smugglers in the Romulan Empire, with few peers in many other crimes.

As two of the figures hung back, one alone approached. He pulled back the hood of his black robe, and Spock saw a Romulan with a cadaverously lean face, accentuated by a scar that ran from cheekbone to chin, dimpling the bone beneath it.

"Greetings, Tr'akul," Spock said.

The Romulan crime lord glanced at him as if he were only a commodity. He reached out, took Spock's jaw, and pushed the Vulcan's head back and forth as if inspecting livestock. As with Snell, Spock set aside Tr'akul's casual, violating touch.

Tr'akul smiled as he flicked his hand like a sleight-of-hand magician and a knife materialized in it. Spock remained silent as the knife scored his cheek.

The hot green blood that trickled from his wound cooled rapidly in the rising wind.

Tr'akul, still smiling, gestured again and the knife was gone. In its place, a small medical sensor. With a flourish, he touched it to Spock's cheek, to Spock's blood.

After a few seconds, the sensor chimed.

Another flick of Tr'akul's hand and the sensor was gone.

Without looking back at his companions, Tr'akul raised his hand and snapped his fingers twice. Then he stepped back.

One companion, also concealed in a fluttering black robe, approached Tiral. He handed her a small case. Opened it for her. Still nothing was said.

Spock shifted his gaze to see what his price had been.

A limbic accelerator.

He mourned Tiral's death, even more so because she could not see its approach.

Tiral fumbled eagerly with the accelerator. Its contact point reflected the light of the searchlight so powerfully that it was like looking at a chemical flare.

Snell took it from her as she struggled to unfasten the second contact. Tiral wrested it back from him.

Spock watched with fascinated despair.

What had Romulus become to give birth to people who had so little sense of history, so little hope?

Tiral looked at Spock. She held the accelerator tightly against her chest.

"Tiral, don't," Spock said quickly. "It will—"

Snell hit him so quickly and so hard in his solar plexus that he saw flashes of light in the corner of his vision.

Felled by primal shock, Spock dropped to his knees, unable to keep his face from falling forward and slamming into the shale.

A small gasp escaped him before he achieved the state of *n'kolinahra* and banished the pain of the assault.

He lifted his head and peered up through the blowing dust and dirt in time to see Tiral and Snell both connected to the accelerator through their transducer implants.

"Just a taste," Tiral warned Snell. "We've got a long drive back."

Spock tried to speak, but there was no air in his lungs.

I grieve for thee, he thought. It was all he could do. A century ago, he could have slipped from his bonds, dropped Tr'akul and his thugs, saved Tiral and Snell, and still learned what he needed to know. And at Kirk's side, there would have been nothing that could have stopped them from going on to . . .

Snell switched on the accelerator. Tiral and Snell embraced.

For the briefest of instants, pure joy lit their faces.

Then they clawed frantically at the transducer contacts on their scalps. Their mouths yawned open without sound.

Green blood exploded from their noses and lips.

Their limbs trembled in a terrible rictus of agony, then went limp as Tiral and Snell slid to the shale, still bound together.

The background whine of the waiting craft swallowed whatever death rattles escaped them. The ending of their lives no more than a troublesome detail, easily dealt with by Spock's buyers.

Spock forced himself to his feet before anyone could touch him again.

He stood before Tr'akul, tasting the copper of the blood that ran from his own nose across his lips.

Tr'akul brought the knife to his hand again,

reached around Spock as if to embrace him, and cut the ropes that bound his wrists.

And just before he stepped away, Spock felt the Romulan whisper in his ear—the first words he'd spoken.

"T'raylya ohm t'air ras."

Spock fought to maintain his neutral expression.

The words were a form of Ancient Vulcan, a spoken tongue unknown to all but scholars. From a lament that dated thousands of years before the teachings of Surak.

Forgive me, my brother. . . .

Tr'akul stared deep into Spock's eyes, then dropped his gaze.

Tr'akul's cryptic phrase told Spock that the notorious smuggler was no longer in charge of what would happen next. He was not even in favor of it.

For the first time since developing this plan, Spock conceded to himself that he might have miscalculated.

Spock had expected to find himself ransomed by Tiral and Snell, and he had been. To a logical choice, Tr'akul. But Spock had expected that whichever party bought him would be the same that had supplied the micropulser to Kirk. And that whoever bought him, in turn, from the supplier would be the group that had restored Kirk.

So if not Tr'akul, then who was in control?

Tr'akul gestured to the third member of his party still silhouetted by the searchlight's concealing glare.

The third figure walked forward.

And he drew a disruptor and fired it in one fluid motion so seamless that Spock barely had time to register it before the orange beam crackled through the night and reduced the person who had carried the transducer to a cloud of disrupted radiation.

The disruptor turned toward Spock.

Spock had no concern for his own safety. There would be no logic in killing him in this way at this time.

But the third figure swung his arm out with the precision of a machine and fired again.

"*T'air ras!*" Spock shouted, "*bral!*"

But before Tr'akul could run, orange fire flickered over the shale and the smuggler was consumed.

The third figure put the disruptor away.

"You will come with us," the figure said to Spock.

Spock calculated the odds of his surviving a trip with the figure. They were not in his favor.

In a heartbeat, he brought his hand to the base of the figure's neck, positioned his fingers, and pinched the nerves beneath them.

The figure did not react or try to defend himself. And the nerve pinch did nothing.

To test his hypothesis, Spock pinched again.

Still nothing.

Spock raised an eyebrow. "Fascinating," he said. He removed his hand.

The figure moved, pulling back his hood to reveal the cranial implant plates that cruelly puckered the flesh of his Romulan features.

Spock recognized their origin.

"Resistance is futile," Vox said.

"Indeed."

TWENTY-SEVEN

In Deep Space 9's infirmary, Dr. Julian Bashir folded his arms and waited impatiently, as if everyone in the infirmary could interpret the Cardassian medical display as easily as he could.

But Riker wasn't interested in the doctor or the display. His attention remained fixed on the patient on the diagnostic bed, kept asleep by means of the small somnetic inducer on his forehead.

Deanna touched Riker's arm. "You believe now, don't you?"

As unhappy as it made Riker feel, he couldn't argue with Deanna.

"Yes," he said.

Dr. Bashir shrugged. "That *is* what I've been telling you, Commander."

Riker rubbed at his sore jaw. For a dead man, Captain James T. Kirk still packed one hell of a wallop.

"Is this some aftereffect of being in the Nexus?" Riker asked. Kirk had been swallowed by the energy-ribbon phenomenon when he had vanished seventy-eight years ago on the maiden voyage of the *Enterprise-B*. Somehow, Kirk had continued to exist in a dream state until Picard had also entered its realm. Picard had been successful in convincing Kirk to reenter the physical world, to help him stop a madman from destroying the Veridian sun.

Their joint effort had been successful, but fatal for Kirk.

Yet here he was. Again.

Surely the only explanation possible involved some kind of alien metaphysics.

But Bashir had said, "No." Politely. Riker had first met the young doctor three years earlier, when Starfleet had taken over the administration of Deep Space 9. At the time, he had thought Julian Bashir one of the most annoyingly arrogant youngsters he had ever met. But life on the frontier had obviously had a positive effect. Bashir was maturing well.

"I tracked down the El-Aurian who used to run the recreational facilities on the *Enterprise*," Bashir now explained. He leaned back against one of the infirmary consoles, a disarmingly informal posture. But Riker had learned that Bashir's casual mien hid a keen and disciplined mind worthy of Starfleet's best officer material.

"Guinan," Riker said.

"Exactly. She experienced the Nexus at the time of the *Lakul* disaster, and she is quite adamant that if Kirk left the Nexus of his own volition, unlike her and the others who were forcibly removed, there can be no . . . echo of him left within it. He came out as he went in, flesh and blood and all it is heir to."

"Then how . . .?" Riker said.

Bashir crossed over to a second display above

Kirk's diagnostic bed. He touched the incomprehensible Cardassian controls and the screen changed to display a quantum-phase interior view of Kirk's skull and brain.

"Two possibilities," Bashir said, "both of them unusual. This. . . ." The display zoomed in to show a dense structure the size of a pen snaking around Kirk's medulla. It branched into a fractal network of smaller structures, absolutely impenetrable to the medical sensors. "And these . . .," Bashir concluded. The screen shifted to what Riker recognized as an interior view of an artery. Mixed in with the blood cells that surged rhythmically by, there were smaller objects, no larger than single pixel dots compared to the relatively huge blood cells.

"Those dots?" Riker asked.

"Computer, enlarge current view by two factors."

Now Riker recognized the dots, but he still didn't understand. "Nanites?"

"Of a type," Bashir confirmed. "I've never seen this precise configuration before, but they are clearly nanotechnology intended for medical treatment. In this case, repairing the extensive damage to the patient's tissue."

Riker fixed Bashir with a skeptical look. "With respect, Doctor. The patient wasn't 'extensively damaged.' The patient was dead. I would think that what has happened to Kirk is a bit more complicated than a medical treatment."

Bashir grinned. "Perhaps that was an understatement. But take another look at the device in his brain stem."

The display over Kirk returned to the image of his skull and the object within it.

"What is it?"

"According to the scans I can make, perhaps the most sophisticated neural implant known to medical science."

Riker's senses went on alert. He saw Deanna give him a quizzical look, responding to the sudden change in his emotional state.

"What's its purpose?" Riker asked. It was too much of a coincidence that just as one Starfleet captain disappeared on a mission with a neural interface, another from the past came looking for him. Also with an interface.

Bashir frowned. "All I know for certain is that it's killing him." The doctor moved his finger over the outer fractal tendrils of the device. "These contact points are being modified by the nanites to extend further into the patient's cortex. It's like a cancerous tumor. At the rate it's growing, I give him no more than a week."

Riker gave the doctor a sharp look. Most cancers were as easy to treat as contact dermatitis. "Remove it."

"*I* can't, Commander. What's required is far beyond my skill as a surgeon."

"Can't you use the transporter to filter out the extraneous material?" Deanna asked.

"That is a valid treatment, Counselor. But to carry it out, we'd have to create a complete cellular map of the patient's nervous system in order to ensure he would be correctly reassembled. And that, I'm afraid, would take months. Which we don't have."

Riker went back to what the doctor had stated earlier. "You said *you* couldn't remove the device by surgical means. Does that mean someone else could?"

Bashir nodded. "Possibly. I've made another enquiry into Starfleet's medical archives." He grinned again. "They're getting to know me there after everything I put them through just to get Kirk's old records. But there are a handful of devices as complex as this that have been encountered before . . . and have been successfully removed by Starfleet doctors."

"Are any of those doctors available to us?"

"Only one is on active duty," Bashir said. "Beverly Crusher."

Riker understood at once. "She removed the Borg implants from Captain Picard."

Bashir nodded.

Riker's chest tightened. "Are you saying the device in Kirk is a Borg device?"

"I can't even venture an opinion on that, Commander. All neural interfaces share similar design features simply because of what they're designed to do. Does this device resemble a Borg implant? Certainly. Is it identical to Captain Picard's implants as recorded in Starfleet's archives? No. Could it therefore be of Borg manufacture? Perhaps."

Riker thought over his options. "This is an obvious question, but does Kirk know where the implant came from?"

"I only spoke with him briefly, but he has no idea who he is. And any questions I ask him about his activities in the past few days, or his reported

265

compulsion to kill your Captain Picard, simply trigger a violent response. That's why I'm keeping him under the somnetic inducer. It's preferable to modifying his aberrant behavior through drugs, until we know what's causing his behavior."

Deanna made the connection. "Has he been programmed?"

"Conditioned," Bashir said. "Yes."

"The implant?" Riker asked.

Bashir was emphatic. "Yes. Of that, at least, I *am* certain."

"So the only way we're going to get past whatever blocks have been put on Kirk's memories is by removing that implant. And unless that implant is removed within a week, at most, Kirk will die."

Bashir's next question was what Riker had been waiting for. "Commander, where *is* Dr. Crusher? According to Medical, she's on extended leave. But no one will tell me where."

There was no more time to waste. If Picard had taught him anything, Riker thought, it was that not only must a good leader make correct decisions, he must make fast decisions.

He drew himself up, understanding that there would be no stepping back from what he was about to do. Shelby be damned.

"Dr. Bashir, Counselor Troi, under Starfleet General Order Three, I am now invoking the official secrets regulations of stardate 7500, as amended, stardate 42799."

"But . . . those orders have to do with . . . invasion," Bashir said hesitantly.

Riker pressed on. He was speaking for the

record now. "Starfleet has reason to believe the Federation is facing imminent attack. Captain Picard and Dr. Crusher are on special assignment to prevent that attack. It is my opinion that James T. Kirk is in some way involved with these events, and I am taking it upon myself to transfer him to the last known location of Dr. Crusher. I am taking this action in order to facilitate the removal of the implant which is preventing me from questioning him."

"You are both hereby seconded to my command aboard the *U.S.S. Challenger* and ordered to prepare for immediate departure to Starbase 804."

Deanna headed for the infirmary door without a single question. Riker had expected no less from her. But Bashir was another matter.

"Commander Riker, this ultrasecret business is all very interesting, but since everything we say from now on *is* ultrasecret, may I ask just who Starfleet thinks is about to invade us?"

Riker had no time for junior officers who questioned orders in a crisis, no matter how personable. But just this once, he would make an exception. If only to see the color drain from the young doctor's face.

"The Borg," he said.

Bashir's expression was worth the exception.

TWENTY-EIGHT

The *Starship Challenger* eased back from the upper docking pylon which had been its berth at Deep Space 9.

Her Vulcan captain, Simm, a twenty-year veteran of Starfleet command, exchanged polite farewells with the station's traffic controller, then had the helm bank the ship away, setting course for Starbase 804.

As the *Challenger* came about, the Bajoran wormhole irised open again to admit a Klingon mining survey vessel. In the flood of exotic radiation that the wormhole itself emitted, a single directed pulse of tetryons was easily and understandably overlooked.

The faster-than-light particles could exist only in subspace and were an expected, if not regular, phenomenon of any wormhole.

But in this case, the directed beam did not come from the Celestial Temple itself, but from a point four light-years distant from Deep Space 9.

Aboard the *Avatar of Tomed*, Salatrel leaned to the side in her command chair, nervously stroking its arm.

"We're receiving a passive return from the tetryon pulse," Subcommander Tran reported.

He turned from his helm board to face her. "He is being moved."

"On the station?" Salatrel asked.

"On the *Challenger*," Tran answered, smiling coldly.

Salatrel wouldn't give the upstart the satisfaction of seeing her fear. She had not been able to risk outfitting Kirk with a transmitter or a locator beacon, for fear his signal would be detected. But so close to a wormhole with its constant fluxes of broad-spectrum radiation, it had been a simple matter to realign her Warbird's sensors to use tetryons to search for and detect Kirk's implant each time the wormhole opened.

"Heading?" Salatrel asked.

Tran checked his board. "The only port of call that makes sense is Starbase 804."

Salatrel turned in her chair to face her white-haired centurion, Tracius.

"Is Starbase 804 of any particular significance?"

The grim-faced Romulan looked up at the ceiling of the bridge, accessing memories he was too old and too stubborn to commit to a computer. "Another bastion of the Federation's intent to plant her flag and fascist rule on free space. A small frontier outpost. A Klingon contingent of scientists." He returned his attention to her. "It is of no special value or importance."

"Then why is Kirk going there?"

Subcommander Tran rose to his feet. "I submit Kirk is being *taken* there. Unless you wish

269

us to believe he has successfully taken over a *Galaxy*-class starship."

Salatrel bit her lip. If anyone could, Kirk could. "Regardless of whether he's in control or a captive, the question remains, Tracius. Why take him there?"

The centurion's brow furrowed as he put all his years of experience and knowledge about the hated Federation to use. "If they have identified Kirk's implant as a Borg device, they would be taking him to Starbase 324 for study, as they do all Borg technology. If they have executed him, they either would not be taking him anywhere— they'd disintegrate his body and eject the molecular dust into space—*or,* they'd be continuing with their plans to return him to his home planet for burial."

Salatrel struggled to be patient with the old soldier. "I need a third possibility, my friend."

"He is going to meet with Picard."

Salatrel sat up on alert.

Tran took a step toward the centurion. "Impossible!"

Tracius held his hands behind his back. Salatrel recognized the pose. It was an unconscious affectation from his days of study of Vulcan, in an effort to understand the enemy of the Romulan people. In such a pose, the centurion would not be moved.

"These are the facts," he reminded Tran. "Picard's whereabouts has disappeared from all available Starfleet computer networks. Our spies cannot find reference to him anywhere. It is proper to assume that he is in some manner connected to Starfleet's efforts to build defenses against the Borg." Tracius looked meaningfully at Salatrel. "And where better to hide an ongoing and, perhaps, illegal weapons research program than at a remote starbase of no particular importance?"

Tran would not be moved, either. "Starbase 324 is where Borg defenses are being developed."

The centurion stood his ground. "With the cooperation of the Klingons *and* a Romulan team of cloaking specialists. From the Federation's viewpoint, it cannot be a secure location. Especially when some of the weapons they wish to develop could be used against the Star Empire."

Tran and Tracius both turned to Salatrel.

Her decision was swift. "Lay in a course to Starbase 804. Remain cloaked, but stay in the *Challenger*'s sensor shadow."

Tran made no move to return to the helm. "I believe Vox should be informed of . . . our new course of action."

Salatrel held his gaze, daring him to defy her leadership. "Vox has other matters to attend to. I will send word back to the Dante Base."

"Other matters!" Tran protested. "You don't even know where he is. You don't even know what he's doing. You're as much a puppet as Kirk is."

Salatrel leapt to her feet. Tran didn't back away. So in full view of her bridge crew, she struck him with the back of her hand, crashing him back to the deck.

Then she placed a boot on his chest and ground its toe into his throat.

"If this were a Klingon ship, you would be food for the captain's *targ*. If this were a Federation ship, they would be performing medical experiments on you before you were dragged off the bridge. But this is *my* ship. And we are Romulans. The only way we will crush our enemies is if we learn to do it together." She pressed harder on Tran's larynx to be sure she had his attention, as well as her crew's. "Do you understand, Subcommander?!"

Tran grunted. Salatrel took that for a yes.

She lifted her boot from his chest and returned to stand beside her chair.

Tran stumbled back to the helm and laid in a course to pursue the *Challenger*.

Tracius leaned close to Salatrel as she sat back in her chair.

"To keep your crew and ship, you will have to provide a clear example of the cost of defying you," her centurion said. "And soon."

Salatrel knew Tracius was right, but for now, all she cared about was tracking Kirk.

She had no idea why he was being taken—or taking others—to Starbase 804.

But if the history of the Federation held any lessons, it was that where Kirk was concerned, things were never as they seemed.

After working so long with the Borg, she almost found that lack of clarity . . . enticing.

TWENTY-NINE

Picard ducked low behind a sharply angled cube of mechanical components that jutted upward from the deck of the Borg corridor, like a forgotten protrusion from some long-ago collision. Beside him, Beverly set her medical tricorder for distance.

The dark corridor in the hypercube station echoed with the monotonous clanking of the Borg work crew marching past. They were a species Picard had never seen. A meter and a half tall, gray-skinned, one enormous and almond-shaped dark eye set below a swollen cranium. If the other eye matched, Picard didn't know. Borg implants obscured the other half of each creature's face.

Beverly passed him her tricorder. The readings told Picard that not only did he not recognize the creatures, Starfleet's xenobiology records didn't either. But the Borg were clearly established and taking victims in sectors other than those known to the Federation.

When the work crew filed by, Picard once again resumed moving along the corridor, Beverly at his side.

Far ahead, the hallway seemed to twist off into a corkscrew, but Beverly and he had already determined that the illusion of distance aboard the Borg station was just that—an illusion caused by whatever dimension the hypercube station existed within. For the most part, they were trying to keep their eyes focused only on what was nearby.

They came to an intersection. Passageways curved off like the vanes of a pinwheel in six different directions. Picard studied his tricorder. The section of the hypercube station under the Romulan ships they had seen prior to docking was to the right.

They hurried on. And the closer they came to the sector that Picard believed held the captive crews of the Romulan ships, the worse the cloying scent of rotting flesh became.

Another intersection brought them to an enormous railed walkway that skirted the edges of an open reservoir, at least a kilometer across.

Picard looked over the railing and immediately swayed back in horror.

The reservoir was a lake of what appeared to be writhing entrails. The squelching, sucking sounds that rose from it were enough to make Picard gag.

Beverly scanned the hellish scene with her tricorder. Her voice was low and unsteady. "It's a recycling tank, Jean-Luc. The atmosphere is being cleansed, and waste products are being removed from the water."

Picard understood the concept. But most colonies relied on plant-based systems to recycle air and water. It was most unnerving to see the same process undertaken by reclaimed animal flesh.

They moved on, carefully following the path laid out by their tricorder, ignoring all else, hiding from the work crews, breathing through their mouths to escape the ubiquitous stench.

Until they rounded a corner and halted as they saw a ten-meter-long section of burnished green metal corridor which could only have been lifted intact from a Romulan ship.

Picard ran his fingers over that wall. Even though it was Romulan, the fact that it was smoothly finished and recognizable made it a welcome relief from the nightmare of flesh-enrobed rods and pipes and conduits they had come through.

Beverly rapidly scanned the area. "I'm getting a strong life-sign reading in that direction. In excess of a thousand. Most likely Romulan." She pointed down the corridor.

They started forward again. But Picard stopped suddenly, when they encountered the Romulan bulkhead.

"Jean-Luc?" Beverly said anxiously, turning back to join him as soon as she realized she had gone on alone.

Picard stood in front of a Romulan display screen. Beneath it was a control board. Its virtual configuration of command keys glowed, indicating the board was still active.

"The Borg are very efficient in their assimilation process," Picard murmured, staring at the screen.

"You think that computer terminal is operational?" Beverly whispered.

"We won't know until we try." Picard pulled off his armored gloves and tucked them up under one arm. Then he took a moment to reacquaint himself with the fat squiggles of Romulan script and pressed the activate control.

The screen came to life above the board. Picard mouthed the script written across it, which identified the ship whose computer network this terminal had once accessed.

"This is from the ship named *Claw That Rends Our Enemies' Flesh*," Picard told Beverly.

"Sounds like a Warbird to me." Beverly tried to smile, but failed.

Picard knew he had to avoid any request which might prompt the system to ask for his crew member I.D. or password. He thought for a moment, then began by asking for a display of the day's general orders. On the *Enterprise*, that type of inquiry would have generated a menu providing access to the day's shift assignments, entertainment and education options, and notable events—birthdays, special meetings, and all the other milestones of a community of one thousand individuals.

Picard had no idea what the request would turn up on a Romulan vessel, but it was a reasonable first choice.

He began to read the menu that appeared on the screen.

And he gasped.

"Beverly . . . this terminal isn't connected to the Romulan ship's system . . . it's connected to the *station's* system!"

Beverly pushed closer to look over his shoulder. "But why?"

Picard lifted an armored panel from his forearm sleeves and, on his tricorder, quickly called up a programming screen for his universal translator.

"My best guess is that when the Borg incorporated this deck unit into the station, they connected the air-supply conduits to their own air-supply conduits, the power cables to their own power cables, and the computer's ODN network to . . . whatever computer system they use."

He could hear the real smile in Beverly's voice. And the relief. "How efficient of them."

Picard set his tricorder for field transmit, then held his breath. If the Romulan computer system had an intelligence file that contained standard translation protocols . . .

It did.

The virtual keyboard shimmered and was replaced by a Starfleet standard configuration. The onscreen Romulan text melted into Federation Standard.

"Jean-Luc," Beverly said in awe. "It's like . . . opening a window into the Borg collective."

But Picard shook his head. "The collective isn't computer based. It's a shared neural network that's distributed among the Borg's organic components. But *this* is the mechanical heart of it."

Adrenaline surged within him. He typed in a request for the current docking schedule.

The Borg system did not request an identifier code. After all, who else but a Borg could access it?

Then Picard smiled grimly as the station's docking schedule began to scroll across the screen. At least half the lines were composed of square bracketed tags reading [TRANSLATION UNAVAILABLE]. Traffic from systems as yet unknown to the Federation, Picard guessed.

But here and there, he saw names he could recognize. From their belligerent tone, Romulan Warbirds. Picard could barely contain his excitement.

"Beverly, this is astounding. Those Warbirds we saw . . . they've all docked here within the past thirty hours."

"The Borg captured ten intact Warbirds in less than two days?"

Even Picard knew that couldn't be right.

Fingers shaking, he typed in a request to ask for the status of the crews. The screen shifted to a visual display.

Of barracks.

Picard pored over the images intently. He recognized the Romulan style of asymmetrical bunks. He saw food replicators, entertainment screens, exercise simulators. The crews of the Romulan vessels hadn't been removed to the hypercube station; they were still onboard their vessels.

"They aren't prisoners, are they?" Beverly said slowly.

Picard shook his head. He pursed his lips.

He asked for the flight plans of the Warbirds.

They were to depart in one hundred hours, towed through the [TRANSLATION UNAVAILABLE] conduit to Sector 3-0.

"Sector 3-0?" Beverly said. "Isn't that near the Romulan Neutral Zone?"

Picard nodded. "It's also the location of the Borg's first attacks in our region of space."

Beverly looked at Picard. "The Neutral Zone isn't well defended these days, is it?"

"No," Picard said, seeing the first broad strokes of the Borg strategy. At the moment, he knew, there was a slowly building rapprochement with the Romulan Empire. Starfleet had welcomed the opportunity to demilitarize the Neutral Zone. Such action meant Starfleet vessels were freed for duty near the Cardassian sectors that were threatened by the Gamma Quadrant's Dominion. So what better place from which to launch an invasion than the poorly defended Neutral Zone?

Still, ten Warbirds, however formidable, weren't enough to invade the entire Federation.

Picard asked the computer to list any other vessels that would be departing at the same time as the Warbirds.

The screen scrolled with a seemingly endless row of:

[TRANSLATION UNAVAILABLE]

"Ships that have no name," Beverly said.

Picard knew what she meant. "Borg ships."

"Then Starfleet was right," Beverly said. "The Borg are going to invade."

"But not by themselves. They've somehow . . . allied themselves with the Romulans. They're going to come at us from the Neutral Zone, where we have no defenses, and where the Romulan outposts won't lift a finger to help us."

"But how can the Borg . . . *cooperate* with an unassimilated race? That isn't possible. Is it?"

Picard contemplated the unthinkable. "Perhaps the Borg decided it was the only way to defeat the Federation."

His own words suddenly came back to him, hideous in their new context.

Or perhaps they thought the Romulans could be a valuable resource in a galactic civilization.

Picard felt cold. "Beverly, is it possible that the Borg did get the idea from me, when I was part of the collective?"

Beverly immediately sought out Picard's hand. "No, Jean-Luc. If they had, they would have acted faster."

But Beverly sounded no more convinced that Picard felt.

He held his fingers over the keyboard, poised to enter another request.

"I have to know," he said. "I'm going to ask it to show me the unit responsible for this plan."

Beverly nodded, making no move to dissuade him.

Picard typed in his request. He prepared himself to see an image of himself as Locutus.

But when the screen cleared again, it displayed a different visual.

"Dear God," Beverly said. Her face mirrored the shock that both of them felt.

Picard could say nothing.

In response to his enquiry, the screen showed two individuals, walking in a corridor somewhere in the hypercube station.

One was a Borg-Romulan of no particular importance.

The second was Ambassador Spock.

THIRTY

Spock paused at the intersection of four passage-ways leading from the Borg docking chamber which had just received him. All about him, the maintenance crew of the Warbird which had conveyed him here strode off into the depths of the hypercube station, as confidently as if they were on shore leave on their homeworld.

It was a disturbing scene, given all it implied about the state of affairs between the Borg and the Romulans.

But not unexpected.

Spock had already accepted that nothing he could see would match the shock he had felt, though not expressed, when he had realized his investigation into what he had thought was a criminal enterprise had delivered him into the hands of the Borg.

In retrospect, the logic of it was irrefutable.

It required no heroic leaps of faith to accept that Borg technology had reanimated James T. Kirk.

And the purpose of that reanimation was elementary. Kirk had stated it himself.

His mission was to kill Jean-Luc Picard.

Most likely, Spock concluded, to keep Starfleet from accessing some Borg secret still contained in Picard's mind. Some secret, thus far unsuspected, that could lead to the Borg's eventual defeat.

The only question remaining unanswered was why, of all the hunters who might have been set into motion against Picard, had Kirk been chosen?

Since there was no logical answer, Spock felt certain that emotions would provide a key. The captain had had many run-ins with Romulans during his career. Somewhere in the web of circumstance that had brought Kirk back again was the one Romulan who hated Kirk enough to create the irony of one great hero of Starfleet pitted against another.

A Vulcan would have simply dispatched a trained assassin to eliminate Picard. But then, a Vulcan would never have knowingly allied himself with the Borg. Which is, Spock decided, exactly what logic dictated was under way at this hypercube station.

A Borg-Romulan alliance.

"You will continue walking," Vox stated.

Before responding as ordered, Spock took a final moment to analyze the curves of the passageways stretching into the distance. Once more matching Vox's pace, he continued to organize his thoughts about the Borg-Romulan alliance, while at the same time his mind pursued the more concrete challenge of the station's existence.

"This station is constructed in a Thorne subset of eleven-dimensional transpace, is it not?" Spock asked.

Vox did not look at him as they moved along

the corridor. "That is correct," the Borg-Romulan said.

"The power requirement for entering such a subset is generally calculated to be greater than infinity," Spock observed.

"The general calculations are wrong."

Spock thought that over for a few steps. He had made some of those calculations himself, when he had still been an active worker in scientific pursuits. He regretted he would not have time to review his earlier work to look for his mistakes.

But on their voyage here from Romulus, Vox had made it clear that Spock's fate would be, and it would not leave room for pure research.

Just as Vox was Speaker for the Borg in the collective's relationship with the Romulan Star Empire, Spock was to be assimilated to become Speaker to the worlds of Vulcan.

Spock was without question prepared to fight assimilation. He was prepared to die to prevent the collective from accessing the secrets contained in his mind. But he much preferred the option of escaping. And he had not yet come to the moment at which he believed escape was no longer possible.

Another intersection loomed, and Vox stepped to the side to let a work crew pass.

Spock was intrigued by the work crew. What he had thought was a single-file line of humanoids was in fact a single organism somewhat like a terrestrial centipede. Each bipedal segment was linked by its thorax to the one ahead and behind. Each segment's head was little more than a vestigial knob of flesh. Only the more developed segment at the head of the creature appeared to have multiple functioning eyes and sensory inputs, though most of them now were covered by implant plates.

Since there was no logical advantage for such an inefficient shape to have arisen by self-organization or natural selection, Spock deduced that the life-form had been engineered.

"What is the purpose of that entity?" Spock asked.

"It feeds the tubes," Vox said.

Spock chose not to ask for clarification. He had other things to consider.

"When will I be assimilated?" Spock asked.

"By standard Federation units, within eight minutes."

They had come to an open turbolift. Spock recognized its awkward design as having originated on a Pakled vessel. Vox and Spock stepped into it. Vox spoke his command to it, and the turbolift dropped.

Spock decided it was time to see how robust Borg programming was. He began his first line of defense.

"I do not wish to be assimilated."

"That will be corrected."

Spock tried another tack, looking for any logical opening. "Do you enjoy being assimilated?"

"That is irrelevant."

"Why is the crew of the Warbird not being assimilated?"

"It is not yet their time."

Spock found that interesting. Everything he

had read about the Borg indicated they had voracious appetites. In the material he had reviewed, there had never been any such idea as "later." Yet the idea of an alliance implied that the Romulans expected some benefit from their relationship with the Borg, other than assimilation.

Spock had read Jean-Luc Picard's reports on being part of the collective. Supposedly, there were no secrets among them. Thus Spock determined it was likely that, this close to his own impending assimilation, Vox would consider him as almost a Borg himself, and be just as candid as he would be to one of his own.

"Do the Romulan crew members know they are to be assimilated?" Spock asked.

The steadily descending turbolift afforded Spock a view of an endless series of metal panels encrusted with tortured mazes of pipes and conduits. None hinted at what lay beyond the levels they shielded, yet Spock knew that whatever the activities, they would all share in one purpose: advancement of the collective.

"No," Vox answered. "They are an experiment. They are not to be assimilated until they aid us in assimilating the Federation. Many resources have been expended on correcting the misunderstandings the Federation has of the collective.

"It appears you wish to take advantage of the Romulans' emotional dislike of the Federation."

"Precisely," Vox agreed.

"Do you not find it a contradiction to acknowledge that emotions confer an advantage?"

Vox didn't hesitate. "That is irrelevant."

"You argue like a physician I once knew,"

Spock said. "You discount all data except those which support your thesis. It is most illogical."

"Logic is irrelevant."

Spock abandoned that approach.

"What will happen to your alliance with the Romulans once the Federation has been assimilated?"

"The Romulan Star Empire will be assimilated as well."

Even without knowing who was involved, Spock instantly understood how this alliance had come about, and he had no doubt that the Romulan government was fully ignorant of what was being promulgated in the Empire's name.

"In other words," Spock said, "you will betray the Romulans when your goals have been accomplished."

"We will not betray them," Vox said. "We will correct their misperception of the collective."

"I do not believe they will find that reassuring."

"Their beliefs are irrelevant."

The turbolift stopped and its safety gate swung open onto yet another Borg passageway.

"Vox, in that part of you which is still Romulan, do you at least understand the concept of betrayal?"

Vox hesitated. He did not step out of the turbolift. For once, he appeared to be thinking about his response to Spock's questions.

"Yes," Vox finally said. "That is my function as Speaker to the Borg. To bridge between that which is known and that which is unknown. Between the collective and the Romulan people."

"Do you also understand that the Romulan people will feel you have betrayed them?"

Spock was fascinated to see a muscle tremble at the corner of Vox's mouth. He recalled that Picard's reports had indicated that assimilation did not lead to the total extinction of personality. Perhaps there was a spark within Vox which could still be reached.

"They will feel betrayed," Vox agreed. "But that will pass." Surprisingly, Vox still made no move to leave the turbolift. Spock quickly continued his attack. . . .

"But if they *suspect* you will betray them, what will be their response?"

Vox cocked his head as if caught by Spock's argument. He turned to Spock, who ignored the Borg laser scanner and concentrated on the dark, living, Romulan eye. The only window to what was left of Vox's true self. "The Romulans will attempt to betray the collective," he said.

Spock struck another blow. "Then, since the Romulan government would never agree to such a joint undertaking, logic dictates the Borg have entered into an alliance with a group of disaffected officers. Knowing Romulans as I do, these renegade officers will have developed two plans, both leading to a different victory. If your Borg-Romulan alliance defeats the Federation, the Romulan Armada will attack you without mercy, while the Borg forces are still weakened by the conflict. In turn, if the Federation once again defeats the Borg, the victorious but badly weakened Starfleet forces will be set upon by the Romulan Armada."

Vox seemed unimpressed. "That is an illogical scenario."

Spock lifted an eyebrow. "Explain."

"The Federation cannot win. The Borg fleet will not be weakened."

The flaw, to Spock, was obvious. How could the Borg fleet win a conflict with the Federation without sustaining heavy damage? The Federation, after all, had already gathered considerable information about the Borg.

"The Federation will not fall in battle. It will be betrayed," Vox said. "By a highly placed member of Starfleet."

Spock was startled.

"Who is that individual?" he asked, although he suspected the question was futile.

Vox stepped out of the turbolift and gestured to the side.

"You will be assimilated now."

Spock decided that dying here was no longer a useful alternative course of action. He must return to the Federation with his knowledge of a highly placed traitor. But how?

Spock chose the obvious. "Turbolift," he said firmly, "return to the hangar level."

The safety gates began to close.

But just as quickly, the floor of the turbolift car lurched and Spock stumbled against the wall.

"The collective is in control of all functions on this station," Vox said. "Resistance is futile." The Speaker for the Romulans had not moved from his position outside the turbolift.

"You have stated that before," Spock pointed out.

Vox lifted his arm graft and a blue spark leapt out to encase Spock in a halo of radiant energy. Spock collapsed to the floor without sensation below his neck. Yet he remained conscious.

Vox's weapon had been some type of neural blocker. The effects were likely to be short-term, otherwise interference with his breathing, heart function, and endocrine system could be expected.

But even in the short term, Spock realized, his potential range of actions had been severely limited.

Four Borg stepped up to him and lifted him, one Borg for each of his limbs. They carried him along the corridor and into a nearby chamber.

Spock heard another spark discharge, and at once sensation returned to him.

The Borg released him, and he stood by himself.

"Sit down," Vox said.

Spock glanced behind himself. He saw an unusual chair frame that appeared to be fused with a medical examination table. He looked up. Surgical equipment hung from the ceiling.

"That would not be a wise decision for me to make," Spock said.

"Sit," Vox said and fired his neural blocker.

Helplessly paralyzed, Spock fell back into the assimilation frame, as the other Borg adjusted his position. Above him, the surgical equipment whirred into life.

An incision arm snaked down, exposing a circular blade and three laser cauterization tubes.

Neural waveguides sprang forth from a cranial

drill, like silver threads held apart by a static charge.

Excavation scoops connected to suction tubes dropped in incremental jerks until they were poised millimeters above Spock's chest.

A head brace clamped down and tightened around his skull, leaving his temples exposed. He heard multiple drills moving in from either side. A pool of bright light surrounded him.

Though he felt no fear, he allowed himself regret.

There was still so much he had wanted to do.

For Romulus.

For Vulcan.

And for Kirk.

As Vox watched impassively, Spock heard the hum of a surveillance lens as it zoomed out at him from the far wall.

Spock had one last strategy to try.

It had little chance of success. But he long ago had learned that desperation had a logic of its own.

"Starfleet knows about Kirk," Spock said.

Vox's hand rose into the air and the machinery of assimilation stopped.

"What do they know?" Vox asked.

Spock pushed his bluff to the next level. He knew both his father and Kirk would say this was not the ideal time to bluff. But Spock had nothing more with which to wager. Except his wits.

"Kirk is the highly placed member of Starfleet who will betray the Federation. His murder of Picard will deprive Starfleet of the knowledge which can save it. Because Starfleet is aware of this, they will anticipate any action Kirk might make. Therefore, Starfleet will protect Picard and be able to fight the Borg-Romulan attack. You must withdraw, or be defeated. All else is an inefficient expenditure of resources."

Vox studied Spock for long moments. "What you say is relevant."

Spock allowed himself to experience a moment of hope.

Then Vox continued. "When your implants have been attached, we will know if you are telling the truth."

He lowered his hand.

The equipment began moving, whining, racheting closer.

Spock composed himself, waiting.

Not just for death, but for something worse.

The conscious annihilation of his identity and his volition.

Logically, he knew he should accept defeat and prepare himself for the loss of his existence.

But in a final act of will, he refused. Even as the first slender waveguides punched through his skin and the drills sang as they readied to pierce him.

Jim Kirk had never accepted defeat.

And for his sake, neither would Spock.

THIRTY-ONE

Picard and Beverly jogged endlessly through the dimensionally distorted passageways of the Borg station. The Romulan computer terminal had shown them Spock's location, but the layout of the corridors did not match the map it had displayed, as if the station were in a constant state of growth and change.

"Jean-Luc, stop!" Beverly panted beside him. "We're going in circles."

Together, they halted to rest against a wall of metal mesh. Its complex weave of optical wire flashed with intermittent light signals. Beverly checked her tricorder, reset it, checked it again. Shook her head with a sigh.

"The deeper we go into the station, the less sense these readings make."

"Spock was being assimilated," Picard said. The frustration he felt, the maddening helplessness, made him tremble with rage.

It was one thing to have experienced such a violation on his own. But to see it about to happen to another, especially someone whom Picard knew and respected.

He had to do something.

He had to save Spock.

"According to the map on the Romulan screen, the assimilation chamber should be right here," Beverly said. "But everything's twisted up."

Picard heard the clang of heavy boots on the Borg deck. He didn't have to think about what to do. He touched the side of his face to make certain his neural plate was still in place, then stepped out into the middle of the corridor before Beverly could protest.

The Borg who was approaching stopped.

His laser sensor scanned Picard's face.

"Locutus," the Borg said, "you are malfunctioning. We cannot detect you within the collective."

Picard felt himself slip into his alternate persona far too readily. But there was no time to consider what that meant.

"There is no malfunction. Some units are being suppressed in order to avoid detection by Federation forces when the attack begins."

The Borg remained motionless, giving no clue to whether or not it accepted Picard's lie.

"Where is the closest assimilation chamber?"

The Borg's mechanical arm shifted in its socket. "That information is available in the collective. You are wasting time by asking meaningless questions. You are wasting resources."

The Borg glanced down at Picard. The laser played over Picard's right arm.

"You have been modified," the Borg said. "That is why you are malfunctioning." His arm swung up. "You must be repaired."

"That assessment is correct," Picard said quickly. "You will escort me to the nearest assimilation chamber for repair."

The Borg's arm lowered, and it changed direction as if it were on a turntable.

"You will follow us."

The Borg began marching down the corridor. Picard matched its stride. He heard Beverly's light footsteps behind him as she hurried to catch up.

The Borg heard them as well. It stopped and faced Beverly.

"What is this?" the Borg asked Picard as it scanned her. The Borg's arm began to rise.

"This is a prisoner with information about the Federation. It will be assimilated after repairs have been made."

The Borg lowered its arm, satisfied by the answer. "That is relevant."

Picard felt Beverly's hand brush his as they marched. He glanced down. She carried a photon grenade.

He nodded his understanding. If he had placed them into a no-win situation, they would not allow themselves to be assimilated. It was that simple.

The Borg turned a corner in the passageway and appeared to begin walking up a steep slope without leaning forward. Following directly behind, Picard tensed, expecting to feel the stomach-wrenching sensation of stepping between two different artificial gravity fields. But he felt nothing. The gravitational gradient itself was curved.

Picard marvelled at and cursed the Borg's ingenuity. How could the Federation ever hope to withstand beings with control of such technology?

Through knowledge, he answered himself. The

knowledge that he and Beverly could bring back. And the knowledge Spock might have.

If he could be rescued in time.

The Borg turned sharply into yet another corridor. The walls appeared to stretch into infinity.

"The assimilation chamber is ahead," the Borg announced. He continued walking purposely forward.

Picard walked past an open turbolift which he recognized as a characteristically ungainly Pakled design.

The lift platform was rising, and a familiar figure was on it.

Picard's pace faltered and Beverly stumbled into him from behind.

The figure looked their way. For the moment before the platform disappeared into the next higher level their eyes made direct connection.

Spock.

But his flesh was unmarked.

His skull bore no neural plates.

All his limbs were intact.

Beverly plucked at his arm. "Did you see him?" she asked urgently.

Picard's silence was answer enough.

"Jean-Luc . . . he wasn't assimilated."

The Borg ahead of them stopped. He gestured to an opening in the corridor wall.

"The repairs will be done here," it said.

Picard stood in the entrance to the chamber. He saw the assimilation frame. Beside him, Beverly shuddered.

Picard's heart raced. He had to get away. He

had to go after Spock. But if they ran from this Borg, he knew an alert would flash through the collective. Every Borg on the station would be searching for them.

He decided to go to the source.

"This assimilation chamber has malfunctioned," Picard said.

The Borg took on the faraway gaze that indicated it was communing with the collective.

"This assimilation chamber is operational," the Borg replied. "You are in need of repair."

"No," Picard said, daring to argue although the Borg never did. "A Vulcan was here. He was placed in the frame. He was not assimilated. Explain."

For the moment it took the Borg to access the collective, Picard stood on the brink of an exceptional discovery. Perhaps Spock had found some way of defeating the assimilation process. Perhaps some trick of Vulcan mind control could—

"The Vulcan was not assimilated because the effort would have been a waste of resources," the Borg said unexpectedly.

The Borg's statement was mystifying. "Explain," Picard said again.

"The neural waveguides identified the presence of the collective in the Vulcan's mind. Conclusion: The Vulcan is already part of the collective. To assimilate him would be redundant."

Beverly gasped. Picard felt as if he had stepped into free fall.

Spock was *already* a Borg?

And then the awful, hidden pattern instantly became clear to both of them.

A Borg-Romulan alliance.

Spock spending eighty years working with Romulans.

A new era of peace dawning between Romulus and the Federation, leading to a reduction of the forces defending the Neutral Zone.

Making the Neutral Zone the perfect place from which to launch an invasion.

Could it be possible?

With all the new behaviors the Borg had learned, had one of their branches discovered a new way to assimilate an individual's mind? Without the telltale neural plates and bioneuronic implants that made Borg so instantly identifiable?

Or was Spock's incredible treachery the result of some perverse application of Vulcan logic, by which Romulans and Vulcans would be spared the ravages of assimilation by betraying the Federation?

Either way, the answer was the same.

It was why the Borg computer had shown him Spock when he had asked who was responsible for the Borg-Romulan alliance.

"He's one of them," Picard said softly, overwhelmed by the enormity of that knowledge. Starfleet would have to be warned.

"It just can't be true," Beverly said.

"Delay is a waste of resources," the Borg said ominously.

"We certainly don't want to do that," Picard replied as the anger built in him. Then he lunged out and snapped the Borg's interface cable free.

The Borg arced in a spasmodic dance of misfiring muscles. Sparks sputtered from its neural implant plate and the power connections on his chest and shoulder.

Its high-pitched scream was piercing. Agonized, inconsolable, appalling. Because it was alone.

With instant pity, Picard swung the unresisting creature by its shoulders and pushed it into the assimilation frame beyond.

The Borg thrashed and struggled there, without control. Its laser scanner pulsed erratically.

Above the frame, the surgical arms began to descend.

The multiple drills and blades spun and flashed in the light.

With one swift motion, Picard took the photon grenade from Beverly, twisted the activator, and threw it at the keening Borg.

Then he grabbed Beverly's hand and he ran.

The explosion erupted into the corridor behind them like a solar flare. The searing heat was intense.

Three more Borg appeared in the corridor.

"There's been a malfunction!" Picard told them. "The collective is in danger. Communications are breaking down!"

The Borg pushed past them to the burning assimilation chamber. They ignored Picard.

Picard sprinted ahead of Beverly to the Pakled turbolift, hit the wall command-panel to call a new platform. From somewhere below, he heard a platform whine to life.

"Where to now?" Beverly asked gamely.

Picard felt flushed with purpose.

"Spock," Picard said. At last, he had a clear direction to follow. "If we want to save the Federation, we have to stop him."

Beverly regarded him with incomprehension. "How?"

Picard drew his phaser.

"By whatever means possible."

THIRTY-TWO

As Spock waited for the Pakled turbolift to stop, he dabbed a corner of his robe against the pinpricks of green blood on his temple. Despite the fact that the Borg were a life-form dedicated to efficiency and logic, he had rarely been subjected to more unanticipated developments in any of his journeys.

If he were merely human, he might say he was astounded, astonished, *and* bewildered.

If he were merely human.

But as a human and a Vulcan, he would admit only to a mild sense of unease.

The worst of it had begun with the withdrawal of the Borg's neural waveguides from his flesh.

He had read Picard's reports.

He knew what assimilation by the Borg entailed.

Yet, none of it had happened.

The wires had entered his skin. He had felt

them press through the layers of his temporal fascia to make contact with his skull.

And then . . .

Nothing.

After less than a minute, the surgical devices had returned to their storage positions on the ceiling. His restraints had opened. And Vox and the other Borg attendants had left.

As Spock slowly sat up from the frame, he had wanted to ask questions of Vox. But with logic having little to do with his situation, he decided not to draw attention to himself.

If the Borg collective had for some reason forgotten him, or lost interest in him, he was not inclined to encourage it to change its groupmind.

Still the problem remained.

Why had he not been assimilated?

And what was Picard doing in the heart of the collective?

Or more accurately, why was Locutus back among the Borg?

When Spock had seen Locutus from the Pakled turbolift, in the company of another Borg, so much of the mystery he had been faced with had suddenly been revealed.

Picard's current situation did much to explain why Commander Riker had been so uncommunicative on Deep Space 9. The commander must have been aware that Picard was missing. Perhaps he had known that his captain had returned to the Borg.

Spock accepted that the Borg had continued to advance their knowledge in the time that had passed since their first encounters with the Federation. It was quite probable they had perfected a new means by which to assimilate an individual's mind. Without the use of neural plates or other bioneuronic implants.

It was also possible that Starfleet by now might be riddled with such assimilated individuals.

Indeed, if, according to Vox, an act of treason was going to set the stage for the Borg-Romulan attack on the Federation, who better than Picard to be that individual?

Spock reflected on the consequences of this line of reasoning. If Picard had remained assimilated since his first encounter with the Borg, then everything Starfleet had accomplished since that time, each new defensive tactic and each new weapon, had been passed on to the Borg.

In the face of a Borg-Romulan attack, the Federation would not stand a chance of surviving.

The Pakled turbolift stopped on the hangar bay level. Spock paused. Locutus was somewhere below in the station. Logically, Spock understood it made no sense to try to go after him. All that Picard knew would already be part of the collective, so killing him would serve no purpose. Also, assuming that Spock could even find Locutus again, he doubted he would survive for long after attacking him.

Thus, Spock could see only one logical course of action available to him.

He must return to Federation space and warn Starfleet of Picard's treason.

Spock stepped off the lift platform and began walking toward the hangar bay. The immediate problem he faced was to find a way to return to the Federation.

The Warbirds docked with the Borg hypercube station might be useful. Somehow, they had traversed a transwarp conduit to arrive here. Logically, there must be some way to reverse their course.

Spock paused at the entrance to the hangar. Unassimilated Romulans worked side by side with Borg-Romulans, as well as Borg of other races and configurations.

With less than a moment of serious consideration, Spock ruled out a physical confrontation. Even a century ago, such a proposition would have been foolhardy.

Thus, the only weapon remaining to Spock was logic.

He felt his was up to the task.

Spock assumed the efficient attitude of the Borg. It was not difficult for a Vulcan. Then he chose a single Borg attending to a repair in a floor access panel. The Borg had been a humanoid once, but its race was now impossible to identify.

Spock stepped up to it. The Borg looked up at him, no expression in its one organic eye.

"Are your optical sensors intact?" Spock asked. He knew the risk he was taking, but there had to be some reason why he had not been assimilated. This was the perfect time to find out

The Borg withdrew its manipulator arm from the floor opening. A welding tube glowed on the tip of it.

"Yes," it replied.

"Can you identify me?" Spock asked.

"You are Borg," the Borg answered. "Are you in need of repair?"

For a moment, Spock wondered if he had uncovered a joke of cosmic proportions. Could it be possible that to the Borg, the emotionless, disciplined, and logical mind of the Vulcan was indistinguishable from their own? But he quickly dismissed the idea. The Borg groupmind was based as much in technological implants as in brain matter. If the Borg had misidentified him as one of them, it must be for another reason.

"I am not in need of repair," Spock said. "I am in need of transportation."

The Borg stood up. "Where do you need to go?"

Spock thought for a moment. Could it really be this straightforward?

"Locutus is aboard this station," Spock said.

"That is correct," the Borg answered. "He cannot be found in the collective because . . ." The Borg hesitated, taking on a distant look, as if listening to voices only it could hear. "Because some units are being suppressed in order to avoid detection by Federation forces when the attack begins."

With this confirmation of what he had already concluded, Spock felt a new urgency to his mission. He had to trace Picard's—*Locutus's*—treachery to the source. Starfleet had to know if there were others like him.

"I require transportation to the point at which Locutus began his journey to this station," Spock said. "Speed is of the essence."

"Resources must not be wasted."

Spock's counterargument was prompt.

"The Federation might be tracing the route Locutus has taken. We must inspect that route at once if the invasion is to succeed."

He sensed the hesitation in the Borg.

He spoke to it in its own language.

"Resistance is futile."

The Borg cocked its head, then turned like a soldier on parade.

"A scoutship is available," the Borg said. He began to march away.

Spock looked around, saw that his exchange had not attracted any attention, and followed the Borg.

Logic appeared to have won the day. However, he couldn't help wondering if the same rigid logic which had made the Borg so easy to manipulate could, in the same way, someday bring ruin to Vulcan.

Perhaps Vulcan had been fortunate to meet the emotional humans. Each race tempered the other with the quality most needed, both becoming stronger.

Spock decided he shouldn't be surprised by that.

Somehow, his need to answer Kirk's call and his subsequent search for his lost captain had led to the discovery of an imminent Borg invasion of the Federation, made possible by Locutus.

What connection any of this had to Kirk's as yet unexplained return was beyond even Spock's ability to surmise.

But he did know that a connection existed. And when he discovered it, knowing all that he knew of Jim Kirk's remarkable life, he knew it would have its own logic. Sometimes, beyond reason. But successful in spite of that.

From his captain and his friend, Spock would expect no less.

THIRTY-THREE

Captain Lewinski tapped the arm of his chair as he regarded the static backdrop of stars that filled the *Monitor*'s view-screen.

His ship was among the fastest and most powerful in Starfleet. Being forced to remain in orbit of New Titan for the past three days, doing absolutely nothing, had been his most difficult duty assignment in years. As far as he was concerned, there was nothing he disliked more than waiting. But then, he shared that dislike with most other starship captains. It was probably what made them starship captains in the first place.

Land's Earth-born accent cut abruptly through the background hum of the bridge. "Here she comes, Captain. And is she fast!"

The viewscreen image shifted, making the stars swim past, until a rainbow thread of light shimmered in the upper corner. And as quickly as that, the *U.S.S. Challenger* appeared dead ahead, smoothly dropping from warp no more than five hundred kilometers away.

The massive vessel banked as it came about,

adjusting its orbit, its gleaming white hull glowing in the combined radiance of the clustered core stars.

"And she's beautiful," Lewinski said. Then, because he couldn't resist engaging his Vulcan science officer in a teasing debate, he added: "Wouldn't you agree, Mr. T'Per?"

But T'Per did not respond with a comment about the illogic of applying a relative term like "beauty" to an artificial device whose shape was derived from the mathematical realities of warp velocities. Instead, she said: "Captain, we should run a full diagnostic on our cloaking device."

Without prompting, Ardev opened hailing frequencies to the *Challenger*.

"You've had three days to do that," the captain complained to T'Per. "Why now?"

T'Per was unperturbed. "When the *Challenger* dropped from warp, I recorded a tachyon surge. Our cloaking field might have reacted to the *Challenger*'s subspace backwash. If so, it must be recalibrated in order to remain functional at warp speeds."

Lewinski sighed. "Any other source possible for a tachyon surge out here?"

T'Per considered the question for a moment. "Only if the *Challenger* were operating a cloaking device. Other than that, we're the only source."

"Do it," Lewinski said, then turned back to face the main screen and Captain Simm of the *Challenger*.

Except that the old Vulcan wasn't on the screen.

It was Will Riker.

"Will, it's good to see you again."

"I wish it were under other circumstances, Captain. And I don't mean to be so abrupt. But we are now operating under General Order Three. Commander Shelby will have provided you with encrypted orders to open at this time. Please do so, then report to the *Challenger* with your science officer in thirty minutes. Riker out."

Riker disappeared from the screen, replaced again by the *Challenger* poised against the unchanging stars.

Mr. Land turned around from his helm position. "What was all that about?"

Lewinski stood up and stretched, as if Will Riker's request were unremarkable. "I guess we're about to find out. Take us in to match orbits, drop the cloak, and . . . I'll be in my quarters reviewing our orders."

Lewinski left the bridge, feeling the eyes of his crew upon him. General Order Three or not, it was a strange experience to have a captain being told what to do by a commander.

But then, this entire mission had been strange. And whatever was to happen next, it had to be better than just waiting.

High above New Titan, the space-black disk of the *Monitor* rippled out of nothingness, less than half the size of the *Challenger's* command saucer alone. It appeared against the larger vessel's full-spectrum gleam like the featureless shadow of a moon passing over its planet.

Together, these two sides of Starfleet—explo-

307

ration and defense—kept station over the desolate world beneath them.

And they did not go unnoticed.

On the bridge of the *Avatar of Tomed,* Tran turned to Salatrel in surprise.

"Commander, a vessel has decloaked beside the *Challenger!*"

"Onscreen." Salatrel left her command chair and went to the helm to confirm the readings herself.

The blocky Starfleet vessel they had followed from Deep Space 9 fluttered into focus on the main viewscreen. It was no match for a Bird-of-Prey, let alone a Warbird, and Salatrel felt no concern about facing it in battle.

But the ship that had appeared beside the *Challenger* was a different matter.

Salatrel recognized it at once as a *Defiant*-class vessel, specifically designed, built, and equipped to fight the Borg. From the intercepted data which had been transmitted from the spies among the Romulan cloaking team working with Starfleet on that class of vessel, it was well suited for its task.

"Identification?" Salatrel asked Tran.

Tran's screens flickered with Starfleet ship identity charts, but the main window remained blank.

"It has not been encountered before," Tran said. He paused. "And it does possess a functioning cloaking device."

Salatrel was well aware of the dilemma that placed her in. Starfleet had clearly gone beyond the limits of the Treaty of Algeron and was deploying cloaking technology on its warships.

Fortunately, the Borg had not determined the weaknesses of the latest generation of Romulan cloaking devices. They had yet to assimilate a Romulan with that knowledge. But unfortunately, that meant a fleet of cloaked *Defiant*-class vessels could be an effective force against Borg ships.

It would be simple enough to provide the Borg with the specific tachyon patterns to scan for, which would reveal the presence of cloaked Starfleet vessels. But then, when the Star Empire moved against the Borg, as was inevitable, the greatest advantage of the Romulan fleet would have been negated.

Salatrel turned to her centurion, who had remained at his post behind her chair. "Tracius, can you offer any explanation for that ship's presence?"

She was surprised by the tone of contempt in the centurion's voice. "Look at the scans of the planet's surface."

Salatrel called them up on Tran's board. The radiation signature of a Borg tractor beam flared brilliant white at the coordinates of Starbase 804.

Salatrel's temper flared just as brilliantly. "The Borg took the starbase!" She whirled to face Tracius. "Why?"

His face was clouded with anger. "How can you be surprised that the collective doesn't tell us everything?"

"Because they need us to conquer the Federation!"

Tracius shook his head, shifting from contempt to sorrow in that moment. "Have you learned nothing from me? Before you can defeat your enemy, you must understand your enemy."

"I understand the Federation," Salatrel hissed. The old centurion was presuming on the ties between their families and would continue to do so at his own risk.

"And what of the Borg?"

"What is to understand?" Salatrel flung the words at him. "They are consumers. Single-minded accumulators of technology and living flesh. Ferengi without subtlety. Vulcans without remorse."

Tracius looked tired, as if all the years of living on the run with his former student, the child of lifelong friends, had caught up with him in the seven days since Kirk's return.

"You understand nothing about the Borg," he said. "If they were that direct, then they would not deal with us at all. They would be a school of *trasanara* come to strip our flesh from our bones. And when was the last time a single *trasanarit* emerged from the water and tried to negotiate with its victim?"

Salatrel felt the mood of her bridge change. This was not the Imperial Armada. There were no misconduct tribunals. A breach of the chain of command could be dealt with as quickly as the time it took to fire a disruptor. She could not allow Tracius's challenge to go unmet.

"If you have a point, make it quickly, old one," she warned, trying to undercut any authority Tracius might have among her bridge crew.

Tracius lapsed into the singsong cadence of a tutor. "Why do the Borg prepare a Speaker for each race they contact?"

Salatrel said nothing. She knew from experience that once in teaching mode her centurion would answer his own question.

"To make the assimilation process easier. More efficient. Less wasteful." He raised a weathered hand of sinew and bone to point an accusing finger at her. "And what could be more efficient than becoming our ally, then striking at our heart when our guard is down?"

Is that all? Salatrel thought, feeling relieved.

"Of course I expect the Borg to try and betray us," she said.

"Not *try!*" Tracius insisted. "Do you think they are standing still, waiting for the war with the Federation to conclude? Salatrel, they are betraying us already! This assimilation of the starbase, it's just *one* action that they've taken without informing us. How many others do you suppose there to be?"

"None," Salatrel said. "Vox told me—"

"Vox is one of *them!*"

Salatrel tightened her fists at her side. "Vox *told* me—"

"Your lover told you only what you wanted to hear!"

Without thought, Salatrel drew her disruptor and aimed it at Tracius.

But it was as if her former mentor didn't notice. As if he were sitting on the porch of her father's estate, debating the duty of the individual to the state versus the duty of the state to the individual.

"Can't you see what you've done?" Tracius argued. "The entire movement to overthrow the cowardly appeasers on Romulus has been set aside in order for you to pursue your revenge against one human. The Borg have never truly been committed to our joint venture—to attacking the Federation with such devastating force that the Empire would have no choice but to join in the war. If they had been, do you think Vox would have permitted you to subvert the entire plan?"

Salatrel's hand tightened on her weapon. "The Borg brought us the device which returned Kirk to life!"

"To distract you from everything else they do!"

Salatrel's teeth clenched. "The Borg want Picard dead. Kirk can do that."

"Are there no other assassins in our movement who could have done the same?"

"It would not be the same thing!"

"For history—of course it would be the same. Only for you would it be different."

Some of the bridge crew had stood up from their posts. Salatrel glanced at them. Saw their expressions. She had seen their like before, on the crew of this same Warbird when she had killed the admiral in command and joined the movement to restore pride and purpose to the Star Empire.

"Leave the bridge, Centurion."

But Tracius pointed to the screen, instead. "The Borg are playing their own game against you, moves within moves, intrigue on top of intrigue. And what better diversion to throw you than one you chose yourself?"

"Tracius . . . leave the bridge now."

The old centurion returned his hand to the edge of his cloak and stood proudly, like an orator in Dartha's court.

"You have abandoned the movement, Salatrel. You have become exactly what our Vulcan cousins accuse us of being—emotional, head-strong, swimming in blood, trapped in the past, and unable to grasp the future."

Salatrel closed her eyes. Heard the whine of her disruptor.

Felt the heat of its discharge as Tracius fell.

When she opened her eyes again, a single spike of green light flickered by her chair, then faded, and was gone.

She looked around her bridge again.

All crew members, even Tran, were back at their posts.

Order had been maintained.

She couldn't stop to think about the price.

Salatrel returned to her chair. "Is the *Challenger* in standard orbit?" she asked.

"Affirmative, Commander."

Salatrel hadn't heard that respectful tone in Tran's voice for months. Ironically, Tracius's death had restored discipline to her ship.

"Very good," she said. "Each time it crosses the terminator and comes into line of sight with the local sun, send a tetryon pulse to confirm the location of Kirk."

Tran did not look up from his board. She saw his hands hesitate on the controls. "Commander, they will be able to detect that pulse. We have no wormhole to hide it."

"They'll worry about it until they see it happens each time they come out of New Titan's shadow. Then they'll catalogue it for later study." She smiled tightly. "Know your enemy, Tran."

"Yes, Commander."

Salatrel settled back in her chair. She realized she still had her disruptor drawn and in her hand. The barrel of it was warm where it lay across her leg.

Her old friend had defied her, she told herself. He deserved to go quickly. As did anyone and anything else that would dare deny her her revenge.

And that included the collective.

THIRTY-FOUR

Everywhere he went on the *Challenger,* Riker faced the ghost of the *Enterprise.* There were subtle differences in the wall coverings between his old ship and this newest one. The computer systems had been updated to incorporate the latest neural gel pack circuitry, replacing the supposedly antiquated isolinear chips of the past. The bridge module was yet another generation beyond that to which the *Enterprise* had been upgraded, prior to its mission to Veridian. And the recreational facility called Ten-Forward on the *Enterprise* was here known as Shuttlebay Four, probably because most *Galaxy*-class ships had only three.

But sickbay was virtually unchanged. And as Riker entered, he half expected Beverly Crusher to step out of her office.

But instead he saw Julian Bashir at Kirk's bedside. And that scene once again viscerally reminded him that the past was gone and irretrievable.

Bashir looked up from a complex medical scanner as Riker approached.

Kirk was still in induced sleep. En route to New Titan, Bashir had confirmed that reducing the reanimated patient's metabolic rate slowed the nanites as well. Each hour Kirk remained unconscious was an hour longer he would live.

But he still had no more than a handful of days left.

"I'm due in a briefing in ten minutes," Riker said. In present circumstances, there was no time for pleasantries, and fortunately Bashir didn't take offense. "What couldn't you tell me over the comm system?"

Bashir frowned. "Under General Order Three, I can't tell you anything over the comm system. Enemy interception and all that."

Riker sighed. "I'm here. Tell me."

Bashir pointed to the scanner. Riker recognized some of the technical schematics on its display—Starfleet's reverse engineering of the Borg implants that had been recovered from Captain Picard.

"I've been going through the classified files you provided," Bashir explained. "They have far

315

more detail than the papers that were published in—"

"Doctor, I've got a missing starbase I have to deal with. The Borg could return at any second. And I just don't have the time for lengthy explanations."

Bashir gestured with open hands, indicating his helplessness. "Bottom line, Commander— the implant in the patient's brain *is* a Borg device."

Riker put out a hand to the scanner to steady himself. "Why would the Borg reanimate James T. Kirk?"

"I don't know if it *was* the Borg who did this."

Riker blinked at Bashir. "You said it was a Borg implant."

"But the nanites aren't. And the nanites are what restored him . . . physically, at least. Whatever brought his . . ." Bashir looked uncomfortable as he pronounced the Vulcan term. "Whatever brought his *katra* back to his body is beyond any science I know. And not within the realm of what either the implant or the nanites could have accomplished."

"Any idea where the nanites came from?" Riker asked.

Bashir looked weary. "It took some time, but I've been able to isolate and disassemble some of them. If anything, I'd say they're based on an original model designed by the Daystrom Institute, then modified for a different manufacturing process."

Riker forced a smile. "So someone stole a

design and figured out a different way to build them?"

"Essentially."

"Are they of Borg manufacture?"

"That's just it," Bashir said. "According to these classified files, all Borg computer circuits encountered up to now universally contain traces of a distinctive tridithalifane doping agent in their subprocessors. The implant has it, but the subprocessors in these nanites do not."

Riker felt a sudden wave of apprehension. Even if the Borg had assimilated the technology behind the nanites intact, the modifications arising from assimilation would have laced them with tridithalifane. The fact that the tridithalifane wasn't present could mean only one thing. "Do I understand what you're saying here? *Two* different technologies are present in Kirk?"

Bashir nodded glumly. Riker could see the doctor had reached the same conclusion he just had.

"Someone's working *with* the Borg."

"It would appear so," Bashir said.

Riker felt as if the *Challenger*'s artificial gravity was fluctuating. The only characteristic of the Borg which gave Starfleet any hope of defeating them was that at a certain base level, the collective was absolutely predictable.

That was why Picard had been chosen for his mission.

Starfleet already knew how the Borg reacted to Locutus. Everything Picard hoped to accomplish was predicated on the Borg reacting exactly the same way again.

But what if the Borg were no longer operating on their own? If, in some unfathomable fashion, the Borg had learned the behavior of cooperation, then a most unwelcome unpredictability had just been added to the equation.

"Doctor, with the additional information in the classified files, do you feel it is possible for you to remove the implant from Kirk?"

"What about Dr. Crusher?"

"Dr. Crusher is missing. We have no idea where she is, or when she might return."

Bashir looked at his patient.

But Riker didn't have time for thoughtful consideration.

"Dr. Bashir—if the Borg have allied themselves with another race, then all of Starfleet's efforts to develop adequate defenses are at risk. It is imperative that we release Kirk from his programming, so we will be able to interrogate him about who did this to him, and why." Riker held Bashir's gaze with an intent stare. "Now, I ask you again. Can *you* remove the implant?"

Bashir lowered his voice, as if afraid his patient could hear him.

"There is no question that I can remove it, Commander. I just don't know if the patient will survive the attempt."

Riker closed his eyes for a moment. There was no time to weigh pros and cons. No time to calculate the odds.

He looked at Bashir, daring the doctor to question him. "Do it."

"You're asking me to perform a procedure which might kill him."

318

"You may consider it an order, doctor."

Bashir hit the main control on the scanner, shutting it off.

"With respect, I feel compelled to file a formal protest with Starfleet Medical."

"By all means," Riker said. "*After* the procedure."

Riker saw the moment of decision in Bashir's eyes. He would do it, against his better judgment.

"I'll need an hour to familiarize myself with Dr. Crusher's notes and to have the necessary instruments replicated."

"The full facilities of the *Challenger* are yours."

"You'll pardon me if I'm not thrilled at the prospect."

Riker left without replying. It was surprising how much he liked the doctor. Lots of attitude, but he could follow orders.

He decided young Dr. Bashir would go far in Starfleet.

Provided Starfleet survived.

THIRTY-FIVE

Data had participated in many medical procedures in the past, though they had usually involved emergency care. The extraction of the Borg implant from James T. Kirk was one of the few times he had actually assisted in a surgical bay, and part of him looked forward to the experience. He found it brought anticipation of enjoyment.

However, another part of him recognized the seriousness of the procedure, because the outcome could have a direct bearing on the survival of the Federation. That brought anticipation of a different type.

Data decided that having emotions was indeed making it easier for him to understand why humans so often seemed confused. The experience of both wanting and dreading something at the same time was akin to contemplating the wave and particle nature of light. Unfortunately, there existed no quantum equations to describe the duality of conflicting emotions.

Yet, Data thought.

But then he wondered if that question had ever been addressed on Trilex. And whether the answer had somehow contributed to that society's destruction.

"Mr. Data," Bashir said, interrupting his musings, "if you would please inspect the primary branch of the implant's main core."

Data immediately concentrated on the task at hand.

Dr. Bashir had requested Data's assistance in this procedure because of the android's ability to remain in direct contact with the *Challenger*'s computers. Thus, all Starfleet's information about the Borg, as well as Beverly Crusher's analysis of the implants she had removed from Captain Picard, would be instantly available.

Data did regret that even though he had the medical knowledge to guide Bashir's surgery, he did not have the motor skills to perform it himself. After observing Bashir once, Data would, of course, always be able to re-create the identical operation, in the same way he could re-create great musical performances, note for note. But since human bodies were so varied, inside and out, the ability to exactly reproduce certain movements would not guarantee the next patient to receive the exact same operation would survive Data's ministrations. A successful surgeon's fluid skill depended on being able to adapt to constantly changing conditions—and bodies.

However, Data could still contribute to Bashir's success, and he began his work.

Before him, in the glow of the sterilization field surrounding the surgical table, Dr. Bashir had reflected a flap of Kirk's scalp to expose the occipital bone at the base of the skull. A small, rectangular opening, two centimeters by three centimeters, now punctured the skull. The excised bone fragment was floating in a nutrient bath, to be replaced at the procedure's end.

Within the opening, the dull yellow dura mater had been peeled back to expose the occipital gyrus of the cerebrum, sitting atop the cerebellum. A computer display screen was suspended from the ceiling, over the patient's head. On it was displayed an enlarged, three-dimensional sensor model of the skull's interior, in which the main branch of the Borg implant could be seen at the boundary between the two components of the brain.

Bashir had threaded eight molecular wires through the brain tissue and made contact with

321

the implant at eight key points. The wires would draw off any power-discharge the implant might make in response to being disassembled.

Data verified that the placement of the molecular wires matched that described by Dr. Crusher as those least likely to cause harm to the patient. "The implant's power source has been correctly isolated," Data said.

"Thank you," Bashir replied. He rubbed the back of his gloved hand against the red cap he wore, then held the small cylinder of a number two tractor scalpel near the exposed brain tissue. With deft movements of his fingers, he began to use the miniature force field projected by the scalpel to gently ease apart a path through the brain tissue along the wires.

Data and Bashir both watched the progress of the pathway on the sensor screen. Neurons were being disconnected with each pulse of the scalpel. But the disruption was so minor, no permanent damage would result. At least, if the patient survived.

As Bashir continued with the procedure, Data multitasked his observations among the display screen, Kirk's skull, and Dr. Bashir, while constantly reviewing Crusher's notes, confirming each step Bashir took, and suggesting refinements when Bashir requested.

Data was constantly impressed by Bashir's calm and proficiency. However, one hour into the procedure, he began to wonder when the young human would realize he was facing a hopeless task.

An hour and a half into the procedure, Data

took it upon himself to inform the doctor of his conclusions.

"Dr. Bashir, it is clear by now that what you are attempting to do is hopeless."

Bashir responded by glaring at him. "What is the condition of the implant?" he demanded.

"Eighty percent of the implant has been separated from the brain tissue," Data confirmed. "Bleeding is minimal. The patient's vitals are stable."

"Then that means only twenty percent to go," Bashir said.

Data was puzzled by the challenge in the doctor's voice. Data was not questioning his expertise, only commenting on the inescapable facts.

"Dr. Bashir, the remaining twenty percent of the implant cannot be removed by the procedures Dr. Crusher used on Captain Picard. Please recall that many of the Borg implants in the captain were connected to secondary nerves located outside of the brain. In those instances, Dr. Crusher was able to sever and remove nerve sections for later replacement and regrowth. That is not possible with the brain. That is, if you are hoping to retain the integrity of the personality currently inhabiting it."

"Is there anything you can tell me in ten words or less?" Bashir snapped.

"If you continue using the tractor scalpel on the remaining sections of the implant, you will also cause irreparable harm to the patient's cerebellum. You have reached the point where the implant's fractal tendrils are too tightly entwined to remove from either the blood supply or the brain matter itself."

"That wasn't ten words or less."

Data was prepared to go on for an hour, citing all the pertinent passages in Dr. Crusher's notes. But given Bashir's mood, he simply said: "If you continue, Kirk will be dead in twenty minutes. Ten words exactly." Data wondered if he had been understood correctly. "Except for those words at the end. And these words."

"That will be enough, Mr. Data."

Bashir looked down at the exposed brain of his patient. Data used a sterile pad to draw away the blood that collected in it.

"I've gone too far," Bashir said. Data sensed Bashir wasn't directing his words to anyone. He was thinking aloud. "A partially functioning implant will completely paralyze his brain-wave activity. He'll never wake up."

"My cursory examination of the *Challenger*'s medical library suggests that other techniques are available," Data volunteered.

Bashir looked up at him with hope. "Well . . .?"

Data felt contrite. "Unfortunately, they would require extensive study and experimentation before they could be applied in this case."

Data saw Bashir's shoulders sag beneath his surgical gown. "Then I have no choice, do I?"

"You could place the patient in stasis," Data suggested.

"Check the literature," Bashir said with a sigh. "Stasis won't slow down the type of nanite he's filled with."

Data gazed down at the bleeding opening into

the patient's body. He was suddenly struck by the terrible certainty that he was going to witness a human being die. And there was nothing he could do about it.

He looked at Bashir, wondering if the doctor had reached the same realization.

But Bashir kept his eyes on the patient. He picked up a more powerful tractor scalpel.

Data supposed that was the difference between them.

Bashir still thought there was something he could do.

Data did not look forward to the next twenty minutes.

After drawing a deep breath, Bashir held the tractor scalpel close to the opening. Data saw the gentle pressure he used to activate the force field. Despite the urgency the doctor felt, he was still proceeding methodically.

Until the *Challenger*'s collision alarm sounded.

Data's subsystems accelerated to critical speed as he anticipated a spray of blood erupting from the opening. No human he knew could have suppressed a reflexive response to the sirens that warbled throughout the ship, and Data fully expected the scalpel force field to have torn a hole through the patient's brain. Death wouldn't take twenty minutes. It would take twenty seconds.

But against all of Data's expectations, the opening did not disappear in a spray of blood.

Data looked across at Bashir. The doctor's eyes were clenched shut.

Data felt astonishment.

The doctor had actually held his hand steady. His skill and self-awareness had been that great.

"Bashir to bridge," the doctor growled, barely containing his fury. "What the *hell* was that?!"

"Sorry, doctor," Riker's voice replied from the overhead speakers. "We just had a ship drop out of warp nine point nine five, two kilometers off our bow. The computer responded on automatic."

Bashir slowly drew his hand away from the patient's head. "I don't care what it was," he said in low and angry tones. "If you don't want me to decapitate my patient, shut off all alarm systems to sickbay *now!*"

In the silence that followed, Data couldn't help himself. He was designed to acquire knowledge. "Commander Riker, what kind of vessel can travel at that speed? Are we being attacked by the Borg?"

But the tension of battle wasn't detectable in Riker's voice. "It's an experimental Starfleet transport, Data. Two big warp nacelles and not much else. From Earth."

Bashir gazed up in exasperation at the sickbay ceiling and the speakers there. "Does any of this have a point, Commander?"

From his tone of voice, Data could almost picture Riker smiling. "It seems you were premature in concluding there was only one doctor in Starfleet who could deal with Kirk's neural implant."

Data saw the immense confusion on Bashir's face.

"That wasn't *my* conclusion, Commander.

Starfleet Medical said Beverly Crusher was the only physician on active duty with experience in—"

Bashir and Data both turned to look into the center of sickbay as they heard a transporter harmonic begin.

"We're beaming a consulting physician directly to sickbay, doctor. He's been fully briefed. And should be able to help."

Data watched as the transporter cloud took on the shape of a squat pyramid. For a moment, he thought a Medusan might have been beamed on board, though that ephemeral race was hardly known for its physical skills.

But then he saw the cloud resolve into a humanoid sitting in a mobility chair.

Data felt his emotion chip accelerate as he realized he recognized the figure.

The mobility chair spun around on its treads and then bounced slightly as it headed for the surgical table, motor humming.

The figure it carried was thin and stooped, his hair a dull gray, his admiral's uniform so loose it appeared to be two sizes too large. Deep creases crosshatched his face, except where a sparse white beard mottled his cheeks and chin.

But there was an intelligence and a quickness in his eyes that belied the age that hung around him like a cloud. Whatever shape his body was in, a much younger person dwelt within it.

"Admiral McCoy?" Data asked.

"*Leonard H. McCoy?*" Bashir croaked.

The admiral ignored Data to squint in disdain

at the young doctor. "Who were you expecting? Dancing girls?"

Data was surprised to see Bashir actually tremble and blush. The young doctor had held his scalpel steady when the collision alarm had sounded, but this visitation by the greatest doctor to have served Starfleet had apparently triggered a loss of control.

Data saw the admiral look over at him. "You I know," McCoy said. His voice was low and hoarse. "Bet you're not surprised, are you?"

"Actually, I am, sir."

McCoy narrowed his eyes. "Thought you were an android."

"I now have an emotion chip, sir."

McCoy rolled his eyes. "What they won't build these days. Mind you, I could've put one of those chips to good use in an old friend way back when. . . ." McCoy turned his attention back to Bashir. "Correct me if I'm mistaken, doctor, but don't you have a patient on that table?"

Bashir nodded, quickly checking Kirk's vital signs on the display screen.

McCoy rolled up beside Bashir at the head of the surgical table. "Well, pull back the sheet. Let me see."

Bashir understood what McCoy meant. He lifted the sheet covering Kirk's face.

Instantly McCoy's eyes filled with tears. Data saw his jaw wobble. "Ah, Jim," he sighed, almost inaudibly. "Scotty was right after all."

Then McCoy abruptly sat up straight in his chair, all sign of emotion dropping from his face. He looked up at Bashir.

"Julian Bashir?"

Bashir nodded.

"You're the one who's been pestering Starfleet Medical for all the old records on Jim Kirk?"

"Yes, sir."

"Anyone think of calling his personal physician?"

Bashir's eyes were wide. "Uh, sir, to be honest . . . we thought . . . well, I thought you were dead. . . ."

"Well, I'm not!" McCoy barked. He thumped his chest. "One hundred and forty-four next month. On my third heart, if you can believe it. Grow a new set of lungs every year. And I've got ten new meters of cloned intestines writhing in my guts. And you know why?"

Bashir shook his head.

"Neither do I, son." He slapped the arms of his mobility chair. Then his hand went to a small box at his waist. Data heard microservos whine, and the ancient admiral rose easily from his chair and stepped forward with the characteristic deliberate motion of someone wearing an exoskeleton.

McCoy braced himself on the edge of the surgical table, studying the display screen. "Neural implant. Fractal tendril growth. You've isolated the power supply, but that's not enough. Too entwined in the vascular supply, artificial dendrite entanglement—"

"Artificial dendrites? Is that what it is?" Bashir asked excitedly.

"I've seen it before," McCoy said. "Sigma Draconis VI. Or was it VII? Anyway, had to disconnect a complete cerebellum by pass and

329

then *re*connect an entire brain. Had some help, mind you. But the details aren't important. Don't remember them anyway. This new Borg rubbish, it's just a variation. Lot simpler, too."

Bashir held out his scalpel.

McCoy looked at him and, from somewhere in those craggy features, found a warm smile.

"Why, thank you, son. But those days are long gone." He held up his hands. Once they had worked miracles, Data knew, but now they were skeletal and shaking.

McCoy tapped one thin finger against his temple. "But I've still got it up here. You listen to what I tell you, and we're going to do just fine."

Data could see the wonder in Bashir's eyes. But the young doctor stared at McCoy just a moment too long.

"Well . . .," the admiral said with annoyance, "get a move on. You're a doctor, not a Horta."

Bashir nodded and brought his tractor scalpel back to Kirk's skull.

But McCoy laid a gentle hand on the young doctor's arm. "Tell you what, son. First you want to trade that scalpel in for a number eight. We're going to forget about Jim's gray matter for a bit, concentrate on shunting some of his arteries, then we're going to use a laser . . . an honest-to-God laser beam like we were some kind of witch doctors. And once we get in there, we're going to section a path on the other side of the implant."

As McCoy began explaining the techniques they would use, Data stepped back from the surgical table, knowing that his assistance was no longer required. He was content to watch the effortless blending of raw talent and seasoned experience that unfolded before him.

Riker and Deanna Troi arrived a few minutes after the doctors began working together. La Forge and Worf followed shortly after. Together they watched as the hands of Starfleet's youngest generation, guided by the wisdom of Starfleet's oldest, worked a new miracle that neither could have performed without the other.

As the final section of the implant was removed, and Bashir quickly closed the wound, pronouncing the procedure a success, Data watched as a teardrop escaped McCoy's glittering eyes.

A teardrop of happiness, Data knew.

And he wondered who, in eighty years, might cry for him.

THIRTY-SIX

Kirk heard the metallic shriek of the bridge hit the rocks of Veridian III, and he opened his eyes.

He smelled dust. Felt the heat of the Veridian sun. Heard the twisted struts creak as they settled.

As something groaned and moved within them.

Kirk stepped closer. His boots crunched on small rocks and gravel, each sound crisp and pure. He peered into the tangle of twisted metal. There was someone trapped inside.

Oh, yes, Kirk thought, *I'm there.*

The duality of his existence in this place did not trouble him. It seemed the way things should be.

The desert wind picked up, and he felt it like the hot breath of a pursuing predator.

"It is getting closer," a voice told him, confirming what he felt.

Kirk turned away from the sight of himself feebly struggling in the wreckage of the bridge.

Someone else was approaching, the sun behind him.

Kirk held his hand up to protect his eyes from the glare of the light. Dimly he realized that the sun was in a different part of the sky and that he had no idea what was shining so brightly behind this . . .

. . . Vulcan?

Kirk recognized the jewels and script on the robes.

The Vulcan raised his hand, exposing his palm, separating his fingers in a gesture of both greeting and farewell. Duality again.

From somewhere on top of the rocks towering over him, something exploded. A band of energy rippled through the sky, sparking and crackling. And then it was gone.

But the Vulcan remained.

"Spock?" Kirk asked.

"He is not among us," the Vulcan explained. Then he stepped closer.

Kirk smiled as he recognized him.

"Ambassador Sarek!"

Spock's father inclined his head, as if he had not heard his name spoken for a long time.

Kirk felt he had to make some apology for the condition he was in. If not for himself, then for his other self, lying in the wreckage.

Dying, Kirk thought.

"I'm afraid things are . . . a bit of a mess," Kirk said.

The ambassador studied him, as if he were about to speak. To impart great wisdom. He did. "There is no need to concern yourself, Captain."

Kirk knew, then. The reason that both he and Sarek must meet like this. He heard scrabbling on the rocks. Someone else was climbing down. Sarek waited, the breeze stirring his robes.

"You're dead and I'm dying, aren't I?" Kirk asked.

Sarek looked up at the sky, staring at something Kirk couldn't see. "Have you had this dream before?"

Kirk looked down at his hands. Flexed them. Watched the muscles and sinews move beneath his skin. Everything was in exquisite focus. Each movement perfect. Far too real. "*Is* this a dream?"

Sarek turned back to him. "That is not the question. Logically, you should ask yourself: Is this *the* dream?"

"You mean, the dream where I die."

"You have had it all your life, have you not?"

"When we melded minds," Kirk said with sudden understanding. "When you came to me so long ago, looking for your son. . . . You saw my dreams?"

"It is the way of things."

"Is that why you're here now?"

"What do you think?"

Kirk smiled. "Ah, then this *is* my dream. And I'm the one who makes the rules."

Sarek looked at Kirk with a skeptical expression that only a Vulcan could make. "I do not believe rules are what you are noted for."

Kirk stepped aside as Picard rushed past him, hurrying to the other Kirk, beneath the wreckage.

"He thinks I'm dying. The other captain of the *Enterprise.*"

"I have melded minds with him as well."

Kirk was intrigued. "Is that what brought you here? Because there's something we've all shared?"

"Or will share," Sarek replied.

Kirk was growing impatient with this dream. "I don't like riddles."

"There are none here."

Kirk watched as Picard lowered his head in sorrow.

"That's wrong, isn't it? Picard thinking I've died. Because . . ." Kirk held out his hand, struggling to complete his thought, trying to remember something he knew he should know. "I didn't die here."

Sarek folded his robes closer to him. Kirk was surprised by how frail the elder Vulcan suddenly seemed.

"Ask yourself this question, Captain. You have always known how you will die." Sarek's eyes seemed to burn into him like phasers. "Is this *the* dream?"

Kirk didn't even have to think about the answer. "No. You know that."

Sarek nodded once. "As do you."

Then a light shone out from behind the Vulcan once again. He turned toward it, robe fluttering, as if the light blew against him like wind.

"Sarek, wait!"

The Vulcan hesitated.

"If not here . . . then where? When?"

To Kirk, it seemed as if Sarek's eyes were as bright as the light which engulfed them both.

"You know, Captain. You have always known."

"Then the dream I've always had is real?"

Sarek smiled then, the first time Kirk had ever seen his face express anything other than a stern stoicism.

"You taught my son a song once, Captain." The years melted from Sarek. He was young, strong, and his smile was dazzling. "Life is but a dream. . . ."

Kirk held his hand up to block the brilliance that came for Sarek. All of Veridian dissolved around him. His voice, their voices, became something else, as they became something else. What they had always been.

Live long and prosper, Captain. . . .

But for how long . . . ?

Look to the stars, James T. Kirk . . . second on the right . . . straight on till morning. . . .

Kirk squinted at the blinding light that shone past his hand and clenched eyes. He tried to turn his head but felt a sudden pain, as if someone had punched a hole clear through it.

"Turn it off," he said. His throat hurt. He coughed.

The light vanished. He watched the silhouette of a lamp on the end of a folded armature move away.

There was someone leaning over him.

"Sarek . . . ?"

"Seventy-eight damn years floating around in God knows where. Then you come back from the dead, and the first thing you do is insult me."

Kirk's eyes opened wide.

"Bones? *Bones!*"

He ignored the pain and sat up, grabbing his friend's arm.

But it felt so thin and . . .

Kirk saw McCoy's face.

"What happened? You look . . . so old."

McCoy grimaced. "Good to see you, too, Captain."

Kirk looked around. He was in some kind of sickbay. Different from what he was used to. Larger area. Smaller equipment.

There were other people by his diagnostic bed. He recognized them.

And why not? He had tried to kill some of them.

Geordi La Forge. The android, Data. Worf, the Klingon who was no longer an enemy. A woman he didn't recognize, with solid black pupils. And . . .

Kirk stared at the tall man with the dark beard. "Commander Will Riker?"

Riker stepped forward. Held out his hand.

Kirk shook it.

"Captain Kirk. It is a pleasure, sir."

Kirk took a breath, hardly knowing where to begin. "My first impression is that I've been dreaming. But . . . I haven't been, have I?"

Riker smiled. "No, sir."

"This *is* the twenty-fourth century?"

Riker nodded. "Then you do remember what happened on Veridian?"

Kirk rubbed the back of his head. Felt something covering his skin there. It was where the pain came from. "Is that where I was? Someone was going to launch a missile, I recall. We stopped him."

"Yes, sir. You and Captain Picard."

Kirk stiffened as he heard that name.

"Are you all right, Captain?"

McCoy clanked around by Kirk. Kirk didn't know what made the noise. It sounded as if McCoy had something mechanical strapped to his legs, beneath his clothes.

"Of course, he's all right," McCoy muttered. "He's just had his head opened up and his brain cut into. Why wouldn't he be all right? It's not as if he's ever used it."

Kirk looked at McCoy with narrowed eyes. "Bones . . . how old *are* you?"

"Don't start with me. I'm still your doctor."

"Captain Kirk," Riker began. "I'm going to leave you with Admiral McCoy to get you caught up on . . . present conditions. But, I have to know, sir. Do you remember what happened to you *after* you assisted Captain Picard on Veridian?"

Kirk felt every muscle in his body tense at the

second mention of that name. And he suddenly knew what he had to do. "I remember falling," he said. "Someone spoke to me . . . and then I woke up here."

Riker nodded glumly. "I see. Well, if anything comes back to you, it's of critical importance for us to know how you came to be here."

"Believe me, Commander. I've got some questions I'd like answered, myself." He turned to McCoy. Stared at him in disbelief. "*Admiral McCoy?*"

McCoy waved a frail hand. "It's a long story."

Kirk didn't smile. "How about . . . Spock?"

McCoy sighed. "Let's start at the beginning." He leaned forward. "With the wake Scotty threw for you."

"A wake?"

McCoy grinned. "You should have been there, Jim. We had ourselves a time."

Kirk glanced at Riker and shrugged. Then he settled back in his diagnostic bed and let his history lesson begin.

Once the sickbay doors had closed behind them, Riker stopped in the corridor. He had to know.

"You heard what he said," he told Deanna. "He remembered Veridian, then waking up here. And nothing in between."

"Yet he knew your name, Commander," Data said.

"He's very confused," Deanna offered. "His feelings are in great turmoil. Especially in his reaction to seeing Admiral McCoy. Kirk remembers him as a much younger man."

"But is he lying about not remembering anything?" Riker asked.

"Yes," Deanna said. "I believe so."

"You believe so. But you're not sure?"

"Will, he's suddenly jumped almost eighty years into his future. We should expect his feelings to be erratic."

"Erratic. In what way?"

Deanna looked embarrassed. "Both times when you mentioned Captain Picard's name . . . I felt such . . . hatred coming from Kirk."

Riker polled Data, La Forge, and Worf to see if they had any similar observations to offer. "Is it possible Kirk blames Picard for his death on Veridian?"

"It wasn't a focused impression, Will." Deanna thought for a moment. "It was similar to the impressions I get from Bajorans when they think about the Cardassian occupation of their world. How they feel when they think about the atrocities the Cardassians committed. That was Kirk's reaction to Captain Picard."

"There's no reason why Kirk should feel that way."

"Unless," Deanna said, "he is still under the influence of whatever programming he was subjected to."

"Even with the Borg implant removed?"

Deanna nodded.

Riker turned to Worf. "Mr. Worf, I want Kirk under constant surveillance. But don't let him know. He's not familiar with our techniques. If he doesn't know he's being observed, maybe he'll slip up."

"Sir," Worf said, "since my encounter with Kirk on Qo'noS, I have studied his historical record quite extensively. He does not seem the type of individual to 'slip up.'"

"We had better hope someone does," Riker said. "Because if we don't find out who's working with the Borg soon, we're all going to be programmed. Just like Kirk."

The rest of his crewmates remained silent as Riker looked back at the doors to sickbay.

The man behind that door had once been one of Starfleet's greatest heroes.

Now he might be its greatest enemy.

And to save the Federation, Riker knew that if the moment came, he could and would deliver Kirk to his final death, without a moment's hesitation.

He saw Deanna sense those dark thoughts within him and turn away.

Riker felt the sting of isolation.

He wondered how Kirk felt.

THIRTY-SEVEN

In an instant, blazing like a sudden sun, the *Challenger* moved from the shadow of New Titan, into the light.

A tetryon pulse accompanied the moment of

transition, as it had for every orbit the great ship had made of this planet.

In the *Challenger*'s astrophysics and astronomy labs, the anomalous radiation spike was noted, commented upon, but set aside in deference to other, more pressing concerns. Specifically, the analysis of the transwarp conduit opening which had been recorded by the *Monitor*'s sensors.

Thus the tetryon pulse came and a small part of it returned to its source, after interacting with and reflecting from the tridithalifane in what was left of Kirk's implant.

On the bridge of the *Tomed*, cloaked one hundred thousand kilometers from New Titan and the *Challenger* and her companion ship, Tran read the sensor return on the tetryon pulse he had sent. It wasn't good news.

"Commander," he said, not daring to look up. "The implant has been removed from Kirk." He prepared to die, anticipating the first shock of the disruptor beam that would disassemble him.

Instead, he became aware of Salatrel standing behind him, studying his screens over his shoulder.

"I was told that would be impossible," she said.

There was a flat tone in her voice. It had been there since she had killed her centurion. To Tran, it reminded him of Vox.

"Do you want me to send a finer pulse, Commander?"

"Would it be detected?"

"I believe so," Tran said.

"And if it were detected, how long before the Starfleet vessels would suspect that a cloaked ship was nearby?"

Tran knew there was no answer he could give which would please her.

"Starfleet has more experience with cloaking devices than we suspected, Commander. I believe they would detect our presence within minutes."

Salatrel walked forward until she was a shadow against the main viewscreen. She held her hands behind her back. Tran saw she still carried her disruptor. She had not reholstered it since she had fired it last.

"I was told the implant would be impossible to remove," she repeated. Speaking to herself, Tran knew. "I was told that even if it malfunctioned, Kirk's programming would hold." Salatrel turned to face Tran and the rest of her bridge crew. "It appears I was lied to, does it not?"

No one said anything.

"There is only one chance we have to succeed," Salatrel said. She paced back and forth in front of the image of the *Challenger* and the smaller, dark ship at its side. "And that is for Kirk to kill Picard. Only then can honor be restored to my family. Does anyone disagree?"

No one did. No one even breathed.

"Picard must die. The Borg and Federation must destroy themselves. And then the wings of the Romulan Empire will embrace all the stars of all the galaxy."

Salatrel turned to face the *Challenger*.

"Take us in, Subcommander. Full impulse. Flood both ships with high-resolution sensors, then take an evasive course behind the sun." She glanced back over her shoulder. "They'll look for us. But they won't find us."

Tran braced himself for what he must do. "With respect, Commander. What shall I set the sensors for? What, exactly, are we looking for?"

"I want to know Kirk's position and location. Other than that, I want to know if any other Borg are on that ship."

"Borg?" Tran said. "On a Federation vessel?"

"The Borg have lied to us, Subcommander, by claiming to be our allies. What if they've played the same game with the Federation? What if another Speaker is there on that ship, helping to prepare Starfleet for a sneak attack on our Empire?"

Tran was appalled by the possibility. By working with the Borg, the Romulan dissidents had revealed almost all the military secrets of the Star Empire to the collective. If the Borg did decide to move against the Empire with the combined might of the Federation. . . . "We would have no defense," Tran said. "We would have . . . nothing."

"Except honor," Salatrel replied. "Tracius and I agreed on that lesson, at least. Honor is the one possession which no enemy can take from you, unless you allow it to be taken." Her eyes grew dark. "And I will not allow mine to be taken. No matter what the price."

Tran thought over his commander's words.

Perhaps she was right.

Even if all the dreams of the dissidents were lost, even if the appeasers in power had led the

343

Empire to its doom, at least Tran could still claim an honorable death.

Or, he thought pragmatically, he could assassinate Salatrel and take command of the *Tomed* himself.

He set a flyby course to intercept the *Challenger.* The war against the Federation wasn't scheduled to begin for another two days.

There was still time to make a decision.

Tran was certain it would be the right one.

His honor depended upon it.

THIRTY-EIGHT

Kirk stood in front of a mirror in an alcove of sickbay, examining himself in his uniform—white sweater, burgundy jacket, black trousers with their pinstripe. He turned around once, then looked back in the mirror. After a moment, he saw his reflection turn, on a three-second delay. The uniform was a perfect fit. All that was missing was his Starfleet insignia.

He looked again at the tiny badge he had been given instead to pin onto his jacket—the Starfleet delta set on an angled rectangle. Supposedly, it functioned as a communicator, as well as allowing the ship's computer to track his every move. Kirk decided he missed the old handheld model. Getting set in his ways, he supposed.

He slipped out of the patient alcove and found McCoy back in his mobility chair, nodding off

344

in front of a desktop computer terminal. The chair was a considerable improvement over the one Chris Pike had been confined to. But McCoy was in better shape than Pike had been. And the exoskeleton support frame he wore beneath his clothes gave him the ability to move around as if he were still under his own power.

The old doctor jerked awake as Kirk came near. It was still a shock for Kirk to see his friend in such frail condition. But then, his own condition wasn't much better. Before the selective pain-killers Dr. Bashir had given him, the pains in his joints from the nanites had been almost unbearable.

"Bones . . . you say they . . . 'replicated' this uniform?"

McCoy blinked at him, as he were still unused to seeing Kirk. "Fancy new name for synthesizers, far as I can tell."

Kirk gently probed the incision on the back of his head. McCoy said that with the latest advancements in medical science, the bone and skin would heal scarfree in less than five days.

But Kirk didn't have five days.

"You give any more thought to what I said?" McCoy asked.

"You think they'd go for it?"

McCoy smiled. "Don't ask me how it happened, but you're a hero to these people. Hell, all of us fossils from the *Enterprise* are."

Kirk shrugged. "We were just doing our jobs."

"The point is, Jim, these people would do anything in their power if they thought it would help you."

Kirk thought it over. McCoy wanted him to take a modified shuttle, switch off all the artificial gravity and inertial dampening, then accelerate up to near light-speed and let relativity take its course. Einsteinian time dilation wasn't a factor in faster-than-light warp travel, but it still existed at slower-than-light velocities. And McCoy believed that if Kirk went off on a one-week flight, in the three years that would pass during his absence, Starfleet Medical might have developed a way of removing the nanites from his body.

"The point is, Bones, you have no guarantee I'll even live a week with these nanites inside me."

"It's worth taking the risk, isn't it?"

Kirk shrugged. "There has to be an end to it sometime, Bones."

"I didn't get to be one hundred and forty-four with a defeatist attitude like that."

"What's the record?" Kirk asked.

McCoy grinned. "You're looking at it. *And* I've got my one hundred-and-fiftieth birthday party all planned."

Kirk looked around the sickbay again. So much to digest. Almost eighty years of history had passed him by. This ship, what he could see of it, looked like it would put both his own *Enterprises* to shame. And the new friends, the new enemies.

Especially the Borg.

Though he couldn't remember much of what McCoy had told him about the Borg. Almost as if he wasn't supposed to remember . . .

"What happened to everyone, Bones? You still get together for reunions. Curse the old captain?"

McCoy managed to smile and look sad at the same time. "Sit down, Jim," he said.

Kirk sat on the edge of the table as McCoy once again slipped into his memories.

And what memories they were.

Admiral Pavel Chekov, commander in chief of Starfleet. The books he had written after his retirement, detailing his adventures on the *Enterprise*, the *Potemkin*, and the *Cydonia*, had made household names of all his crewmates.

Hikaru Sulu, president of the Federation Council for an unprecedented three terms. Kirk had known his helmsman had always had a fondness for politics, and it pleased him to think of Sulu continuing his work, steering the ship of state.

And Dr. Uhura, two-time winner of the Nobel and Zee-Magnees Peace Prize. After her retirement, she had devoted herself to recruiting the best and the brightest for the Academy, tirelessly traveling the worlds of the Federation to make sure the promise of the stars and the challenge of humanity's adventure would be available to all.

And Scotty, who had been trapped in a machine—which seemed all too fitting a fate for him—so that he, too, had survived to meet this next generation of bold explorers and was somewhere out among the stars, still doing what he loved. Flying between the stars, too busy to ever think of actually retiring as he had so often threatened.

Then there were Rand and Chapel, Kyle, M'Benga, Carol Marcus, and Ruth. On his

347

journey here, McCoy had even called up the old computer records of Kirk's nephews, his admirals, his lost loves, friends, distant relations.

All passed before Kirk like the tail of a comet, bright and sparkling one moment, a memory the next.

"It is quite a lot to take in in one sitting," McCoy said.

"All those lives," Kirk said. "I was part of them . . . but sometimes it feels like I didn't know them at all."

"You won't get an argument from me."

Kirk smiled. "That's a first." Then he looked at McCoy to let the doctor know he couldn't avoid what he had been trying to avoid since the moment Kirk awoke here.

"Spock," Kirk said.

"Still alive and kicking," McCoy answered. "And . . . could be he's part of the problem that's got everyone so worked up."

"I'm listening," Kirk said.

But before McCoy could say anything more, red alert sounded, and Riker's voice reverberated from the speakers ordering all crew to battle stations.

THIRTY-NINE

Riker sat beside Captain Simm on the bridge of the *Challenger*. Every sensor display was lit up, flashing its warnings.

Simm sat with steepled hands. He was a black Vulcan from his world's Regar district. The severe features of his face remained placid amidst the noise and appearance of confusion. Nothing surprised him. But whether that was because he was a Vulcan, or because he had spent twenty years as a starship captain, no one could be certain.

"Report," Simm said. And though his voice was neither raised nor strained, it cut through the cacophony of alerts and warning chimes as if he had spoken in the ear of every member of the bridge crew. And some of those crew members were very familiar to Riker. He had taken great pleasure in reassembling them to share his duty on the *Challenger*.

Worf's voice thundered from his security station at the rear of the bridge. "We have been subjected to a full sensorsweep, Captain."

Data reported from his ops board. "I am recording an anomalous tachyon surge, consistent with a cloaking device."

"Is it from the *Monitor?*" Simm asked calmly.

"Negative, sir," Data replied.

Simm turned to Riker. "Your analysis, Commander."

"Flyby of a cloaked vessel, sir."

"That much is obvious," the Vulcan said. "What was its purpose?"

"It was . . . looking for something," Riker guessed.

"And that would be . . . ?"

Riker hated the Socratic method. "I have no idea, sir."

Simm stood up, acknowledging that the lesson was over. "Three possibilities, Commander. In arriving at them, we must assume that we have been under passive observation for a given period of time, since the probability that a cloaked ship encountered us and decided to scan us at the same instant is remote." Simm folded his hands behind his back. "We must also assume that the decision by the commander of the cloaked ship to scan us was triggered by a precipitating action, and not a random event." Simm glanced back at Riker. "A precipitating action implies that conditions have changed from those which did not require a scan, to those which did. What conditions have changed upon this vessel in the past thirty minutes?"

Riker thought frantically. The Vulcan captain was making him feel like a first-year Academy student. He had no answer.

"James T. Kirk became conscious."

Riker wasn't convinced. "How could anyone know that, sir?"

"Precisely," Simm said. "Hence, in increasing order of probability, we have been under observation by a cloaked ship operating with a telepathic crew. *Or* we have a spy on board, who has reported on Kirk's condition to the cloaked ship. *Or* the cloaked ship's actions were not triggered by the act of Kirk becoming conscious, but by another, related act."

Now Riker understood. "The removal of the implant."

"Very good, Commander." Simm looked up at Worf. "Mr. Worf, earlier there were reports

350

of tetryon pulses accompanying our emergence from the terminator. Was a pulse recorded on our most recent orbit?"

Worf accessed his security displays. "Yes, sir."

Simm wheeled around to face Data. "Mr. Data, Kirk's implant was of Borg manufacture. Therefore, it contained traces of tridithalifane. Will tridithalifane reflect a properly tuned tetryon beam?"

Data angled his head as he accessed the *Challenger*'s main computers. "Yes, sir. It appears possible."

Simm turned back to Riker and raised a finger. "Hence, logic dictates we have been under surveillance by a cloaked ship that knows Kirk is aboard, knows Kirk has an implant of Borg manufacture, and knows that the implant has been removed. That ship is our enemy. Its commander has information that is valuable to the Federation. Hence . . . Commander?"

Riker could feel himself getting caught up in the intellectual game Simm had made out of the encounter. "Hence, we should try to capture that vessel."

"But before we capture it, we must find it." Simm angled an eyebrow as he studied Riker. "As commander of the cloaked vessel, where would you go after scanning us?"

"If I had seen the *Monitor* decloak, I would assume the *Challenger* had the capabilities of detecting the tachyon surge common to cloaking devices. I would set a course at maximum warp leading out of the system, then angle back and come in from another direction on impulse."

351

"You're forgetting the enemy has been influenced by the Borg. That maneuver would be a waste of resources." Simm turned back to the viewscreen. "The enemy is hiding on the other side of the sun, out of sensor range. Mr. Worf, hail the *Monitor*."

Riker and Worf exchanged a look of grudging appreciation for Simm's analysis as the captain of the *Challenger* ordered Lewinski to cloak the *Monitor*, leave the system, then double back to the other side of the sun.

If possible, he was to identify the ship which Simm had concluded was lying in wait there, then return. If necessary, he was to engage it.

"Any idea what kind of ship it is?" Lewinski asked.

"A Romulan Warbird, *D'deridex* class or better." Simm glanced back at Riker. "Its commander knew we would detect the scan, but proceeded anyway. Romulan cloaking devices are the best, hence the ship is Romulan. And only the commander of a *D'deridex* Warbird would feel confident enough to risk exposing his ship to an encounter with the *Challenger*."

Riker remained sitting in his place on the command bench—unlike the *Enterprise*, the *Challenger* did not have individual seats for its senior bridge officers. With Simm as her captain, he wondered, why had Starfleet even bothered to install computers on the ship?

Lewinski signed off and the port scanners showed the peculiar sight of the *Monitor* rippling like liquid, then vanishing from view.

"*Monitor* away," Data reported.

Simm sat back in the center section of the command bench. "I believe you should now check on the condition of Kirk. We cannot rule out the possibility of two-way communication with the cloaked vessel."

Riker stood up. The captain was correct. But the captain also read the hesitation in him.

"You have a question, Commander?"

"Sir, we came here to bring Kirk close to Dr. Crusher, if Dr. Crusher had returned in time to help him. But now, with the implant removed, it might be better to take Kirk back to Starbase 324 for study."

Simm looked amused, in his limited Vulcan way. "Are you asking me, or ordering me, Commander?"

Riker remained silent.

"Under General Order Three," Simm continued, "Shelby's orders do give you authority over this ship in regard to any action involving the Borg."

"It is a suggestion, sir. We are not yet in contact with the Borg."

Another alarm chimed on the bridge. Riker and Simm both looked up at Worf.

"Sir," the Klingon announced, "a transwarp conduit has just opened before us and a Borg scoutship has emerged." He looked up, eyes wide with surprise. "And sir, it is requesting clearance to land. . . ."

Simm turned to Riker. "You were saying, Commander?"

★　★　★

Riker checked the power setting on his phaser for the tenth time. Worf noticed. In the cold air of the *Challenger*'s main shuttlebay, Riker could see the Klingon's breath cloud with vapor as he whispered, "The shuttlebay is sealed, Commander. Nothing will happen."

Riker knew Worf was correct. But he checked the power setting one last time. It wasn't every day that Starfleet invited a Borg vessel to board one of its starships.

Riker, Worf, La Forge, Deanna, and Data waited by the cleared landing platform as the main bay doors opened onto empty space. The ship's atmosphere was contained by the annular force field that remained in place. Riker could see the curve of New Titan to the side. Then he saw the dark smudge that was the Borg scoutship, heading closer.

Deanna broke the silence. "Do you realize that there is not one person on this deck who feels this is the right thing to do?"

Riker smiled at her. "Captain Simm is standing by to decompress the bay if anything goes wrong."

"I feel so reassured," Deanna said. Then grimly added, "We should be talking to them with at least a light-year between us."

Worf cleared his throat. "I was able to communicate with the scoutship only through Linguacode," he explained. "It is not equipped with audio or visual communications channels."

Riker realized that made sense. Why *would* a groupmind based on a subspace link require any other type of communications device?

The scoutship glided in between the *Challenger*'s nacelles, then slipped through the atmospheric force field.

Instantly, the hard walls and deck of the shuttlebay reverberated with the hum of the scoutship's engines, and Riker felt the blast of heat from its exhaust ports. Then the scoutship became silent as it switched over to antigrav maneuvering units and floated to a perfect touchdown in the center of the platform.

Riker led the others to the hatch opening in the patched-together ship.

A Borg stepped out and methodically scanned them with his laser as a second figure came out behind him.

"Should I be surprised?" Riker muttered to Deanna as he recognized the second figure. Then he stepped forward. "Ambassador Spock. Welcome to the *Challenger.*"

Spock raised his hand and gave the traditional salute. "Peace and long life, Commander. May I introduce my pilot"—Spock gestured to the Borg beside him—"Six of Twelve."

"You will be assimilated," the Borg said by way of greeting. "Resistance is futile."

Spock stepped in front of the Borg. "You will guard the scoutship. I will make arrangements for the efficient assimilation of this ship and her crew."

The Borg lowered its manipulator arm. "That is relevant." He returned to the scoutship and the hatch hissed shut behind him.

Spock joined his surprised welcoming committee. "Six of Twelve is an extremely literal-

355

minded entity, and I doubt he will have any independent thoughts while I am away from him. However, in the best interests of everyone, I suggest you commence jamming all communications channels to prevent him from signaling his presence to any other members of the collective who may be in this region of space."

But no one facing Spock moved to act on his suggestion. Spock studied them all, then pursed his lips.

"Is there a problem, Commander?"

"The last I heard, you had returned to Romulus."

"I did. While there, I attempted to infiltrate a criminal organization which I believed would lead me to whoever supplied James Kirk with his micropulser weapon. Instead, I uncovered a Borg-Romulus alliance which intends to attack the Federation from the Neutral Zone, following an act of treachery by a high-ranking member of Starfleet."

Riker felt momentarily overwhelmed. "And that would be?"

"Jean-Luc Picard."

Riker smiled coldly. "Nice try. But Captain Picard and Beverly Crusher are on special assignment to *fight* the Borg."

"Then I regret to inform you that they have lost their fight. I encountered Captain Picard on a Borg transwarp station. He is Picard no longer. He is Locutus. Indeed, it is possible that he has always been Locutus."

"No . . ." Riker said.

"Six of Twelve was in full contact with the

collective until we left the Borg station," Spock said. "He will confirm all that I have told you."

Riker glanced at Deanna. She gave him an apologetic look. As far as she could tell, Spock was telling the truth. But whether it was the actual truth, or simply a story that had been programmed into his consciousness by the Borg, Riker knew that not even a Betazoid could tell.

"If your story can be confirmed, what do you propose we do?" Riker asked.

"I am not a tactician, Commander. And as you pointed out earlier, I have been away from Starfleet for many decades. However, I would surmise that the first step would be to mass a defensive fleet at the Neutral Zone."

"I'm sure the Romulans would enjoy seeing that," Riker said.

"And," Worf added, "it would leave the entire frontier undefended."

"So that's our dilemma, Ambassador. Are you telling the truth, or are you diverting our attention from the real attack?"

"I am telling the truth," Spock said. "But I do appreciate your position. Unfortunately, since you must suspect that I have been the victim of Borg programming, I am not aware of any procedure which can be used to prove my veracity to you."

Data stepped forward. "Ambassador, if I may, how did you manage to escape from the Borg station where you say you saw Captain Picard?"

As he heard Spock's answer, Riker was surprised that the ambassador could keep a straight face.

"I asked Six of Twelve to transport me to the place from which Locutus had arrived."

"And he brought you here? As simply as that?"

Spock looked pained. "Commander, I cannot explain why, but the Borg somehow believe that I am already one of them. They took me to the station with the intent of assimilating me and making me Speaker to the worlds of Vulcan. But in the midst of the assimilation process . . . they stopped."

"Stopped?"

"As I have said, I have no explanation."

Riker turned to Worf. "Mr. Worf, escort Ambassador Spock to sickbay. I'll want Dr. Bashir to scan him for implants and nanites. And I want you to be in attendance the entire time."

Deanna interrupted. "Will, what about Captain Kirk?"

Spock instantly turned to her, the façade of his Vulcan reserve momentarily disturbed.

Riker watched Spock carefully. "Ambassador, you should know. Kirk is here. In sickbay. With another old friend—Admiral McCoy."

For an instant, Riker could have sworn that he saw Spock smile.

"I must see them at once," Spock said. "Please, make whatever medical tests you feel appropriate."

Worf stepped to Spock's side. "If you will follow me, Ambassador."

"What is Kirk's condition?" Spock asked.

"Not well," Deanna said. "He is infested with nanites that are reconfiguring his body at a molecular level. We have no way of stopping the process in time to save him."

"How much time?" Spock asked.

"A few days," Deanna said. "I'm sorry."

Spock nodded, then turned his attention to Worf. "I am ready, Mr. Worf. Please—"

Riker's commbadge chirped. Riker tapped it. "Riker here."

It was Simm. "Commander, I thought you would be interested to know that another Borg scoutship has emerged from a conduit and requested permission to dock."

Everyone looked at Spock. Spock lifted an eyebrow. "It is possible I was followed, but I have no knowledge of it."

Riker touched his commbadge again. "Captain Simm, I want a constant update sent to Starbase 324, starting now. I want the *Challenger* brought up to full standby on maximum warp, and I want the *Monitor* standing by to come to our assistance."

"You are expecting another Borg vessel to emerge from a conduit?" Simm's disembodied voice asked.

"Put it this way," Riker said as he looked over at Spock's unreadable expression. "Given what's happening here, I'm expecting the worst."

FORTY

Captain John Lewinski tapped out the rhythm to an old blues tune on the side of his command chair. If there was anything better than two-hundred-year-old Andorian blues, he had yet to hear it. Unfortunately, his crew had taken a poll, and he had been asked to no longer pipe it onto the bridge.

"How are we doing, Mr. Land?"

The navigator studied his controls. "Still no sign of anything, Captain. No tachyon surge, no massless sources of heat, no intercepted communications."

Lewinski sighed. He was back to waiting.

Ahead of him, on the main screen, the New Titan sun pulsed, a roiling sphere of superheated gases. Somewhere within a tenth of an AU of its surface, a cloaked vessel was hiding.

But it wasn't doing anything to make finding it any easier.

Ardev spoke up in his Andorian rasp. Even he thought the captain's choice in music was hopelessly out of date. "Sir, we're receiving a microburst transmission from the *Challenger*. We're to go to battle stations and prepare to render immediate assistance to the *Challenger* when called."

Lewinski sat forward. "Is she under attack?"

Ardev's blue hearing stalks twisted forward,

disturbing his perfect cap of shiny white hair. "Not yet, sir." He frowned. "Though apparently two Borg scoutships have landed in her shuttlebay."

Lewinski smiled and smoothed his goatee. "Good. Maybe they'll cause some excitement. What are our immediate orders?"

"To continue our search for the cloaked ship, while maintaining our own cloaked status."

Lewinski's smile faded. "In other words, keep waiting."

"Yes, sir," Ardev replied, then turned back to his communications board.

Lewinski leaned back in his chair, tapped out another few bars of "Aladevto's Infirmary." "Anyone feel like some music?" he asked.

As if they had rehearsed, the answering chorus came back without a moment's delay. "No, sir."

Lewinski frowned. He hated waiting. But with the Borg nearby, he doubted he would have to wait for long.

The scoutship in which Spock had arrived had been hidden from view by several pallets of modular crates, a common-enough sight on a busy shuttlebay deck.

In addition to the defensive precaution of standing by to explosively decompress the shuttlebay, Worf had arranged for a Type-6 personnel shuttle to be locked down, with its attitude thrusters rigged to fire at the landing platform cleared for the second scoutship's landing. In addition, transporter control was keeping a real-time coordinate update on every commbadge, ready for an emergency beam-out at any second, should any of the extraordinary defenses be required.

The Borg were not known for asking for anything, and Riker felt he was now prepared for the moment they decided to start taking what they wanted.

Once again, a Borg scoutship, slightly different in configuration from the first, eased in through the shuttlebay door force field. Once again, it switched over from thrusters to antigravs and touched down perfectly.

Once again, Riker kept his hand on his phaser as he, Deanna, Data, and La Forge waited for the hatch to open.

For a moment, Riker didn't recognize the configurations of the two Borg who tumbled out of the craft. They seemed exhausted, hurt. The third Borg, which remained in the hatchway, stoically watching the others leave, was more typical.

But Data ran forward at once. "Captain Picard! Dr. Crusher!"

"Data!" Riker shouted. "Get back here!"

Data turned, halfway to his captain. "But they require help."

"They'll get it," Riker said. "When it's safe."

Data reluctantly turned back to join the others. "I was just happy to see them, that is all."

La Forge clapped him on the back. "It'll be okay, Data."

Picard and Crusher approached Riker cautiously, as though both were attuned to the tension in the air. They wore space-black battle armor. Riker recognized the gear as belonging to the intelligence units established by Shelby.

"Will," Picard said. "Geordi, Data, it's so good to see you again!"

Riker noted that Data had been right. The captain did sound exhausted.

Perhaps the neural implant plate attached to his face and head had something to do with it.

Picard faltered, realizing where Riker had focused his attention. Then he dug his fingers beneath the edge of the plate and began to pull.

On the *Monitor,* Lewinski jumped to his feet as he heard the sensor chime.

"What do we have, Mr. Land?"

"Tachyon surge at search coordinates alpha mary bravo."

The image on the viewscreen expanded to show a section of the New Titan sun. The surface seemed pebbled and pitted with dark granules— each large enough to swallow the Earth, Lewinski knew.

"Mark it, Mr. Land."

An overlay grid flashed onto the screen at the point from which the tachyon surge had originated.

Science Officer T'Per spoke from her station. "I have isolated an anomalous heat reading, Captain. There is a cloaked object at those coordinates."

Lewinski leaned over Land's board, looking past him at the screen. "Is it on the move?"

"Negative, sir. It's in a standard near-solar orbit. I think we caught an engine purge that streamed outside the cloaking field." Land grinned up at the captain. "They weren't expecting us."

Lewinski felt all his senses heighten. The hunt had finally begun. "Take us in, easy, Mr. Land. If *you* need to purge the engines, do it now. I want to get close enough to clean their windshields."

Land's fingers danced over his board as he lay in the *Monitor*'s new course. Then he looked back at the captain. "Is a windshield anything like a tailpipe, sir?"

"Eyes ahead, Mr. Land."

The *Monitor* eased forward, closing in on its enemy.

In the *Challenger*'s main shuttlebay, Riker went on alert, half-expecting to see raw flesh laced with a filigree of neural implant wires, as Picard ripped the plate from his face.

But instead he saw innocuous threads of surgical glue and unmarked skin.

The Borg plate was the duplicate which had been made by Shelby's researchers.

Riker lowered his phaser.

Picard gave him a questioning look. "Will, did you think . . . I had been assimilated again?"

It was Spock's voice which answered. "Not again, Captain Picard."

Everyone turned to see Spock emerge from behind a pallet of modular crates, Worf at his side with a phaser drawn.

"Very good," Picard said. "You've apprehended the traitor responsible for the Borg-Romulan alliance. Ambassador Spock."

Spock and Picard faced each other, almost within reach of each other.

"Captain Picard is the traitor who has betrayed the Federation," Spock said.

Crusher broke the impasse. "Will, we were on a Borg station in transwarp. We saw Spock put into an assimilation frame. But he wasn't assimilated because he is *already* part of the collective!"

Spock turned to Riker. "As I told you, Commander, I was not assimilated. And though I do not have an explanation for the Borg's failure to act, I assure you I am not one of them."

"Neither am I," Picard said.

Riker turned to Deanna. Her face was a mask of confusion. "They're all telling the truth."

"Or they've all been programmed," Riker said angrily.

Picard stepped toward Riker. "Will, I understand your predicament. But surely you can't believe after all we've been through together since . . . since that first time, that I'm still part of them.

Spock also stepped toward Riker. "But there is no logic in what you're suggesting is my contact with the collective, Commander. The Borg and the Romulans are within days, if not hours, of attacking the Federation."

Spock and Picard turned to face each other at the same time. Both spoke at the same time. Their words were identical. "And *he* is the one responsible."

On the bridge of the *Tomed*, Salatrel leapt to her feet as she heard the communications chime.

"Commander," Tran called out. "We are receiving a coded signal!"

"What's the message?"

Tran turned to his commander with a smile of disbelief. "Picard is on the *Challenger*."

Salatrel felt a thrill of hope run through her. "What is the signal's source?" Could it be possible that Vox had returned? That Vox had told the truth?

But this truth was even better.

"The signal is coming from the *Challenger* herself," Tran said. "Commander Salatrel . . . it's a signal from Kirk!"

"Yes!" Salatrel exclaimed. Without thinking, she holstered her disruptor. "Battle stations!" she cried out. "For the glory of the Empire and the House of Chironsala—*battle stations!*"

"She's powering up her engines!" Land called out.

T'Per added, "Picking up Bell discontinuities in subspace, sir. She's got an artificial singularity."

Lewinski pounded his fist into his hand. "She's a Romulan! Distance, Mr. Land?"

"Five thousand kilometers, sir!"

"Lock on all passive target systems. We're going to keep a low profile till—"

"She's moving out!"

"Then so are we. . . ."

With only an almost-imperceptible flickering in the charged plasma flares that leapt from the surface of the dying star to show its path, the

Avatar of Tomed slipped from orbit and banked away in a course that would return it to New Titan.

But she was not the swift and silent raptor of vengeance her commander believed her to be.

The *Monitor* moved through space behind her, not even disturbing the light of the stars it crossed, as it came about to match its course to the Romulan's.

Braced for battle, both ships flew for the *Challenger*.

Riker tightened his grip on his phaser. "You're both going to sickbay for analysis. Captain Picard, what's the status of the Borg on your scoutship?"

"He thinks I'm Locutus. He piloted the scoutship here."

Spock gazed indignantly at Picard. "How is it possible for a Borg to think you are Locutus unless your mind is among the collective?"

Riker gestured with his phaser. "Ambassador, as I recall, a Borg piloted your scoutship here as well. Is your mind among the collective?"

Spock glanced away. "The Borg appear to think so."

A tremor rumbled through the deck. Warning lights flashed as the shuttlebay doors began to slide shut.

Then the red alert sirens warbled and warning lights flashed.

"Will, what's happening?" Picard asked.

"We seem to be in the middle of a Borg expressway," Riker said. He hit his commbadge.

"Riker to bridge. Is there another Borg ship in transit?"

Captain Simm answered. "Negative, Commander. The *Monitor* has just informed us we are about to be attacked by a Romulan vessel."

Riker frowned at Spock. "Friends of yours, Ambassador?"

"Commander Riker, it is evident your emotions are being heightened by the danger we are in," Spock answered. "It would be wise for you to consider all your actions in a more dispassionate manner to avoid saying anything which you might later regret."

"Tell it to Kirk in sickbay," Riker said.

Then he saw Picard's shocked expression.

"What did you say?"

Riker didn't know where to begin. "It's Captain Kirk, sir. He . . . didn't die."

Picard seemed stunned. "Will, I buried him."

"He was . . . brought back somehow. By the Borg."

Picard faced Spock. "Is *that* why you have done this? Betrayed the Federation so the Borg would give you back your captain?"

Spock's arm moved back. If Spock had been human, Riker would have expected him to make a fist.

But then Spock relaxed again.

"Do you know *nothing* about me?" Spock said, with absolutely no pretense of hiding his emotions, as if he let loose a lifetime of buried resentment. "We have melded minds, Captain. Has my work, my life, meant so little to you that you can you even consider that I would be capable of such an act?"

Even Picard was taken aback by the cold fury in Spock's tone.

Beverly Crusher put her hand on Picard's shoulder. "That didn't sound like a Borg speaking, did it?"

A profound silence lasted until Riker asked Worf to have the Borg in the scoutships beamed to the brig, making sure to deactivate any built-in weapons systems they might have.

"And for the rest of you," Riker said, "sickbay." He turned to the personnel airlock leading back into the ship.

A shadow moved there, as if the airlock had already been opened. Even though Captain Simm had ordered it sealed until any potential Borg threat had been dealt with.

Riker was momentarily confused. Then his confusion became action as he saw the glowing tip of a phaser node swing out from the edge of the airlock.

"Deanna!" he shouted as the blue wave seared his vision.

But there was no time to know if she had heard his warning. Riker didn't even have time to feel the hard metal plates that rushed up to meet him as he fell.

FORTY-ONE

Picard heard Riker shout, "Deanna!" and then he felt a sudden wave of heat and static charge pass around him.

He shook his head to clear it, then looked around in amazement. Beverly and Data were still standing beside him, Beverly dazed, but they were surrounded by unmoving bodies that littered the hangar bay deck.

"Have we been hit?" Beverly asked.

"I believe we have been shot with a wide-beam phaser discharge set to stun," Data said. "Your armor appears to have protected you."

Picard touched Data's shoulder. "What about you, Data?"

"I require a higher power setting to be immobilized," Data answered.

"Thanks," a voice said from the airlock behind them. "That's good to know."

Picard's hand jerked back, burning, as an orange beam blasted Data from his grasp. The android skidded across the deck like a broken doll.

Picard and Beverly turned to face their attacker as he emerged from the shelter of the airlock frame.

"Kirk . . . ?" Picard said.

The captain of the first *Enterprise* smiled.

"What did I tell you on Veridian? Call me Jim."
Then he raised his phaser again and fired.

The phaser beam struck Beverly, and she crumpled, moaning, to the deck.

"Beverly!" Picard exclaimed.

"As long as she stays there, she'll be fine," Kirk said. "And you step back from her." He pointed the phaser at Picard and adjusted the power setting. Picard could see his finger work the firing stud.

Picard clenched his fists in frustrated rage. "You're not Kirk!" Picard said. "You're a monster!"

The shuttlebay deck suddenly lurched as the *Challenger*'s impulse engines came online. The shuttlebay rang with the discharge of photon torpedoes.

"Perhaps I am," Kirk said. He glanced down at the phaser he held, adjusted its setting again. "I keep setting this to kill," he complained, "but then I can't fire it. Why is that?"

Picard eyed Kirk incredulously. "The ship's security field prevents unauthorized personnel from discharging phasers onboard."

Kirk glanced at the bodies that littered the hangar deck. "Then how was I able to shoot them?"

"The field must have been modified in here, in case there were trouble with the Borg." Picard felt dizzy. The scene and discussion were surreal. Kirk was *dead*.

"The Borg were the ones who brought me back," Kirk said, almost conversationally. "So I'm told."

Picard looked at the monster before him. At Kirk. He knew that if he had faced this moment a year ago, he would never have accepted that a dead man could return to life. But since then, he had met a dead man in the Nexus, fought at his side on Veridian. He knew he could no longer doubt the evidence of his own eyes, nor his knowledge of the Borg.

"Do you have any idea why they brought you back?" Picard asked. His only option was to keep Kirk talking, not acting, until he had help.

The *Challenger*'s deck heaved as the great ship shuddered beneath her wildly fluctuating defensive shields. Picard's ears were perfectly attuned to each specific sound a *Galaxy*-class ship could make. He tried not to imagine what sort of maneuvers the *Challenger* was being forced to perform to account for what he heard now.

"As a matter of fact, I do," Kirk said.

"You see," he said, each word a greater struggle than the one before, "if I'm to have any peace . . . I . . . must . . . kill you."

"Captain, you know that's not right. The Borg have somehow *made* you believe that. But—"

The inertial dampeners roared as everything not locked down was suddenly thrust to starboard. Picard and Kirk stumbled, but kept their footing.

Kirk threw his phaser aside. "Nobody *makes* me do *anything!*" he shouted.

Kirk looked at him wildly, as a series of conflicting expressions washed over his face—frustration, rage, anguish, finally sorrow.

Picard regarded him with the sympathy that could only come from shared pain and memories.

"The Borg can. I know. They've made me do terrible things, too." Those images would never leave his own mind. The Battle of Wolf 359. Eleven thousand deaths. Because of him.

What would *Kirk* do to be free of that pain?

Picard held out his hand to his fellow captain.

"I can help," he said.

"I know," Kirk answered. "By *dying!*"

Then Kirk leapt at Picard and smashed him to the deck, striking out with unthinking rage and hate and . . .

The *Challenger* twisted, engines screaming. Light channels exploded with flares of sparks from an uncontrolled power surge.

Picard and Kirk rolled across the shifting deck, knees digging, fists pummelling, two bodies locked together in the strobing lights and shadows. Picard heard the screech of duranium against duranium as unsecured shuttles began to slide free along the deck.

He looked up just as Kirk was about to land one last, telling blow. He swung up his armored forearm and heard the solid thunk of Kirk's fist against it. Heard Kirk's cry.

The *Challenger* bucked. Kirk flew forward, jarred by the impact. The shuttlebay went dark.

Picard scrambled to his feet as the emergency lights flickered on, but Kirk had already vanished in the shadows.

Picard paused, looked at his crew, still lying helpless on the deck. If he went to them, Kirk would have him and the useless fight would begin again.

He needed assistance. But his armor's communicator was not functioning, overloaded by the phaser hit he had taken. He sprinted to the airlock. Hit the commpanel there.

"Picard to bridge!" He heard only static. "Picard to Security!" The communications system was out. "Picard to Emergency Transporter Control!"

The whistle of a polysonic crowbar sang in his ears as it swung toward him and he ducked. The commpanel erupted in sparks, torn apart by the impact of the tool Kirk had swung.

Picard pivoted on his left foot and rammed his elbow into Kirk's chest as, with the face of a madman, Kirk raised the polybar to strike again.

The polybar spun from Kirk's hands as he stumbled backward.

Picard had no choice. He charged through the airlock, turned to the left, and ran toward the shadows beyond the flickering corridor lights, hesitating just long enough to be certain Kirk followed.

And Kirk did, face distorted by rage.

Picard rushed on into the darkness, enticing his attacker to pursue him. Setting his trap in place.

High above New Titan, the *Challenger* hung dead in space.

"It is a trick," Tran said. "They are lying in wait for us to attack again."

Salatrel bit her knuckle, considering her

strategy as she paced in front of her command chair. "The captain is a Vulcan," she pointed out. "And Vulcans don't bluff."

"Our victory was too easy," Tran persisted.

"It was a sneak attack," Salatrel said, monitoring her bridge crew's reaction to her subcommander's opposition. "Remember the *Farragut* at Veridian." She knew she would have to quickly determine if Tran was arguing with her because he was a coward, afraid of death, or because he really did have some valuable insight to share with her.

Tran pointed to his sensor boards. "Look at the damage pattern!" he urged. "There! There! And there!"

Salatrel checked each point he indicated on the *Challenger* schematic he had called up.

"There is no structural damage to account for her loss of propulsion," Tran said. "No environmental overload to account for the crew death figures we're reading. Commander, I don't believe we've caused a single casualty. I submit the captain knew we were coming and has been transmitting false sensor returns."

Salatrel looked at the main screen. The *Challenger* spun slowly, off-axis. Its propulsion lights were out. Only a few running lights still flashed.

"Then how do you explain that?" She regarded the other ship with scorn. "Only a fool would leave his ship in such a vulnerable condition."

"I say the captain of that ship has taken every hit we've thrown at his screens, and he's diverted the power into his generators to create the power surges we detected. The real damage is meaningless. He can have his primary generators repaired in an hour."

"Look at the shields, Tran." Salatrel gestured at the power readouts on the screen. "They're at less than thirty percent. Two more good hits, and the ship is ours."

Tran stood up to face her. "I promise you he has more power offline than our sensors can pick up. Commander, he is baiting us. Remember the Battle of Icarus IV. It has been a Starfleet tactic for a century."

The reminder of Icarus IV drove rational thought from Salatrel. She made her decision. "Then we will see him power up his weapons when we make our approach, and you will be able to break off our attack in time."

"It is not *his* weapons we must be concerned about."

Salatrel snarled a warning at Tran. Nothing would stop her from achieving her goal this close to victory. "The other ship is gone, Subcommander." She returned to her command chair.

"The other ship is cloaked."

Salatrel stiffened. She could feel her bridge crew tense, wondering if Tran would follow Tracius. "Can you detect its tachyon signature?"

Tran regarded her steadily. "No. Which could mean Starfleet has modified it."

Salatrel had had enough talk. She was ready for action. "Think, Tran! If the other ship is here, cloaked, watching us, what is its purpose? Any commander would have come in behind us on our first run when the *Challenger* fired her torpedoes back at us. The other ship is *not here*."

Tran sat back at his board, jaw set. "Then, for the glory of the Empire," he said in the formal tongue of obedience, "I embrace my death."

Salatrel smiled. Tran would live for the battle. He wasn't a coward. Only impetuous.

"Prepare for final approach," she said. "Target the support pylons to break her apart. Set sensors to scan for life-support suits and escape pods." She leaned forward in her chair. "No survivors. No prisoners. Proceed."

Tran turned back to her, one last question for his leader. "Commander . . . what if the other ship held back because they do not wish to destroy us? What if they wish to capture us?"

"Starfleet takes no prisoners, Tran. They are murderers, plain and simple."

Tran turned back to his controls. The *Avatar of Tomed* began her final run.

"We've got her!" Lewinski said.

The mood on his bridge was electric.

Captain Simm of the *Challenger* had played his ship like the magnificent instrument it was. Absorbing incredible energies by diverting the Warbird's power to the areas where it would do the least damage.

And the commander of the Romulan ship had fallen for it.

"Put us on intercept," Lewinski said. The time for waiting was finally over.

But T'Per stepped up beside him. "If I may, Captain, the Romulan vessel clearly has capabilities we have not seen before. Her disruptors for one. They are not standard."

Lewinski gave T'Per a long-suffering look. "If that thing were a standard Romulan vessel, do you think it would be attacking a Starfleet ship?"

T'Per returned to her station in silence.

Lewinski beat out a drum solo on the arm of his chair.

"All I want you to do is fuse its disruptor cannons, tear apart its torpedo tubes, then target its exhaust ports," he said.

"I thought you wanted us to do something hard," Land replied.

"Decloak at your discretion, Mr. Land. As my noble ancestors once said—*Yee-hah!*"

The *Avatar of Tomed* dropped her cloak in preparation for firing, her Borg disruptors powered and locked on each key structural component of the *Challenger*.

Simm sat patiently on his command bench. Captain Lewinski was a brilliant tactician. The *Challenger* would not absorb another erg of Romulan energy.

The Warbird rippled against the stars, taking on its solid, visible, threatening form.

But just before Salatrel could give the command to fire, an all-too-familiar sensor disturbance obscured her forward scanners as she heard a savage, alien battle cry flooding subspace on all frequencies.

Her shields flared with a sudden overload, allowing Starfleet phasers from the decloaked ship to pierce her defenses and fuse her weapons ports.

Then, before Tran could alter course, the decloaked vessel—the vessel Salatrel had sworn had abandoned the *Challenger*—performed a spinning loop over the top of the Warbird to target her exhaust ports.

The bridge of the *Tomed* echoed with the warning sirens that filled it.

Tran gave her a running commentary on what had happened.

Thirty seconds more, Salatrel knew, and her ship would be dead.

And Kirk would survive her.

This was no longer a battle she could win by herself.

"Engage transwarp," she ordered.

"In front of the enemy?" Tran's shock was apparent.

"The knowledge of our capabilities will give them no advantage," Salatrel said. The real war was that close to beginning.

"Take us out of here, Subcommander."

Salatrel's fingers closed over the handle of her disruptor.

"Transwarp engaged," Tran confirmed.

On the main screen, the *Challenger* diminished, until it was no more than a single point of light, no larger than a star.

Salatrel held up her thumb and blotted that light out.

She would return for Kirk.

And when she did, the full force of the collective would be with her.

Lewinski's mouth dropped open as the Warbird dissolved into light before him, outlined by the faint glow of what he now recognized as a microdurational transwarp conduit, which put the ship completely beyond pursuit.

"Whew . . . how long have the Romulans had that?" he asked.

"I do not believe it is part of the Empire's traditional armada," T'Per said. "Coupled with its nonstandard weaponry, it is logical to assume that the Warbird has been extensively retrofitted by the Borg."

Lewinski thought about the ramifications of that, then dismissed them. "Just tell me they didn't know we were here until we dropped out of cloak," he said.

Mr. Land confirmed it. "The cloak modifications worked, sir. They had no idea we were here at all. Otherwise, they wouldn't have fallen for Captain Simm's ambush."

Lewinski patted the side of his chair. "Then there's still hope for the Federation, after all. Right, Mr. T'Per?"

T'Per remained silent.

FORTY-TWO

Kirk paid no attention to the starship that appeared to be tearing itself apart around him.

All he saw was his prey, farther along up the corridor, almost within his grasp.

Nothing else mattered.

Except killing Picard.

He tried not to think why that was so. He tried not to think at all. Locking McCoy in a stateroom, disconnecting the controls to his exoskeleton, taking away his old friend's communicator pin . . . it all felt wrong. Wrong but still necessary.

Manipulating McCoy's communicator to send out the coded alert signal, though—*that* he had almost enjoyed, because of the technical challenge it had given him. And he had correctly deduced the workings of his own communicator pin. First by using it to listen in on the ship's internal security channels to learn that Picard had arrived in the shuttlebay, then by simply leaving it behind in sickbay so that the ship's computer would not be able to keep track of his movements throughout this vast ship.

And just as Kirk had anticipated, no one person and no automated system had detected his presence in the shuttlebay as he had arrived to take care of Picard. It appeared the twenty-fourth century held no especially great challenges for him.

Except for the phaser-suppression system.

One quick burst could have taken care of Picard once and for all. It had been a disappointment to learn that this future Starfleet had taken safeguards against such actions. Kirk realized that as long as Picard remained on this starship, he would have to deal with his target by hand. Which was fine. He'd always preferred the personal touch.

Up ahead, Kirk saw Picard pause near a large entryway that looked like an airlock. Kirk wondered if the ship had more than one shuttlebay, if Picard were thinking of escaping.

But Picard couldn't escape. Kirk knew that. As certainly as if it had been engraved on his waking mind.

Picard must die. Picard *would* die.

Picard ducked through the large door.

Kirk chased after him.

But when he reached the entranceway, he stopped, suspecting the worse. The door was still open. Sloppy on Picard's part? Or a deliberate prelude to a trap?

Beyond lay another corridor. Except its traction carpet was a different color, and it did not exhibit any of the signs of battle damage that Kirk had seen in the darkened corridors he had just been through.

Picard appeared for an instant at the end of the new corridor. His presence was enough to spur Kirk on, again without thought.

He ran along the new corridor until he came

to the intersection where he had seen Picard. No sign of him now.

Kirk looked behind him. Turned, stopped. There was no sign of the large doorway through which he had entered, either.

He leaned against the corridor wall, head throbbing. He touched the sterile covering at the back of his head. Felt it thick and sticky with blood. The surgery, he remembered. But what had it been for? And what was it McCoy had said? Only days remaining? Why was he spending them this way? Why did he want . . . *need* to kill—

The mere thought of Picard's name spurred him to action again. But the corridors he was in were unfamiliar. He needed a plan. He needed to know where to run.

Kirk looked around. Saw a computer access panel. Remembered seeing Picard try to use a communicator in the armored suit he wore. Would the new captain of the *Enterprise* be foolish enough to let the computer know where he was at all times while he was being hunted?

Kirk went to the computer panel.

"Computer, tell me the location of Captain Picard."

"Captain Picard is on the bridge."

The computer spoke to him in almost the same voice he remembered from his first *Enterprise*. Once again, Kirk felt unsettled that with all that had changed in this future, some things remained the same.

"Where is the bridge?" he asked the voice from his past.

"Follow the light path on the wall panels to the turbolift," the computer explained.

A dark panel along the corridor wall suddenly came to life with a pulsing pattern of light. The twenty-fourth century was making it all too easy.

Kirk ran to the turbolift. The light speeded up to keep just ahead of him.

The turbolift had no controls.

"Bridge," Kirk said, then rocked gently as the lift car moved sideways, then up.

When the turbolift doors slipped open again, Kirk stepped forward into an alcove, then paused as he swiftly took in the sweep of this new bridge.

There were no steps. The outer support-station ring sloped up from the ops level to a raised area at the back, marked by a dramatically curved railing of what appeared to be real wood.

Superficially, the design remained the same as those bridges with which Kirk was familiar—the circular arrangement, the forward screen.

But he noted that instead of one captain's chair, raised in the center, there were three seats, five if he counted the smaller, backless seats to either side. Kirk was puzzled by what that implied. Could it be the captain wasn't as important to a ship in this time?

Kirk stepped out of the turbolift alcove, scanning the bridge for any sign of his enemy.

But it was deserted. Odd. Especially since the ship had just been under attack. What if there were an emergency bridge elsewhere in the ship? He decided he should have asked the computer to distinguish between the two.

As he looked for a computer access panel, Kirk

saw a dedication panel to his right. He recognized a faint familiarity in the silhouette of the vessel depicted on it.

Then he read the name on the plaque.

U.S.S. Enterprise.

He stopped. He read the next line, the smaller type.

Galaxy Class. Starfleet Registry NCC-1701-D.

But this ship was dead. McCoy had told him. It had been destroyed above Veridian as he and Picard had—

Waves of agony pulsed through Kirk. Picard must die. Kirk gasped for breath. Was this another dream? Was there any other way to explain his presence on a ghost ship?

Another set of doors opened. Picard stepped out and to the wooden rail. "We have to talk," he said.

As quickly as that, Kirk's conflict was gone again. Instantly, he decided on his strategy. "I know. You're right." He sagged against the wall. Touched his wound again. Held out his blood-coated fingers. "I need . . . help."

Picard came down the slope of the bridge. Trusting.

"Captain Simm appears to have his hands full," Picard said. "All secondary services are offline. But perhaps I can do something about that."

He went to a padded drawer-front on the wall. Opened it. Withdrew an oddly shaped case marked with the Starfleet caduceus.

First aid, Kirk thought. *Perfect . . .*

"Come over here," Picard said. He opened

385

the medikit on one of the chairs in front of a ridiculously small operations console. "Let me see if I can stop the bleeding."

Kirk smiled, nodded, got within arm's length of Picard. Began to stumble, as if trying to brace himself against the chair.

And when Picard reached out to steady him, Kirk rammed his forehead against Picard's face, amazed that a captain of the *Enterprise* would fall for such a trap.

Picard fell backward, catching himself on the other chair.

He straightened up, straightened the chest piece of his armor, raised his hands as if to surrender.

"Captain Kirk, I think there's something you should know before you carry this any further."

Kirk rubbed his face, as his compulsion to simply jump on Picard and begin swinging became unbearable.

"I believe we can reach a consensus here," Picard said. He glanced up at another set of doors on the bridge. Kirk followed his gaze, recognizing Picard's trap in the same instant Picard leapt forward, fist swinging, catching Kirk on the jaw to flip him over the console.

By the time Kirk pushed himself to his feet, Picard had already run into the turbolift.

Kirk followed and stopped by the closed doors. He had no doubt he could defeat his enemy, but the trick was going to be finding him. And how could he find a captain on his own ship? A ship that Kirk knew nothing about, other than it had crashed in . . . Kirk gasped.

This ship couldn't be Picard's *Enterprise*. Which meant, there was only one thing that it could be. Kirk smiled.

He turned to face the empty bridge.

"Arch," he said.

A standard Starfleet holodeck control arch appeared before the command chairs.

Kirk rushed to it, now clearly understanding Picard's strategy.

He hadn't wanted to let Kirk remain loose on the *Challenger*. So he had lured his attacker into a holodeck in order to keep him occupied until the real ship returned to normal operations. And what better maze to place Kirk in than that of a state-of-the-art, twenty-fourth-century vessel of which he had no knowledge?

"Very clever," Kirk said, as he accessed the arch controls. They were exactly like those he had seen Salatrel use on her ship. He was pleased he had paid such close attention.

"Computer, prepare to change simulation programs."

"Holodeck systems, standing by," the familiar voice confirmed.

Kirk grinned with anticipation.

Captain Picard had been good enough to show him the future.

Now it was Captain Kirk's turn to show him the past.

FORTY-THREE

Picard burst out of the turbolift and skidded to a stop.

He had been heading to his *Enterprise*'s battle bridge. It could be completely sealed off from the rest of the ship—even in this holodeck simulation. Kirk would be free to roam the endless corridors until Picard could once again make contact with the *Challenger*'s bridge and have Simm beam Kirk to a detention cell.

Except . . . this wasn't the battle bridge.

Picard looked around, breathing hard in his armor, until he suddenly realized that somehow Kirk had succeeded in changing the rules. Somehow, the legendary captain had worked out how to alter the holodeck's program.

Picard was on the bridge of a hundred-year-old relic—a *Constitution*-class starship, one of the greatest series ever built.

Knowing what he would find there, Picard turned to the dedication plaque by the turbolift. He smiled in spite of what the inscription meant to his odds of survival.

U.S.S. Enterprise.
Starship class.
San Francisco, Calif.

Kirk had gone home, and he had brought Picard with him.

But that was all the time Picard had for sentimentality.

"Computer," he announced.

"Working." The familiar voice was somehow cooler, more mechanistic. Not quite the response Picard had been expecting.

"Arch," Picard ordered.

"Unable to comply," the computer answered.

Picard sighed.

"Computer, identify your make and model."

"This unit is a D-6 duotronic computer comprising—"

"That's enough," Picard said. Kirk had even called up a simulation of the original *Enterprise's* limited computer, effectively blocking access to the *Challenger's* system and the holodeck controls. How had he had time to become so proficient?

"Do you like it?" Kirk asked.

Picard turned around slowly as Kirk rose from a chair at some kind of operational station with an antique holographic imager. One that actually required the user to peer in through a narrow blue slot, rather than seeing results on a screen.

"I remember seeing one in a museum," Picard said.

He placed his hand on the red railing and began to ease backward, even as Kirk approached.

"This is the way exploration was meant to be," Kirk said as he looked around the recreation of his first bridge.

"No carpet. No replicators. None of the comforts of home." Kirk stepped down to the center deck, rapped his fist against the back of the command chair. "This was a *machine*," he said, almost as if Picard weren't present. "You felt it back then. That you were actually going somewhere. The way the deck pitched when the inertial dampeners couldn't keep up."

"They still can't," Picard said dryly.

His mind raced, trying to remember whatever he could about the safety features in these antique bridges. They must have had fire-suppression systems. Emergency egress panels. But all he could see was the single pair of turbolift doors he had entered through. How many bridge crews had been trapped because that single access route had been blocked?

"I'm going to die in your time," Kirk said as he stood in front of the command chair. "So I thought it only fitting that you die in mine. Or at least, a simulation of mine."

"I'm sure you're aware twenty-fourth-century medical science has made fantastic strides," Picard said.

Kirk looked off to the side with a frown. "Twenty-fourth-century medical science is what brought me here." Then he stepped away from the command chair. Picard calculated how many seconds it would take Kirk to circle the combined ops and navigational console in the center of the bridge. He wondered how long it would be before Simm realized that Picard and Kirk were both missing. With Worf unconscious on the shuttlebay deck, Picard worried that it might take too long.

"Kirk," Picard began, "you don't know what you're doing."

Kirk shrugged, almost in resignation. "I used

390

to think that every day of my first five-year mission. Each crew member who died. Each opportunity missed. I'd ask myself, why? Who was I to make those decisions?"

"Those were the risks of the job," Picard said, knowing what the other captain meant all too well. "They still are."

"You mean the twenty-fourth-century isn't perfect?"

"No age is. It's our hope for the future that drives us on, inspired by the accomplishments of the past."

Kirk walked slowly around the console, idly running his hand over one of the two chairs there. "But this is my future."

"You're seeing it through distorted eyes."

"Am I?" Kirk asked. He looked around his bridge again. "Who's the observer here? Who's the visitor out of time?" He glanced back at the turbolift. "If I step through those doors, who's to say I won't find Spock in the recreation room, waiting by a chessboard? Or McCoy, complaining that I haven't been in for my checkup?"

"Is that what you *want* to find? The past?"

Kirk stared at Picard. Shook his head. "A tempting offer. But the past is the past, never to be lived again. I don't belong there." He glanced behind at the waiting command chair. "No one who sits in that chair does."

Picard had the sudden, heartfelt realization that despite the years between them, he was looking into a mirror.

"Then join us in the future. Fight what they've done to you," Picard said.

Kirk swallowed hard. "I've tried. I can't."

"You've come so far, accomplished so much. Don't let it end here."

Kirk took a step forward.

"It has to end sometime." He spread his arms to encompass the bridge. "Why not here . . . where it all began?"

Picard prepared himself for Kirk's attack. He frowned. "Captain . . . if I have to, I will kill you. . . ."

Kirk grinned. "You can try. . . ." And then he attacked.

He ducked under the railing, grabbing Picard's legs and pulling them forward, sending Picard down on his back.

Before Picard could roll to his side, Kirk pulled him off the raised platform and swung him into the console.

Picard kicked to flip Kirk away before he could lunge again.

He pulled himself to his feet.

Saw Kirk crouching, ready to—

Picard ducked to take the force of Kirk's attack on his shoulder.

Kirk brought both elbows down on Picard's back.

The armor saved Picard from the worst of the impact, then Kirk brought his knee up to hit Picard's jaw. However, before Kirk's knee could connect, Picard threw himself back, to rollover the console, landing on his feet.

His movements must have activated some

control, because an old-fashioned targeting sight unfolded from the console surface.

He could see that Kirk had now gone beyond reasoning. Blood trickled from the corner of his mouth. His breath came like the panting of a lion on the hunt.

Picard felt the same. Tasted blood in his own mouth. Brought his hands up, ready to gouge, to tear, to defeat this enemy.

With a roar, Kirk attacked again.

This time Picard did not attempt to deflect him.

The captains met head on.

The impact of their collision carried them back to the command chair. They struggled against each other, neither giving thought to defense. Their hands found each other's throats. Their eyes were mere centimeters from each other.

Picard heard the pounding of his heart. His vision was narrowing, dark stars flickering in from the sides. But he would not let go. He saw the same loss of focus coming to Kirk's eyes.

Bound forever in a death grip to Kirk, neither captain willing nor able to yield, Picard was astounded to feel the old bridge swirl away from him. Together with Kirk, he was plunged into an endless black hole from which there could be no escape, trapped in a titanic struggle that would last through all time.

And then the command chair disappeared beneath them and both captains dropped to the floor of the holodeck, gasping with surprise.

FORTY-FOUR

"That is *enough!*" Riker said.

He pushed past Dr. Bashir and kept his phaser aimed at the impossible sight of Kirk and Picard locked in mortal combat.

The two captains looked up at him, then looked around in a daze, as if they had forgotten they had been in a holodeck. Slowly, almost reluctantly, their hands fell away from each other's throats.

"The next one who moves gets a force three stun," Riker said.

But Ambassador Spock stepped forward, into Riker's line of fire. "I do not believe that will be necessary."

"Ambassador, believe me, it goes for you, too."

"Oh, calm down," McCoy grumbled.

Riker heard the whine of the old admiral's exoskeleton as he rose from his mobility chair and walked forward, one sure step after another, until he stood at Spock's side. "No one's shooting anyone," he said.

Riker was tempted to stun *everyone*, but Deanna put a hand on his arm and shook her head in silence.

Riker lowered his phaser so it was aimed at the deck. Deanna was right. Something beyond what they could see was at work here. He could almost sense it himself. Behind him, even La Forge,

Worf, Data, and Dr. Crusher maintained a respectful silence. All had recovered from Kirk's attack in the shuttlebay. But Riker had no impression that any of them desired revenge. They only seemed spellbound by the scene before them.

Kirk and Picard stood side by side, spent, breathless. But where Picard silently acknowledged the presence of his old command crew, Riker noted that Kirk's attention was absolutely riveted on Spock and McCoy.

"Spock . . . ?" Kirk said, his voice a low and raspy whisper.

"I am . . . most pleased to see you again, Captain," Spock formally replied.

McCoy shook his head in disgust. "Oh, for crying out loud, Spock. It's been eighty years!"

"Seventy eight point four years, Doctor."

"Can you help me?" Kirk asked.

"Yes," Spock said.

Riker saw the look of relief on Kirk's face. Then Kirk glanced at Picard beside him. "Good. Because I don't think I can kill him by myself." Riker raised his phaser again and aimed it at Kirk.

Spock moved quickly to stand between Kirk and Picard. "That is not what I meant, Captain."

Kirk lifted his hands to push Spock aside. "But, Spock . . . I have to . . ."

"No," Spock said, glancing back at Riker. "You are under the influence of Borg programming. The implant responsible has been removed, but the patterns it laid down are still affecting your thoughts and your actions."

Spock raised his own hand, but not in the traditional Vulcan salute.

"A mind-meld?" Kirk asked.

Spock nodded. "You will be able to draw strength from me, until the Borg patterns have faded."

But Picard protested. "Will—you can't allow this. If they're both under Borg control, this could be a way to cover their tracks."

Spock turned to look back at Riker.

"There is another way," he said. There was silence in the holodeck after Spock's explanation. Even Data had nothing to say.

Riker had no idea what to think, it was so audacious.

"Has it ever been done before?" he asked Spock.

"Not to my knowledge," Spock said.

Riker saw Kirk look past Spock to Picard. He saw the raw need in Kirk's eyes, the desire to attack Picard once more. The pressure he was fighting to retain some self-control.

"Remember what it says on the plaque?" Kirk asked Picard, hoarsely, even trying to smile.

Picard nodded, the same tired expression coming to his face. "To boldly go . . ." he said.

And Kirk finished the thought, with the words that had defined both their lives. ". . . where no man has gone before. . . ."

Spock took a moment to compose himself, then reached out to Kirk. The fingers of his right hand sought the *katra* points of Kirk's face, establishing the connection that would allow their minds to merge.

Kirk stared at his friend, wide-eyed. His

struggle to clear his mind for Spock to enter safely obvious to all who witnessed it.

"My mind to yours, Captain Kirk," Spock said.

Then Spock turned to Picard.

With his left hand, Spock sought the same connection with the second captain.

Riker caught his breath.

"My mind to yours, Captain Picard."

And with that, the two generations joined. Mixed and merged in the one mind that knew both, could contain both. The only mind that could bring them together.

Spock's mind reached deep into the experiences and emotions of both captains, seeking the commonality of their drive, their dreams, their experiences.

He absorbed the urgency of Kirk's run through the *Enterprise-B* . . . the shock of his being claimed by the Nexus and the bliss of its embrace . . . and the stirring promise of Picard's arrival to free him from the stagnation of eternal perfection within it.

He absorbed Picard's agony of assimilation as the biochips of the Borg grew into his tissues . . . the detached horror of instructing a fleet of machines to destroy all that he believed in, in a war against the Federation . . . the guilt for those deaths. . . .

He shuddered as in both minds he experienced that same sterile, absolute joy . . . and the revulsion and strength of will that had enabled both to resist it.

And still he went deeper. . . .

To Veridian III . . .

To the death of Kirk through his own eyes and Picard's.

Picard's fear as Shelby laid out the interface.

Kirk's fear as he rose, unprepared, from the liquid of the alien ark.

Then the torture of Kirk's programming . . . the lies Salatrel wove to entrap him . . . twisting the truth of his grief for his murdered son and lost loves . . . to create an automaton with but one, perverted purpose. . . .

Spock touched the deadening, frightful power of the Borg in both minds. Took its measure. Met its challenge.

He reached out to them both.

Giving each his strength . . .

His wisdom . . .

His logic. . . .

Three minds joined. No barriers among them.

Until a dark shadow rose from the depths of their exchange.

A shadow of the Borg, not from Kirk nor from Picard . . .

But from Spock. . . .

He gasped in pain as the impact of that lost memory seared his conscious mind.

Overwhelmed, he sank to his knees and Kirk and Picard knelt with him. They held his hands to their faces, maintaining connection. As one, they reached out to Spock, to heal and save him, as he had healed and saved them.

"I have seen them. . . ." Spock whispered. "I have . . . walked with them. . . ." His body shuddered with the impact of the truth revealed as his voiced lowered and took on the eerie harmonics of the collective.

"We are Borg," Spock intoned.

"We are . . . *V'Ger!*"

FORTY-FIVE

Except for the almost subliminal hum of the air circulators, Captain Simm's austere ready room was silent. Kirk was already there when Picard stepped in. He held his hands behind his back, gazing out an observation window at the stars.

Picard hesitated, not wanting to disturb him. But Kirk turned, his serious expression fading in a welcoming grin.

"It's all right, Captain," Kirk said. "I don't want to kill you anymore."

Picard smiled and went to Kirk, to shake his outstretched hand. They each had been examined and treated separately by their respective physicians after Spock had been taken to sickbay. This was their first chance to talk alone. And the opportunity would remain for only a few minutes more before the briefing session began.

"I cannot even begin to imagine what you must be thinking," Picard said.

Picard saw a flicker pass through Kirk's expression and knew he was masking the pain the nanites must still cause. Dr. Bashir had told Picard that he had reached the limit of what neural blockers could do without degrading Kirk's awareness. And Kirk had steadfastly refused to go to that next step.

Kirk narrowed his eyes for a moment. "Do you ever ask yourself why you're out here?"

Picard hesitated. It was unusual for him to feel so comfortable with someone he really barely knew. But what secrets could there be between them? What had one done that the other had not? "Sometimes," Picard admitted. "When I think of other paths I might have taken. Or those I've left behind."

"Family?" Kirk asked.

But Picard did not have to answer. He could see that Kirk sensed the loss he endured. Or his nephew and his brother in the fire that had claimed them.

Kirk looked at the stars again. "All the worlds we've seen, all the beings we've known, and it still comes down to that," he said. "Being alone." He glanced back at Picard. "When you lost your ship, Captain, how'd that make you feel?"

Picard wasn't sure how to answer.

A flicker of mischief played in Kirk's eyes, as if he shared a scandalous secret no one else could ever know. "Not as badly as you thought you should. Right?"

Picard waited for Kirk to continue, as he knew the other captain would.

"When I lost my first ship," Kirk said, "I was numb. I kept waiting for some uncontrollable sense of loss to . . . overwhelm me. It never came. You know why?"

Picard felt as if a burden had been taken from

him. Kirk *knew*. He had gone through the exact same experience. "Because, in the end, it's not the ship that matters."

Kirk nodded. "It's the mission."

Picard looked out at the same stars, for the first time allowing himself to ask a question he had never voiced aloud.

"Has it been worth it for you?" Picard heard Kirk sigh, as if it were a question he had often confronted, yet never voiced. "The lack of roots. Of family."

"When I was . . . hunting you," Kirk said, "I thought that if I could just find you, I could . . . find myself."

"You mean, you could find yourself by completing the mission."

The two captains turned from the stars to face each other.

"But the mission never ends, does it," Picard said.

"This one will," Kirk said. And whatever was in his eyes now, even Picard could not decipher.

Two minutes later, James Kirk stood at the head of the conference table, in the observation lounge off the *Challenger*'s bridge.

Behind him, on the viewscreen, was an image he had hoped never to see again.

"V'Ger," he said. "A corruption of *Voyager*, the name given a space probe launched from Earth at the end of the 1900's. Earth lost contact with the probe a few years after it passed outside the boundaries of the solar system."

Kirk nodded at Data, who sat in the first seat on the right, yellow hands folded on the tabletop.

"According to Mr. Data, later findings indicated the probe had been trapped by what was believed to have been a black hole. Though Data says the phenomenon could very well have been a transwarp conduit."

The image on the screen changed and Kirk took a moment to admire the sleek lines of his refit *Enterprise*. It was hard to believe such a magnificent ship could be considered an antique in this time. "Nearly three hundred years later, the space probe *Voyager* returned to Earth— searching for, it said, its creator."

Riker interrupted. He sat at the back of the table, between Julian Bashir and Deanna Trio. "*It* said? I didn't think twentieth-century science could construct a self-aware machine."

"It couldn't," Kirk replied. "Somehow, the *Voyager* probe encountered . . . something which attempted to repair it. Those repairs gave it self-awareness."

McCoy's gravelly voice spoke up. His mobility chair didn't fit beneath the conference table, so he sat to the side, behind Dr. Crusher. "And you're guessing that 'something' was the Borg? That's a helluva theory, Jim."

Kirk didn't have to defend his theory. Spock did. He sat beside Picard, subdued, recovered from his ordeal in the holodeck. For a moment, Kirk could almost believe he and Spock were back on his old ship, as if time had stood still.

Spock's voice sounded as dry as it always had when he had tangled with McCoy. "There is no guesswork involved, Doctor. I mind-melded with V'Ger. I saw where it had been, a planet filled with living machines. At the time, I had no context for that knowledge, and it was so alien it faded from my mind. But when I joined with Captain Kirk and Captain Picard, whose minds both held strong and recent impressions of the Borg, the connection between V'Ger and the Borg became clear and self-evident to me."

"Looks like you're rewriting history here, Ambassador," La Forge said. "Our *Enterprise* wasn't the first to contact the Borg—yours was."

But Spock shook his head. "V'Ger was reconfigured by the Borg, or more correctly, by a different branch of the collective—that assimilated by direct conversion to patterned energy. The Borg we know in this time assimilate by physical means. But V'Ger clearly possessed the same Borg root-command structure that derived from whatever original groupmind that linked them all."

Kirk looked around the room. "What Spock's trying to say is that V'Ger was part of the collective."

Spock looked at Riker. "And because I mind-melded with V'Ger, the tendrils of that collective remained within me."

Picard took over. "Which explains why the Borg would not assimilate Spock on the hyper-cube station." Picard paused. "I don't know how I can apologize to you, Ambassador. . . ."He looked up at Kirk. "Or to you, Captain."

Kirk waved the apology aside. "No need, Captain. We were each put in play by a different aspect of the Borg." There was a stir in the room. Kirk knew he had their attention now. "Though

Mr. Spock . . ." Kirk stopped to correct himself. He must remain up to date. "*Ambassador* Spock could put it more eloquently: What better way to defeat the Federation than by internal dissension? What better way to save it than by the sharing of knowledge? And what better way to defeat the Borg?"

Riker was the first to bite. "Excuse me, Captain Kirk. Are you saying the Borg *can* be defeated?"

Kirk grinned. "Never underestimate the power of a Vulcan. Each of us had a piece of the greatest puzzle facing Starfleet. My contact gave me background data on transwarp conduits and the hypercube station that somehow maintains them. Captain Picard had all the technical information about their ships—which was necessary for him to lead them into battle. And Ambassador Spock has seen their homeworld."

The room filled with excited and confused conversation. Kirk turned back to the viewscreen as the final image appeared. A starchart, with one star marked in red. Kirk pointed to it.

"This, gentlemen, is the Central Node of the Borg groupmind. Destroy it, and each branch of the collective will be cut off and alone."

La Forge voiced an objection. "Captain Kirk . . . that's a chart of the Delta Quadrant. To get that far would take more than a century at maximum warp."

Kirk walked over to Picard and put a hand on his shoulder. "Fortunately, while we were all playing cat and mouse, Captain Picard and Dr. Crusher were performing their duty. In the shuttlebay of this ship are two Borg scoutships with functioning transwarp engines."

Captain Lewinski stepped away from the rear wall of the conference room to complete Kirk's explanation.

"And the *Defiant*-class ships were specifically designed to accept transwarp drives, should any ever be recovered or developed."

Captain Picard stood up beside Captain Kirk, poised on the brink of the Starfleet's greatest mission. "In ten hours, the conversion of the *Monitor* into a transwarp vessel will be complete. And then . . ." Picard smiled at Kirk.

"And then," Kirk said, "we're going to kick the Borg clear into the next galaxy."

As one, every individual in the conference room, even McCoy, stood to immediately ask to be part of that mission.

"Look at them," Kirk said to Picard. "When it comes to people, nothing's changed between our times."

"The best things never do," Picard said.

FORTY-SIX

The four captains stood on the bridge of the *Challenger* as the viewscreen showed the *Monitor* coming about—Kirk, Picard, Simm, and Lewinski.

Lewinski observed his ship with a pang of regret. Because it was his ship no longer. Shelby had sent his new orders by subspace. The second transwarp engine had to be transported to Starbase 324 at once. He was in charge of that operation. In his absence, by order of Starfleet Command, the *Monitor* would be turned over to Picard.

But Lewinski wasn't one to hold grudges.

He touched his commbadge.

"Lewinski to *Monitor*. Come in, Mr. Land."

Land acknowledged and Lewinski told him to angle the *Monitor* seventeen degrees off the *Challenger*'s horizontal axis. "We want to get some glare from the sun," Lewinski explained.

Kirk and Picard looked at Lewinski without understanding what he meant. But after a few seconds, Captain Simm said, "Of course."

Lewinski gestured to the screen as the black disk of the *Monitor* slowly eased forward to fill it, angling gently so that a dull band of reflected sunlight moved over her upper hull, revealing the details of her duranium skin.

"In an operation such as this," Lewinski explained, "when a ship receives a substantial refit and is sent on such a noteworthy mission, it's not unheard of for it to receive a new code designation for the duration."

He saw the band of sunlight hit the first of the new pattern that he had had his refit crew etch into the ship's black microcoating. He turned his attention to Kirk and Picard beside him.

"It'll never turn up in the record books that way, gentlemen," Lewinski said. "But I wanted to give you both a good send-off."

Both captains' gazes were fixed on the viewscreen as they saw what Lewinski had done.

The fabled name flashed across the hull of the starship, as ephemeral as a ghost, but never to be erased from the minds and hearts of those who saw it.

U.S.S. Enterprise.

"Least I could do," Lewinski said.

FORTY-SEVEN

Spock turned from the new *Enterprise*'s science station as he heard the bridge doors slide open behind him.

Without hesitation, he stood as Captains Kirk and Picard stepped onto the bridge.

He noted that Worf, Riker, Troi, and Data did the same.

It seemed the appropriate thing to do.

As Kirk and Picard surveyed their new bridge, Spock's acute hearing picked up Picard's whispered words to Kirk.

"Captain, once again, you mustn't feel you have to do this. Julian Bashir is a fine—" Picard was cut off by Kirk.

"You're still asking me if I want to spend what might be the last few days of my life in a diagnostic bed? Waiting for a miracle that might not happen, instead of being out here, doing something useful?"

"Or foolish," Picard said.

"Captain Picard, I've done a great many foolish things in my day already. What would you do?"

Picard smiled. "Welcome aboard, Captain."

Spock looked ahead at the viewscreen as Commander Data moved the *Enterprise* away from New Titan and the *Challenger*. The android turned in his chair. "We are ready for transwarp injection at . . ." Spock saw a look of consternation cross the android's face. "Uh . . . at the captain's discretion."

Everyone on the small bridge looked to Kirk and Picard.

Kirk and Picard looked at each other.

They stood on either side of the starship's command chair.

Its empty command chair.

Spock raised an eyebrow. Knowing what he did about both captains, he expected the next few moments to be fascinating.

Kirk was the first to offer Picard the chair.

"Captain, please."

But Picard shook his head graciously, returning the gesture with a flourish.

"No, Captain, I insist."

"Really, Starfleet turned over this mission to you."

"But you were the first to defeat a branch of the collective. The mission is yours."

For an instant, both captains were frozen in place. Then Spock saw the surreptitious movement both made as each began to slip into the chair, stopping at once when they realized the other was about to do the same.

"How long do you two intend to keep this up?" Riker asked.

Picard and Kirk both looked embarrassed, but just as neither was going to be the first to sit in the chair, neither was going to be the first to step away.

Then Kirk saw Spock watching him.

He smiled.

"*Mr.* Spock!" He patted the back of the command chair. "I believe your seat is over here."

Spock was startled. "Captain, I am no longer in Starfleet."

"Retirees are always subject to call-up in time of war." He patted the seat again.

"Sir, I have never sought command."

"Then who better to lead?" Picard said, seeing the same end to the impasse.

Riker looked meaningfully at Spock. "Someone had better get us on our way."

Spock rose reluctantly, smoothing his robes.

"I shall have to rely on you both for guidance," he said diplomatically.

Picard angled the chair around to meet him. "That's what we're here for. Please, Ambassador, take command."

With great reluctance, Spock took the chair, Kirk on his right, Picard on his left.

Only Data looked relieved.

"Captain?" the android said. "We are ready for injection."

The response sounded like a confused choral reading as everyone replied at once.

"Take us out," Kirk said.

"Proceed," Spock ordered.

"Make it so," Picard pronounced.

"Yes . . . sirs," Data said.

Then he turned back to face the viewscreen, and Spock watched with interest as he saw a ripple shimmer among the stars, making it appear as if the depths of space had been painted on a canvas that was suddenly split apart and folded back.

Inside, a pool of multicolored light expanded, as Spock felt himself rocked back in his seat with a kick of acceleration even the battle-hardened systems of this new *Enterprise* could not compensate for.

"We have achieved transwarp," Data announced.

"Decrease the resolution of the forward viewscreen," Spock said. "The effects of observing the transwarp dimension can be disturbing for those who have not experienced it before."

The viewscreen abruptly changed to a undulating wireframe model of energy densities.

"Speed, Mr. Data?" Spock asked.

"We have exceeded the speed of subspace radio and are continuing to accelerate."

Spock looked to the ceiling. "Bridge to engineering. What is the status of the Borg engine?"

La Forge answered in a voice tinged with awe. "Sir, I couldn't begin to tell you how this thing's working, but it's drawing less power than one-quarter impulse."

"Is there any indication of an operational limit being met, Mr. La Forge?"

"No, sir," the engineer replied. "Diagnostics

show we're running at twenty percent of capacity."

"Bridge out," Spock said. "Mr. Data, assuming we continue to accelerate through this medium until the Borg engine reaches eighty percent of its capacity, what is our estimated arrival at the Borg homeworld?"

"Six point two hours, sir."

Spock stood up and faced Kirk and Picard. "Gentlemen, I will be in my cabin. I suggest you take this opportunity to rest."

"Very well done, Ambassador," Picard said.

"Taught him everything he knows," Kirk said with a grin.

Spock left the bridge, wondering if he had done the right thing by healing the rift between Kirk and Picard.

One starship captain was still quite enough as far as he was concerned.

FORTY-EIGHT

The Borg world orbited a sun long dead, a white dwarf star little more than a core of degenerate matter, spinning rapidly, accomplishing nothing except serving as the center of gravity for a paltry system of three planets.

Untold ages ago there had been more.

But some of those planets had been consumed.

One that remained in the dark and sunless system was the Borg world. Whether it was the

411

world on which the Borg had first arisen, or whether it was simply a planet they had chosen near the beginning of their march across the galaxy, no one would ever know.

All that mattered was that, here and now, it was the center. The node to which all branches reported. The wellspring from which all branches emerged.

There were no natural life-forms left on it. No free water. No stones or soil. Everything was engineered—the results of millennia of work and reconfiguration. Each molecule now had a function, each shape a purpose. So that now even the world itself was living, if only in the sense that Borg themselves were alive.

The surface of the solitary planet was banded by rings of light, flickering with the thought processes of a computer that encompassed a sphere larger than the Earth. What thoughts it held were unfathomable except to others who might share its size and structure.

But whether others like it existed was unknown even to its great mind. And so it sent out its children to remake the galaxy, to remake the universe itself if need be.

Anything to escape being alone.

In standard orbit above that world, the *Avatar of Tomed* coasted in space one hundred thousand light-years from home. If not for the Borg-built transwarp engine tied into her warp drive, it would take her almost three and a half centuries to return to Romulus, instead of a mere ten hours. But that great distance was what made this Borg system the perfect staging arena for the invasion that was within hours of beginning.

Spread out before Salatrel, secure from attack, was a vast Romulan armada—not the Empire's, but *hers.*

Eighteen *D'deriderex* Warbirds were among it, their whereabouts a constant embarrassment to the Empire, which publicly declared them as missing on voyages of exploration, while privately acknowledging that never before had they faced such numerous incidents of mutiny.

Forty additional single-hulled Warbirds of older classes hovered at their sides. Five classes of Bird-of-Prey. One hundred seven vessels in all, all outfitted with Borg transwarp capability and self-modulating Borg disruptors, all their controls and functions tied together in the Borg collective.

And assembling with them, joining the spread-wing formation of Romulan victory, was the key to absolute victory—eleven Borg cubeships.

Soon to be more.

Because even as Salatrel watched her fleet assemble in the viewscreen of her bridge, swift Borg scoutships converged on the assembly coordinates, showing the reason why the cube was the Borg's most common shape of choice.

Salatrel changed the focus of the viewscreen to watch as four scoutships met, docking inner face to inner face until a single larger cube was formed, the generalized control mechanisms of each scoutship now combining so that the task of controlling of the entire larger cube would be distributed among four accumulation points.

Then those four scoutships moved as one to join another combination of four, and two more.

The new cubeship comprised sixteen vessels.

And they would combine again.

And again.

Until another single, mammoth cubeship had emerged to serve the collective.

The first time Salatrel had seen the impressive, but so simple, assembly of the Borg vessels, she had instantly understood why they were so difficult to destroy. It was like scratching a holographic plate. Since every element on the hologram was encoded with the whole image, a single point of damage could not do any harm. On a cubeship that had experienced minor damage, every other undamaged part contained information enough to continue every function.

That was the power of the collective.

Groupmind.

Group function.

Destined to conquer all.

Except the Romulan people.

"Victory," Salatrel pledged as she watched the mighty cubeships slip in to join the spread-wing formation.

"Perhaps," Vox said beside her.

"How can *you* doubt the triumph of the collective?" Salatrel asked.

"We do not," Vox said. "We doubt the victory of the Romulan Armada. Picard and Spock escaped from the transwarp station. You were unable to detect the new class of Starfleet vessel. You were unable to destroy Picard. You are weak."

"I took a chance," Salatrel said.

"Chance implies risk. There is no risk. There is only success."

Salatrel felt a chill. Hadn't she said the same to Tracius? The day Kirk had been reborn?

"There will be success."

She felt Vox turn to her, and she forced herself to look up at him.

Surprisingly, his scanner eye was dim. He looked at her only with his real eye. The one she was certain still connected somehow to his Romulan heart.

"Run," he whispered.

"I'm sorry?"

"Nothing can stop them."

"Vox?"

The Borg-Romulan reached out to her with his organic hand, took hers, squeezed. Gently. Just as he had before.

"Leave while you can," he said.

Salatrel stared at her former lover. She had no understanding of how he might be able to defeat the influence of the collective for the length of time it had taken for him to say those words, in the unaltered voice of the warrior she had loved.

"Tell me what I must do," she asked quickly.

But the scanner eye rekindled and painted her with its inquisitive red beam.

"Do not fight us," Vox said, with the harmonic of the collective once again underscoring his words. "Resistance is futile."

Salatrel turned away from him, assailed by old doubts about her future and the future of her people. But her course had been set long ago, when James T. Kirk had entered into the tail of the comet Icarus IV and murdered her grandfather. Everything that had happened since was the responsibility of the Butcher of Icarus. Even the Borg-Romulan invasion of his brutal Federation.

A warning chime sounded. Tran looked away from his board.

"Commander—a transwarp conduit is opening."

Salatrel leaned forward, puzzled. "Aren't all ships accounted for?"

"Yes, Commander."

"Then what is it?"

"That's just it, Commander. The transwarp conduit opened, then it closed. But sensors didn't show that anything came through it."

"That is not possible," Vox stated.

"Did you scan for a cloak?" Salatrel asked as she rose to her feet.

"Yes, Commander . . . but I found nothing."

Salatrel turned to Vox. "It must be an anomaly."

Vox stared at her coldly. "Or James T. Kirk."

On the bridge of the new *Enterprise*, McCoy was the first to speak as they emerged from transwarp. Kirk thought it was typical. McCoy was always the first to react to a situation. Spock was always the first to think a situation through. And Kirk was always the first to put the two extremes together and come up with the winning plan.

Or, at least, *a* plan.

He still hadn't figured out Picard's crew, other

than that they worked as a team—and as a team, they seemed unbeatable.

"One ship . . ." McCoy sputtered. "Against all of *them?!* You've got to be kidding, Spock."

"May I remind you I did not request your presence on this journey, Dr. McCoy."

"You needed ballast. And these days I'm the next best thing." McCoy looked up from his mobility chair at Kirk. "What do you think, Jim?"

Kirk shrugged. He had spent the past six hours digesting the specs on this ship. From his twenty-third century perspective, its capabilities were mindboggling. He smiled at McCoy. "I've read what this ship can do, Bones. That fleet out there doesn't have a chance."

McCoy frowned, never one to appreciate Kirk's hyperbole.

"Is there any sign we have been detected?" Spock asked. He was back in the center chair, behaving as if he had always been in command of the ship.

"No, sir," Data said. "I am picking up an increase in intership communication, though. Obviously, they saw our conduit open and are trying to determine why."

Kirk saw Spock check the displays on the arm of his chair. "Helm, take us in to the second planet. I believe it is the one I saw when I melded with V'Ger."

But Picard stepped up to Spock. "You said you would depend on our guidance, Mr. Spock."

"I am listening, Captain."

"Save your analysis of that planet for later. Right now, we owe it to the Federation to inflict

417

as much damage as possible on these ships." He pointed at the screen. "That's a Romulan spread-wing formation. They're on the brink of launching into battle."

"How do you propose this one vessel take on such a fleet?" Spock asked, with no trace of rancor.

"These Romulan vessels are clearly working *with* the Borg ships," Picard said. "Therefore, they are tied into the Borg communications system."

Spock understood. "Ah, and this vessel's deflector array is configured to deliver a subspace pulse to effectively blank out all operative subspace transmitters."

"Will that destroy them?" Kirk asked.

"No," Picard said. "But best-guess estimates say it will be fifteen minutes before the Borg are able to reform the collective enough to coordinate their attack. In the meantime, we would be able to proceed, unhindered."

"If you don't mind me asking," Kirk said. "If you have the ability to blank Borg communications, why didn't you do that on New Titan?"

"Because individual Borg recover within seconds. Each ship will reestablish its own internal systems within a minute. It is the sheer complexity of reestablishing the intership subspace network that will slow the Borg down."

Spock nodded. "It is a logical decision. Mr. Data, prepare to fire the deflector pulse."

Data glanced back at the captains with an expression of surprise. "Captain Picard, I have just realized that it was precisely this kind of pulse which could account for the erasure of all computer records on the world of Trilex."

"I will be quite fascinated to discuss archaeology with you *later,* Data. Now, proceed with Ambassador Spock's order."

"At once, sir."

Kirk looked down at McCoy as the doctor shifted uncomfortably in his mobility chair. "Talking archaeology when we're facing the biggest fleet this side of Utopia Planitia," McCoy muttered. "I still say he has pointed ears."

Spock glanced back at McCoy. "I am sure you intend Mr. Data to consider that a compliment, Doctor."

Kirk grinned. It was good to be back in action, even if he were little more than an observer.

He flinched as a searing pain shot through his legs. The inexorable nanites, still at work. Kirk took a breath to steady himself. Given present circumstances, he reminded himself, it was good to be anywhere.

Salatrel sat beside Tran, double checking all her subcommander's sensor readings. "The ship *has* to be somewhere in the system," she said.

"Most logically, it will attempt to map the Borg world," Vox said. "You should concentrate your search there."

"Why don't *you* concentrate a search there?" Salatrel snapped.

"You remain ignorant of the resources that this armada has consumed for the collective," Vox said. "We are limited in what we can do here."

At one level, Salatrel was pleased by that

admission. It was the first time she had heard any Borg admit there were limits to what they could accomplish. If the Federation were able to withstand this armada, the Borg might be defenseless, exactly as Salatrel had hoped.

"Tran—order all Birds-of-Prey into tight orbit of the Borg world. They are to scan for tachyons and fire on any sources."

"But that will break the attack formation," Vox said. "The formation must be maintained to balance its entry into the transwarp dimension."

"We've come this far," Salatrel said. "A few more minutes won't hurt. Unless you want to risk a Federation ship's dropping a few quantum torpedoes on the Borg homeworld."

Salatrel watched Vox carefully for a reaction. The Romulan Speaker for the Borg wasn't pleased. She took that to mean that the homeworld *was* vulnerable to attack.

Perhaps the Borg had become too complacent here, never expecting that anyone could do to them what they did to the galaxy.

"Tran, send the order."

"At once, Commander."

Tran began to change the configuration of his control panel to bring up the subspace radio link that united the armada. "Attention all Birds-of-Prey. For the glory of the Empire, you are ordered to—"

The Warbird rocked as every ODN circuit lining the bridge arced with a power discharge.

Collision alerts sounded.

"Tran! Report!" Salatrel demanded.

How could the Starfleet vessel know enough to target *her* ship?

"That was an extremely powerful subspace pulse," Tran reported. "A useless gesture, if it was the Starfleet vessel. All of our circuits are shielded. No damage."

Salatrel was puzzled. "Then what was the point of . . . ?"

She stopped as she saw Vox bent over, clutching his head and circuitry.

"Vox?"

The Borg-Romulan looked up in agony.

"The collective is gone from our mind. . . . We are alone."

Tran shouted, near panic. "Commander! He's right! The entire Borg communications system has been overloaded. The whole fleet is out of contact."

Salatrel lurched toward Tran. "Then *reestablish* contact!"

Tran shrugged helplessly. "I can't. Every Borg system will respond by moving to a new method of communications. By the time we all match frequencies . . . it'll be too late."

Salatrel spun to the screen. Clenched her fist. "Kirk," she said.

It was the only answer.

FORTY-NINE

Silent, unseen, the *Enterprise* sped toward the Borg homeworld.

On her bridge, Spock still held the center chair, with Kirk and Picard still beside him, and McCoy to the side. Riker served as science officer, Worf as communications, Data at the helm. Beverly Crusher and Deanna Troi both arrived from the ship's spartan sickbay to witness the historic voyage firsthand. La Forge labored in engineering, guiding the intricate meshing of Borg technology with Starfleet's latest wonders.

And a crew of Starfleet's finest, trained by Shelby and Lewinski for the worst the Borg could throw at them, held their stations throughout the sleek and deadly ship.

The Federation had never faced a more menacing threat than the Borg collective. But if this ship proved worthy of her namesakes, that threat might end, here and forever.

"That is the world I saw," Spock said. "Without question."

"I wonder why V'Ger didn't return with a crew of Borg," Riker asked.

"Who knows? V'Ger was here a long time ago," Kirk said. "Maybe the collective followed different strategies then. Maybe there were no Borg as you know them now." He paused and regarded the new crew of the new *Enterprise*.

"What we need to remember is, if this world *is* a single, living creature, then it's doing what all living things do—evolving, growing, learning."

Picard frowned. "Which means that somewhere down below could be the start of something even more deadly and relentless than what we've faced already."

"Destroy it," McCoy said. "While that damn fleet is immobilized, burn away its surface. Sterilize the place."

"If it is a living creature, doctor," Spock said, "that would be a crime against everything the Federation stands for."

"Then we cut it off," Kirk said.

"I agree," Picard added. "The power of the collective is in its organization. If we can make this interruption of its communications system permanent, then we deprive it of its ability to organize its conquest of the galaxy."

"Who knows?" Kirk said. "If we slow it down enough, maybe we can even try to reason with it."

"Reason with the Borg?" Riker asked.

Picard made the argument. "Destroying them will always be an option, Will. But an option we can never go back on."

"Are you sure, sir?" Riker asked.

Picard looked at Kirk. "After what I've been through recently, yes. I am."

"The problem still remains," Spock said, "how do we make this interruption of their communications permanent?"

Picard stepped forward to better see the viewscreen and the world of light upon it. "From my time with them, I now know that somewhere down there is the Central Node of the entire collective. We must find it. And we must . . . destroy it. Beyond any chance of them reconstructing it."

Picard turned to face Spock. "If you agree, sir. This ship does have that power."

Kirk thought Spock's response was noticeably grim. "Provided we utilize it within the next ten minutes, Commander. If we attempt to act once the Borg and Romulan fleet are functional as a united force, I estimate our useful lifetime in the system at less than two minutes."

Picard turned to Data and Riker. "Gentlemen, I suggest you begin a full sensor sweep of the Borg homeworld at once."

Kirk raised a finger. "Um, I'm not an expert on this ship, but won't our sensors reveal our location to the Borg?"

"Only if they're looking for us this close to the planet," Picard said.

"I would be," Kirk replied.

Picard smiled. "Then I would suggest you take the weapons console."

Kirk moved there directly and found the layout familiar enough to hope he'd have a chance to use it.

Spock addressed the helm. "Mr. Data—estimated time to scan the Borg planet?"

"Eighteen minutes, sir."

"Full Borg communications will be restored in eight minutes."

Data turned to Spock. "Sir, may I try an experiment?"

Even from his position at the weapons console, Kirk could hear McCoy groan.

"Do you believe it will decrease the time necessary to search for the Central Node?" Spock asked.

"I believe so, sir."

"Will you just get on with it!" McCoy snapped. Then he started coughing uncontrollably, and Kirk smiled as he saw both Dr. Crusher and Deanna Troi rush to McCoy's side.

On the viewscreen, a schematic of the Borg homeworld appeared to one side. On the other side, the schematic of another planet Kirk did not recognize. Though he did find it familiar.

Picard recognized it, though. "Data, that's Trilex, isn't it?"

"Yes, sir. A reconstruction of its landmasses, seas, and population centers, prior to the disaster which claimed its sun."

"Very interesting," Picard said. "But what does it have to do with the situation at hand?"

"Sir, I submit that the organic and machine intelligences of Trilex did not perish in a war against each other. I believe that they were involved in a war against the Borg. Or, at least, the Borg as they existed at that time."

"Go on, Mr. Data."

"The damage that was done to the Trilex computer infrastructure was the result of a subspace pulse similar to what we have just used to temporarily incapacitate the Borg fleet. If we accept that our technique is one which can be independently developed by any who fight the Borg, then the ruins of Trilex could indicate that the inhabitants of that world used a massive subspace pulse to incapacitate a Borg invasion force in their system."

"Mr. Data, are you saying that the people of Trilex, organic and artificial, deliberately triggered the deadly explosion of their sun."

"Yes, sir. They might have thought there was a chance some of the population might survive. But if the Borg were not stopped, then none would survive."

"It would be an act of terrible desperation for a people to gamble the existence of their world," Picard said.

"I find it is an act of hope, sir."

"In what way?"

"What better indication could there be that organic and artificial beings can live together, than by their decision to fight and die together, for what they believe in? Surely that shows they were united in a common purpose."

Kirk had watched and listened to the lengthy exchange between Picard and the android. He felt certain that on his bridge, he and Spock had rarely indulged in such introspection. He wondered if things had moved faster in his day. No one else on the bridge seemed as impatient as he felt with the inaction. He checked the time readout. Six minutes remained before they would come under fire.

"You may have answered the Trilex Question, Mr. Data," Picard continued. "But how does it apply here?"

"The Borg are not imaginative, sir. They follow preset patterns. If we overlay the pattern of

426

destruction on Trilex—" On the viewscreen, the two schematics merged. "—on top of the Borg homeworld, I believe that since the people of Trilex were intending to destroy the Borg center of communication on their world, the area of the worst destruction should line up with the location of the Central Node on this world. Assuming that the Borg followed the same pattern, that is."

Spock turned to Riker. "Commander Riker, if you would scan those coordinates, please."

Kirk watched Riker work with intense concentration. Then Riker looked up, almost in surprise. "Ambassador Spock, we have located the Central Node." Perhaps, Kirk thought, there was a place for introspection on a captain's bridge.

Picard pounded Data on the back. "Well done, Data."

Data smiled. Kirk found it disturbing to see an android exhibit emotions. But when in the twenty-fourth century . . .

"Thank you," Data said. "But we must really thank the people of Trilex, both organic and synthetic."

Spock nodded at Kirk. "Captain, if you would target the Central Node."

With relief at the call to action, Kirk checked the coordinate readouts. With a few commands, he successfully locked the *Enterprise*'s phasers on the center of the target and laid in a torpedo barrage to encircle any backup connections that might be linked into it.

"Target locked," he confirmed.

"Four minutes to reacquisition of communications," Worf announced.

"I'll be damned," McCoy said, slapping his leg. "It's not even close. We're going to make it after all."

And then the *Enterprise* shook as the first barrage hit, sending half the crew to the deck as the ship began to dive.

Tran shook his fist in the air in triumph.

"Direct hit, Commander!"

"Stay on it," Salatrel said. Alone of all the armada she had brought her ship in close to the homeworld. And her suspicions had been correct.

On the bridge viewscreen, she saw the rippling effect of a cloaking field dispersing and knew she had caused considerable damage to the Starfleet vessel, whatever it was.

She turned to Vox.

"See? A single ship is of no concern."

"Did you not read its sensor returns?" Vox said. "It had located the Central Node. The collective could not hold."

"What about the famed Borg redundancy?"

"There can be only one collective," Vox said.

Salatrel smiled in fierce satisfaction. At last, she knew. The Borg had a fatal weakness after all.

"Fire at will," Salatrel commanded. Then she sat back in her chair and dreamed of victory.

"Where the hell did that come from?!" Riker shouted.

La Forge answered over the bridge speakers.

"It's this transwarp drive, Commander. It interferes with our tachyon detection modes."

Worf confirmed La Forge's analysis. The cloaked ship that had attacked them would remain undetectable as long as the transwarp drive was engaged.

"Disengage the transwarp drive," Spock ordered matter-of-factly.

"And pull up," Picard suggested.

Data was already involved in doing just that, leveling out the *Enterprise's* path so she would not repeat the ignominious end of her predecessor by crash-landing on the Borg world.

"As soon as we have a fix," Kirk said, "torpedoes are ready for launching."

Everyone on the bridge worked in perfect balance. The instant the transwarp drive was offline, Riker reconfigured the sensors for maximum tachyon sensitivity. The instant the sensors picked up the tachyon signature of the cloaked ship trailing them, Data transferred the coordinates to Kirk's weapons controls. Kirk launched the torpedoes less than an instant after that.

The *Avatar of Tomed* spun twice on its vertical axis as a quantum torpedo struck its outer starboard hull support.

Only its structural integrity field kept it together.

Only its artificial gravity and inertial dampeners kept its crew from being crushed.

Tran brought the Warbird back into trim and

continued its pursuit. But its cloak dissipated as quickly as had the *Enterprise's*.

"It's a Warbird," Data announced as the image of the pursuing vessel appeared on the screen.

"I know that ship," Kirk said. "Can you get a closer image? Give me a name?"

The viewscreen fluttered as magnification was enhanced.

Data read the Romulan script on its raptor prow.

"The *Avatar of Tomed.* A poetic reference to the battle in which—"

"That's her!" Kirk said. "Salatrel."

"Fascinating," Spock commended. "*She* is the one who set all of this in motion."

Kirk punched the controls and fired more torpedoes.

The Warbird swerved to avoid them.

But the moment her port side was exposed, the *Enterprise's* phaser dug into that hull support as well.

"Excellent shooting, sir," Data said as the Warbird wobbled erratically. "Without hull integrity on both supports, it will be unable to withstand the compression of its defensive shields."

The *Enterprise* shook as the *Avatar* struck out again.

"We're going into overload!" La Forge shouted.

"I thought this ship was shielded!" Riker shouted back.

"Not with this damn transwarp drive! All our power curves are off."

Kirk targeted the Warbird's rear hull support, planning to put a shot through the gap between her upper and lower hulls the next time she swerved.

He fired two more torpedoes.

The Warbird swerved as he had anticipated, and he fired.

Plasma streamed out from behind the *Tomed*.

"Direct hit!" Data cheered. "Her shields are fluctuating . . . fluctuating . . . *gone!*"

Spock sat forward in his chair. "Mr. Worf, open a hailing frequency to the Romulan ship."

"They are refusing to answer," Worf said.

"Can they hear us?"

"Yes, sir."

Spock spoke loudly. "Attention, Romulan vessel. Your shields are disabled. If you withdraw, we will not destroy you." Spock looked over at Worf. "Is there any answer, Mr.—"

Spock's answer came as the bridge filled with streamers of power sparks.

"Direct hit on us," Data said in disbelief.

Kirk watched as his control board shut down. "The phaser banks are offline!"

"Good work," McCoy said. "They don't have any shields. We don't have any weapons. What are we supposed to do? Ram them?"

Picard turned to McCoy. "Actually, I have—"

The collision alarms wailed.

On the screen, the Warbird accelerated forward.

"*They* are attempting to ram us!" Data exclaimed. He jabbed his fingers on his controls. "The helm is not responding! We have stationkeeping thrusters only! Too close for torpedoes!"

"All hands, brace for impact!" Riker ordered.

But Kirk left his station to seek out Data. "Data—do you trust me?"

"That is a curious question to ask at this—"

"Then move over!" Kirk said, and slid in beside the android. "Now get me La Forge in engineering and stand by on the cloak."

Data blinked. "Sir, in twenty-eight seconds, we will be spinning debris."

"Trust me," Kirk said.

Then he turned to the board and did the only thing he could.

He changed the rules.

Moments before impact, the *Enterprise* rippled within its cloak and disappeared.

"They've cloaked," Tran reported.

"A meaningless act of desperation," Salatrel said. "They can't go anywhere. Stand by for impact."

"Five . . ." Tran counted, "four . . . three . . . two . . . one . . . impact!"

The Warbird moved smoothly on course.

Salatrel was out of her chair and by Tran in a second. "Where did they go?"

Tran looked at his board in helpless confusion. "Nowhere, Commander. They're so badly damaged, we would have picked up any attempt to leave their position."

"Activate all external scanners," Salatrel said.

Vox stepped up beside her. "We told you James Kirk was not to be underestimated."

"You don't know Kirk is on that ship!"

"Then how does it keep evading us?"

"Luck," Salatrel muttered.

"Luck is irrelevant."

The viewscreen flickered with rapid views of the volume of space surrounding the Warbird. There were no sensor traces anywhere.

"That is impossible!" Salatrel said. "It's not as if we swallowed him whole and . . ."

She stopped talking as the horrible truth hit her.

Tran turned to her in disbelief.

And Vox, through his implants, even seemed to smile.

On the bridge of the *Enterprise*, Picard shook his head as he watched the viewscreen. On it was the back hull of the Warbird's raptor prow.

Kirk had slipped the *Enterprise* between the Romulan vessel's double hull.

"I'm seeing it," Picard said, "but I'm not believing it."

"What's the matter?" Kirk asked. "You don't tell the story of the Trojan Horse anymore?"

"Captain Picard, Captain Kirk—the Warbird is activating its internal sensors," Riker said. "They must have guessed our strategy."

The captains turned to Spock. "It's up to you," Kirk said.

Spock nodded. "Mr. Data . . . on my mark, you will use stationkeeping thrusters to initiate a

433

three-hundred-and-sixty-degree lateral rotation. Drop the cloak to put full strength into the structural integrity field."

"Yes, sir."

Kirk smiled as Spock shifted in his command chair.

"Mark," the reluctant commander of the *Enterprise* said.

Salatrel grabbed the helm as she saw the Starfleet vessel shimmer into view between the *Tomed's* hulls. She knew that in seconds it would begin to rotate and gut them. There was nothing left for her to do.

"This is your fault!" she screamed at Vox.

And this time, Vox did smile. "No. this is all the fault of James T. Kirk. And since you are the one who brought him to us . . ." Vox stopped speaking as he saw something to the side.

Salatrel turned to see Tran aim a disruptor at her.

"You did this," the subcommander raged. "All you old people making wars . . . you make me—"

The bridge groaned.

On the viewscreen, just before the image winked out in a flurry of static, Salatrel saw the starfleet vessel begin its rotation.

The bridge shook.

Salatrel heard the hiss of escaping air.

And with an endless cry of denial, she was sucked out through the rent in the hull, knowing she fell through stars that still shone on Kirk, but which would never shine on her again.

Nestled in between the double hulls of the Romulan Warbird, Starfleet's newest *Enterprise* slowly continued her lateral, lethal roll.

Her streamlined profile and reduced size had made it possible for her to ease inside the Warbird, skirting her prow, to take up stationkeeping above the ventral and below the dorsal hulls.

By rotating within that enclosed space, without having to fight the force of the Warbird's shields, the *Enterprise* opened the ship like a hatchling splitting an egg.

The shell of the Warbird spun away in a glittering cloud of tumbling wreckage, fogged by a frozen, sublimating cloud of escaping atmosphere.

And from that cloud, like a phoenix reborn, the *Enterprise* broke free and continued on her mission.

FIFTY

"One minute to acquisition of communications," Riker announced. "But we have no weapons left to destroy the Central Node."

"Unless we ram it ourselves," Spock said bluntly.

There was a moment of silence on the bridge. To save the Federation from the Borg, there was no one on board who would not agree to such a drastic sacrifice. But was it the only way?

Kirk left his weapons station. "Send me down, Spock. There has to be a self-destruct mechanism . . . or a power generator I can put on overload. . . ."

"You will be sacrificing your life," Spock said.

Kirk grinned. "You're the one suggesting a suicide dive. Beam me down. I'll take my chances with the Borg."

Picard stepped up beside him. "I'll go with you."

Kirk shook his head. "Don't forget, I'm the one with the nanites eating through me. You have a life ahead of you."

"Not if the Borg are allowed to continue unopposed." Picard matched Kirk's grin. "Besides, with what you know about the Borg, you're liable to help them *fix* their Central Node and not destroy it."

Kirk studied him in silence, then nodded, sealing their pact.

Picard sought out Crusher at the back of the bridge, still with Troi and McCoy. "Beverly. I'll need the interface in the transporter room. At once."

Kirk stepped out of the armorer's storage room laden with phasers and photon grenades.

Spock and McCoy were waiting for him.

A hundred glib remarks came to Kirk. Light things. Easy jokes. Anything to ease the burden of these last precious seconds. But somehow he knew the time for that had passed. Decades ago.

So instead, he reached out to them, gripping one of their hands in each of his.

"It's all right," Kirk said. "I had a second chance. Not a lot of people can say that."

Even after all their years together, Spock's expression was unreadable. But McCoy's eyes glistened.

"The way I figure it, you're working on your fiftieth chance by now," the doctor croaked. His old-man's voice trembled with unexpressed emotion.

"A second chance," Kirk said softly, realizing the enormity of the gift he had been given: to see his two friends again, even for these brief hours. "And there's still not enough time. Never has been."

"I am . . ." Spock began, then faltered.

Kirk understood. "And always will be . . . your friend."

Then he let go of them, stepped back, fixing them both in his mind's eye to hold them there for the rest of his life. "Look after each other. Never give up." Then he turned and hurried to the transporter room, unable to look back.

In the transporter room, Kirk found Picard burdened by the same array of weaponry on his own equipment harness. He also held a black carryall pouch which Crusher had given him.

Crusher watched as Kirk stepped up on the platform.

"I can do this myself, you know," Kirk said. "You can tell Starfleet what we've found here."

Picard shook his head. "I have faith in my crew."

Then Kirk saw Dr. Crusher staring at Picard. Suddenly, she ran over to him, hugged him, hard. He eased her away, gently.

The deck rumbled underfoot. A weapons impact. Spock's voice came from the speakers. He was back on the bridge. "We have been engaged by a Bird-of-Prey. Communications capability is returning to the enemy fleet. Please transport at once. We will loop back in precisely eight hundred seconds for an emergency beam-out."

"Energize," Picard ordered.

The cramped transporter room dissolved around Kirk, then reformed as a dark warren of ugly black metal struts and walkways. He tested his footing in the gravity of the Borg world. It was lighter than he had expected.

"Is the whole planet like this?" Kirk asked. The metal framework seemed to stretch to the horizon, lit only by glowing and pulsing emanations from below.

"If we're lucky," Picard said, "we won't have to find out." He glanced around to get his bearings, then headed off to the right. "This way."

"Why not?" Kirk said and followed him.

Above the Borg homeworld, the *Enterprise* went to full impulse, deliberately directing itself toward the densest accumulation of Borg and Romulan ships. Spock had concluded that that was where they would find those few ships which had not yet rejoined the newly restored Borg communications network, and where those that had would be least likely to use their weapons, for fear of hitting allies.

The *Enterprise* flew on toward that mass of ships, swerving as closely as Data dared take them to Borg cubeships and Romulan formations. And because Data navigated with the precise control of a machine, his maneuvers were daring enough to alarm even Spock.

On the homeworld, Kirk and Picard stood outside a massive metal door, at least ten meters tall. It was covered in intricate scrollwork. Writing of some kind, Kirk decided. Faintly reminiscent of old circuit designs. Picard checked his tricorder. "The Central Node is through here. According to the tricorder, the door hasn't been opened for at least two hundred thousand years."

"Good," Kirk said as he drew his phaser. "Then you've come far enough. Wait here for the beam-out. Let me go on."

"And let you have all the fun?"

Picard drew his own phaser and blasted the door's locking device.

It swung open with a gust of foul air.

Picard waved to the dark passageway beyond. With a smile he said, "After you . . ."

Kirk returned the gesture, and the grin. "Oh, no . . . after you. . . ."

With shared laughter, the two captains stepped through together.

The *Enterprise* streaked through space, avoiding those few ships that fired on her. Her

439

restored shields protecting her from the shots that didn't miss.

"The enemy fleet still appears to be in confusion," Riker said. Spock had already deduced that the subspace pulse from the deflector array had been more destructive than Starfleet had anticipated.

Data amended Riker's assessment. "Except for the Borg vessels directly ahead."

Spock called for them to go onscreen.

It was not an encouraging image.

Once again the cubeships were reassembling themselves, not into larger cubes, but into other, more ominous shapes—some long and bristling with disruptor cannons, some resembling vessels with twin nacelles formed as if from a child's set of building blocks.

"They are adapting to us," Worf marvelled.

Spock had no need to check a time readout. "As long as they take more than six hundred seconds to do so, Mr. Worf, we will have a chance to recover Captains Kirk and Picard."

The *Enterprise* flew on. But now the reconfigured Borg ships took up the chase. And the distance between hunter and prey grew smaller.

The dark passageway beyond the ancient door smelled worse the deeper Kirk and Picard penetrated. But at last, no more than two hundred meters later, the passageway opened up into a vast interior space that made Kirk think of the Grand Canyon turned upside down.

A Grand Canyon of black metal and endless pipelines.

But that oppressive technological mass was above them, lit only by gouts of flame, as if oil wells were being vented. Below them, on a lower plaza ten stories deep, a sunken dome stretched away, kilometers wide, its surface pulsing with flashing traces of cold blue light.

The patterns of that light were the same as those Kirk had seen on the ancient door.

There was order here, and purpose. Though Kirk doubted even a Vulcan could appreciate or comprehend it.

Picard folded his tricorder shut. "That's it," he said.

"*Now* why don't you go back?" Kirk asked. "Now that we've found it, I can deal with it."

"But can you deal with them?" Picard said.

Kirk turned to look in the direction Picard looked, along the wide deck that ran from the passageway in a sweeping circle around the glowing dome and sunken plaza.

He saw what Picard saw.

Borg.

Thousands of them.

Marching toward them.

"Coming up on course change," Data announced.

Spock steepled his fingers as the *Enterprise* shook beneath the onslaught of disruptor fire it was taking from the Borg ship in pursuit.

"Commander Riker," Spock said, "have you noticed the delay in the Borg's response to our course changes?"

"Yes, sir," Riker said. "Their ship is more

massive, less responsive to sudden vector changes."

"I calculate a three-second discrepancy."

"I concur."

Spock put his hands on the arms of his command chair and held on tightly. "Mr. Data, put us on a collision course with the Borg ship, bearing forty-three, twenty-seven, mark eight. I would like you to pull out at two seconds before collision."

"Yes, sir," Data said. "I believe I would like that as well."

Kirk and Picard crouched behind a power conduit more than five meters thick. It ran down from the wall of the immense interior space, across the wide circular deck, then down the ten stories where it snaked into the side of the dome of flashing light traces.

Picard pointed to a switching lever on the side of the stained and mineral-encrusted metal that formed the pipe.

"This lever will do it," Picard said, confirming his guess with his tricorder. "It will cut the power to the Central Node's core and trigger a feedback surge that will burn out all its circuits." He looked around. "This facility was constructed long before the Borg developed redundancy to the extent they practice it today."

"How can you know all this?" Kirk asked.

"I don't," Picard answered. "But Locutus does."

The mass of approaching Borg was coming closer. Not all of them marched. Some rolled, some crawled, some floated as if on antigravs. But the sound of their approach hammered on the metal plates of the deck, making Kirk think of rolling thunder on a planet which could have no more weather.

"Do you think they're going to *let* us cut the power to the Central Node?"

"That is not within the realm of possibility," Picard said.

"Then we should cut the power now."

"No," Picard said. "We have to time it for the *Enterprise's* return. That way there's still a chance for us to get out."

"The *Enterprise* is still eight minutes away," Kirk said. "How do we hold them back till then?"

"You don't," Picard said. "I do."

Picard opened the black carryall pouch that Dr. Crusher had given him. Kirk glanced inside. Saw the Borg interface.

Knew what it meant.

To destroy the Borg homeworld, Picard had to truly become Locutus again.

"Collision in ten seconds," Data said calmly.

Spock made a cutting motion with his hand. "Shut off the collision alarms, please, Mr. Worf."

The bridge of the *Enterprise* fell silent.

The screen filled with the chaotic mass of metal pipes and tubes that would collide with the *Enterprise* in a matter of seconds. Directly before them, submodular cubeships formed themselves into a shape that looked like a spear—a spear aimed at the *Enterprise.*

In contrast, the Borg ship that pursued them

was spiked and blazed with disruptor fire that converged from three emitters into a single, central, stabbing beam.

Spock had Data hold his course, absorbing hit after hit from that beam.

Data continued his countdown. ". . . four . . . three . . . *course change!*"

The *Enterprise* sidestepped the spear-shaped Borg vessel by fewer than three hundred meters.

And as Spock had anticipated, the pursuing Borg ship didn't miss it at all.

The two Borg ships met, blazing like a new sun, shedding thick golden shafts of light on the tumbling cubeships that spiraled away and dissolved into storms of debris as the power of the explosion reached out to them.

The *Enterprise* banked in that firestorm of plasma. Her shields took all the energy of the dying Borg without fail or complaint.

She had been in transit for four hundred seconds when Spock gave the order to return from where she had started.

His captain awaited him.

Picard drew his hand away from the neural plate now attached to his face. The power cell and subspace transmitter were already strapped to his chest.

"Are you sure?" Kirk asked.

"Is there a choice?" Picard answered.

Kirk pointed out the phasers and the photon grenades laid out before them behind the power conduit.

"These could keep them busy for a while."

"And what if one of that horde gets off a lucky shot? And we miss being able to pull on the lever? And the Node isn't destroyed?"

Kirk put his hand on Picard's shoulder. "Captain—I've seen Locutus. Spock took me in there, inside your mind. I know what it means to you . . . put that thing back on."

"Spock showed me things, too," Picard said. "As did you." He held up the interface cord, felt for the slots that would guide it into place. "Some of the courage in here is yours. Some is Spock's. The truth is, I'm not any less afraid of the collective, or of Locutus. But it's been so long since I even allowed myself to feel fear, I unwittingly gave it power over me." Picard held the input jack to the neural plate. "You've shown me how to face fear, Captain. And I will return from that encounter—just as you did."

Picard jabbed the jack home. A faint blue crackle of energy leapt along the input cable to the power cell on his shoulder. His hand fell back. His eyes rolled back in his head until only white remained.

Beyond the conduit, the Borg horde advanced.

Picard rose to his feet beside Kirk, facing the enemy as it approached.

Kirk stood as well. "It is working?"

Picard stared at him as if he were nothing more than the metallic debris that littered this world.

"We are Locutus," Picard said. "We are . . . Borg."

FIFTY-ONE

Kirk grabbed Picard by the shoulders. Shook him.

"Fight it!" he shouted.

Picard's eyes cleared, but just for an instant. "It wasn't . . . supposed to . . . be like this. . . . It's too strong."

Picard's hand scrabbled for the interface cable. Kirk pulled the hand away. "Not yet! You have to send them away!" He twisted Picard around to face the advancing Borg.

Kirk could hear the whine of their servomotors. The awful raspy wheeze of their assisted breathing.

"Tell them to stop or I'll cut off the power now!"

Picard lurched forward, bracing himself against the power conduit. Mouth open. Gasping.

"Resistance . . . resistance . . . *resistance is futile!*" he screamed and swung at Kirk.

Kirk grabbed his arms, held him.

"Picard! You are a starship captain! *Act like one!*"

And Kirk slapped him. Slapped him again.

Slapped him until Picard brought up his hand and caught Kirk's arm in midswing. "I think," he gasped, "you've convinced me. . . ."

Picard faced the Borg, now no more than a handful of meters away.

"Go back," he said. "We are Borg . . . the collective is safe . . . return . . . return to your functions. . . ."

Kirk tensed as he watched the Borg hesitate, swaying back and forth, motors whining.

And then, as one, they turned and moved away.

"It *is* working," Kirk said.

Picard's eyes followed the retreating Borg. "They want me back. And this time they're not asking. They're demanding."

Kirk looked intently at Picard, trying to read his emotions beneath the implant plate.

Picard's answering gaze was firm, unwavering. "And I'm saying . . . *no*."

"Then go deeper into the collective," Kirk urged in relief. "Find out what we need to know about the power cut-off. How long do we have after we throw it?"

"We don't," Picard said. He held his hands to his head. "The feedback is immediate. The instant we throw the lever, the Node is . . . the Node is. . . ."

Kirk pulled Picard around to face him. "Concentrate, Captain. Look into the collective. Is there any way to pull that lever and still get out?"

Picard shook his head. "Whoever pulls that lever will die." His eyes cleared again. "Resistance is futile."

His eyes began to drift away again. His head turned in the direction the Borg had marched away.

Kirk had heard enough.

He grabbed the interface cable and pulled it free.

Picard cried out.

Gasped as if struck.

Then stared at Kirk.

"How long?" he asked.

Kirk checked his tricorder. "We've got sixty seconds till the *Enterprise* does her flyby."

"I can take it from here," Picard said.

"No, you can't," Kirk argued. "In case you don't remember, whoever pulls that lever and destroys the Node gets trapped in the power surge."

"I do remember. It is my job to do it. You've done enough."

"Jean-Luc, I'm dying."

"Who isn't?"

Spock's voice crackled out of Kirk's commbadge. "*Enterprise* to away team. We are at thirty seconds to emergency beam-out. What is your status?"

Picard locked eyes with Kirk. Touched his own commbadge. "This is Picard, *Enterprise*. Break off your approach. Repeat—"

Kirk pushed Picard's hand away from his commbadge, hit his own.

"Ignore that last order, Spock. Bring that ship in."

"I am not leaving!" Picard said.

Kirk was about to shout back, when he suddenly stood down.

"Did you ever try to save the *Kobayashi Maru* at the Academy?"

Picard watched Kirk with deep suspicion. "Yesss. . . . But it can't be done. It's a no-win scenario designed for cadets."

Kirk smiled. "That's what they'd like you to believe. But there is one strategy that can win it. It's just that nobody in your time seems to do it anymore. Spock tells me it's a lost art now."

"Are you suggesting a compromise?"

Kirk thought it over. "You could call it that."

"Well," Picard said. "Go ahead. I'm always open to suggestions."

Kirk nodded. "Good."

Then he slugged Picard in the jaw as hard as he could.

Picard dropped like deadweight.

Kirk dragged Picard away by his collar, until he was well away from the power conduit.

He pulled off his own commbadge, touched the front to activate.

"Kirk to *Enterprise*," he said.

"Spock here."

Kirk smiled.

He felt better already.

"Keep the ship out of danger, Mr. Spock." He studied the Starfleet delta in his hand. Remembered when it had belonged only to the *Enterprise*. But some things had to change. It was the way of the world. Of the universe.

He was glad to have been part of it.

"Lock onto my signal," Kirk said. "One to beam up." Then he tossed his commbadge onto Picard's chest and stepped back.

Picard reacted to the impact of the badge. His eyes opened. He looked up. Started to speak.

Then dissolved in the transporter as the *Enterprise* once more claimed her own.

Kirk turned back to the power conduit. Grabbed the lever in both hands. Tested it once to see how much force he might need. Felt it move easily.

"A second chance," he said aloud.

Then he closed his eyes.

Squeezed his hands tight.

Pulled.

Heard a sudden, deafening roar of thunder coming from the dome.

Then a scrape as quiet as a footstep behind him.

Kirk turned.

Opened his eyes.

Saw the—

"Dear God," McCoy said.

On the bridge of the *Enterprise,* to which he had been directly beamed, Picard shielded his eyes against the sudden glare from the viewscreen. On it, a blinding column of light shot up from the Borg homeworld, directly from what had been the Central Node.

In the intensity of that destructive light, every surface on the bridge that faced the viewscreen was too bright to look at. Every surface that was in shadow was too dark to reveal detail.

But Picard watched with grim fascination as ripples of explosions began to spread across the homeworld's surface, following the strict lines and angles of circuitry.

Beside him, Beverly Crusher took his hand.

Riker stood beside her. Data and La Forge sat together at the helm. At his station, Worf made no effort to hide his eyes from the light. And Picard saw tears roll down Troi's cheeks. He knew the counselor was overwhelmed by the emotions of all who surrounded her, their joy and their grief.

For one crew had been reunited.

While another had at last been torn asunder.

McCoy stepped forward, held up only by his exoskeleton, to stand by Spock's side.

In the flickering of that light, Picard saw the Vulcan rise from the command chair to place his hand on the old man's shoulder. And through it all, Data counted off the uncountable Borg and Romulan ships colliding throughout the system, with no more subspace signals from the collective to link or guide them.

The explosions spread out in a web of fire, encompassing a third of the homeworld as a thousand other cubeships broke from its surface and jumped to transwarp, fleeing the death of whatever this planet had been.

There would still be Borg, somewhere, Picard knew. But not the Borg they had known. Not the Borg that had threatened them in the past.

For today, and with luck tomorrow, the Federation had been preserved.

Because of one man.

Picard rubbed his jaw as he watched the flaming destruction spread over the planet before them. "Perhaps this is a more fitting memorial," he said, "than a simple cairn of stones."

Riker nodded. "A great man died today."

Then Picard saw Spock turn to look at Riker. To Picard, the Vulcan's expression was disturbingly both unfathomable and familiar.

"Captain Picard," Spock said, "Now, I believe, the bridge is yours."

Picard watched in silence as Spock and McCoy slowly left the bridge, Spock supporting his friend, again with no regard for the normal Vulcan aversion to touching and being touched.

When they were gone, Riker turned to his captain.

"Did you see the look on Spock's face?" he asked, astonished.

A flame leapt into life within Picard as he waited for his first officer to continue.

"I've seen it before," Riker said. "At the salvage camp. Spock *still* doesn't believe that Kirk is dead."

Picard looked at the commbadge in his hand.

He remembered fleeting images of what he had seen in Kirk's mind. What Spock had shown him there.

He remembered Kirk's dream. The dream that had always haunted Kirk. Always shown him how he would die.

"There are always possibilities," he said.

The Borg homeworld was a blazing pyre, bringing light to a system that had been dark for a time too long to be measured.

Against that light, a tiny craft came about, its space-black hull catching just a glimmer of that fire, so that all the universe could know its name.

A name which had lived on other ships.

452

A name which would live on ships still to come.

Triumphant, victorious, in the new dawn's light, *Starship Enterprise* set course for home.

One voyage at an end.

The continuing mission far from over.

EPILOGUE

He fell. . . .

But this time, not alone.

The rocky face of El Capitan blurred past him.

The brilliant sun of Yosemite blazed down on him through the pure blue of Earth's own sky.

He shouted out his challenge to the world that raced to meet him.

He would not die today.

And then, as he knew it must, Spock's hand took his ankle in a grip of duranium and held the world—and death—at bay.

That night, by the campfire, three friends sharing shore leave together, McCoy had railed at him. "Human life is far too precious to risk on crazy stunts. Maybe it didn't cross that macho mind of yours, but you should have been killed when you fell off that mountain."

"It crossed my mind."

"And . . . ?"

"And . . . even as I fell, I knew I wouldn't die. Because the two of you were with me."

"I do not understand," Spock had said.

So the falling man had looked into his heart and spoken a truth he had never shared. "I've always known . . . that I'll die alone."

That night, he stares up at the stars, knowing all their names, but still wanting to know more.

He hears the crackle of the dying fire. Breathes

454

deeply of its fragrant smoke mingled with the green scent of pine and the richness of earth.

In this moment, the falling man once more is immersed in life, content to drift beneath those stars, on the planet of his birth, knowing that his ship waits above him for his return. That there are still many voyages left before the dream that haunts him becomes his final reality.

But then, from the shadows of the trees, a figure robed in white approaches and stands over him.

It is the figure from his dream.

The dream.

The figure from whom he has run all his life.

The falling man is troubled, knowing that in some way this is the time in which his hunter will claim him.

"Must I go?" he asks.

For the first time, the figure turns back his hood and holds out his hand.

"There will be time enough for rest, later," Sarek says. "But not here. Not now."

The falling man looks back at the campfire, at three friends resting peacefully beside it.

Spock and McCoy and . . . himself.

"You must leave them behind," Sarek says. "They cannot be with you."

"Why?" the falling man asks, bewildered that he does not remember how he came to this place in his past, though he has always known that it would be to this place and to this moment he would return. The moment when he first spoke of his dream with his friends.

"Sarek . . . why has it always been you in my dreams? Even before we met. Before I met your son. Before I left Earth . . . it has always been you who comes to take me from my friends and to my death."

"Because of what we share," Sarek answers. "Or will share."

"My dream? Or my death?"

"As long as a single mind remembers, as long as a single heart still beats with passion, how can a dream die?"

"But what of the dreamer?"

Sarek smiles. "Look to the stars, James Kirk." He takes the falling man's hand as he has always taken his hand in this dream. Sarek's smile fades. "avenge me."

And then, for the first time, the dream continued. Beyond the shadows.

There would be one last journey for him. One last voyage. One last mission.

And as he had always known he must, James T. Kirk turned his back on the past and rushed to embrace his future.

IF YOU HAVE ENJOYED READING THIS LARGE PRINT BOOK AND YOU WOULD LIKE MORE INFORMATION ON HOW TO ORDER A WHEELER LARGE PRINT BOOK, PLEASE WRITE TO:

WHEELER PUBLISHING, INC.
P.O. BOX 531
ACCORD, MA 02018-0531